LONGSWORD: EDWARD AND THE ASSASSIN

DIMITAR GYOPSALIEV

2017

ISBN 978 619 90851 0 3

"With love to my son, Brani, who helps me enormously and challenges me every day to be a better father and person."

CONTENTS

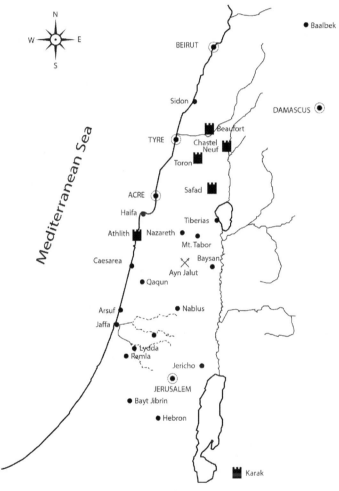

THE HOLY LAND IN 1272

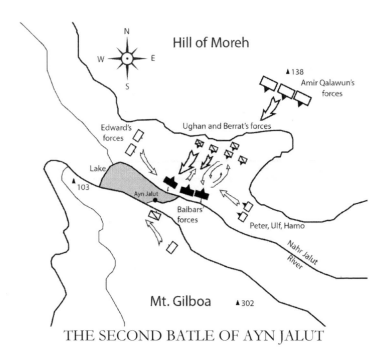

THE SECOND BATLE OF AYN JALUT

Dimitar Gyopsaliev

GLOSSARY OF CHARACTERS

Lord Edward - Eldest son of King Henry III and the future king of England, also known as Edward I Longshanks

Lady Eleanor - Eleanor of Castile, wife of Edward, daughter of Ferdinand III of Castile;

Otto de Grandson - Knight, diplomat, and close friend of Edward; member of the House of Savoy

Edmund Crouchback - Edward's brother

Peter - An orphan, raised in Acre by an old Hospitaller

Ulf Magnusson - Also known as the Desert Wolf, or *Diyaab al-Sahra*; a Northman and an experienced warrior employed on various occasions by the sultan

James of Durham - A Scottish Knight, also known as Red Herring

Edward the Saracen - An assassin

Sultan Baibars - The fourth sultan of Egypt from the Mamluk Bahri Dynasty, a former slave warrior who rose from the ranks

King Hugh III - King of Cyprus and King of Jerusalem

Balian of Ibelin - Lord of Arsuf

Thomas Bérard - Grand Master of the Order of the Temple in Acre

Hugues de Revel - Grand Master of the Order of the Hospital in Acre

Jean de Grailly - A Knight and the future Seneschal of the Kingdom of Jerusalem, member of the House of Savoy

Pope Gregory X - Teobaldo Visconti from Piacenza, a friend of Edward

Marco Polo - A Venetian merchant traveler

Izz al-Din Ughan Samm al-Mawt - A powerful amir from the north and an old friend of the sultan; his name literally means "Poison of Death"

Barak - One of Ughan's officers

Berrat - Baibars' most trustworthy spy

Julian of Sidon - A Knight Templar

Nickolas - Lady Isabella's valet and a chronicler

Isabella of Ibelin - Lady of Beirut

Githa - A female Knight Hospitaller and a personal guard of

Lady Isabella

David - A Scottish sergeant in the service of James of Durham

Owen - A Welsh archer in the service of Lady Eleanor

Andrea Pelu - A Genovese captain

Roger of Sicily - A mercenary warrior in the service of the Templars

Hamo Le Strange - A lord from the Welsh Marches and a companion of Prince Edward

William Longsword - An English Crusader who died in the Battle of Mansurah in 1250 during the Seventh Crusade

Brother John - An old monk and a participant in the Seventh Crusade led by King Louis IX of France

Alexander Giffard - A follower of William Longsword, a participant in the Seventh Crusade of King Louis IX of France

King Louis - King Louis IX of France, who died in 1270 in Tunis, Leader of the Eighth Crusade

Charles of Anjou - King Charles I of Sicily, brother of King Louis IX of France

Amir Qalawun - A powerful amir, close to Sultan Baibars

Ibn Abd al-Zahir - Sultan Baibars' clerk

Ibn al-Nafis - A personal physician of the sultan

Shams al-Din - Son of Nonagenarian, the leader of a faction of assassins; his name means "Sun of the faith"

Siraghan al-Tatari - A commander of Mongol horsemen, on service of the sultan

Anna - Sultan Baibars' youngest daughter

Ivar the ostringer - Anna's personal falconer

WHY?

"The War must be for the sake of Peace" —Aristotle (Politics, book VII: 14)

"The Templars and Hospitallers were said to deliberately prolong the war between Christians and Muslims in order to collect more money from pilgrims ...." —Anonymous Christian Contemporary of the Crusades, recorded by Matthew Paris in his Chronica Majora volume IV

CHAPTER ONE

City of Acre, Holy Land, Friday, 17th of June, in the year 1272 of the incarnation of Christ

Peter opened his eyes.

"Where am I?" he asked himself as he stared at the night sky full of stars. There wasn't a single cloud in the sky. The sound of the night was dancing around him. Insects were buzzing, the summer breeze whispered its song, and the sea waves were kissing the rocks near the harbor. The Crusaders' city of Acre was sleeping silently in peace.

"Ah, the peace," Peter remarked.

Egypt and Syria were under the control of the Mamluk Sultanate – and their leader Sultan Baibars. Over the last few years, he had been gaining success against the Crusader States. After Lord Edward's arrival last year, King Hugh of Jerusalem and other Crusader leaders had agreed to a peace with Baibars. The truce was sealed a few weeks ago. An agreement had been reached between the Crusaders and the sultan. Ten years, ten months, and ten days of peace lay ahead for the Kingdom of Jerusalem and concerned the city of Acre, the plains around it, and the road to Nazareth. The city of Jerusalem was in the hands of the sultan.

Peter was part of the royal household of Lady Eleanor—a Spanish princess, the wife of the English crown prince, Edward. This was his first day of service. He was honored to be part of the household of the foreign lady, whose husband was a notorious Crusader.

1

Peter was an orphan raised in the streets of Acre, a bastard with a miserable life so far, a novice in his job, which he had received thanks to Brother John, the old monk, who had looked after him while he was a child. Now he lay in the dark with a terrible pain.

He had a splitting headache. He was on duty to guard the western gate with another soldier—What was his name? Peter struggled to recall the names of all the new people he had met recently. He also tried to remember how he had gotten here.

His sergeant had given him instructions, along with some rusty soldier's gear; a mail shirt; a dirty white surcoat, a long, sleeveless, linen garment worn over the armor; and a cheap, one-handed sword. Once he had received his equipment, he had departed to join another guard for night service.

A raiding party had returned early in the evening from the south and there were adventure stories to be heard in the taverns. Barrels of ale and wine were waiting to be drunk, for an evening full of stories, humor, and warring deeds was always accompanied by food and drink.

Jealous of those involved in the storytelling at the taverns, he had gone in search of a quiet place to take a piss, and he had found a dark corner with an old tree without leaves. Before he could accomplish his task, someone had hit him from the back in the dark and he had lost consciousness. Now he lay with opened eyes, wondering if this was his first and last day of service.

The muscles in his neck were on fire from the pain. He blinked a few times and took a deep breath. The pain was brutal. Peter looked around; he was somewhere between the fortress wall and the street near the gate of the castle.

He instinctively reached under his mail shirt to check his pouch. It was there, untouched. His sword was also in his scabbard. So, it hadn't been a thief. He rubbed his neck and realized blood was running down the back of his head.

"What a bloody mess," Peter thought, touching the wound gingerly. He decided that he would survive. He noticed the cold of the wet on his worn-out pants. Peter remembered that he had been about to relieve himself and realized grimly what had happened. His face twitched in an ironic smile; his attacker hadn't waited for him to relieve the pressure.

Why? Who? Questions descended on his thoughts like a sudden, summer rain. An alarm rang in his mind—the royal chambers in the castle were near.

The newly-hired guard—clad in a bloody mail shirt, a surcoat bearing the royal household guard's colors, and pissed trousers—ran to his post, his rusty sword in hand.

The same post he had abandoned to take a piss.

***

The Crusaders called him a Saracen, as they called all Muslims and Arabs that way. He did not care how they addressed to him. He was a renowned assassin. He never hesitated to slit someone's throat with his blade. He had heard his master telling another man that he was a valuable member of his company. Now, he walked with confidence toward his next task and hoped to earn a promotion soon.

He moved calmly and swiftly as he approached a sentry, put his hand on the guard's mouth and killed him with his knife from behind in the dark. Murdering people in the shadows was his job, a job done as easily as a hunter chasing his prey or a brewer making his ale. Or so he assumed; it was the job he had been doing all his life and he had never worked at anything else. He executed his task with calmness and with precision, never questioning the reasons behind the tasks he received nor caring enough to ask. He never left traces and he never met difficulties because he was always prepared.

His occupation allowed him to travel, to explore unseen lands and cities, to meet new people. The services he provided to his master were rare and his knowledge gave him some rank and freedom. He was a wolf amid a herd of lambs and he loved it. And he didn't fail his master's trust so far, and he didn't think there would be a time when he would not dare to use his talent.

Nevertheless, he had always admired his next victim. And that admiration held his dagger hidden in his vambrace, a forearm armor of leather. He asked himself questions, one of them rising in his mind and making him uncomfortable.

"Why him?"

"Why this one?" His brow furrowed but he quickly made his face placid; years of training would not permit him to reveal any inner doubt. In his mid-thirties, he thought he had seen enough for several lifetimes, but he wasn't prepared for this challenge.

He needed a new strategy.

The crown prince of England was his target. Edward the Longshanks, as his people called him. Lord Edward, at six feet two inches tall, towered head and shoulders above the average man. "Mighty tall," as Sir James would put it. He was broad-browed and broad-chested, blond and handsome despite having inherited a drooping eyelid from this father.

But, for the shadow killer, he had become close a friend.

Nearly a week after the truce agreement, he had received an order to kill Edward. He knew that the time to act was close and he must make his move soon, lest his master doubt him. But the assassin wasn't ready to fulfill his duty. Not yet. His stomach twisted and he had trouble sleeping; over the past few months, suspicion had grown in his heart along with an unstoppable storm of questions.

He had spent more than a year blending in with the Crusaders, spying. He had been integrating well, spending hours surveying the enemy and their plans. After he gained the trust of the target himself and got him alone to complete the task, now he hesitated. He had thought it would be another target, not Edward. After the peace agreement, it had been expected that the Englishman would leave to return to his homeland. Moreover, the assassin liked Edward. Last year, on his way back to Acre, he had saved his target's life to prove his loyalty. The prince had repaid him with recognition and trust, making him one of his most trusted spies and advisers. The short blade attached to his belt was a gift for his bravery from the prince of England. The scabbard was inscribed with the year 1271 and the words "Honor bound, Edward of England."

Such irony. The shadowy killer calculated his options and

assessed his future risk. The future of his family was at stake. His mother and sisters were under the protection of his master. He should not fail if he wanted to see them again. Unwillingly, he decided that he had to act.

He moved like a silent plague through the night, killing guard after guard under the cover of darkness with his poisoned dagger, hiding the short blade in his left leather vambrace. He approached through the western gate, the route he had chosen to withdraw by after his job was done. The Saracen always took precautions ahead of a job to clear those who could be obstacles to his escape.

The only thing he had not predicted was Peter, the young man, the orphan he had taken a liking to during his time in the Crusaders' city of Acre. How had he gotten here? The assassin felt pity for the young man. Leaving his blade in its sheath, he reached instead for his club and stunned him.

The assassin walked through the corridor of stones straight to the door of the prince's chambers. The last guardsman stood in front of the door. He was nearly asleep. The single sentry recognized the Saracen; everyone knew him as the infidel who had saved the life of Lord Edward. Now he was one of the most trusted men of his retinue. With his rank, he could visit the prince without a preliminary appointment— even during the night, if necessary.

"I need to see Lord Edward right away," the Saracen said.

The guardsman blinked and scratched his forehead, noticing the famous gift, but said nothing.

"It is a matter of urgency which requires the attention of the prince himself!" the Saracen added. It looked as if the sentry would fall asleep again, but he overcame his fatigue and told the visitor to wait. The guard opened the door and slipped inside. After a couple of minutes, his face appeared again, nodding in the direction of the lord's chambers, and he allowed the infidel to enter.

The assassin stepped into the middle chamber, which was connected to the prince's private rooms. The sound of the night was playing and he anticipated his target to come to him from his bedroom, through the door in front of him. He wasn't disappointed; Edward emerged, wearing only his underclothes.

It was time for the Englishman to meet his fate.

***

There was a rumor about a specially-trained spy and assassin hired from the Mamluks' Sultan Baibars to take away the prince's soul.

Rumors circulated around the Crusaders' camp all the time. But this one had been fading since the truce had been negotiated.

The orphan was running and had almost reached his post. Near the gate, to the right of the door, Peter found his partner sitting on the ground, motionless, his kettle helmet tilted in a strange position on his right side. Peter shook his shoulder to wake him up and his hand touched something wet and sticky. Blood.

He quickly realized that the guardsman was dead. He barely knew him, never could remember his name. Blood bubbled from the open wound on his throat. It was fresh; the killer was near, a few moments ahead at most. A quick thought ran through his mind and he asked himself why he had been spared and not killed like the other guard. Peter had no time for a proper answer during his savage run to Edward's chamber. An answer would be found soon.

Peter climbed the stone stairs in haste. He rushed into the antechamber like a hurricane, pushing aside the lone guardsman, who had almost fallen asleep. There wasn't time to scream a warning or to explain what was happening. Peter was tired to the bone, but he drew his rusty sword and kicked the massive wooden door open, rushing forward without pausing for thought.

After the blow he had received earlier that night, he was moving in what felt like a trance. Everything around him shifted slowly, his body flying like a feather fighting with the wind.

Peter saw Edward, who was near the table, stabbed on the

hip with a dagger. The assassin was about to deliver the final blow with his blade, but the sound of the door breaking open made him turn his head. The distraction gave the prince a chance—Edward angrily slammed his fist into the attacker's temple. The Englishman was tall and mighty and even wounded, his arms' long reach gave him a massive advantage. The blow was delivered with such rage that it knocked the assailant to the ground for a moment. Peter sprinted toward the assassin and hit him with the pommel of his sword— a vengeful blow on the back of the head—as the man tried to get up. The assassin's body collapsed on the ground and Edward kicked him and kicked him again as he growled. He grabbed a dagger from the nearest table and moved as if to finish him.

But fate was unpredictable; Edward's face jerked, he fell and went into convulsions. Before he closed his eyes, he looked at his rescuer's face.

"Eleanor, the baby, they ...." Edward whispered and fainted.

The lone guardsman who had followed Peter looked at the prince then back to the orphan.

"You saved his life!"

"If he lives," Peter said, doubtfully eying the unconscious lord.

"Have you served him long?"

"It's my first day, and I hope it's not my last."

CHAPTER TWO

City of Acre, Holy Land, Friday, 17th of June, in the year 1272 of the incarnation of Christ, Lord Edward's Chamber

Peter was shivering like a child before a punishment. He sat with his back to the wall. Although the wall was nicely cold that summer night, Peter dripped with sweat. His head still pulsated with pain. His right hand still held tight the hilt of his sword, the pommel covered in blood. Suddenly he hoped that no one would smell the piss on his pants.

What had just happened? Peter wondered. Somehow, he felt important, no longer regretting that he had missed the night in the tavern. He felt as if he were in the center of the known world. He had prevented an assassin from delivering his final blow.

He was a common man with a sword, but his act of courage had made him a key figure tonight and he was elated. He didn't want to lose this sense of excitement. He was part of something great; the feeling was surreal.

This was a new experience for him. He had never been involved in such events. He had never been in a battle, or on a battlefield, or in any military action. He had dreamt of being in a real battle and shield wall one day. He wanted to feel the fear and the danger himself, to unhorse a wealthy knight and take his warhorse and gear. To win renown.

Someday he would become a knight and be able to afford a decent piece of land he could call home. Peter was fantasizing like a child, with an innocent smile on his face.

Now he had been involved in defeating an assassination attempt, a killing ground, making fast and important decisions that had saved a life. "A life of a prince …" Peter smiled; he was proud of himself. Until now, he had been an ordinary man with no war experience. Having recently joined the royal household guards attached to the Lady Eleanor, his main duties consisted of delivering messages and some other general chores.

"Life is unpredictable," Brother John had used to say to Peter. "You will never be ready for the future so you must embrace whatever unfolds; you must face life without fear." Peter thought fondly of the man who had raised him "God has a plan for all of us and nobody has to be afraid." The old man used to say this whenever the time was right. The orphan liked him, and he was his closest friend.

But now Peter was in the center of the world, in the city of Acre, the de facto capital of the remnant Jerusalem kingdom, the Holy Land, and he had saved Prince Edward's life. Or so he hoped.

In front of his eyes, everything was moving at a glacial pace. The newly arrived servants and guards were in a panic because of the prince. They lifted Edward, moved him to the next chamber and placed him on the bed. Peter followed them as he saw that the wounded man's face was pale. One of the servants examined the dagger and smelled it.

"Poison," the servant said.

Edward's blood must have been poisoned by the assassin's dagger. And now the hope for his life was evaporating like a morning mist. Peter realized that his courage and deed might mean nothing if the prince dies.

The closest members of his household had entered the chamber moments after Peter. One of them pushed him aside; another kicked the Saracen on the ground. A third immediately started asking questions. The whole place was in disorder than minutes ago.

Lady Eleanor entered the room.

She froze for a moment, her eyes filled with horror as she started to shiver like a nervous rabbit. She went to her husband. She took his hand and started talking to him, sobbing.

"My love …." Her eyes filled with tears. "Stay with me, please."

Edward stared at her while another convulsion passed through his body.

Time began to speed up again. Lord Otto appeared like thunder in the room. Otto De Grandson, a Savoyard knight, an adviser, a diplomat, and close friend to Lord Edward was in his mid-thirties, not as tall as the prince, but almost an inch above the average.

He approached Edward, and Peter thought he saw a pain in his eyes when he looked at his friend convulsing on the bed. From the moment he entered, all the fuss stopped and all eyes were on him.

"Bring some fresh water, call the physicians, restore the guards' posts, and close the city gates." Otto's voice was calm. He stopped his surveying eyes on Peter, gave him a nod, and turned to Eleanor.

"Save your tears, milady; he is not dead yet," De Grandson said.

Sir John de Vescy kicked the body of the assassin who was unconscious, once more. He pulled out his sword menacingly. But Otto stopped him.

"Please, John put the blade away." Otto's words were cold. "Make sure that no one touches him; we need him. Tie him up, move him to the next room, and put him under guard."

It was as if someone had put a spear between De Vescy's ribs. Peter had heard that the Scot rarely obeyed; he was used to giving commands, not obeying them. He turned quickly with a burst of anger to Otto. He opened his mouth to say something, but De Grandson was a step ahead of him once more.

"Yes, I know, my friend. I want to kill him, too. But first, we need to find some answers. We have responsibilities. Now, go and find de Grailly."

His stone eyes were so determined that nobody could cross him, not even the Highlander.

"Peter," Otto said, "I need you to find a man and to bring him here for me. Do you know Sir James of Durham?"

The orphan nodded.

"He just returned from a mission; he must be in the English tavern. Now, go."

The common man was feeling important again after having received the order. He stood up from his resting place to obey.

"Run fast! We have a life to save," Otto shouted after him.

A flicker of hope was still breathing in his mind, as Peter fled the room.

***

A warm, summer breeze from the sea stroked Peter's back as he left the castle. He was on the same route he had passed earlier. The bodies of the dead guards were still there. Peter's mind was working again.

Why had the assassin acted now? The peace was sealed; there was no logical reason to cause trouble by killing one of the Crusade's leaders. And why the hell had the Saracen killed these guards, but not him? Despite the turmoil and chaos, he had recognized the attacker's face. He wasn't a stranger to the Crusader's camp; he was an insider. Peter shuddered at this thought. This provoked new questions and new thoughts, which would have to wait till later.

"This must have been an escape route for him," Peter decided, running with his gear, his pain, and his new task.

He turned left after passing the gate, without slowing down. The only sound present was from his rhythmic steps and from the scabbard rubbing his tattered pants. His heart beat fast; his head pulsated from the pain and drops of sweat were running down his temple and the back of his neck, but he didn't bother to wipe them off.

He was used to running; as a boy, he had chased other children down these streets. He often used to deliver messages from the old monk to the castle or other parts of the city. Most of the streets and shortcuts were familiar to him. Peter took one of the side streets to avoid the main road and get to his destination faster. All the paths in the city were narrow, even the key ones.

He was following the escape route of the assailant. Had the assassin been alone? A moment later, Peter turned left and entered an alley darkened by the surrounding buildings and a few bushes and headed to a nearby big old tree in the middle of a small square.

It was a crossroads. Southward led to the Venetians; the Hospitallers were to the west, near the Genovese Quarters. The running man was the only source of sound in the square for a few heartbeats.

Suddenly, four shadows appeared from all directions.

Devil's shadows, without faces, blades in hands—with surprise on their side, they encircled the courier. Peter, the common guard with only half a day of experience at service, was hit from the back again.

"Not again! Twice in a single night," thought the member of the royal household guard as he fell to meet the dusty, cold street with his face.

He was stunned, but he didn't lose consciousness. After the first blow that night, the excitement of the following events was strong and he refused to pass out.

"Is it him?" a throaty voice with a French accent asked in the dark.

A hand grabbed Peter's hair and raised his head to examine it. The orphan felt the power of the man over him.

"By this time, it must be done already." He felt his surcoat being tugged at.

A younger voice split the silence. "No, some bloody, stupid royal guard, looking for a tavern—"

The first voice, cold and older, interrupted the second one. "He didn't look like a man searching for a drink, did he? Look at his gear; there are spots of dry blood along with the fresh ones you just made. It's too early to be changing off the guards. Does anyone know him?"

No answer came.

"Kill him! He is not our goal," a calm order was spoken in the same cold, commanding voice. "He might recognize us.

Get rid of him."

"What about the body?" the younger voice hissed into the night.

"That's your concern, not mine. That's why I'm paying you." The older man turned away and retreated into the dark. "And Julian, please do it fast and come back here. We need to wait a little bit longer, I guess. We need assurance."

So, the younger man was called Julian. The orphan held his breath, trying not to move, but to listen and memorize the distinctive marks of his assailants. This small party must have been waiting to ambush someone in the dark, and it wasn't hard to guess who their target was. They knew what was going on.

How did they know? Only a few minutes had passed since the events in the castle. Peter's right cheek laid on the pavement and, for a short moment, he opened his eyes and saw the man's boots, the one called Julian. He was wearing soldier boots—expensive ones. Peter would not be able to afford boots like these in a lifetime. He knew he could find decent used leather shoes at the market for a coin, but these were rare gear: pricey, custom-made for their owner. From the moment he saw the boots, he envied his attacker. The orphan felt ashamed of his desire to have them. A different matter should have troubled him now.

Peter had to find a way to survive this. He was alone in the dark with Julian.

"Hey! What's going on there?" A sharp voice came from the southern road leading to the tavern that the Englishmen frequented.

Loud steps were approaching. Julian had been holding him and dropped him on the ground. Peter opened his eyes and saw the dark figure had vanished in the night. His life was saved and, once again, he could relax.

He tried to stand up and continue his mission, but two hits on the head were too much for him. His body collapsed to the earth again like a rotten plank. This time he lost consciousness.

CHAPTER THREE

City of Acre, Holy Land, Friday, 17th of June, in the year 1272 of the incarnation of Christ

Peter opened his eyes again.

Everything was foggy and a strange smell lingered around him. A small light from a candle was dancing to his left. The smell was familiar, yet he couldn't place exactly what it was. He took a deep breath and tried to determine where he was.

Peter was lying on a hard bed in a dark room. He struggled to remember the last time he had rested on a bed. The scent remained, sharp and acrid, making Peter's skin tingle. It was like a looming, fatal end that couldn't be avoided.

He lay on his back, eyes open, with a strange feeling of déjà vu. Peter examined a bandage on his head. His motions were hard to coordinate, but he felt the gluey blood spots on the back of his skull. There was a pain, albeit fading, which reminded him of the night's events.

His eyes turned around, looking for a window, and when he found one, he smiled at the Moon. The Moon smiled back at him, it seemed. He was alive and he had survived an assault. Was this the same night or the next? He had lost his sense of time. He tried to remember what had happened.

Peter remembered the need to piss, then the assassin and the prince. He recalled the task he had received from Otto, the shortcut he had taken, the trap he had fallen into, and the feeling of an inevitable end approaching his soul. He remembered he had been saved before he passing out. He was a lucky one.

Peter slowly turned his gaze to a wooden door, which was barely outlined in the dancing darkness. The sound of steps approaching could be heard. At least two men were outside the room in the corridor. A sound of wood scratching the floor as the door opened woke up the night.

The cold night air entered the room; the vivid flame of the candle flickered but a little spark survived and the light was restored. Peter tried to focus on the dark figures that entered. They were most likely men. Not that women weren't allowed to work in the hospital, but it was rare. One of them was particularly familiar to Peter, but somehow, he couldn't remember from where.

"You're awake," the first man said as he revealed himself, stepping into the candlelight.

"Peter? How's your head?" His hard and harsh accent sliced the night.

The first man was one of the tallest Peter had ever seen. His broad chest added to his presence: that of a giant oak. "A red oak," Peter thought. His bushy, dark-red hair and his vivid brown eyes were absorbing everything. He looked like a man who was closing the chapter on his thirties but was still solid as a rock. His ironic smile, combined with his Scottish appearance, made him the most unforgettable knight from the North. He was one of the few who had followed Lord Edward from beyond the sea and his name was James. Sir James of Durham.

Everyone knew him, even Peter. He was one of the distinguished knights from Edward's household. A loud one, with brutally dark humor, but nonetheless a brave soldier with a fearsome reputation. Most of the men called him Red Herring, because when he got angry, his pale face turned red, like the fish from the northern sea—a herring, kippered by smoking and salting until it turned reddish-brown.

"How are you, lad?" the Scot asked again.

Peter was already rising up, using the wall for support and groping about in the dark with his right hand. He took a deep breath and opened his dry mouth.

"Like an oak tree, sir." Then he swayed and searched for some support. The man behind Sir James approached and caught Peter before he collapsed to the ground. The orphan from Acre looked at the short man who held him.

"David, sit him down on the bed! But where are my manners, this is David, my sergeant."

James scratched his chin while the sergeant moved Peter effortlessly. David was short and stocky and had a cold, chubby face with enough minor battle scars that his age was indiscernible. He wasn't talkative; he was one of the men that you could never remember.

"A dancing oak tree, as I see," James said as he chuckled. "You are still bleeding. Give him a cup of water."

While the short man was fetching the water, James said, "You know, lad, while you sleep your body dries up, and the first thing to do in the morning is to kiss some water like you are kissing a virgin." He gave Peter a dark smile and patiently waited for him to empty the cup.

"So, lad, I think you have a story to tell. You were unconscious for almost an hour. What happened before that?"

Waiting eyes were on Peter, and he felt that now was his turn to say something, but the words didn't come easily. He ran his fingers through his hair, touching the bandage that reminded him of his first adventure of the night.

"Do you need a little help, young man?" Red Herring asked. The knight scratched his beard again. "Let's start with this. How did you find yourself on the street with an enemy upon you, near that beloved tavern of ours?"

"Ah …." Peter searched for words. He wasn't that shy, but the presence of the short sergeant somehow made him feel nervous.

"You decide to take a walk with your royal household guard dress on this enjoyable night, lad?" Sir James was grinning in expectation.

Peter told them everything—even the fact that he had been absent from his post in search of a place to take a piss. While he was telling that part, his face flushed and he secretly took a look at his pants, hoping no one noticed the stain. He was ashamed for leaving his post and for his pissed pants. He also felt stupid for being so easily knocked down on the street earlier and trapped. He was lucky Red Herring had shown up from the nearby English tavern in search of a place to unload the ale he had drunk. Peter smiled for a moment. What a pissing night; his life's fate twisted twice. After he finished his tale, he paused and took a deep breath. He raised his eyes in search of some reaction from the men in front of him.

The knight was dressed in an expensive mail shirt, a white surcoat with a red cross on the front, and a red scarf tied around his right arm below the shoulder. What had once been white was now worn out and looked more like yellowish dust. The sergeant's mail shirt, in contrast, was a cheap one, riddled with rust. He obviously spent more time cleaning his master's war gear than his own clothes. Red Herring was wearing war mail boots, reaching below the knee and tied up with laces. When he moved, the iron rings of his mail produced a mild, singing sound. David was wearing dull leather boots, finishing below the calf with the laces wrapped around them. Similar boots had been given to Peter when he had been put on the list of the royal household early that day, but his were much dirtier and older.

James' face was serious, pondering the situation and scratching his beard with his left hand. His right hand was on the pommel of his sword. Peter had heard that wealthy knights bought the best swords. And the best swords were purchased from a German master blacksmith. There was a cross on the round pommel, encircled with a gold decoration. The sword was simply a masterpiece. Peter wished for one desperately. He wished not simply to own it, but to be a master of using it.

"A strange coincidence," James thought out loud. "At this interesting hour for a walk, four strangers—obviously soldiers or mercenaries, according to your description," he continued with his eyes dancing in the dark room. "These men are waiting for someone and the story of what happened in Lord Edward's chambers ... Ah, isn't it supposed to be a calm night, David? My arse sure isn't." A hard laugh came out from his big chest.

"You are a lucky bastard, lad, aren't you? What are the odds that I should happen along just then? The streets are full of nasty jerks at this time of the night. Ha ... and I was also going for a piss." His laugh and good mood helped Peter to feel a bit better.

Over the past few weeks, most of the Crusaders had been leaving, ship by ship. Daily affairs were arising in Acre once more. Merchants' interests were again above all others. The contracts formed between the merchants and most of the knights following the prince had expired long before. Spirits were low. Only the most loyal of Edward's retinue were still with their lord. Red Herring was one of them, Peter assumed, although most of his fellow Scots were now gone. Events such as the ones which had transpired this night were curious for a bored man, especially a knight from another part of the world. Red Herring had recently returned from a raid southward, outside the territory concerning the Peace treaty, and now he was needed again.

"Sir Otto asked for you and sent me to find you," Peter said, trying again to stand up.

"Yes; however, I found you," Sir James replied.

The orphan's eyes opened wide, and he realized that the man was right. The orphan owed his life to the Scottish knight.

"Thank you," Peter said, "for saving my life."

"I didn't do anything. Besides, you are the man of the day, or rather the night, eh lad?" The knight put his hand on Peter's shoulder.

"A brave deed, lad, and in your first day of service." James smiled as he studied Peter's young face. "De Grandson wants to talk, so when you feel strong enough, lad, we will go to him."

"Lord Edward?" Peter asked.

"I hope he is still alive. He is a strong man, lad; you should know that. Some people say Edward was repeatedly sick as a child. But he grew up and matured. It would be a terrible death, to die like that—like a rat in a poisonous hell. A horrible story."

Peter rose from the bed. He was tired to the bone. His head

was heavy on his shoulders. But the orphan was energized by the fact that he was still alive.

He hoped Edward had a chance after all.

"I do not know another man with such mental strength and such determination in his eyes. Whenever he went, he drew respect. And Lord Edward's devotion to his beloved wife Lady Eleanor is so strong," James said.

Peter felt good about saving his life. The orphan from Acre had saved a precious life. Every life was precious. But Peter was proud to have received recognition from a knight like Sir James as well.

"I'm ready," Peter said and he took his belt from the floor, geared up, took a look at the candle, and went out the door, following the knight and his sergeant.

He had always wanted to see the Hospitaller Quarters from the inside, the beautiful mosaics, decorations, and tapestries. But today, he was on the lowest level—the hospice, where the sick and dying lay, waiting for their last sacrament, and where most of them would face their final peace or something worse. One could tell by the smell here that these poor souls belonged to the lower layers and Peter was one of them.

Peter was of low origin, one of the urchins who had lived in the streets of Acre all their lives. He had never known his father or mother. Brother John had taken care of him every time he got involved into a trouble. He had mentioned once that Peter's father had died far away on a battlefield many years before—the year he was born, to be more precise. But Peter never cared to hear about his parents. Deep down, he was hurt that his family had left him to his fate.

There were times when Peter hadn't listened to the words of the old monk. He had been a bad child sometimes, causing trouble with his ruffian friends on the street. His scraps and adventures had given him a plethora of scars over his body; others were internal, invisible to everyone but himself but which had made him strong, mentally. He remembered a recent incident in which he had lain on the street in a pool of his own blood, beaten half to death by some mercenaries whom he had tried to steal from. This episode had forced him to try to change his life for the better. He used to work for a local bandit who organized young lads to do his dirty business for him. And for what? A few pieces of hard, inedible bread? Pathetic. Remembering this, Peter smiled to himself. He thought about where he was now. Sometimes it wasn't easy, but he got used to smiling and laughing at himself because it gave him some hope and courage. Hope that the world wasn't so dark after all.

***

Peter, Red Herring, and the sergeant walked along the street in the direction of the castle. The Moon was bright and silent and the stars were vivid, looking at Peter and his previous encounter with Julian. David held a torch, walking in front, investigating the darkness. The city of Acre at night wasn't pretty; it was dark and scary. A man had once described Acre to Peter as a sinful city filled with all uncleanness, and that was true. It wasn't marvelous in the daylight either, but Peter liked it, as it was the only home he had known. He knew most of the city districts—where bad men gathered, where merchants worked their business, where Crusaders walked, and where the local representatives of the king passed their time.

Peter was in deep thought, wondering about the assassin. He had been shocked to recognize the attacker's face. It was the Saracen who had saved Edward's life about a year before. Peter didn't know what to think.

Everyone knew the story.

The newly-arrived Crusaders from a land called England had set a raid to a village, 15 miles to the east. The raid turned out to be a disaster. The Sun, the heat, the sand, and the shortage of fresh water combined with fatigue were devastating to any army, no matter its size. Their bodies and their horses were not yet accustomed to life in the Holy Land, neither to the food nor the weather conditions. This had cost them determination, motivation, and, ultimately, many horses and men.

On their way back from the sacked village, they were

ambushed. Their low energy and spirit almost cost them their lives. But somehow, they managed to repel the infidels. During the fight, a small force detached from the main body of the enemy raiding party and engaged Lord Edward's private bodyguards. The impact was brutal, fierce, and bloody. One of the Mamluks' soldiers unhorsed the prince by putting a spear into the ribs of his stallion. He almost succeeded in killing the Englishman.

But one of the merchants who followed the army stepped in. He stood against the attacker with a spear he had taken from the nearby dead raider. He struck the chain mail of the horseman using all his strength. The spearhead pierced the assailant from chest to spinal cord, splashing the ground with blood. Edward's life was saved.

A new hero was born, a Saracen, an infidel, an ordinary merchant. As a sign of gratitude, Lord Edward bestowed a present on him: a short, encrusted blade. Edward asked the Muslim about his homeland and he was always offering valuable information about the locals and their customs. He became the prince's local spy. Edward gave him some tricky tasks and after the Saracen had done it, he soon became one of the trusted spy advisers employed by the prince.

Young lads, hungry for stories, always followed him. He would tell them some news, stories or gossips, and the kids loved it. Peter was one of the lads who enjoyed the Saracen's tales. Even Peter had heard all the details about how a local inhabitant had become a hero by saving a lord's life. Most of the Crusaders were envious of him and many admired him, too. It was a brave act indeed. Peter had never met such a hero before. He was always intrigued while watching the Saracen in the city. He was always interested in local activities, as the logistics in the harbor, the merchants' taxes and prizes. He traded in medicines and, as such, he was useful to the hospitals and the monasteries. He often visited the Merchants Quarters, the Templars, and the Hospitallers. There was an incident one day at the harbor, a broken wagon wheel collapsed near the Saracen, but he managed to evade it as he jumped left, agile for a man in his mid-thirties. He was a strong man, energetic, clever, and polite.

He was the same man who had visited the old monastery daily and talked to monks, selling them goods and ingredients. He used to talk to Peter as well and the orphan liked the fact that someone noticed him. Once, Peter helped the man carry luggage from the harbor to a merchant. The orphan got a coin for his work.

Lord Edward had baptized the man, naming him Edward, following the old custom whereby a new Christian would be given the same name as the person baptizing him. Most of the people now called him Edward the Saracen, to distinguish him from the original name-bearer. He quickly became a hero and he was the personal advisor to the foreign Crusader, the future king of England.

Seeing this man covered in blood on the floor after trying to assassinate the prince was a real shock. Peter was unable to speak, stunned by the fact that Edward the Saracen was the assassin. The world had turned upside down in a night. The hero had been reduced to a traitor, the prince lay dying, and Peter had earned renown. He now understood why the assassin hadn't killed him. He hadn't expected Peter to be there at his new post. Maybe Edward the Saracen felt some sympathy for him. Peter felt strange.

Peter would remember this night all his life. But it wasn't over yet; sunrise was still far away and, for Peter's bravery to have any meaning, Lord Edward would have to survive.

As he walked with the two older men through the city streets, Peter thought about the assault upon his own life, as well. He had taken the shortcut, bypassing the main street and fallen into a trap. A trap or meeting point destined for someone else.

"If I were in an assassin's shoes," Peter wondered, "how could I arrange my own withdrawal unnoticed?" His mind worked busily.

"Sir …. Can we go on the merchants' street?" The question was shot like an arrow in the dark.

"What's in your mind, lad?" Red Herring slowed down the pace.

"I ... I've got a feeling, sir ... that ...."

"What? You want me to circle around the city like a homeless dog because of a feeling? Listen, lad, I'm tired to the bone; I've just returned from a raid with my men ...." Herring stopped for a moment. "I'm explaining myself to a one-day service guard, like a—" Suddenly, his mood changed.

They stopped for a moment.

"Why?" His eyes struck Peter like a hunting spear to a wild boar. "You want to check a possible exit route of this bastard," Herring guessed and Peter noticed that the knight's eyes brightening. "The assault near the English tavern wasn't for you, I guess, but for that treacherous bugger. To disappear fast enough unnoticed, he couldn't do it through any of the gates, even though there was no guarantee that the body of the prince would be discovered quickly. But this one is a clever one, eh?" James said.

"He would need assistance!" Peter said.

"If you're thinking what I'm thinking, then we need to take a look." The knight grinned, showing his yellow teeth. "To be sure you don't walk alone in the dark, you know." The Scot laughed again.

The party of three men—the knight, the sergeant, and the orphan—decided to postpone their meeting with Otto for the moment.

Peter now led the group. He was determined and focused, knowing exactly where he would take them.

The three men were equipped with swords, and the two high-ranking soldiers also carried daggers on their leather belts. In the city, shields weren't used often, especially when going to the tavern to get drunk. Peter held his sword hilt tightly, quickening his pace.

> *My desire is to die*
> *But not in the tavern drinking*
> *My sword must be in my hand*
> *Ready when I need it*
> *Angels when they come*
> *I shall cry out loud*

Spare this fighter, God, he's mad
Fighting your battle and absolutely glad!

Red Herring surprised everyone with this drinking song about battle—even the night and his guardians, the stars. He finished with a throaty laugh. He looked at the shorter sergeant, who said nothing.

"Wishing you were on the tavern table with a cup of wine, David?"

"Not at all, sir."

"Glad you share my thirst for troubles, man." Sir James' love of laughter intrigued Peter. He noticed this was the first time he had heard the sergeant's voice.

Peter liked Red Herring—his undisguised humor, his laugh, and his presence. He had used to watch him when he came to the hospital to see the wounded and to talk to the brethren. There was a spacious courtyard in the headquarters of the order, where a man could see knights of the hospital train with sergeants and the men-at-arms in their war skills. The orphan had spent a time observing them while helping Brother John.

Myriad Crusaders passed through the city. Most left after visiting; rarely, they settled here. People called them by one name: Franks. But Peter understood from the monk that this was a collective name for the invaders from beyond the sea. They came from different parts of the world: France, England, the Low Countries, Venice, and many others. Strangers, all together with the pilgrims and merchants.

The orphan knew only his world, the city of Acre and its vicinity. His limited knowledge of the outside world made it hard for him to understand why so many men arrived from the sea to visit this sandy land, to see holy places from long-ago events. He was curious to know why. He wasn't religious, although the monk had tried hard to make him so. His poor life so far had taught him that if he wanted to eat, he must fight for every piece of food. To him, there was long-vanished God who couldn't provide him with food or a warm bed on cold nights.

The monk disagreed, but Peter wasn't stupid. He saw the

donations monasteries received and the military fanatic orders too. The friars also cultivated their lands and earned revenue by selling goods.

They were almost there.

"There is a Saracen merchant who lived there, near the Venetian Quarters," Peter said. "I used to see Edward the Saracen often in the company of this man in the market and talking on the street." The orphan felt that these two men were somehow connected. They must check the merchant.

"This is it," Peter said.

He stopped and looked at the two-story building in front of them. On the right side, there were wooden garret windows, closed for the night. On the left was the stable. The building was silent. He stepped forward to the wooden door and lifted his hand to knock. He paused, an alarm sounding in his mind, as his hair rose up on his neck

Something was not right.

Peter turned around slowly, examining the doors of the nearby buildings and the warehouse across the street. A light came down from the clear Moon and they had the sergeant's torch, but it was still dark out. There was complete silence. Even the sea breeze felt asleep.

The feeling was lying, Peter decided. His hand reached again to the door. He wondered whether he should knock or shout to wake up the dwellers. And he moved his fingers an inch closer to the door.

The door opened when he touched it. The wood creaking as the inside of the house was revealed. Darkness lay in front of them. Red Herring stood still and whispered, "be quiet, lads. Something's wrong here."

In one move, all three unsheathed their swords. The pommel of James's sword-blade reflected the moonlight and made Peter blink. The knight pushed the door with his boot.

It wasn't wise to leave one's door open at night. The merchants' street was close to the Italian Quarters, near the harbor. The harbor was the mercenaries' world; untrustworthy men abounded.

The three of them stood still on the threshold of the front

door. The Moon reflected their short mail sleeves under their dirty and dusty surcoats. As they entered, James took the lead. Nobody leapt from the shadows at them. Still, the soundless stillness was dancing in the night, too hushed.

The torch was left outside. They stopped and waited for their eyes to adjust to the darkness. Red Herring and his sergeant were experienced men; Peter assessed from their calm movements that this wasn't the first time they had done this.

For the orphan, however, this experience was new. Peter felt again that time was slowing. His heart rate was high; he felt his pulsating heart would crash through his chest and come out to see what was happening with its own eyes.

"Take a breath, lad." Red Herring said. "And stay close."

Peter tried but didn't feel much of a difference.

The noise of moving furniture scratched the soundless background. It was coming from the upper story. Some light slipped through the upper wooden planking. Peter quickly examined the room around him. He saw empty shelves; nothing on the table on the right.

"Follow me," the Scottish knight said. He jumped onto the wooden staircase. David was a step behind his master. A few heartbeats later, James stood on the second story, in front of a closed door with his sword pointed onward.

Red Herring kicked the door and stormed the upper story.

Peter was the last to enter the first room on the second floor. There were a few pieces of wooden furniture, scattered and upended. Three men in mail shirts and sleeveless, leather vests appeared to be ransacking the place. Their dark cloaks made them appear bigger. One of them was carrying an oil lamp; the other two stood there, swords naked.

"Put down your weapons," Red Herring shouted, "in the name of the King!" He stopped for a moment to wait for the opponents' answer.

"We do not take orders from you," the tallest of the swordsmen replied boldly. He was dressed in an expensive battle dress with rich decoration that distinguished him from the others. A thick, black leather sword belt tightened his armor against the waist. His boots were of an excellent quality—pricey and custom-made.

Peter knew those boots.

Their bearer was named Julian. The orphan and the assailant faced each other. Julian blinked and stared at Peter as if at a poisonous snake. The orphan was now able to assess his enemy from feet to head; his opponent's blond hair was tied in a ponytail and ran down to his shoulders. His glasslike eyes were cold, Peter noticed. He was broad-chested, in the end of his thirties, taller than the orphan, and almost the size of the Herring, but more broad-shouldered.

Red Herring bided his time. He waited for the opposing party to make a move. And they did.

Julian nodded to his followers.

"Kill them all." His voice was overconfident.

His calmness was strengthened by another couple of men who arrived from the next room. That wasn't something Peter or his companions could have predicted. A raiding party of at least five men was there, searching for someone or something.

They were clearly desperate to finish their task. But there was no merchant in sight. Julian was in charge, the orphan assumed, as he had given the killing order. He wondered what had happened to the strong, older voice from earlier that evening, which had given Julian orders.

The room became a battlefield; the two parties faced each other and clashed like children with wooden sticks. Except the sticks were real weapons designed for killing men and Peter had not received any lesson how to use it.

Herring attacked with his sword from above. David parried with his weapon, cutting a blow from the left, leaving Peter to cover him from the right flank. Peter stood, staring at the enemy. He hadn't expected to see the man who had wanted to kill him earlier on the street. This man wanted to kill him without mercy like he was nothing. Like a bug which Julian wanted to smash.

Peter managed to take his position and push aside a third assailant, who was charging toward the sergeant. He glanced at James. Red Herring's face turned vicious, true to his nickname, as he hurled insults at his opponents, provoking and goading them on. Peter realized with awe that the Scot was fighting two men at once. But James was also a tavern fighter and knew some dirty tricks. He struck out with his elbows and legs, throwing his opponents off balance, slowly influencing the skirmish to his favor. The sergeant, seeing the combat prowess of his mentor on full display, rose to the occasion as well, raining down fierce blows upon his opponent in a storm of steel.

Peter was struggling. The art of sword fighting was new to him and he held his blade like a child holding a stick. He needed to learn fast. He remembered observing the men-at-arms in training. For a moment, he felt he looked stupid and clumsy. But he pushed these thoughts aside; right now, he needed to win and to survive, no matter how. He swung his weapon as he had seen the soldiers do it in practice. But this was not a practice. This was real—and deadly.

Julian smiled at the clumsy actions of Peter. The blond man watched the fight. The savage actions of Herring made him join the fray. He drew his long blade, which looked custom made. Julian's one-handed sword was much larger than average. He waited for a moment and calculated. One of the men engaged with Red Herring lost his balance. James swung his sword and hit the crossguard of the owner's weapon. The man felt and the blond knight took his place.

Julian advanced and kicked the Scottish knight on his left thigh, trying to push him down. Peter watched, feeling like the moment was lasting a lifetime. He saw the danger to Herring. The orphan made a feint in an attempt to divert his face-to-face attacker; he pushed him out of the way with his two hands like a child fighting for a bread as David struck the man with his sword. Peter jumped over to assist James. He put his left shoulder forward like a battering ram and hit the enemies' leader from the back.

Julian's mantle managed to soften the hit and he quickly got back up to his feet. As he rose, he saw Peter's sword coming from above. The orphan had aimed at his neck but Julian easily deflected the clumsy swing. Peter cursed himself; he didn't know how to use the weapon properly. The sound of swords kissing fiercely filled the room.

Julian restored his position and counterattacked. Peter fought off the blows but his opponent was too good; he was too fast. The blond warrior lowered his head as his eyes looked through a lowered brow as he tried to cut Peter down. The lad tried to parry the blows. Julian's weapon met his rusty sword a few inches above the crossguard and broke it. The orphan froze.

Julian closed in on his target and swiftly moved his blade to the orphan's neck. Peter stepped back, as the sword reached his right cheek. The edge cut the flesh like a knife through butter. The orphan felt the blood on his face as he tripped on something on the floor, lost his balance and fell on his backside.

In this moment, the frightening sound of flying arrows put this fight to sleep.

CHAPTER FOUR

FOUR DAYS EARLIER

Holy Land, the Kingdom of Jerusalem, Monday, 13th of June, in the year 1272 of the incarnation of Christ

Red Herring was on a trail.

He had received an important mission.

Intelligence about the Desert Wolf and his lair had arrived. Everyone knew of the Desert Wolf's extraordinary skills and knowledge and the fact that he worked for Sultan Baibars. Either his lair had been discovered or he had been betrayed.

The rumors that the Desert Wolf had provided the warring leader of the Mamluks, Sultan of Egypt and all of Syria, Baibars, with drawings of new siege engines, which could throw larger stones were giving the Crusaders trouble. Even if they were unfounded, which were not yet clear, they threatened the castles of the Kingdom of Jerusalem. He also possessed knowledge of the Franks' castles' plans and their weak spots. This was a rumor, but a dangerous one. King Hugh of Cyprus and Jerusalem also felt uncomfortable. His barons had caused him enough trouble, and he had no strength left to think of a new threat from the sultan. After all, the Crusaders and the Mamluks had signed a peace treaty.

Still, the intelligence about the Desert Wolf's lair and the rumor were a good reason to arrange an investigation party to check it. A damned good reason, indeed.

Sitting on the saddle on his gray destrier, his big warhorse,

Red Herring looked to the Sun, whose vibrant, smiling face was rising from the horizon. The Sun's warmth transferred to his mood and Sir James smiled back at him. He scratched his newly-shaved face and dropped his hand to pet the neck of his horse.

This raid was controversial. Otto, James, and the English prince had discussed it passionately. James had voted against it, but the Savoyard knight and Lord Edward had voted for going.

"Why?" Red Herring had asked them. "The peace treaty is signed. We must think about going home."

Edward wasn't in a rush to set off from the Holy Land once the truce had been agreed upon. He was concerned about Lady Eleanor's health; she had just given birth to a baby girl, Joan of Acre. The Saracen physician, who oversaw the royal couple's health, and who was recommended personally by the master of the Order of St. John, took care of Edward's wife. Lady Elanor looked happy with the physician. Red Herring assumed that this was the reason for the choice of name. He didn't give a coin about the name. Why were his thoughts leading him to that? Edward and Eleanor needed a little joy in this sandy land, and the face of their newborn girl baby finally gave them that joy.

James reflected on the mood of the royal family before the arrival of the baby Joan. After the death of their last infant, he could see the traces of sadness on the faces of the royal couple. Richard, the Lord of Cornwell—the renowned uncle of Edward and brother of King Henry—had also passed away. He was a great man for the Kingdom and his friends. Indeed, morale had been low for some time; the crusading campaign had been a series of disasters. Sir James had heard grumblings in the Crusaders' camp for some time; Edward's followers worried about the lack of action and were restless from a lack of opportunity. The men craved battles and adventures to fill their pockets and appease their wild, English souls.

Red Herring had been with Edward from the beginning of this campaign, unlike some, who had been hired here, in this forsaken place. Almost two years before, thirteen ships with Edward's men had set sail for the Outremer -the French word for "overseas. Almost a thousand followers accompanied Edward; one fifth were knights. They spent months at the galleys. The Crusaders were followed by misfortune all the way.

At first, the Crusaders intended to set sail to the Christian stronghold of Acre, but King Louis had been diverted the Crusade to Tunis. The French King and his brother Charles of Anjou decided to attack the emirate. Why? James had no idea, only suggestions. The plan failed when the French forces were struck by an epidemic.

When Edward and James arrived in Tunis, they were greeted by a shock: King Louis of France, the leader of the Crusade, was dead. Al-Mustansir, the Caliph of Tunis, offered a peace treaty and agreed to pay tribute to Charles, Louis' brother. Charles was satisfied; he had been through one campaign before and had no desire to go forward with this one. Without King Louis of France and his brother, the Crusade, the preparation, and logistical arrangements fell apart. Edward and his men spent the winter in Sicily. The Crusade was postponed until next spring, but a devastating storm off the coast of Sicily dissuaded Charles of Anjou and Louis's successor Philip III from any further campaigning.

James could see the fierce drive in the Lord Edward's eyes to reach the shore of this dreamland called the Holy Land—or what was left of it. He and his Lady Eleanor—the daughter of a notorious Crusader—were following their dream and their fate. They had survived a sea storm, which the voyagers felt was a good omen. Edward had decided to continue alone, and on 9 May 1271, he finally landed at Acre with nine ships.

But since then, nothing had occurred as the prince had hoped. Corruption and daily troubles lay everywhere Edward turned his eyes. Money ruled all; it superseded man, pilgrim, kingdom, and faith.

James saw his prince and how he looked devastated. Edward's vision of the land beyond the sea clashed brutally with reality. The prince had counted on support from the people of Acre and the rest of the Cristian's cities and fortress. James and Edward realized that they had not enough knights and men-at-arms to defeat the sultan. So, the prince was forced to look for support elsewhere. He turned his eyes to the Tartars, who had previously sought his cooperation. Upon Otto's advice, he sent envoys and waited for a response. Together with Knights Templar and the Knights Hospitaller, Edward and James emerged a raid against an important Mamluk village advised by aforesaid experienced defenders of the realm. King Hugh has involved in his internal affairs as usual and had no desire to participate. He preferred to stay on his island, Cyprus.

Red Herring was snapped out of his thoughts by one of his scouts. David, a short sergeant who had been in Sir James of Durham's pay for many years, approached to report.

"Sir, there is a Mamluk raiding party a few miles ahead. They are heading south, in our direction."

James took a minute to consider this.

"We continue as we planned," he said.

He was leading a small party of ten knights, ten men-at-arms, and ten archers. Most of the men had been specially chosen for this journey. No one was a member of the fanatic military orders; most of them were Englishmen, some were from Scotland, some from Gascony. A single Welshman named Owen was in the party. Most of them were from Lord Edward's personal household.

Otto and Edward advised slightly by Red Herring, had gathered the intelligence and laid the plan. The religious orders certainly couldn't be trusted with this task. Their thirst for land, money, and power was well known.

They had traveled southward via the road to Nazareth, skirting the sand beach to their right, starting this dangerous journey early in the morning because of the Sun. They intended to travel light and fast, speeding in the dark, slowing under the heat. When the Sun was high, searched for shelter to avoid heat exhaustion.

Proximity to a fresh water supply was vital to his men, especially in the summer. They packed sufficient supplies for a week. As Otto put it, this mission was to be done quickly, they go, grab the Wolf, and go back to Acre. They needed to go unnoticed. They wore simple surcoats, free of distinguishing marks, over their coats of mail. All of them were equipped with linen hoods to cover their western faces, like a band of mercenaries.

If they were tracked down by the sultan's scouts, they could be accused of breaking the truce, which concerned the coastal city of Acre and the safe passage to Nazareth only.

They passed Roman ruins, a testament to that ancient culture which appeared wherever they traveled both here and at home.

They rode in the wilderness until they reached Mount Carmel. Soon, they passed the river Kishon. The Sun touched the sky and they stopped to rest. When the Sun went down to sleep, the party continued their quest.

James was observing the landscape and saw a destroyed fortress from the sultan. After Baibars became ruler of Egypt and Syria twelve years ago, the Crusaders' estates and fortresses had fallen, one by one, into his hands. The sultan despised the untrustworthy Christian military orders, especially the Templars and the Hospitallers These military orders were the guardians of the faded Holy Land. They served the kingdom of Jerusalem and were devoted to its protection. But power had corrupted the pure intentions born 200 years before. In recent years, the religious orders cared only for donations, lands, estates, and the opportunity to fight infidels. Their desire to plunder was fatal to their original purpose; the Latin kingdom was falling apart. Piece by piece, the surrounding enemy encroached on them irreversibly. Although Edward had brought some hope, after a year, things hadn't changed. People who had the power and authority to bring change and hope were ruined by themselves. The end was near.

No one cared for this forsaken land except the merchants and mercenaries whose motives weren't hidden. They wanted only profits; they fought for money, their license to trade and to overpower the competition.

James thought about Edward. He admired the way the prince kept his men together. His organizational skills and prudent actions were like a light in the dark. He wasn't the fragile boy James had met long before. One day, he would rule

England, after his father. If he ever returned to his homeland.

Red Herring had used to think that, for Edward, all this adventure was a game. A game of chess, a tactical figure's playground, where one positioned oneself and waited for the opponent's next move. The kings moved their troops and officers. Ordinary men suffered, but not the rulers; they were above every law except the laws of nature. No man could fight the heat, even a king; no matter how hard he tried, that was a battle he would never win.

After midday, they were on the trail of another mounted raiding party. Owen, the scout, counted them and reported them to number over 100. They were Mamluks, slave children, raised and trained as a professional army of merciless warriors with strong discipline and morale. They were the fearsome warriors of Egypt, the same soldiers who had crushed the previous Crusade of King Louis of France twenty years before, at the battle of Al-Mansurah.

James spat some sandy spittle from his dry mouth.

An entire battalion of English souls had been killed at that bloody battle due to the commanding officer, a French count, who had led the advance without waiting for the main body of the army to cross the river. It had been a real blow, but that was the fate of the Crusaders.

On the next morning, they met with their spy, a Turk horseman who worked as a messenger, spy, guide, and interpreter for whomever paid most. James assumed he earned some gold from selling them the information about the Desert Wolf's hideout. His swarthy skin and Turkish gear distinguished him from James' men. His powerful voice was calm and sagacious. His eyes wore the signs of sleepless nights. There was something unforgettable in his gaze; James felt strange every time he looked in the spy's eyes. The Scottish knight couldn't determine the man's age, masked by his garments and the dust and dirt glued to him.

The spy guided Red Herring's men.

As the Sun retired again, they approached the place. It was a hilltop manor, well hidden from men to the west by cliffs and rocks. Their guide was short of words but he led them to a secret passage through the cliffs which led directly to the backyard of the manor. Before they started to climb, the spy drew them a map in the dust with his curved sword, indicating the location of the buildings and the dangers they may face.

"Danger?" Herring asked. "Are there a lot of guards?"

"The Desert Wolf and his family. Only he and his wife are important."

"Why? What haven't you told us?"

"He has certain skills," the spy said, after some silence.

"We have some, too," David said.

"Like fishing?" Owen joked. The men laughed.

The plan was simple: to approach the estate, kidnap the host and his wife and go home under the cover of the night. They left the horses in a place well-guarded by trees near the passage, ready for their withdrawal. They left two men to guard their belongings. They needed to leave behind anything which could on the moonlight betrayed their presence, taking only what was necessary. They had to be silent, not drawing weapons until they reach the target. Red Herring had warned his men. He didn't want someone to slip into the dark with an unsheathed sword and hurt himself or to make noise.

While approaching slowly up to the manor, Red Herring and his men saw flames blazing above the trees. They sped up. They needed to change their plan. Now, they had to remain unseen, to scout the place in the dark and to block all the possible exits. Then with surprise still on their side, Herring hoped to find and capture the infidel and his wife quickly in the dark.

He had been trained to respond quickly to a change in plan and had likewise trained his own men to do the same.

But they were too late. And they not accounted for such a scenario, meeting another raiding party attacking the same place.

Events were moving quickly in the eye of the night.

Herring rushed forward a few paces, scouting the area quickly with bated breath.

"Halt!" He grinned to his men. "Owen, take six men to the west side," James turned left. "David, to the north with another six. Robert, you have the honor to approach from the east with another six." James turned to the remaining men. "You, follow me. The main entrance from the south is our goal. Hurry, men. Gathering point is in the courtyard of the manor. Stay close. Shields up and don't do anything reckless."

They would wait for his signal and would not start to plunder without permission. His share of the strategy had been to obtain the right men. He was the best organizer in Edward's ranks and he knew it. When he noticed the flames, he was sure that most of the job was done; someone had arrived first with the same plan. The flames were covering their deeds and tracks.

He thought for a second that the Templars were ahead of him. These treacherous bastards were brainwashed and their hearts filled with blind faith and obedience. The Templars were like an ideal Spartan society but with a small difference: Spartans fought for their city but the religious orders fought for someone else's amusement.

In return, they were denied everything from wealth to the simple pleasures of life—all except killing in the name of God and dying bravely for their faith. You couldn't reason with these religious fanatics. It was no wonder that Sultan Baibars didn't negotiate with them but used their only weak point to exterminate them.

But Mamluks were a different breed. They were professional soldiers, trained to obey and kill.

If they were here, someone had sent them. Herring had heard that the Desert Wolf worked for the sultan. But now the elite Mamluk's regiment interfered in a small manor. Why?

Later, he would seek answers. Now, he needed to organize and lead his men to encircle the manor. Red Herring reached the front entrance and looked into the courtyard.

Bodies were everywhere—men, women, servants, even animals were scattered on the ground, cut to pieces, lying in a river of blood.

Most of the Mamluks were rushing off, half a mile away already.

But some stayed behind; twelve men remained to finish the

nasty job. They were fearsome-looking Mamluks in mail armor, with curved swords attached to their leather belts. Their captain had a white cloak. Some of the men searched for loot. Two of them prepared horses for their departure. The rest were engaged in a conversation with their captain.

Near the center of the manor lay the dead body of a pregnant woman. The captain looked at her face and murmured something to the soldier next to him.

Sir James was about to show himself when two Mamluks dragged an unconscious man to the captain. He looked like a Frank—one of James' own—and his hands were tied with rope. The man was bedraggled; blood leaked from a wound on his neck, his plain robe was torn, dirty, and reddish. His gold hair, almost white, was bloody, too.

A tall Mamluk and another with a scar on his face dragged the Frank forward and stood him up like he was made of hemp straw. They threw him at their master's feet. One of the soldiers spat at the captive, the other kicked him in the ribs. Another Mamluk brought a bucket of water and poured it into the man's face. The captain bent down and hit him across the cheek with the back of his hand, then grabbed the man's chin and said something to him.

The captive opened his eyes and stared at the dead, pregnant woman. After a moment, he rose from the ground and focused on the captain.

James noticed that the Mamluks laughed like they were enjoying their task. Their faces showed that they almost tasted the victory. They looked confident. Most of them had left their spears and shields on their horses. The captain had dark brown skin, burnt from the Sun, and his white beard was short. His fine mail armor and expensive leather rider's gloves were something every knight from the west dreamt of. Herring would have loved to catch such a prisoner and to strip him of his possessions.

James waited a few moments. The others must have been in position by then. All his men, hardened by war, would be ready to rush in with naked swords and flat-topped kite shields. They waited for Red Herring's signal.

But the spy was missing.

"Where is our guide?" James asked angrily.

He stepped out of the dark, almost forty paces from the Mamluks, and hit his sword to the metal rim of his shield, shouting, "Bastards, you are dancing on our playground!"

The Mamluks looked surprised, but not the captive. The Frank headbutted the captain in front of him and pushed him aside. He took the knife attached to the Mamluk's belt, his hands still tied together. He lunged at the next soldier, struck him with his left shoulder, turned around and stuck the knife to the hilt in the neck of the scarred Mamluk to his right. As the Frank retrieved the blade, a fountain of blood splashed on his face and he cut the rope from his hands. The Mamluk captain restored his balance and tried to stand, but the Frank struck him with his knee, turning quickly to the tall one, who held a naked sword over his head and slicing his throat with the knife.

Red Herring could not even blink.

The tall Mamluk fell to his knees and put his hands over his wound, but the newly-freed man pushed him with his right foot out of his sight and turned his gaze to the next victim. His face was as pale as a corpse. Perhaps he was Death, wielding his legendary scythe, hunting for victims.

The main building of the manor collapsed under the flames that inexorably eaten the wooden beams. The hot wind was blowing harshly on all of the men. Red Herring felt the heat as small burning pieces of ash stuck to his face. He ignored the irritation and lunged forward.

"Advance!" James shouted, and the Crusaders attacked. The captive had surprised them all.

The Mamluk captain's eyes widened and his jaw hung as he looked from the liberated Frank to Herring and his men. He reached for his knife, which was missing, then tried to find a sword. He stepped backward and stumbled. He rose and turned to the rest of his men, starting to shout something. The Frank caught the captain's cloak and pulled him back to him, stabbing the Mamluk in his armpit. He withdrew the knife and stuck it into the neck of his victim. The blade emerged from the other side of the new corpse. The unknown warrior left his blade where he had put it and unsheathed the captain's own sword with his right hand. The closest Mamluks drew their weapons and ran to the wretched man.

Red Herring was almost twenty paces from the fight. Three big Mamluks surrounded the pale stranger. James ran to the nearest enemy, using his shield and speed to deflect the spear pointed to his belly and swung his sword toward the infidel's face. The man fell. The rest of the Mamluks, realizing their leader was dead and observing Red Herring's men approaching, attempted to flee.

David and his followers took care of them. Owen and his archers shot down the enemies on the horses. Their arrows pierced them like practice apples.

In a few heartbeats, all the Mamluks were dead.

The pale Frank looked tired and was covered in blood, but not his. He didn't turn to his saviors. He fell on his knees and stared at the dead woman a few paces from him.

"Sir?" Owen, the Welshman, spat on the sand. "What is going on?"

"Search it fast, and let's go home," James shouted. "They will look after their comrades soon."

Red Herring sheathed his weapon in the scabbard.

"Come on men, do not waste time."

"What do we do with him?" Owen nodding to the unknown Frankish captive.

"Tie him. We take him with us. David, you and your men prepare the horses, strip the bodies of their valuables and the useful gear. I want all of you to be ready for travel in half an hour."

The whole place was on fire—death, blood, and terrible annihilation reigned.

"We were late," David said.

"Yes, and our guide is missing. We didn't know who our target was. The whole raid was a disaster," James said.

"Some of our men have a few scratches and bruises," David said.

"At least they are all alive," James said.

"And we found some booty," Owen said and grinned.

James observed the flames. He had bitterness in his mouth. He and his men had almost taken part in a fight. They had almost turned their blades red. But it wasn't a proper fight. The joy of battle was missing. The stranger had stolen the show and something in their hearts was missing. They had come to this faraway place, evaded dangers, and slept in the wilderness, and for what? They had achieved nothing.

And the Crusaders rode back.

CHAPTER FIVE

Ughan's Camp, near Arsuf, Holy Land, Saturday, 18th of June, in the
year 1272 of the incarnation of Christ

Berrat entered the main door with his bodyguards. He
scanned the room through the smoke. Darkness and smoke
twirled in the air. Dancing figures in the center of the room
entertained the amir and his guests. The fat and drunken ruler
was focused on a young girl. The loud music made Berrat's
ears vibrate. Most of the guards stood with their backs to the
show.

The fat man was laughing at her; nevertheless, his attention
wasn't pure. The guests were in a trance of liquor and some
strange smoke. The blonde girl was pale and scared but tried
not to show it. She smiled at the drunken amir.

Berrat was a tall man, but not as tall as his guards. His
warrior gear was expensive, but not only used for a parade.

The amir started to sing with his thick voice, emphasizing
certain words.

"You can put yourself to death listening to that," Berrat
thought and looked at his followers.

The cold night air had entered with him. The music
stopped and everyone froze and stared at the newcomers. The
newly-born atmosphere was killing everyone's emotions except
the amir.

In his mid-forties, Berrat looked like a true warlord in his
prime. And he was. His skin wasn't as brown as the rest of the
Mamluks'. His chin was shaved and perfectly clean. No

distinguishing scars marked his face. Although most of the men knew him, his hairless skull alerted the rest when he came. His mail armor accentuated his broad chest and almost reached his knees. A red leather belt was on his waist and a richly decorated scabbard was attached to it. His excellent cavalry riding boots were one of the precious things he possessed and were a gift from the sultan himself—the sultan liked to give his men a little prize in front of the public to show his gratitude for some brave or important deed.

Berrat was one of the trusted advisers in the sultan's court. They had been raised together on the island where the Mamluk regiment was trained. They had lived together, shared food, fought alongside each other, bled together, and shared almost everything. Almost.

After Sultan Baibars had made himself ruler of Egypt, he had made Berrat one of his amirs.

When Berrat was involved, it meant Baibars was personally interested in the matters. Some people called him the sultan's dog, but he didn't care. He didn't know a way of life except to serve and work for Baibars. Even if that meant being woken up late at night by his spies and sent ahead of the entourage to prepare the Ughan's camp for the arrival of the sultan.

His task was to investigate the news that had arrived and to check the security before the arrival of his master, Sultan Baibars.

"Ughan!" He omitted the word "amir" on purpose. "You became fat." The two men embraced each other. "When was our last meeting?"

Ughan rubbed his eyes with his hands and smiled.

"My friend, a lot of water has flowed since then ... and I can tell that time has been kind to you, not like me."

"Life on the northern border is harsh, I see," Berrat said. "Prepare yourself to meet the sultan; he will be here soon."

The night was charged again with the stir of nervous buzzing. The guests were dispatched and the two amirs— Berrat and Ughan—were left alone.

"I am glad to see you. How are your family and your lands?" Berrat asked.

"They are fine, thank you. Life goes on, inexorable and merciless, as usual. And you, Berrat, I hear you are a sultan's dog now?"

The hairless Mamluk left the last comment unanswered.

"A few days ago, on returning from the north, you and your entourage were stopped at a certain hilltop manor not far from here," Berrat spoke slowly, locking eyes with Ughan.

"Is it forbidden to visit a Frankish manor these days?" Ughan asked with an innocent smile.

"To be precise, you destroyed it, ransacked it, and killed everyone in it. May I ask why?"

"Don't be so angry you missed the fight, Berrat. It was just a Christian and his servants. Why would you allow this infidel to live freely, so close to the border? And please, do not thank me for doing your job." Ughan's voice was arrogant.

Berrat looked like a spear, but Ughan was more like a round shield.

"Baibars let him, not me. When I heard of your actions, I hoped you had done the job perfectly and that all the Frankish inhabitants in the manor were dead. Especially the manor's master."

The door opened again and another man entered. His savage and expressionless face revealed nothing. It was a Mamluk, the chief officer of Ughan's retinue.

"You remember Barak? He was the last of our vanguard at the manor, so you can ask him personally," Ughan said.

Barak didn't wait for an invitation, but turned to the interrogator and began to speak, nodding. "We were searching for shelter for the night. One of our scouts took us to the manor. But it was Frankish. We took care of it."

"Interesting. You must have been lost to be so far from the road on your course. Please tell me about the manor's master"

"He is surely dead. I left some of my men to finish the job and traveled this way."

"How many men did you leave?"

"Twelve."

"Not enough." Berrat's heart was palpitating as he kept his face blank.

Ughan continued to smile arrogantly.

"Why are we discussing this?"

"You will see," Berrat said.

The sultan entered. His personal bodyguards—a few dozen men—spread throughout the space, surrounding the men.

The fat host widened his eyes and his eyebrows slanted upward. He focused on Baibars' appearance.

The ruler was a giant of a man with a husky voice, light blue eyes, and a large white spot in his right eye. His personal qualities—above all, his complete absence of scruples—had made him the sultan of the kingdom.

Baibars possessed boundless energy. His ruthlessness—and occasional cruelty—made all men fear him, even his closest friends. He was nearing his fifties but was a strong and mighty warlord. He was the sultan of the whole of Egypt and Syria. A former slave, now he was the most powerful man in these lands. He had tasted defeat from neither the western Crusaders nor the Tartars.

"I was enjoying a game of polo when I received word that my old friend, Ughan, had arrived." His tone didn't show his mood yet. He talked vividly but it seemed as if he were waiting for something to happen.

Ughan's drunken smile disappeared. He didn't seem sure what to expect from the sultan.

"I took my fastest horse to salute him." Baibars took a step forward and embraced the fat man.

He was almost a head above him and the spot on his eye made him look vicious. He was Mamluk, too, but his skin and hair were unusual. The hardened life of a mounted warrior and captain of his regiment had made him the man he was now. Ughan was dressed in an expensive, embroidered robe showing his status; in contrast, the sultan was in his war gear, with a saber attached to the belt around his waist over his fine, mail coat.

The three men in the middle looked at each other. The mood of the room had changed.

"Tell me, my friend, did you receive an order to attack the Frankish manor? I don't remember giving such a command."

"My vanguard was searching for shelter and they found it," Ughan said, with confidence. "If this offended you, I will pay for your losses."

Baibars glanced at Berrat and his loyal captain shook his head.

"So, as I understand it, you didn't finish the job properly?"

"Your highness …. Why are you so upset about one Frankish manor and his master? The peace will hold; the Franks hadn't enough manpower to defend themselves." Ughan said.

"Don't interrupt me. The peace isn't your concern. The manor and its inhabitants were in my protection and my service. Tell me, what will people think when we start attacking our own? Give me one good reason to have attacked the household."

Anger slowly seized the sultan's face.

"As I said, I will pay for your losses." Ughan started to sweat.

"Now, that is not important. Who made the decision to annihilate them?" Baibars asked.

Ughan eyes betrayed Barak.

With the speed of an attacking cobra, the sultan struck Ughan's officer with his riding gloves and there was a flurry of movement. Ughan's guards took their swords, but the royal guards were faster.

A dangerous mood surrounded them.

Berrat, as usual, played the peacemaker and stepped between the two parties.

"My scouts reported that Barak's men killed his pregnant wife in front of his eyes. Butchered all the servants and animals, too." He took a breath, searching for his next words. Berrat finished the tale, describing the Crusaders and their arrival.

"He is alive," Baibars said, "but not her?"

"She is dead, yes," Berrat confirmed.

Baibars' face was stone cold but he said nothing.

"Who is this man you care so much about?" Ughan dared to ask.

"This man worked for me. He was designing new siege engines—bigger, more precise, and more mobile. But that is ... not the problem," the sultan said.

"You know that when we have had a problem with some amir or a western lord, we have sent a word to the mountains and the assassins have taken care of it," the bald Mamluk said.

"So ...?" Ughan's face was puzzled.

"But when we have had a problem with a whole division of assassins, we have sent the Wolf. *Diyaab al-Sahra*, the Desert Wolf," Berrat added.

Silence conquered the room.

"The master of the manor? That reckless soul?" Ughan asked.

The sultan looked at the ground.

"Now he knows your Mamluks have crushed his world, killed his wife. What you think he will do next? He is in the Crusaders' hands with only one thought: revenge," Baibars said.

"Did the Crusaders know his identity?" Ughan asked no one in particular.

"They think he is one of them, I suppose," Berrat said.

The tension in the room abated; the guards put their weapons away and the mood lightened. Baibars glanced to Ughan.

"Bring twenty men from his regiment and hang them for punishment," the sultan nodded to Barak.

"They just had followed orders!" Ughan's officer shouted.

Baibars observed the faces of Ughan and his officer. Barak's face turned red and his head was slightly dropped as his eyes looked through a lowered brow. Ughan placed his hand on Barak's shoulder.

"I hope this is enough to satisfy your loss," the fat amir said.

"I will decide this, not you," Sultan Baibars said and stormed out of the room.

***

Ughan was stunned. The evening had begun so pleasantly. One minute, he had been dancing drunkenly. The next, he was surrounded by royal guards, being accused of breaking an international treaty and—much worse—wronging the Desert Wolf. How had Berrat gotten this news so quickly?

He had heard about the sultan's new secret intelligence system—that it was able to transport information from the northern part of the kingdom to the south in just four days. Nobody knew how it worked. He had heard that it had been developed and organized by the sultan's secret regiment, Qussad. It was modeled after the assassins' system, but more professional and had been reformed by Baibars himself. After several unsuccessful assassination attempts on Baibars' life, he took precautions.

Ughan thought about this message system. Maybe it used water transport or pigeons. It must be something like this. Baibars surprised him with his speed intelligence.

Everything was almost perfect in their plan. The only piece missing from the flawless move was the head of the Wolf. But nothing was lost, yet. A new opportunity would arise soon, and someone had to seize it.

He smiled. His mentor was right; they must be patient and careful.

Berrat and his men also had retired to his chambers, Ughan turned on Barak like an angry, wild boar, jumping toward him.

"Why he is still alive? Your first job was to kill him, not to ransack the manor. Why did you entrust the work to someone else? The responsibility was yours!"

"The men I left behind paid with their lives, and they were also my men. Next time, we will succeed." Barak's face looked red and strained.

"You just lost another twenty of your men," Ughan said. "I hope Baibars' rage will not last long."

"But…" Barak tried to say something, but his master waved his hand.

Ughan's anger was satisfied for now. He called the guards.

"Bring her to my chambers." Ughan wanted the pale young girl, to taste her heat. He needed to relax.

"Tomorrow morning you will ride to Acre," he said to Barak. "I want you to be close to the vicinity of the city and to lead our men and allies. And please find out what you can about the Desert Wolf."

He turned his back to his officer. Sometimes Barak angered him.

But it was a time to turn his attention to the young beauty who awaited him in his bed. The desire to taste her fruit had arrived again.

***

Baibars was in his private tent for the night, discussing events with his friend and adviser.

Lord Edward's life was hanging in the balance; there had been an attempt on his Crusader's soul. This news had arrived a few moments before. Baibars' message system worked well, but he knew it could be better and faster and he had plans to improve the network.

"Are the two events connected? The attempt to assassinate Edward and the attack of the manor?" He turned his gaze to Berrat.

"We cannot be certain."

The sultan called his private clerk.

"Send a letter to congratulate Edward for escaping death and to wish him a fast recovery. Use a diplomatic tone to assure him that our hands and thoughts are clean."

Why now? Who was so bold as to perform this act and what was his purpose? These questions troubled his mind. It wasn't necessary to speak out loud; his friend, Berrat, could guess his thoughts. They knew each other well.

So many questions needed to be answered. But the most troublesome worry was the fate of the Wolf. Baibars had witnessed the fury of this stranger, the fighting and tactical skills he possessed, and the dedication in his eyes. He had never failed before.

But now he had failed to protect his family. Perhaps he had become lazy and was caught off guard. Or Ughan's forces had been lucky.

"Why was the Crusader's party there?" Berrat asked.

The scouts had reported that the Crusaders' gear was without any distinguishing marks. One thing the Franks loved was to show their colors before a fight. These men had come with a plan. It couldn't be coincidence, two mounted parties from opposite sides attacking the manor of the Wolf in the same evening.

The ink on the peace treaty wasn't even dry and war songs were on the horizon once more.

He needed peace with the Christians to strengthen his position and amass forces against the Tartars. But for now, he also needed the Crusaders' most important maritime port to provide him goods. He had access to his own harbor, but it was smaller.

So many rivals and enemies, but life was too short.

The merchants had made themselves richer during the war. The fanatic, military religious orders of the kingdom of Jerusalem always benefitted from war. Everyone wanted war—everyone except Baibars. He wasn't getting any younger and he couldn't afford to be surrounded by the enemy. He was familiar with the changing tides of men; his instinct sensed a great change on the horizon.

"Send two battalions to the plain of Acre to watch the movement of the Crusaders. We need to be prepared," he ordered Berrat. "Something will happen soon, with or without us. There is a chance that these events are somehow connected. Maybe not, but we must take precautions. We must investigate it. Someone has started a song. I want to finish it myself."

Baibars raised his gaze to his friend and ordered some water to clear his throat.

"You know, he saved my life once."

"The Wolf?" Berrat asked.

"I was hunting in the forest near Arsuf. I was on the trail of a beautiful hind and I was ambushed. The Wolf appeared from nowhere and killed the traitors single-handedly—all of them. He never hesitated, just did it. I survived that day because of him."

Baibars took a cup from the wooden table.

"He wanted a bucket of green apples for thanks."

"Apples?" Berrat asked.

"I felt powerless after that; I couldn't repay him for saving my life. Sometimes, the world is a strange place. Fate plays with us like grains of sand in the desert."

"You were lucky back there," Berrat said.

"Yes, I was, but I was also terrified. I never met another man in my life like him. He made my flesh crawl." Baibars continued, "That day, I imagined for one second what it would be like if he were on the other side. If he were my enemy. My blood froze, just as it did when I heard what happened at the Wolf's manor."

And he drank some cold water.

****

Barak was humiliated.

The sultan was merciless; he never forgot failure or a man he couldn't trust. Ughan hadn't told Barak who the target was. He thought there was little chance his master didn't know but he couldn't be certain. Barak understood that his life was on the line for this mistake. He hadn't known the real reason they went so far away from the main road but he wasn't stupid; they hadn't needed shelter. They could have made it to the main camp.

Yet, he felt that he and his men were sent there with a reason. He had misjudged the situation. He hadn't been prepared and had made a bad decision. If the whole party had stayed together, the westerners wouldn't have stood a chance. But he had decided to divide his force, to retreat with speed and to reach the main body of the army. He had wanted to reach the main camp quickly. He had wanted to see the pale girl who stole his thoughts these days.

And now he had to figure out how to avoid the Sultan's wrath.

Barak knew his master well and knew what his name meant:

Ughan, the poison of death. He knew that his master would sacrifice Barak's life if he needed to stay clean from this mess.

He also understood that his master regularly received messages from the north but he didn't know from whom. Now he had a chance to discover who this source was. He needed to quickly organize his regiment; their morale was low after the casualties on the hilltop manor and the men hanged by the sultan's soldiers.

The sultan would be a formidable opponent. Barak needed to be careful. Into the middle of this story, the Wolf had been involved. Barak had heard fairy tales told about this man: *Diyaab al-Sahra*, the Desert Wolf, the legendary warrior.

He hadn't imagined that bedraggled man from the manor to be the same. Why had his master wanted to eliminate a retired warrior with engineering skills? After all, the size of the siege engines didn't matter these days. All that mattered was their effectiveness, precision, and mobility. Even if the Crusaders obtained his new designs, could this save their necks? No, they were doomed.

The only reasons the sultan had prolonged their stay in this land were the Tartars and his need for an important logistics center, the maritime port in Acre. Baibars used the greed all men from Christendom possessed against them—especially the Italians, with their desire to control the sea trade.

The end of their Holy Land would inevitably arrive, sooner or later. The old regime would disappear, a new one would be born. There would be a battle; the victorious would be remembered throughout history. Barak wanted to be part of all this, whatever the price.

He touched the cheek which had been struck by the sultan. It was still on fire. His mood was devastated tonight; he was eager for the girl, but what had he received instead? Humiliation and not the woman he wanted.

He had found a reason to smile. "Women can be fatal, even indirectly," he thought.

When he had seen his master's desire for her at the party that evening, he had been disappointed. Thinking back to it, he felt humiliated again. He wanted the girl for himself but now he had to wait for Ughan to satisfy his hunger first. When his master had thrown her away like a rag bag, Barak would have her.

But he was patient; Mamluk life had taught him that. This was the world of Mamluks, where calm, strong friends and delicate political maneuvers meant everything in situations like this. Who knew how things would develop?

One day, he would seize his opportunities. Ughan, his master, would pay for Barak's humiliation. But he had to keep his eyes wide open.

He would take another slave girl for the night to calm him down. The new dawn would rise and new options would come. He must be ready. He needed to give his men a lesson, to teach them not to let him down again.

"Soon," he told himself. He knew fate would give him a chance to earn redemption.

He removed his mantle and called his personal servant. The work could wait until the morning. For now, he needed rest and to gather his thoughts. He had to leave the camp early in the morning toward Acre.

CHAPTER SIX

*City of Acre, Holy Land, Saturday, 18th of June, in the year 1272
of the incarnation of Christ;
Lord Edward's Birthday*

The city of Acre woke up; a noise of passing wooden wagons, waking hens, people arguing filled the streets: merchants, pilgrims, travelers, mercenaries, sailors, knights, priests, whores, workers, freemen, slaves, common people, children, and royalty.

The Sun woke up the orphan like the rest of the city. Now he only wanted a cup of water to satisfy his thirst. He rose from the bed. He was in the castle, in an unfamiliar room. The room was big and sunny and smelled faintly of perfume—the trace of a lady.

The bandage from last night's adventures was joined by a new one; his cheek had a knife wound from just below his eye to his chin. The mark from Julian's blade. It wasn't deep. He would survive, but it was a milestone. He had received his first battle scar. He thought it must look just like a barber's cut. He smiled. The irony he used to see himself from another angle made him feel alive. Whatever pain or humiliation he was subjected to, he could always use humor to restore his energy.

Peter had survived his first day of service. Would the next days be equally difficult? Was this what he wanted every time he dressed in his gear and went to work?

"Bloody yes." Peter felt bad for using these words. Yet they were in his mind. Brother John had used to say that whatever was in your mind would come out sooner or later.

What had happened the night before and the way he felt, thrilled, made him want more of the same: adventure and risk, glory and renown, fights and battles. Danger and uncertainty lay ahead and Peter didn't hesitate to embrace them. He wanted this kind of life.

All that had happened to him the night before was like opium for his mind and body, and he wanted more, much more. His desire for more was fresh, like a baby's hunger. Peter felt alive.

When he woke up he didn't want the story to end. He felt there would be more to come, that he was on top of a wave of events. Edward's assassination attempt was just the beginning. Peter wanted to be part of this. Desperately.

Red Herring opened the door and showed his twisted smile.

"How are you, lad?"

"I'm not that young, but thank you, I'm fine."

"We are expected, lad, in the most important chamber."

He followed the Scottish knight out of the room and Peter realized they were on the second story of the palace. It was early but the Sun was shining hard.

"Lad, thank you for last night," James said.

"For what?"

"For saving my poor soul from the sword of that bastard," Red Herring said earnestly.

Peter had saved the life of a bannered knight from Durham. Now realizing how close to death he had been in the fight in the merchant's house, Peter felt surreal. The orphan observed Herring; he looked like a man used to fighting and bloodshed, used to everything connected to death. Now the Scot was indebted to a common man. It was bizarre and Peter almost wanted to laugh at such irony.

Yes, Red Herring had appeared from the tavern in the streets and scared the men away from Peter who had been lucky. The Scot had saved him, and now he had saved James' life during the fight too.

"I envy you, Peter."

"Why?" Peter's face flushed.

"I want to be in your place, to be young again and …."

"Sir James, you are not too old for brave deeds," Peter said and smiled.

"The job of experienced soldiers is to give discipline, to set an example, to lead, and to steady the nervous novices. That's my job." Red Herring looked into Peter's eyes. "I've seen so many men on the battlefield, facing the enemy, break under the fear and pressure. I've witnessed so many men let down their comrades and break their oaths to their fellow soldiers, to their friends, their families, and to their liege lords. Most men are mentally weak. They couldn't stand in the shield wall. They couldn't stand in front of the horse charge, and they couldn't stand in front of the enemy."

Peter tried to understand what the knight was telling him.

"But you stood your ground last night." James smiled. "And I know you would stand by my side again."

Peter didn't know how to react to these words.

"So, Peter, you are not like most men these days," James said.

Their steps sounded through the stone corridor as they walked and talked.

There were ten guards outside the prince's chambers.

One of the soldiers told Herring that their visit needed to wait; Peter and James were supposed to enter, but they were late. Already inside the room were the Master of the Temple, the Master of the Hospital, Otto, and some other members of Edward's inner circle.

Peter recognized these titles and had seen the men before, but never up close. After a few minutes, he observed them as they left the prince's chambers, one by one. The Savoyard knight, Otto, watched the rest of the men depart and invited James and Peter to come in.

The memories of the previous night's events were fresh in Peter's mind as he entered the familiar room. His heartbeat accelerated. He remembered the assassination attempt, the wounded prince, the servants' uproar. He noticed the place by the wall where he had stood, witnessing it all.

The Sun coming through the wide-open window made for

a new atmosphere. The morning's fresh air wafted in and the Sun lit the room with vividness and life. Edward lay on his bed, speaking with his clerk. When their conversation ended, Otto introduced Peter and James.

Edward's face was pale and pained. He wore a plain white silk shirt, but the bandage across his wound was stained red.

Edward tried to smile.

"I have never really understood this," the prince said. He spoke slowly. "Why my written testimony is so important? I could be dead. Why I should care in the afterlife for my deeds when I couldn't control them?"

"James." He nodded to Red Herring, then took a glance at Peter and sought Otto's gaze. Edward's usual confidence and determination usually conquered the room and his followers. But not today.

"Today is my birthday, and what present has fate given me? An assassination?" the prince asked ironically.

"A chance, my lord, and a lad who saved your life," James replied.

"That's Peter. The young man I told you about, lord." Otto's voice was calm.

Edward's eyes focused on the orphan.

"John, the old monk, the Hospitaller I told you about, convinced me to find him a job. I found work for him in the lady's household," Otto added.

The prince's gaze was still on Peter; he seemed to be waiting for something.

The orphan's skin was frozen despite the Sun that played around him. In the presence of Edward, he felt nervous. He knew his place wasn't here with these people. He was an orphan, a lowborn lad who had grown up on the streets of Acre.

"Do you know your father?" Otto asked.

"No, sir," Peter said. His father had died before his birth, his mentor had said.

"So, you were raised by the old monk?"

"I am afraid so," Peter said.

The laugh of Red Herring followed. Even the prince tried

to smile through his pain.

"Did you know he was a knight once, from the Order of the Hospitallers, the old monk?" Otto asked the orphan.

Peter didn't answer. He considered this. He had assumed that the old monk was experienced in war by the way the old man moved, how he stood, and by the way he talked about training and battle. Once, the orphan had tried to ask him about it, but the old man had changed the subject immediately and had never spoken about it again.

"He never talked about it, sir."

Lord Edward gestured to the orphan to come close to the bed. Peter obeyed. Edward tried to rise a little from the bed, but his face showed agony.

"Only one physician was bold enough to propose that they cut the poisoned flesh from my body," Edward said.

Had the Prince agreed? Judging by his red bandage and his pain, he had.

There was gossip regarding who had sucked the poison out of the prince's body. Red Herring had said he believed it to be Otto, the man Edward trusted most. But Peter preferred to think it had been Lady Eleanor.

Even the best physicians in the city feared failure. If a high noble patient died under the care of a physician, his career was ruined. Rumors were born fast and escalated quickly.

Yet, Edward's face looked pale. The prince needed a miracle. Or an antidote.

Now, he tried to find the strength to rise.

"These days, the most important thing is to have loyal friends. Nothing more and nothing less." He looked into the orphan's eyes. "Sometimes you find them in unexpected places and in unusual circumstances."

Peter said nothing. The mighty figure of the prince now looked fragile.

"I am grateful you did what you did last night." Edward's eyes were on Peter—it was a privilege which few common men had witnessed in their lives. The prince spoke slowly and never turned his gaze from the orphan.

"When I understood that it was your first day in our

service, I was even more impressed." Weak, he paused frequently. "Otto has told me about Brother John, who he was and what he told us about you ... I guess I am lucky."

He fell back on his bed again. The red stain spread across his bandages. His face twisted with pain. Nearby servants scurried to take care of their master.

Otto waved his hand at Peter and James, motioning them to follow him into the next room. They obeyed silently and left the servants to tend to the royal patient. The next room was smaller but somehow more vivid and sunnier. There was a small, wooden table near the window. The men sat at the table, the chairs creaking a tragic melody, warning others that everything grew old. Otto sat close to the window and directed a servant to bring them some breakfast.

"You must be hungry," he said.

"Like devils," Herring said. Peter was silent.

"Lord Edward wanted to thank you personally," Otto observed the young man. "The last person to save the prince's life turned out to be an assassin!"

"I am not ...." Peter's face turned red.

"Calm down, lad," Herring said.

"Tell me, Peter. Tell me everything about last night's events, down to the smallest detail," Otto commanded.

The orphan was a little shy, but he described it all. While he talked, the food arrived: bread, salted ham, boiled eggs, carrots, and cheese.

Peter and Herring ate like hungry wolves. Otto didn't touch his plate. He drank a cup of water, listening carefully and directing Peter's story with pointed questions. When the story reached the point where Peter met Red Herring, Otto stopped him. He was interested in the mysterious men who had attacked the orphan.

"So, the ambush wasn't for you. And you were lucky. Julian was the name you heard, is that right?"

"In the fight in the merchant's house, we saw him again, a big ugly bastard," Red Herring said, emphasizing the last.

"I heard you were on the verge of losing the fight in the house?"

"Peter saved my life. They were experienced and damn good soldiers; we underestimated them. I, David, and Peter—we were surrounded, yes. But Owen, the archer from Lady Eleanor's household, led in a dozen shooters to interrupt our little dispute. And they saved us, I must admit it," James said.

Otto smiled.

"Lady Eleanor is a prudent person. She was acting like her husband, disciplined and practical. She wisely sent an archer's party to search Acre in the night and to bring you to the castle."

"The lady?" James asked.

"She has a unique ability to hire the proper people. Owen was the perfect choice—our only Welshman, eh." Otto gave them a half smile. "He told me some interesting news from your journey to the south, too."

"Yes," Herring agreed. "Something is happening behind the scenes. There is a shadow plot to be exposed."

Peter had stopped listening; he was remembering the merchant's house.

They had been in the second-story room. Through the open wooden windows, the cold night air was joined by flying arrows. A small group of archers stood on the roof of a building across the street, screaming something. Peter heard footsteps from the lower story. He turned his gaze to the dark mercenaries with whom they fought; they looked like evil knights. There weren't distinguishing marks and colors on them, only dark garments.

The opponents reacted instantly to the newly-arrived threat. Julian and his men pushed aside Peter and his followers, jumped through the door of the eastern terrace and disappeared into the night. One of the assailants was pierced by arrows like a pincushion full of needles and he fell near Peter. Blood bubbled from the wounded one's mouth. His face looked sour as he examined the arrows that stuck up from his chest, then he died.

"An unforgettable night," Peter thought.

Owen appeared and sent some of his archers on the trail of the enemies. A night raid on the roof was a doomed adventure—most of the experienced soldiers knew that but they knew they must try.

Peter was exhausted, like fish out of water after a long struggle to return to the sea.

He was elated that the archers had shown up. Peter's eyes investigated the merchant's lair. The house had evidently been abandoned in a hurry. It looked as though things had been packed fast; the occupants had left their food and some less important belongings behind.

On the first story, near the stable, was enough forage for two horses for a month. Peter assumed the owner of the house must have been waiting for someone but was surprised. The facts indicated that the dwellers had left earlier in the day.

Something or someone had foiled the merchant's plans. Now, these mercenaries were searching the house. Why? The orphan had many questions but there were no answers.

"He can't be that far," James said, mostly to himself.

"The merchant?" Peter asked. The Scottish knight had opened the wardrobe on the first story room near the kitchen. There were fresh footprints, outlined by sandy grit.

"Someone was hiding here," James said.

"And he left when we started upstairs," Peter assumed. "So, he must be close."

Red Herring was lost in his thought.

"Owen, how many men are with you?" the Scot asked.

"A dozen, plus me," the Welshman replied.

"Well, continue searching the city." Herring didn't hesitate to give the order.

Peter, Red Herring, and David examined the merchant's house again.

Just as the intruders had done, they rummaged through the entire house, the stable, the warehouse, and the store up front. They didn't find anything interesting apart from their initial discoveries.

"Tell me about the merchant," James said.

"He was an ordinary-looking Saracen who traded, imported and exported goods. His face wasn't memorable," Peter said. He knew that merchant's importance now was at the forefront.

"The merchant is our main clue and he is gone. Julian is the second one—gone, as well." James said.

"He looks like an Italian," The sergeant nodded to the dead body, which had been taken downstairs and was lying on the floor.

"And how the hell do you know that?" Red Herring held back his laughter. "Do you know his mother?"

"No, but …" David tried to say something but James didn't let him finish.

"Or is it because of his eyes and his face?" Herring was in a jovial mood. "He looks like an Italian to you? Or to you?" He looked at the orphan. "Maybe it's because of the dried salt on his clothes, David? If there is sea salt, it means he's Italian?" James laughed. "Look at his pockets; maybe you can find a note. 'In case of inflicted death, I'm Italian. Please send my body back home to my mother, over the sea.'"

Sir James and his humor were unstoppable. Peter also smiled. David did not.

Owen returned from dispatching orders to his men. His age was hard to determine, Peter thought. His Welsh face had freckles and brown eyes. His wild, dark-red hair was shaggy. His roguish look seemed to invite trouble. But there had to be a reason he was one of the most trusted men of Lady Eleanor's household.

"What have I missed?" Owen asked.

Red Herring, through a laugh, replied, "Our Italian friend with your arrows in his belly told us a story." And the knight wiped the sweat from his forehead.

"Tell me, please, do you think this is good archery? Four arrows to kill a bastard?" James nodded to the dead body. "I think you should have hit him with at least five arrows to look more like a pincushion, am I right, lads?" Herring laughed harder.

Owen said nothing at first. Suddenly, he laughed, pointing to the corpse.

"So, you want to say thank you? I accept your sincere gratitude."

James grinned and nodded. Then he stepped forward to the

dead body and searched him. They found some coins, a short blade, leather belt, and some dry cheese in his small bag.

There was also a safe conduct letter for passing the guards in the city.

"Where did he get this letter?" Owen asked.

"It's difficult to obtain one, but not impossible," David said.

"Perhaps he worked for the military orders or Italian merchants," Herring said.

"Does anyone know his face?"

No one did.

They had one more lead, if he was still alive: Edward the Saracen.

Peter related all this to Otto in Edward's chambers, with Red Herring adding his humorous commentary. In the end, he felt as if he had emptied his bags of knowledge earned the night before and felt some heaviness lifted from his shoulders.

"Peter," Otto said, "I understand that it was your idea to check the merchant's house. May I ask why?"

"I used to do some jobs for the old monk—shopping, delivering supplies and messages. I remembered I often saw Edward the Saracen hanging around the merchant's house. I just happened to know about him. I had a feeling we should check there." He paused for a moment, then continued, "I tried to put myself in his shoes. I tried to guess how I would manage to escape the city, which route I would use ..., besides the trail of guards marked the assassin's getaway path, led in the direction of the merchant's house."

Otto laughed.

"I see we will have to keep an eye on you," he said and looked at Peter's face with his cold eyes. "You have saved two of the most important people in this household. You think the same way as the assassin, and you know the traitor's habits."

Peter was not sure whether this was criticism or admiration. He hoped it was the second.

"So ...." Otto gave a tiny smile.

Red Herring said nothing.

"What do we have? A name—Julian—a dead body, and the

assassin." Otto said to no one in particular.

Peter turned his eyes to the window, which faced the cursed tower where convicted criminals hanged to death.

"It's a fresh corpse there," Otto said. "I helped the news spread quickly that he was the failed assassin who had tried to kill Lord Edward the night before."

A rumor infected the city that the western prince had evaded the attack and killed his assailant with his bare hands. But nobody mentioned Peter and his part in the story.

"It is difficult to interrogate a corpse, don't you think?" James asked ironically. "Or you have already done it?"

Otto's face showed no emotion. He stood up from his chair, turned to the window, and leaned against the stone wall.

"The assassin is not dead," Otto said, "… yet."

"So, who is that?" Peter asked.

"Nobody important." Otto carefully observed the orphan's reaction.

"If I were you, sir, I would assume that the assassin did not act alone. He had a backup. That's obvious. I would show the traitor's body or someone that looks like him so that everyone can see it," Peter said.

The two knights didn't say anything but listened.

"Judging by the fact that he is a spy, his training, and his dagger skills, it seems it would be hard to make him talk. But that is no reason not to try. I would make the hanging body hard to recognize before hanging it. Then I would have paid men to spread the news that Edward killed the assassin in the taverns and set a bait. And then we wait to see who's going to move out from the shadow. There are many questions to be answered and Julian and the assassin are our only leads now that the merchant is gone. I am sorry if I am out line, sir," Peter added.

Red Herring and Otto were immensely surprised and their mouths hung open.

The two knights started to talk quietly together. Peter could not make it out.

The orphan stood and paced around, observing the room. Something to his left stole his attention. There was a big bookshelf, almost big as the stone wall. On it, stood a book with a bright cover embellished with beautiful drawings of knights. The colorful illustrations on the cover left the orphan wide-eyed. He looked at the book, which seemed to represent his ambition to become a renowned warrior himself. This book might be able to tell him what it would take to become a knight. He desperately wanted the book. It seemed, over the past twelve hours, that he wanted everything he saw, like a child. He had desired Julian's boots, Red Herring's sword, and now this book.

This time the temptation was stronger than he.

Peter drew close to the bookshelf. He took a look at the two knights. They were still talking. He grabbed the book and put it under his tunic. He had learned a few things on the street. In the moment of his decision, he didn't think; he was calm. He was controlled by his desire to have this fabulously-decorated book with its eye-catching cover.

He knew he would regret the theft later. He wasn't proud of what he had done but his curiosity was stronger than he was. Now he needed to learn how to read. And how to silence his conscience.

Brother John had tried to teach him how to read and write, but he had shown no enthusiasm. Now the coin had turned upside-down; now he was motivated. In the monastery, most of the books were in Latin—he wasn't interested in them. This was different; his curiosity and determination had led him to steal and would lead him to learn to read.

It was just a book; nobody would notice it was missing, especially after the events of the previous night. Sure of this fact, he smiled. Yes, he had stolen, but royalty had so many books, surely no one would notice one book missing. His desire to look inside would have to wait until reached his bed in the old monastery.

Thinking of home, he was eager to go there and to share his experience with the old monk. He had always wanted to earn the approval of John, who was like a father to him and had taught him all he knew. The monk was old and barely spoke, but he was the only person he trusted.

Peter was released by Red Herring and Otto. He smiled to the Sun; he was going home. He ran toward the old monastery.

***

Edward had a fever. Darkness was in the room.

The English prince moaned and talked to Otto.

"In this never-ending war between Christians and Muslims, there is no light in the tunnel. Their expansion to the west started with the dying Roman Empire. Slowly, we, the Christians, and our forces managed to return, to retrieve some of our lost lands and establish a kingdom overseas. Now we must defend it because this is our last line of defense against Islam." Edward stopped for a moment. Otto listened; James and Eleanor were behind him.

"Of the five most sacred cities to the Christians, three of them—Jerusalem, Antioch, and Alexandria—are in the hands of the followers of Islam. Only Rome and Constantinople belong to us."

"Times are changing, my lord," Otto said.

"And how many times have Christian forces attacked either Mecca or Medina? The answer, of course, is never." Edward put this strange monolog to his friend but mostly to himself. "Did we ever attack one of their sacred places? Did we ever attack their Mecca?" It was a rhetorical question.

"We are only defending our realm. Sacrificing all—richness, health, family and friends. Perhaps this madness will end after hundreds of years," Edward said.

"This war will never end, as long as there are two main warring religions, my lord," Otto said.

"'Warring religion,' you say, but we just defend ourselves. Is this belligerent?"

Edward paused, turned his gaze to the window, and continued, "Some said we came here to make ourselves rich, to plunder. Look at me, I am a broken man." Edward seemed ashamed to say this in front of his closest friends. "I am forced to beg for funds to finish what I started or just to go home. This is shameful."

"This is what kings do, my lord: borrow money," Otto said.

"Money which someone else has earned," Edward said.

"My lord, monarchs with grand ideas need investments," Otto said and added, "So yes, kings need loans. It's nothing shameful, your majesty."

"It's a necessity, especially in our situation," James said.

"And what is our situation? A few people became rich by crusading. Their numbers are dwarfed by those who have been bankrupted, like me," Edward said.

"You have options, sir. Most people do not," Otto said calmly.

"I owe money to everyone. The Genoese, the Venetians, the Templars, the Hospitallers, and some other traders. Do I look like I could be a great king, lying here, probably dying, with not a single shilling in my pocket? Am I the desired leader of my kingdom? Am I worthy?" Edward tried to stand up from his bed. But he couldn't.

"Crusading has brought deprivation, suffering, and, often, death. We knew this before we set off, my lord," Otto said. "Any greatness has a beginning, no matter what."

"We also knew that seven in ten men would never return home. It is a brutal casualty rate. Yet, we were determined to leave our mark on history. We wanted to be part of the exhausting battle between the religions," James added.

There was silence in the air for a moment. The sound of the street arrived through the window once more.

"Was it wrong, my friend? The decision to come here?" Edward looked into the eyes of his knight.

"Some said we were crude, greedy, aggressive barbarians who attacked civilized, peace-loving Muslims to improve our own lot. Some saw us—the Crusaders—as a glorious song in a longstanding struggle in which Christian chivalry had driven back the Muslim hordes. But my lord, this is war, and soldiers do what must be done. Whether they are Muslim or Christian, every good soldier does what he is ordered to do," Herring said.

"What is our place in history? What?" Edward's pale face was tired.

"Let the people and history decide on their own, my lord. Do not bother your mind and body right now. You need to rest."

"One more thing." He spoke to James. "Whatever happens, kill him, James. Kill the bastard." Edward said. There was no mercy in the prince's heart for traitors. The assassin's fate was doomed.

The English prince lay down and closed his eyes. Lady Eleanor sat near him and kissed his forehead.

The two knights left Edward's chambers.

"What you think of Peter?" James asked.

Otto said nothing.

"He was touched by a lucky angel this day," Red Herring continued.

"The old monk who brought him, do you know him?" Otto shot his question like a crossbow bolt. Red Herring shook his head.

"Should I?"

"There is something that the old man didn't tell us,"

"How could you know?"

"I don't. Call it instinct—an instinct for survival. There is something curious about Peter and his mentor. The way he appeared yesterday before me and talked to me. He reminded me of someone. For now, I can't remember, but I'm sure it will come to me." Otto placed his hand on Red Herring's shoulder.

"I want you to keep an eye on Peter, James."

It wasn't the first time James had been charged with such a task. He grinned and rose.

"You want me to be a babysitter?"

"He saved your life; I think you need to return the favor. And to achieve that, you need to be close, don't you think?" Otto said.

"I will send Owen to search the harbor taverns for Julian and his men. David thinks he is Italian, the dead body." James said. "Julian didn't look Italian; he was more like a knight in disguise. He was arrogant; he felt he was above us. But to me, he looked more like a master's warring dog."

"Now tell me about your last raid, every detail. Do you

think there's a connection between the events?"

Red Herring leaned back in his chair.

"I am still hungry," he said. Otto asked the servant to bring more food and wine.

It would be a long morning.

***

Peter was in the monastery again.

He entered the kitchen from the backyard and sat at the table. No one was there to meet him. There were some dry bread and some cheese on a wooden plate. He looked at the food. Although he was usually hungry, now he wasn't; he had had enough to eat in the castle. The orphan forced the bad memories from his head and sat at the hearth. His mind didn't want to rest, but his body felt otherwise. He lay down to relax, and the heat made him sleep.

When he opened his eyes again there was a tall man with a familiar face above him and a blade pointed at his throat.

There was no sign of the old monk.

Julian grinned at the orphan.

"Get up!"

Peter blinked for a moment.

Where was Brother John? Where was everyone? How had he been found by this man? It was strange that the monastery was empty. It was a mid-day; there must be monks nearby. Was it mid-day? How long had he slept? He decided it was the same day.

Slowly he rose, touching the stone wall with his hands. He caught his opponent's eyes and the arrogant expression on his face. Another man stood on the left of his assailant. A new face; he hadn't been in the merchant's house the night before.

Peter wasn't afraid yet, but he was still groggy from sleep and his reactions were slow.

He was unarmed and caught off guard. He thought he ought to say something, but he couldn't. He opened his mouth, but not a sound was released. Was there a point to saying anything? His enemy, the man who had received an order to kill him, the man whom he had fought against was now standing in front of him with a naked sword pointed to his belly.

Peter wondered if Sir James and David were in danger, and he wondered, if this man wanted him dead, why he wasn't already dead. He stood, unhurried, leaning against the stone wall, and looked at the assailants.

Julian was overconfident. He looked more like a knight than a rogue, although his chivalric marks were missing. Maybe that was on purpose, not to attract attention or reveal himself to others.

"Where is he?" the blond knight asked.

Peter was anxious.

"Where is … who?" The orphan was confused and frozen.

In the same moment, he felt a blow from the right as Julian's follower delivered his fist into the orphan's ribs, hard. He had not expected such force to be used against him. "Welcome to the world of knights, mercenaries, rogues," he thought. He almost lost consciousness and tears appeared in his eyes from the sudden pain.

The man next to Julian had red eyes. He grabbed Peter by the shoulders, picked him up, and pushed him against the wall like a practice target.

"Don't waste our time, dog."

Peter blinked again and took a deep breath. He was ready to answer something. Anything to buy himself some time. Julian's face was expressionless.

The outside door of the kitchen opened.

A fat monk entered. At first, he didn't notice the men inside, perhaps as his eyes adjusted to the dark of the kitchen. Julian and his companion turned on him. This little distraction was enough for Peter.

He kicked his captor between the legs, freeing himself from the grip of the red-eyed man as the man let out a shout. He pushed his assailant aside, kicked him one more time, and ran past him to the next room. His heartbeat was fast and he felt that time had slowed again. He pushed a chair to the floor behind him as he ran. He headed to the inside corridor, which led to the storehouse and the winery.

Peter heard a scream from the fat monk and a muffled sound.

The orphan was almost at the end of the corridor when he turned to look over his shoulder to see whether he had been followed. He stopped for a moment to take a breath, placing his fists on his knees. He hoped they would abandon their pursuit. Julian and the red-eyed man came into view and Peter started to run again. The door leading to the large courtyard was ahead. Peter reached it, thanking his good luck as he found it unlocked.

He entered the garden full of flowers, trees, and sunlight. The old monk, who had looked after him since a child, appeared and grabbed his hand.

"Where have you been, Peter?" Brother John asked.

"I ...." He tried to speak, but he couldn't catch his breath. The surprised monk moved his gaze from Peter to the men running at them from the corridor. The old man pushed the orphan behind him, putting himself between these hunters and their prey like a shield.

"Run, Peter. Find Brother Alexander."

Peter wasn't sure what to do. He hesitated to leave his mentor in danger.

Julian was in front, followed by his hound. He reached the old monk first and tried to push him from his path. But the old man was prepared; he evaded the attacker like a trained warrior, just like the religious knights the orphan had witnessed training in the practice yard. He stood again and swung his wooden stick, striking the blond knight. Julian's face was all surprise and anger as he fell. His follower tried to move past his master, ready to attack. He lunged his naked sword at the holy man's neck. But the old monk used his stick to parry the attack. He made a feint and struck the assailant at his temple. The man cried out in pain and fell.

"Run, Peter!" Brother John shouted.

Peter started running again, thinking about the surprising fight.

He had always known there was something in the old

monk, had always used to think him a former Crusader, but he was surprised by the determination, moves, and stance of Brother John. This wasn't a fight most men could hope to win—one against two.

Peter was already at the end of the inner garden, as he heard the old man cry out and turned to see him on the ground. Julian's face was full of ferocity and a thirst for blood. The blond assailant looked at the fallen man and thrust his blade deep into his chest. Peter heard the nasty sound of a blade delivering pain and death.

"No!" The orphan shouted.

Peter hesitated, open-mouthed and ready to cry, frozen by fear and helpless. The only man who had cared for him, the only person he could call family now lay in a pool of blood. What could he do now?

He hesitated, uncertain. He wasn't ready to confront Julian yet. Not yet, not now, and not here.

Peter ran.

Realizing that the death of the monk would be in vain if he couldn't manage to escape, he sped up. Julian would pay, the orphan said to himself. But now it was time to run. The monk had bought him time but at what price? Peter's heart was dark.

He felt as if he had met black-shadowed Death herself, that her scythe had swung above his head.

Peter had often wondered about death. In his miserable life, he had wanted several times to be dead. When he had been beaten almost to death and left on the street, bleeding. When he had fallen into a well. Memories suddenly appeared in his mind of hard-earned experiences. All those times in his youth, he had been weak, had wanted to give up and not to feel pain.

Now, he wanted to live and to continue his fight.

While he ran, he wiped the tears away from his face with the sleeve of his shirt. He could hear Julian and his follower's footsteps behind him. He accelerated his run. He was already out of the monastery. He crossed the street, hearing his heart pound in his chest with fear.

"Run, Peter, run," he thought.

After a while, the sound of his pursuers faded and was

replaced with the song of the street. But Peter kept running and weeping. His world was broken. In the span of one night and day, his world had changed completely.

What lay in front of him, he didn't know, but he knew that he was part of Lady Eleanor's household. This was his new home: the household of royalty from a kingdom beyond the sea. His tears didn't stop, but Peter didn't care. He surrendered to them. He passed a few streets and finally stopped.

He climbed a tree near the southern wall of a two-story, yellow, brick warehouse and sat on the roof, near the edge. This was a place he had used to hide in his childhood. He gazed at the blue sky touching the azure sea. The picture of Sun and sky dancing in front of Peter's eyes calmed him down.

He felt lonely as he had never felt before. He was alone in this wretched world. Young and inexperienced, he knew there was much to learn and discover ahead. He looked at the sea. He liked this place; he liked the smell of salt and to watch the sea, the blue horizon, and the birds. The sound of the harbor was inviting, filling Peter with the desire to travel and explore the unknown. His spot on the roof gave him a private place to escape from the street and his problems. But he couldn't stay here forever.

What could he do? He hesitated for a moment. He had to report to duty soon at the castle, but this would wait. The monk had told him to see Brother Alexander, an old and strange monk, a friend of Peter's mentor. He wasn't sure why, but it was the last wish of the man he considered as a father.

Peter had survived so far. He would survive a little more; he rose and went looking for Brother Alexander.

CHAPTER SEVEN

*City of Acre, Holy Land, Saturday, 18th of June, in the year 1272
of the incarnation of Christ;
Lord Edward's Birthday*

The Desert Wolf, the Mamluks called him. His mother had called him Ulf, but she was long since dead. Cold sweat was on his neck.

He felt as if there were a thousand blades in his heart, piercing deep into his flesh and mind. The lifeless face of his beloved wife was before him, impossible to forget. It had left its trace for life, losing a piece of himself. He had suffered— and committed—a thousand awful deeds but none compared to this.

Sweat drops fell from his temple and splashed on the stone floor.

He had been left in a cellar under the castle. He had seen such dungeons before; Frankish castles and their structures were unmistakable. The smell of sewage was close, as well as the scent of something rotten. The smell of death hovered in the air. Humidity was high near the coast. The last remnant of the Crusaders' kingdom was the largest maritime port of the region. Most of the prisoners were held at the Templars' and Hospitallers' quarters. But not him. He was in the castle of the city of Acre.

His grief broke his soul in two but his training and his instincts made his powers of observation sharp. His mind constantly calculated, searching for a weak spot, a way out.

While his thoughts were in a distant field of sorrow, his habits and skills knew their jobs.

He shook his head clear of his grief and tried to evaluate his position. His household was lost; the sultan's elite regiment had taken care of that. They had sacked his manor, ruining his present and his future. On the way to the city, from the saddle of his horse, he had listened to the raiders. They had been surprised to find rivals at the same night mission as theirs. It seemed that his manor had been the target of two warring parties at the same moment. This wasn't a coincidence. He could understand why the Crusaders wanted his head, although his identity couldn't have been easy to find. But for the sultan to send his elite Mamluks was a real surprise. He and the sultan had had an agreement. Now it was broken.

There was a traitor playing both sides. A dangerous game had begun whose purpose was still hidden. He had become part of this plot and his beloved one a collateral casualty.

He was weak, he was tired, and he was destroyed—not only physically, but from the inside, as well. His mental strength kept him from falling apart. But his grief was like a spear splitting his chest. He had received such a wound long before, the pain unbearable, yet he had survived it. This wound was a thousand times worse.

His wife was dead. His unborn child was dead. What reason did he have to live now? He hadn't any, only sorrow and pain. Perhaps the time to lie down and surrender was near. He didn't give a coin for his life. In the afterlife, he would meet his beloved one and be granted some peace. He hoped. He closed his eyes, trying to clear his mind.

He felt the relaxing chill of the dungeon wall against his back. The red-haired knight, who was in charge of the Crusaders, was trying to talk to him. But Ulf looked through him with his empty gaze. He had lost an idea of time and reality. There was no window in his cell. Was it day or night? He didn't care.

"Come on, rise up, rats," the guard had shouted earlier in the night. Ulf had paid him no attention; he simply lay on the cold, damp stone floor. He missed the cold sometimes; he missed the thick forest and freezing winter slopes of his homeland, the mountains touching the sea. The distant memory of those unnatural creatures, the fjords, made his heart shrink.

His muscles were in pain, his neck was scratched, his head was stunned, his arms and legs were raw, he was bruised, he had been beaten badly by the Mamluks, yet he didn't care. He was trained to live with pain and he knew that pain was controlled by the mind. Not to think about it was the key.

The Crusaders had taken care of his wounds and given him water and food. He drank the water but didn't touch the food. He was no longer hungry for food or life.

An old friend of his had used to say, "A man changes his life when his mind is open or his heart broken." He saw his life changed at this horrible moment. Again. Perhaps fate did not want him to leave him alone to live his life with his wife.

But seeing his beloved one lying dead, her body covered with blood—this had ripped him apart. He wanted to see her smile one last time. She was the light in his dark world. She was his beauty. She was his crossroads. She had saved him from the dark abyss he once had been. She was his reason to live. She was the person who had opened his mind. She was the face he saw when he woke up in the morning. She was the face who kissed him goodnight. She had born his child. She had born the future.

And that future was dead. His world was broken into thousands of pieces and he couldn't do anything to prevent it.

When the raiding party had come to his house, searching for a place to pass the night, he had known that something wasn't right. The main road was far away and his house was on the top of the cliff. Visits were rare. The only people who came there were officials coming to buy his trade and merchants stopping for shelter. The horsemen had been wearing the colors of an unknown amir. He had heard the name of the man who led the Mamluks: Barak. He would remember that name.

He was asleep but woke up.

Ulf had a look around.

There was sweat on his forehead. The nightmare was gone.

He was in the city of Acre's castle dungeon.

The dungeon was a lonely and scary place but he didn't give a coin. His eyesight was empty but his mind was not. Sorrow filled him from inside. The last time he had cried had been on a cold, northern night, long before. He had been but a scared child back then. He had spent all his tears watching his family burn.

He had had another nightmare. For two years, he hadn't dreamt of it. And the main reason for that was his beloved one. But now she was gone, and the nightmares were back.

Some said that weeping could purify one's soul and heart, but this was not true for him. He doubted weeping could reverse his grief. Ulf wanted to be alone in the dark, untouched. The dungeon was a suitable place.

He preferred his privacy right now, to satisfy his sorrow and sadness. The pain in his belly was indescribable, yet he had survived it once; he would survive again. For he hated unfinished business. He knew himself; he didn't like to lose.

That was the desire to deliver vengeance. But first, grief. He was deeply immersed in it. The revenge would come. He needed time to think and to recover his strength.

Steps on stone sounded in the corridor outside his cell.

A key clicked in the lock of his cell and the door opened.

***

Light from a nearby torch showed the prisoner sitting against the wall. Otto entered, followed by two guards. He looked at the man, waved the sentries away and sit on the steps which led from the door down into the cell. The prisoner's eyes mirrored the fire in a vivid dance.

"So, you are the man called Desert Wolf? I didn't expect you to be a Frank," Otto said.

Prisoner's gaze examined the question giver, but no answer followed. A whining came from the far end of the dungeon as well as the noise of a creeping rat.

The two men regarded each other.

"Strange name, Desert Wolf."

Otto scratched his shaved chin and smiled. He didn't anticipate this being an easy conversation. On his way down the stairs, he had pondered how best to start. In one night, his men had captured one of the most famous and dangerous men of the land, the Desert Wolf, the hidden blade of the sultan, a man whose face and true identity were unknown. It had been too easy. Had he been betrayed, or was it part of some dangerous and clever plot? And a plot to what purpose?

He had Edward the Saracen, the man who had tried to assassinate the prince of England. Otto suspected that the Wolf and the assassin were somehow connected. He wondered how to get the most out of the situation, as his friend, his lord, was on his deathbed.

Four days before, he had received information from one of his spies on the location of the Desert Wolf's lair. This was the most valuable information he could have hoped for to salvage the dying Crusade; it provided an opportunity to capture one of the main players of the enemy and to learn his plans.

Edward, Otto, and James had voted to take the risk of a raid to the south.

They were astonished at the identity of their target—one of their own, a Frank. Was it true or was it a setup? Who was this man? He didn't match his reputation. But what was his reputation, a man surrounded by shadow and mysteries? Some said he was a master builder of siege engines. Some said he was the backbone of the secret Mamluk intelligence organization, Qussad, created by the sultan. Some said he trained assassins, others said he killed them. Some called him the right hand of the sultan, others said he was the only person to strike fear in Baibars.

"Who are you?" Otto asked.

Again, no response. For a few moments, they stared at each other. Otto thought for a while, then changed his strategy.

"Why did the Mamluk regiment attack your place?"

"Why did you attack my place?"

It was a start, the Savoyard knight thought with hope.

"Ah, where are my manners? My name is Otto de Grandson. I am part of Lord Edward's household. And you, what's your name?"

The Frank looked at Otto with glassy, blue eyes.

"Nobody."

"You might think you are nobody, but a few nights ago, there were two parties fighting for you. One to take your life away, the other to save it." Otto took an advanced stance. He decided that the best strategy was not to lie—or not to lie too much. Nevertheless, his time was precious. He stepped closer to the strange Frank. "You are not dead yet, are you?"

"What do you want from me?" the prisoner asked.

Otto tried to guess by his accent what part of the world this man was from. It was obvious that he wasn't a Saracen. He looked like a Frank, but his face, his glassy eyes, and his blond hair, almost white, made Otto think. He definitely had not been born in the Holy Land. His guttural speech suggested he was from the north, but which part of the north? The Desert Wolf didn't look like most of the men one met at the harbor.

There was something about him, something different, but Otto couldn't tell what. He considered the man's character. He had been captured, had lost everything, but he clearly possessed enormous mental strength, as he didn't show any fear or nervousness despite being in a dungeon. He seemed that he would not surrender without a fight.

"Last night, there was an attempt on Lord Edward's life," the Savoyard knight said. He surveyed the Wolf's reaction but there was none.

"Why should I care about one of your own?" The blond Frank sat against the stone wall and placed his hands on his knees.

"Was the assailant one of yours?" Otto asked. It was a shot in the dark.

The prisoner looked at Otto.

"What do you want?" the Frank asked.

"If you're the man I think you are, you were our enemy up until four days. Now it seems you are unallied, in the prison of your former enemy."

Otto looked into the stranger's eyes. He knew that there was no sense in threatening him. Red Herring had told him how this man had lost everything. His heart must have been full of anger, vengeance, and grief. Otto had felt these things long before and, although the feelings had faded, they were still in his mind.

"Whatever this plot is that you find yourself in the middle of, it will be difficult to uncover," Otto said. He nodded to the corridor, and asked the guards to deliver a flask of water.

"I will give you a chance to get out of here and get your revenge." Otto took the risk, but he was running out of time. He had to act quickly in the name of Edward's health.

"Why do you think your dungeon could hold me?"

"Oh, I don't." The knight smiled. "But I am fairly sure that you will make the right decision."

A new figure entered the stone cell, wearing a dark, woolen cloak over a long tunic which reached the feet. A broach held the hood and cloak in place over the figure's face; it was a pure gold, in the form of a lion.

The stranger's disinterest in Otto's proposal seemed to evaporate as the new figure entered. Lord Edward's advisor shifted to allow the figure through. The newly-arrived person carried a tray with three ceramic cups.

She stopped in front of the prisoner and handed one of the cups to the northerner. Otto examined the man's reaction.

The captive was hypnotized by the moves of the woman as she unhooded herself.

"Milady." Otto took a half-bow. The prisoner took the cup. He didn't take his eyes off her as he drank the water and handed the cup back.

She regarded the prisoner with calmness. She looked pure and innocent. She was neither tall nor short. She had warm eyes and small lips. Her handsome, blond hair was tied behind her head. She looked about thirty years old.

"Lady Eleanor." She was introduced by the knight.

After a quick pause and exchanged glances, she said, "I am sorry for your loss."

The prisoner nodded.

"I am a woman who needs help. My husband is dying and I am here to beg you for a favor," she said. The honesty in her trembling voice made the two men silent.

"My beloved was wounded by an assassin with a poisoned dagger. Most of the physicians in Acre don't even dare to try. He needs medicine from one of the best physicians of Jerusalem. We need to know who sent the assassin. Please, help me find a healer. Help me find who sent the assassin. I will be obliged to you." She stopped for a second and added, "With that, I will grant you the opportunity to find out why you have been attacked."

The Wolf said nothing.

City of Jerusalem is in hands of the Mamluks. You know them, you know this realm, you speak their language.... Please, help me save my husband!" Eleanor looked at prisoner's eyes.

"You have no reason to help me, we raided your home too. Someone sold you to us; maybe the same person sent you a present, the Mamluks who attacked your manor too. Help me, and I will give you a chance to find out." She looked determined.

"This is not something you possess to give. If I want it, I will seize it." He didn't act like a common peasant; he was bold.

She moved closer to the stranger, as he stood, his eyesight above her. Otto sensed the smell of sweat, blood, and dirt. He simply gazed at her. Her blue eyes seemed to hypnotize the prisoner.

She spoke, gentle and soft.

"I know what is it to lose something you love, more than you know. I know what are you feeling and yet, I want something from you. I want your oath. Swear loyalty to me."

The Wolf hesitated. There was a little light in the darkness and Lady Eleanor with her blue eyes.

"I want a green apple," the northerner said. Otto was surprised by his request. She nodded to one of the servants that stood outside the cell.

Otto realized what Lady Eleanor had achieved with her innocent eyes. But the apple, what was that for?

Something was brewing from without the city. Someone had dared to make a move in Acre, while others had attacked to the south. He doubted that the stranger's manor had been attacked by accident. Were these two events related? He hated not knowing but he would found out, sooner or later.

He had begun to place his own figures on the chessboard. The lady and the Wolf were ready. The game of kings and advisers. A single move of a man could achieve what an army could not. Otto knew this was his game, and to win against the sultan's intelligence he needed the Wolf on his side. He had hesitated, initially, when Lady Eleanor had asked to be involved. But he had calculated the risk. The legendary Desert Wolf's reputation dictated that there was much to lose. Although the man didn't look so renowned at the moment, Red Herring had emphasized that he was to be feared. He was like a mist; they couldn't know what the Wolf was involved in.

Otto was motivated to be the best spy for his friend, Edward, who gave him that chance. Yet the secret intelligence of the sultan was a real challenge. He had not seen before such an organization. To overcome the Qussad, he would need to understand how it worked and identify its weak spots.

The stakes were high. Edward's life hung in the balance. The peace accord was in danger. The truce concerned the city of Acre, the plains around it, and the road to Nazareth. Outside of the area, there was a battlefield; a war waged for supplies, for power, for estates, for money, and, above all, for influence. The Crusaders, the Mamluks, and the Mongols constantly stalked each other. Not to forget the religious factions.

Once the Crusaders had achieved their goals in the Holy Land, they would go home heroes, enjoying the well-earned glory. A kingdom waiting to be ruled, a life and name to be made. To get there, Otto must win the game of chess that lay before him.

***

Ulf hadn't anticipated this. He had guessed it would be violence and torture, the traditional ways to make a man talk. Instead, he was visited by a woman he had never seen who expressed her sympathy. Ulf regarded the lady. She looked very much like his lost wife; it struck him like lightning when he saw her. His training helped him to control himself; nevertheless, it was hard. He was wretched, bruised, wounded, and unknown in the palace. Yet, a princess stood in front of him, begging him for favors.

A servant brought a plate of fruit. The Frank took a green apple and he ate it. He looked at Lady Eleanor's blue eyes.

Well, another day in hell, another day in this realm.

"To help the Englishmen and the lady?" he thought. A lady who fascinated him and reminded him of his past love. Was it a coincidence? Fate was brutal.

The Northman considered it. His heart was bleeding and he knew from experience that the best way to heal it was to spill the blood of others. But he had to go on the path of his old life. The path of a ruthless killer. His instincts were alive and working.

"God, please help my enemy," he thought. They would need it if this were to be a worthwhile challenge. The chance lays at his feet.

"What do you know so far?"

***

"The city of Mansurah was asleep," Brother Alexander told him, his voice shaking, "in the year of your birth."

Peter listened to him. He hadn't heard any details about the circumstances of his birth before now. He was in the monk's room in the quarter of the Knights of St Lazarus in the northern suburb of Acre.

"We were on one side of the river; enemy forces were on the opposite bank." The old man talked slowly. He looked like a ragged, used book. "A spy showed us a place where the river could be crossed. A place near the city. The French Lord of Artois was eager to advance. He didn't want to wait for his brother, King Louis, to cross with the main body of the Crusader army and to prepare for the battle. The Templars were opposed to the Lord of Artois' decision too, as were the

Hospitaller Knights. Your father, William Longsword, who was in charge of the English regiment, was a proud knight, Peter."

The orphan was silent. Brother Alexander leaned forward, with a twinkle in his eyes.

"Pride. Isn't that the weakness of every knight?" Alexander said and continued his tale.

"He could not leave the French bastard alone under the threat of the enormous enemy forces in the city. Your father's bravery consistently matched the Frenchman's arrogance. William Longsword and the Count of Artois were in constant competition: Who was the better knight? Which had more glory, more renown? Together, they led this brave and stupid vanguard to suicide." Brother Alexander gazed into the distance, remembering.

"They were in their prime, as I once was. We fiercely engaged the sultan's force, which was taken by surprise by our charge; we penetrated their defenses, entering the city and killing all who faced us. Your father, with his long blade, caught the old sultan by surprise and silenced him, rendering the Mamluks leaderless. The sultan was old and fat, without his armor and aware only too late of the turn of events. We were all bold, arrogant, and young, chasing easy victory and easy prize. Yet, that day, a new hero was born. But not in our ranks."

He stopped his tale for a moment, his eyes seeming to see the inevitable as if he were back with his comrades and sword brothers.

"Peter, are you still here?" He reached for the orphan with his left hand, blinded by his age.

"Yes," Peter was hypnotized by this man, who had always avoided the other monks in the monastery. He enjoyed solitude and calm. But Peter and Brother John, his old mentor, had used to bring him food near the ruins of the old Church of St. Lazarus, where he could supervise the reconstruction process. That was long ago; now he was blind and impaired. His right hand had been cut off at the wrist and his face was constantly hooded. He never talked about how he had lost his hand, but the orphan had deduced it. While helping Brother John clean Alexander, Peter had seen the state of his face under the hood; his flesh was unsightly—leprosy had claimed him. Brother Alexander often used to say that this was his destiny and punishment for his early years' deeds.

"God, young man, sees all. You may hope to be forgotten by your destiny but, while He may delay your fate, you have no chance of evading it. He never forgets," the old man said. He had tears in his eyes.

"So, my sword brother is dead?" he asked. "Tell me again how it happened, my child."

Peter retold the story, beginning with his visit to Brother John, the shadow of a once glorious knight. He told of Julian, his enemy, and his dark knights, how they had caught him and how his mentor had bought him time to escape, saving him. How it had cost him his life.

"Julian killed him," the orphan finished.

"Sad. We are like wood, and life is like a fire; it eats us fast. Another soul was released." The old monk began to nod off but, suddenly, he was awake and took up his tale again. He was back on the battlefield of Mansurah, twenty-two years earlier.

"We fought like demons in mail that day. We swung our blades and we crushed the enemies who approached first. It was so beautiful and promising; our raiding party speared the enemy force like a knife cutting through flesh, with speed and ferocity. We penetrated deep into the city, cutting, thrusting, pushing with the strength of our horses and shields and lances ...." Alexander's voice was dreaming.

"We were like God's warriors that day, earning the red crosses on our chests. We showed no mercy and no fear. But some resisted. A young captain of the Mamluk's regiment stood firm and didn't back down. He showed us what a real warlord must do and earned glory for himself. He organized the remaining defenders and ordered most of the streets to be blocked with wagons and wooden planks, forcing our men to gather into the narrow streets."

He took a deep breath.

"Do you know how hard it is to maneuver a mounted army

down a narrow street? It became chaos, then our enemy released hell upon us. It happened so fast—we were cut off and the slaughter began." Brother Alexander shifted painfully in his bed, catching his breath. This was more than he was used to speaking.

"The Mamluks left their horses to block us and took advantage of our position, shooting us down from the roofs with their arrows. Their infantry thrust their spears and shields into our horses. We were surrounded, pressed into this narrow space of death.

"We realized we were doomed," the old man said. "Your father was experienced in war. He knew we couldn't win—he couldn't do anything to prevent our failure." The storyteller took a harsh breath, heavy with burden.

"Some were cowards and tried to flee, leaving their friends and fellow knights. Some of them drowned in the river while running from their brethren; some were shot to death in the back. Such cowardice, these men broke down and showed their true selves. The French count fled and died spineless. But your father refused to surrender or to flee and leave his troops. We would die, one by one, cut to pieces by our foes at close range in the narrow battlefield, but never to surrender our arms."

"Why you didn't retreat?"

"Why indeed? Because we were knights! We were Crusaders. We gave our oaths to each other not to abandon our brothers to danger. The slaughter turned our sunny attack into a reddish song of sorrow and death. The dust on the streets turned to a bloody, stinky mud; it was hard to move, hard to balance. Your father turned to me and asked me to leave the fight—me and one of my followers. He released me from my oath to him and urged me to rescue the plunder from our campaign."

Peter listened carefully.

"But there was more at stake than treasure; he wanted assurance that I would take care of his beloved one and his future baby in Acre. Someone had to deliver his bloody wealth and secure his lady and ...." He clutched at his chest, pain in his tortured face. Nevertheless, the monk continued his tale.

"He gave me permission to retreat and vowed that my honor would rest intact despite leaving that field." He spoke this last sentence slowly and with obvious difficulty.

"You know, lad, back there, I was glad to leave the bloody battlefield and to live another day to see the Sun. I lost my hand on that day, but I also lost my honor, no matter what my comrades and the witnesses might say."

"Year after year, day by day, my soul suffered from my decision to accept the invitation to retreat. Yes, I had received an order but, deep in my heart, I knew I had made a mistake. That day I should have died with my friends and fellow sword brothers. And that thought eats at my heart and soul every single moment. I have nothing left now; my soul is dead, my honor died long ago on that battlefield, and my hand was lost along with my bravery." His eyes were full of tears as he remembered this moment.

Peter had never before learned anything about his heritage or his family and was intrigued to know more. Before now, he had always thought he had been left alone on his own; he hadn't known his mother. Brother John had raised him as far back as he could remember. Now that his mentor was dead, he needed to satisfy his curiosity. Was what Brother Alexander had told him enough? The more he heard, the more he wanted to know about his kin.

He sensed the unbearable pain in the old man's heart and his desire to turn back time, to stand side-by-side once again with his long dead friends, to regain his own self. To win back his honor.

"Peter, remember: never lose your honor and reputation. These are the only important things in this warring world. Never let your friends down; loyalty cannot be bought. Trust can never be regained, once lost."

"What happened to my father?" Peter was anxious to ask.

"Ah ... Your father, he fought like a devil. He was the last man the Mamluks succeeded in unhorsing. On the ground, he stood, petted his favorite destrier's head and threw away his broken lance. He smiled to the approaching enemy and drew his long sword and bore his shield. I will never forget his demonic, fearless smile. He caught my eyes one last time—I was still recovering from the blow that had taken off my hand. A fellow sergeant helped me to rise from the mud on the river bank. We were two sad souls who had lost our horses but, by some luck, the moment your father was unhorsed, a victorious war cry echoed into the valley. This made all the Mamluks and inhabitants turn to observe the fall of the last hero of the English regiment, William Longsword—the man in whose veins ran the same warrior blood as the Lionheart's. This bought us just enough time, me and my companion, your mentor." He paused, asking for water.

Peter gave him a cup.

"We caught a horse running blindly toward us and successfully crossed the river on its back. While crossing, I was able to see the last deeds of your kin. Your father had lost his helmet, and his long, crow-black hair was wind-swept. You couldn't mistake him, even from a long range. The combination of his armor, blackened from spilled enemy's blood, and his dark hair was breathtaking. His long blade rose and fell and with every cut or thrust he made could be heard the haunting sounds of splashing blood, cracking shields and bones, and screaming. He took many infidels with him that day. After every man he killed, another took his place. But, finally, they seemed to be discouraged. They hesitated between assaults," Alexander said. "He had taken their courage away from them, Peter. He was a real daredevil warrior."

"Daredevil warrior?"

"I watched him use the fallen bodies to protect his rear, but leave himself room to move and to swing his blade. He punished men who underestimated him. He was a true warrior, a Crusader, a knight of valor, brave and bold with a bloody sword and black hair and darkened armor. He never showed any sign of fear or lack of bravery. He fought with eagerness. It looked as if he would never surrender."

"But?" Peter asked.

"But, in the end, the enemy prevailed. The same Mamluk captain who stood and organized the defenders now asked your father to lay down his weapon."

Peter raised his eyebrows, captivated.

"But your father wasn't such a man. The Mamluk captain drew his curved sword from his scabbard and he approached William. There were only two of them now, a few paces from each other. The rest of the infidel troops gathered around them to witness the young and ambitious Mamluk captain against a warlord from the west."

Alexander looked tired of talking but continued.

"They lunged at each other, in a death dance of clashing swords. All was still; the wind stopped and the spectators fell silent, fixated on the two fighting men with determination in their eyes and swords and shields in their hands. They clashed in the square. The fight was fierce and brutal and drained down their remaining stamina fast. Even though your father's fatigue, he matched his opponent. One other Mamluk dared to enter the circle and tried to join the fight but the Mamluk captain ordered him to leave.

"Your father became slow, bruised, and wounded from the battle and his fall from his horse. The Mamluk killed him quickly, cutting him down for the amusement of the crowd.

"That was your father's last song and fight, young man. You should be proud of him. He earned glory and honor for his name that day. He could have retreated but he didn't run; instead, he stood and fought to the last blood. He was the last of his regiment to die. The battle was lost, the whole campaign was lost, the Crusade of King Louis was over. So many good and brave men saw the Sun smile for the last time that day. A whole generation of Crusaders had gone."

"Why didn't he retreat? His death was meaningless."

"Your father died like a hero, fighting to the very end, my child."

Yes, but Peter wanted to have a father; he fiercely wished for it. The naïve chivalry of the man who had sired him had deprived him of a true family.

"I shamed myself in leaving the scene, that day. I chose to dishonor myself but to live. Your father chose immortality. Now, lying in this sandy land that feeds on men's blood, I feel regret. The loss of my honor kept me from going home. I couldn't stand in front of my family and my king and tell them that I had abandoned my battalion—even with permission—to bring news and to save myself." He had tears in his eyes.

"Soon after I recovered from my wound, I returned to Acre and decided to await my destiny in this land and to live in the name of my master, raising you. When I arrived, you were already born. Your mother was gone and I faced the challenge of raising a baby in a hostile place, missing home and with my soul degrading." He tried to look into Peter's eyes.

"You knew my mother?"

"No, my child, all I know is that she had abandoned you in the monastery." Alexander raised his hand to Peter's face.

"You are so much like your father. Your black hair and brown eyes are just like his. You have his stubborn pride too."

Peter shuddered but didn't worry about offending Brother Alexander—the old monk could hardly see him. Peter's father obviously had been a notorious Crusader, connected to the bloodline of English royalty.

"Why have you never told me his name?" Peter was eager to know, but the leprous man was somewhere else. The story had driven him back in time and loaded him with fearful emotions. Peter wasn't sure he had heard him.

"Why?" Peter asked again.

"Because of his name. Your father wasn't loved by the French." Brother Alexander took a breath. "William Longsword, or Longespée in French. The name reminded them of King Louis's failed Crusade, and of his brother's death. As you know, the city of Acre was in the hands of the French. I promised your father to tell you the truth about your name when you're ready or when I'm on a deathbed. Brother John, your mentor, and guardian is dead. Soon I will leave this world, so ready or not you need to learn your father's name, young man."

"I feel guilty about Brother John's death," Peter said.

"You should not, my child," Alexander said. "It was his oath to keep you safe."

He knew there was nothing to be done, yet he felt guilty.

His stomach felt nauseated and his chest felt as if a piece of a rock were stuck in it.

What was the main difference between the experienced and inexperienced man? The experienced man had fallen and risen many times that he knew how to do things. But the inexperienced man had not yet started to fall or rise. This thought revived him. This lesson was delivered from his mentor.

He was proud to have had such a mentor.

"Rest his soul," Peter said.

Brother Alexander pointed to an old small leather bag hanging on the wall.

"Before I left the battlefield, William gave me this for you," the leprosy man said. "Take the bag. You will find inside a ring and a letter."

Peter thought about Brother Alexander's words as he looked at the ring. It had six lions engraved on it: three on top, two under them, and a single one below. The sign of his father and his family. The seal of the letter was the same as the ring.

"It belonged to your father. Longsword." Alexander whispered. "This is the most precious present for you."

Peter was silent.

"You are the illegitimate son of a notorious Crusader connected to the bloodline of the Lionheart." Alexander talked with a wheeze. "Your mentor, who was given the responsibility to raise you and to protect you, is dead. The ring will show you the true story of your father, your family, and your curse."

"Curse? But …."

"The letter is only for your eyes, Peter."

The young man looked at the old roll of parchment with its seal. There was only one problem: he couldn't read. He had never wanted to learn, no matter how hard his mentor had tried to teach him. Now he must.

"A curse?" he asked again.

"Now you are on your own, young man. I am too old and sickly for this." The old man coughed.

"Peter Longsword, your journey starts now. I wish you well." With this, the old man fell asleep. The orphan took the bag and stood. He had no sword; his weapon had been broken during the fight of the previous night. He would have to stand in front of his officer and explain how he had broken his sword less than a day after it had been issued to him. He cringed, imagining the scene.

He had heard that today was Lord Edward's birthday. What a sad way to celebrate it, with poison in your blood delivered by a treacherous bastard. The same bastard Edward had promoted and given a new life, power, and his friendship a year before.

The world had gone mad.

Peter needed to continue his quest to find who was behind Julian's orders. Why did they want him dead? Why had the old monk paid with his life?

He was sure it was connected with Edward's attack and with his own destiny.

His determination drove him forward like the waves of the sea. He thought nothing could stop him from his goal, and he went to find Red Herring.

***

Red Herring was worried. The lad had gone missing.

After his conversation with Otto, he had gone to inspect his men in the barracks, then to check on his destrier. It was not that he didn't trust the groom, but he was used to checking it for himself—an old habit from his childhood. The animal was cleaned and fed.

Afterward, accompanied by David and some of his men, he went to look for the orphan. He intended to enjoy the lad's company while they investigated the harbor and the taverns there. But the alarming events from the night before seemed to have continued. They found two monks at the monastery with their bellies split open. One in the kitchen and one in the garden. The second body was the old monk, John, that had taken care of Peter, the same man who had arranged for the orphan's job in Lady Eleanor's household. There was evidence of a fight.

An eyewitness described warriors in dark garments running by with blood on their unsheathed weapons, chasing a young man. That Peter was missing gave James hope, but he wasn't happy at all. He was supposed to look after the man and he already had failed.

After they left the monastery, he sent a word to the castle and continued his task, heading to the harbor's taverns to join Owen in his search for Julian.

Had the orphan been followed? Or was another traitor involved? James was trying to figure out how Peter had been found in the monastery.

"It stinks," he said to David while walking toward the merchant district. He passed by the Templars' Quarter and turned left, walking alongside the sea shore. He sent some of his men to check the harbor, hoping to find Peter still alive.

Saddlebacks were flying all about. The birds' robust voices couldn't be mistaken. They were always in search of food. The Sun was laughing on his creatures and was waiting for the culmination of the day, before retiring to his lair in the sky.

James was reunited with the Welshman, Owen. He liked his humor. But most of all, the archer was a reliable man. The three of them, James, Owen, and David entered the first tavern together. It was crowded with mercenaries, Crusaders, unemployed rogues, sailors, and Genoese crossbowmen. As Edward's Crusade began to fade, most of these men were in search of new jobs or ships to take them home. Templars and members of the other orders also hired men; they always were short on manpower.

They sat and ordered some ale and dried fish.

Ingram, the tavern keeper was an old Scot who had arrived in the city many years before. He was a former Crusader, now was satisfied with his job and his young, Saracen wife. Englishmen liked to frequent this tavern, as the atmosphere reminded them of home. The host's accent and jokes helped, too. Everyone who visited the tavern wondered how this ugly bastard had managed to end up with a pretty, young woman but no one dared to ask him how he had found her. Ingram was a barrel-chested Scot with a fierce temper, although he was no longer young. His long claymore hung on the wall behind the bar, where anyone who entered could see it.

James knew him from a distant village north of Durham. The tavern-keeper was like a brother to him; they were sword brothers who had participated in a war over religious misunderstandings, power, and influence. They were all pawns in this game of kings.

"Herring, where have you been these days? I missed your presence. Not your ugliness, but your humor was much needed." They all laughed. "The girl who warmed your bed almost came here to ask for me," Ingram, the tavern-keeper joked.

"I am here, so hands off her skirt." They joked about everything. Everything except for honor, which was always a touchy topic for Englishmen.

"Send my regards to your lady. Tell her when she is bored of you, she should come to me." James winked.

Together, they drank, laughed, and shared their problems, and of course, they sang.

We are the men from the north
We are here to sing our battle songs
We are the devils from the north
We are the bastards beyond the sea
We are here today to fight
We are here today to drink
We are here to sing out loud
Till the very end of the world.

They laughed again, the rest left behind.

"Hey, curly Welshman, when you will learn to shoot proper, eh?" James asked, drinking his ale.

"Whenever you change your skirt," Owen replied with a devil's smile. "Besides, do you know whose side God is on?"

The table grew quiet for a moment. They all knew the answer but wanted to hear the Welshman say it.

"The best shooters. God is on the side of the best shooters," the archer said seriously.

"Praise God." The men around the table smiled and shouted together. They hit the wooden cups on the table, spilling ale on it.

"To God, and to the best shooters. May they be on our side forever," Red Herring added.

Ingram brought another tray of ale, but this time he sat with them.

"You know, these days here are full of newcomers. Since Lord Edward brought the news he needed stoneworkers, mason, builders, and more workers, it's like the whole world is fighting for jobs on the new construction site."

"What have I missed?" Owen wanted to know more.

James said nothing, but let the old tavern owner do the talking.

"Didn't you hear? The English prince wants to build a new tower of his own, and to rebuild the weakened section of the inner wall of the city," the old Scot said.

"So, he has the money to pay our wages?" the Welshman asked ironically.

"The Italians fight for the right to supply the goods. The Templars want to be under their supervision. The Hospitallers do not want to play the second violin. The whole project would eat a lot of funds. They all want to be involved, to earn a piece of it. Edward has a respectful reputation; even the moneylenders love him," the tavern-keeper said.

Red Herring looked at his friend and said nothing.

"Are you suggesting our lord has money problems?" Owen asked.

They all laughed. Most of the men had not received their wages for the past year of service. Everyone knew the military campaign on this side of the world was a bloody expensive endeavor, even for a future king.

James managed to provide all that was necessary for his own men. It wasn't easy; sometimes, they had to do some dirty work to earn their living, working as escorts or bodyguards. Most of the time they earned by plundering. Peace wasn't a problem; it made it harder, but also more fun. As a hide and seek game. They tried to get contracts from the Templars or other orders, or Genoese or Venetian mercenaries.

"And how, Almighty Lord, he will provide the money for the construction? Or will an army of monks do the work themselves?" He smiled and looked around for any black-robed fellows that might overhear.

Owen tried to imitate one. "O, mighty God, please lift this big stone and put it over there." He grinned. "The black hoods never get their hands dirty. They would pray for someone to build it, some other to fund it, and, of course, they would want extra donations for their help, eh?"

James was an eyewitness to most of the Church's business in his homeland. He doubted that things here were any different, except that here, the scale would be much greater. They were in the last Christian stronghold in the Holy Land.

"Moneylenders," David said. "I heard Edward took another loan, this time from the Templars."

As the men spoke and drank, Red Herring enjoyed the company of his closest companions but Peter remained on his mind.

"Damned lad, where are you?" he muttered.

Owen apparently guessed what his friend was thinking.

"He will be fine. You will see; he will turn up. He is a little rogue; he survived last night, so he'll be fine."

James wasn't so sure. He was supposed to look after Peter. He was indebted to him for saving his life. He was a proud Scot and he wanted to return the favor. Honor and reputation made a man; they could be ruined in a moment.

His mood turned dark. He needed to cheer up a little. A good fight would do the trick or a game of dice. Even some good news. He hoped to find this son of a bitch, Julian, soon.

King Hugh's constable, Balian, and his men were leading the investigation of the last night events.

"That was in his jurisdiction," Otto had told him earlier. "Who are we to take away that honor?"

"We will see," Red Herring thought. Time never lied. James downed his ale at once and asked the tavern-keeper if he had heard anything regarding a band of dark mercenaries passing through, describing Julian with added commentary on his ugliness and the origins of his mother.

But no one had seen Julian or anyone who looked like him.

"Hey," Ingram remarked. "Yesterday, two barges arrived. Venetians, but they had a Genoese captain with his crossbowmen, all hired to escort some merchant. They brought supplies and fresh additions of men. I don't remember the name of the merchant, but one of their men came by for a beer and said something about some kind of a mission."

"Said that to you?" Red Herring was puzzled.

"Oh, no. One of the whores who works for me heard it while he ... you know .... He rode her well." He smiled, and even though his mouth was bare of teeth, it hadn't affected his charm.

Red Herring smiled at the tavern-keeper. "So, you are a lender of whores now?"

"Ah, you insult me. No, I just provide some pleasure for some hungry men; I offer full service, food, drink, bed—full and warm, of course." Ingram grinned, then switched the topic of conversation.

"What happened last night? All anyone has talked about all morning is an assassin at the castle. I'll bet you know." His face looked hungry for gossip.

"I would like to know, too. My men and I were returning from a raid last night," James replied.

"The poor bastard." Owen nodded to the hanging corpse, which was visible from the tavern. James looked at the dead man too. It was a message to all enemies that killing the English prince was not an easy task.

"But why now, so soon after the truce was signed?" The tavern-keeper asked. "This was the most-asked question this morning in the city."

James wondered the same thing; it was a mystery.

The old Scot smiled at him and said, "Did you hear about the assassination attempt against Sir Philip of Montfort, the old Lord of Tyre, and his nephew, Julian, the Lord of Sidon, last year?"

Red Herring snapped out of his dark mood.

"Julian? No, what happened?"

"Sir Phillip didn't survive. It was the same scenario; two infidels entered the service of the lord, earned his trust, and waited for a good opportunity. They split up when the young Lord of Sidon left the city. A traitor exposed the plotters but decided to trade his soul and not tell his master. The old lord didn't survive, but his son killed the assassin."

"A nasty job," Owen said.

Ingram continued, "They sent a messenger and a ship to warn his nephew, Sir Julian. But the other infidel had disappeared and there wasn't an attempt on the young lord's life. They all thought it was Baibars who stood behind the whole plot and had sent his shadow killers, but I doubt it."

"Why?"

"Lord Philip was old. Why would the sultan bother? It makes no sense."

"Yes, God would have collected his soul soon enough," Owen said.

"What about this Julian?" Red Herring asked.

"The Lord of Sidon sold his castle and his lands to the Templars and entered into their service a few years ago."

"Why?" James asked.

"Some said that his lands were devastated by the Tartars and he hadn't the funds to rebuild it," Ingram said.

"Why would a sultan worry about an old lord and a landless one?" Red Herring was curious. Julian of Sidon—this couldn't be a coincidence.

"The old Lord of Tyre was a real man and knight. Prudent and experienced, dangerous for the sultan. But his nephew? I couldn't say," the tavern-keeper said.

"Where is he now?"

"Some say he vanished, I don't know. Why?"

"Nothing, just curious," Red Herring lied.

So, some fresh Italians had arrived the day before. This was curious. Was it connected with the previous night's affairs? He would feel better if he checked it. Where to find Julian, this son of a bitch? He wasn't in the taverns or other places where these types were usually found.

It seemed Julian may have been under the protection of

another. James remembered the letter they had found on the body—a letter of safe conduct. He slapped his forehead. Why had he not thought of that earlier? One could not find an apple in a peach garden. This was simple. He shouted an order and all his men rose at once and followed him.

"They aren't here. We are looking in the wrong place."

A guard arrived with word from Otto at the tavern door. He wanted James back at the castle immediately.

"What's wrong?"

The guard had no further information.

"Owen, take five of your men and check on the Italian captain. You have one hour. Find me afterward."

He and his short shadow, David, hurried toward the castle. The past few days had been confusing, but James suspected that this was just the start of the intrigue.

Today was Edward's birthday and what they were doing instead of preparing celebrations? They were searching the streets and the taverns for ugly bastards and murderers. And where the hell was the orphan?

He felt Peter would play a major role in this quest.

***

He had failed to kill his target.

His whole body ached. He opened his eyes.

There she was. Her eyes could melt anything, even his conscience. Eleanor, the lady from some distant land called Castile.

For a moment, he thought she smiled at him. But he quickly shook off this thought. He had failed; he had been tied up and brutally beaten.

He knew his failure could be attributed to one single mistake: he had felt pity toward the orphan. That was a new feeling for him. Now, his fate had taken a wrong turn. He tried suppressing the fear that arose in his throat, as he had done throughout his career, but it would not be stifled. Now, he was on a verge of collapse.

He blinked again and gazed at the handsome face of Lady

Eleanor.

The small room next to the Lord Edward's chamber was his prison now, not the dungeon or the tower. This wasn't a bad idea; the prince's chambers, after the previous night's events, were the most guarded place in the city.

He looked around the room. He had been here before; this was the place where he and Edward used to talk about the campaign, about the strategy, about many things.

Was he ashamed of what he had done? No. He was a professional killer; this was his trade. He was the best at it and he was proud of his reputation. Although the Christian infidels didn't know his true name and his reputation, his family and his master did.

The brutal knight who had delivered most of his beatings approached the assassin, lifted him to sit on a chair, and threw a bucket of water over him. The cold water froze his face and woke him fully.

"There must be a reason behind what you did last night. Could you share it with us?" The kind voice of the Spanish princess made him felt unruffled.

He was trained not to give up, trained to not to tell the secrets he knew. But in her eyes, he felt the urge to say something.

He looked around the room and saw Sir Otto in one corner of the room, with his guard on his right. Otto de Grandson, the noblest and most trusted of Edward's household—and the cleverest, too—was staring at him. Otto had never liked him. The assassin had spent almost a year trying to blend into the Crusaders' camp and they had always stalked each other. But now, the assassin wasn't sure what his role was.

The brute wasn't important; he was here only to bring pain and obedience. The presence of the lady was a surprise, however. He knew what to expect; if he were on the opposite side, he would do the same. He prayed it would be a fast death.

"If you want to see the sunlight again," Otto took the conversation. "It depends entirely on you."

Edward the Saracen said nothing.

"Who sent you? The sultan?"

To say something or not? Ultimately, it did not matter if one said nothing or everything. The lady's eyes were persuading.

"I am a member of the Qussad." Edward the Saracen said.

"Who sent you?' Was it the sultan?" Otto asked again.

"When I receive orders, I never ask who gave them."

"Why did you attack Edward now?"

"I couldn't say. My primary task was to observe and to fetch intelligence of your plans to my commanding officer."

"But ...?" Eleanor prompted.

"The order for assassination arrived a week ago. The man with the responsibility to do it was injured, and I took his place."

Otto's jaw dropped.

"You are a replacement?" he asked. "How many of you are in our camp?"

"I have no idea; we didn't know each other."

Otto narrowed his eyes. He had never trusted the Saracen.

"Why?" Eleanor asked.

"If one of you is captured, he cannot betray your brothers if he doesn't know them," Otto said.

"Yes, like me, now." Edward the Saracen observed that Lady Eleanor was leaning forward attentively.

"So, you executed an order received from someone you didn't know. What form of orders did you receive—verbal, written, through codes?"

"Every kind."

"And how did you know they were not false?" Otto asked.

"I have my ways of knowing."

Lady Eleanor behaved like a true leader. She nodded, smiled, and underlined some of Sir Otto's questions. The whole scene was unreal—the assassin had anticipated being tortured, brutalized, and, finally, killed, but none of this was happening.

"The merchant?" the lady asked.

Edward the Saracen was surprised by the question.

"The merchant?" he repeated.

Lady Eleanor explained to him, slowly, how they had found

the merchant's house, ransacked.

"So, this black-haired orphan, Peter, turned up at the wrong place at the wrong time for me." The assassin found some strength to smile a little.

"Why do you say that?" she asked, unaffected.

The fallen assassin explained that it was his pity which had stopped him from killing the orphan.

"And this led you to failure—what irony," Otto said. "But maybe he was at the right place at the right time. It depends on your point of view."

After a few heartbeats, Lady Eleanor turned to the door and called for food.

The assassin observed the princess and truly admired her. She possessed an iron will; this little female would be a perfect ruler. But they lived in a world of men. Society wasn't ready to accept a woman as a leader. Yet, this time would come one day.

Nevertheless, she was a real master of organizing her men. He had heard that she had survived the Barons' War a few years before, had lived in a hostile territory, alone and penniless. And she stood before him now. She questioned him without fear. She looked like a woman who achieved her goals.

After the food and the drink were served, she brought a cup of water to the assassin's mouth, as his hands were tied with rope behind his back. She courteously waited while he drank all of it.

With the warmth of her eyes, she looked at him.

"I need your help."

This surprised him. He was speechless. She looked like a goddess and she smiled on him. He feared she would win. He knew that she was at the beginning of her thirties, but she was already a mother, a princess, a war survivor, a land owner, an administrator, a Crusader, and now she was a truly leader of her men. And she would take it all because the winner always took it all.

The silence was strong throughout the dark room.

She continued. "The best physicians in Acre, no matter the religion or race, all speak of an extraordinary healer in

Jerusalem who could cure my beloved husband." Her gaze became heavier. "From the poison that you delivered to his body last night."

She emphasized her last words, like a dagger piercing the flesh. Still, her face looked calm.

The assassin had assumed his target was dead by now; this news shocked him. He had not expected Edward to live more than half a day—maybe a day, if he were lucky.

Someone had taken great care to keep him alive. This was admirable; maybe it was the same Saracen healer who had taken care of Lord Edward's child. But the physician had achieved nothing but to prolong the prince's agony. The assassin had witnessed this horrible pain in some of his previous targets.

"I need to find this Jerusalem physician for my husband." The determination drawn on her face was unbreakable. "Could I rely on you? Your life in exchange for that of my beloved one?"

It was an easy decision: accept the lady's proposal, and live another day.

Fate was unpredictable.

"Allah is merciful," the assassin said, hoping it was true.

***

Julian opened the wooden door and entered.

His master was sitting behind the big, heavy desk, writing on parchment. The newcomer was nervous. He was tired, he was beaten, he had barely slept, and his target had escaped from him for the third time. This was unacceptable, and he knew it, and his master knew it, to be presented three chances and to fail. His pride was hurt too.

Julian approached his master hesitantly, his breath shallow and his heart was pounding.

"Julian, my boy, come near me." His tone was relaxed and showed no evidence of his mood.

The blond man hesitated for a moment but walked on, toward his master. The room was richly-furnished, big, and sunny. The northern wall was a library. This gave the room a strange feeling.

Julian was at arm's reach from his master and was alert to his reaction. The master was one of the most feared men in the Holy Land. Most of his men were afraid of his temper and his frightening decisions. With a slow move, the older man rose and looked at his subordinate with icy eyes.

"You failed me." He said and approached Julian and patted him on the left cheek. But his eyes were focused like an arrow on the blond knight. Julian didn't move.

"I gave you a chance to prove yourself. How many chances do you need?" The master's tone was quiet.

"But—" Julian tried to respond.

"I did not give an order to kill the monks."

"They saw my face."

"Your mistakes made me have to interfere." He sat down near his desk. "Can you ever use your head rather your sword? Just one time?"

The question was covered in irony. The master was a thin and bleak man, in his early fifties. His hair was almost gray, but he took care of it. He sported a rich warrior's outfit, with ornaments showing his high status. There was an inch-long, vertical scar below his left eye. He had never mentioned how it had happened and no one dared to ask. He had saved Julian from misery and starvation, accepting him into his service. The master had helped him to restore some of his pride. But he demanded complete obedience and when he didn't receive it, he became extremely violent and had the power to destroy a man's world.

A knock sounded at the door and a guard opened it. A short man with hooded face entered. Julian's master turned his attention to the newly-arrived person and ignored the blond knight for a moment.

"They leave tonight," the short messenger said.

"Direction?"

"Jerusalem"

"Why?"

"The assassin promised to help them fetch a healer for

Edward, in exchange for his life," the man answered.

"So, he is alive. Who is the healer?"

"Ibn al-Nafis."

"Well, that will be bloody fun. What about the witness, the orphan?"

"He will be with the riding party."

"So, the journey continues."

"There is one more thing," the hooded man said.

"What?" the master asked.

"The Desert Wolf will ride with them, too."

"This is interesting. The most dangerous men in our plan will travel together toward Jerusalem. They will be at a hand's reach from our sword." The master smiled, then murmured something to the messenger. It was only for his ears; Julian didn't hear it.

The master sent the messenger away and turned to the blond knight again.

"You are lucky. You will have another chance. Please do not disappoint me again," he said and smiled. It was cold smile which froze the heart.

Julian didn't need any threat to know what he must do. He was keen to succeed this time and to earn the pleasure of his master. And some fortune, of course.

His master smiled and was in a good mood from whatever the messenger told him.

"Julian, please, prepare two messengers for me right away," the master said. He turned to the window, then back to the blond knight.

"We need a new plan," the old man smiled, "The world needs to be reordered. There is a great chance and we have to grab it."

And Julian went out of the room to obey his master.

***

Otto was on his balcony, watching the party depart.

"Do you trust him?" James asked. "The Wolf?"

"We must have faith, my friend," Otto said. "Besides, we

need a man like him."

"But I don't trust him."

"Nor do I," Otto said. "But Lady Eleanor thinks we haven't much of a choice."

James leaned against the wall.

"After all, it's was his idea to take the assassin with you," Otto said. "We need to spread the rumors that the Desert Wolf and the failed assassin were headed to Jerusalem with your party looking for a physician."

"So, we are baits for the enemy to make his move?"

"Well, yes, my friend," Otto said. "And you need to take Peter, the witness of the last night event, with you."

"First, I have to find him."

"You do not have to. Look over there." Otto pointed down the street. Peter was walking toward the castle.

"You want me to take this inexperienced recruit with me?" James asked.

"It is necessary, we have to wait for all the plotters to come out in the open with a desire to silence the witnesses," Otto said.

"It will be a dangerously interesting week," James grinned. "So, we play a game of predator in a lamb's skin?"

Otto nodded and placed his hand on his Scottish friend's shoulder.

"We will catch all the traitors and plotters with dirty hands and we will punish them, my friend."

"It's a risky business," James said.

"Yes indeed, and I believe you will do fine, my friend." Otto smiled.

It would be a long week. He hoped his friend would be all right. He had debated the plan with Edward and Lady Eleanor. The couple had given their approval.

The intelligence network Otto tried to use was hastily assembled, unlike the sultan's Qussad. The Crusaders used traitorous and weak souls to trade their news and information in exchange for something to eat. The professionals the sultan used were another breed.

From Otto's point of view, this opportunity to overthrow

the Mamluks' spy network was the most difficult challenge he had faced. All previous attempts had been games of swords and spears.

There was something new that intrigued his never-sleeping mind: a ring on the orphan's hand. He had seen those marks before, but where? He eventually would remember.

He hoped not to be too late.

CHAPTER EIGHT

Plains of Acre, Holy Land, Sunday, 19th of June, in the year 1272
of the incarnation of Christ

A new dawn was born. The Sun slowly started to climb toward its throne. With vivid warmth, he touched the land and woke up every living creature.

They had been riding all night. He yawned from his place on the saddle of the brown horse he had received last night. This was the first time he had left the city. Peter was afraid, but also impatient. His dream to see and explore something new was about to come true.

Yesterday, after calming down, he had returned to the castle. Sir James had embraced him but had also slapped his neck.

"I was worried about you, lad," he had said. Otto and the Scottish knight had questioned him about the monastery. His stomach had knotted with guilt during their questioning. Was he a criminal? They had offered Peter their condolences on the loss of his mentor. But there hadn't been much time to talk.

Otto had ordered him to join the newly-formed party. This new task offered Peter a chance to escape another assault from Julian, and James was in charge of it. Peter had felt that he couldn't say no.

The others weren't as inexperienced as the orphan—Red Herring; David; Owen; a pale Frankish stranger dressed in a wretched, dirty robe who looked like a monk; the assassin; and an arrogant knight called Hamo Le Strange. There were five other men that Peter didn't know, as well. Twelve men left the southern gate—a dirty dozen whose only purpose was to bring life for their beloved lord, no matter the cost.

And, thus, their mission began.

The previous night, there hadn't been a feast for Edward's birthday. Instead, there had been a meeting followed by preparation for the expedition. The party was meant to fetch a physician to save Lord Edward s life, the best one around, Ibn al-Nafis.

Their second directive, of course, was to survive. They needed to find the physician who would dare to try to heal the prince. But most of the physicians would not touch a case as dire as Edward's.

Peter was eager to understand. Owen explained it to him.

"Most of the physicians in Acre don't even dare to try," he began. "Some old Hospitaller advised cutting out the poisoned flesh. A respected Saracen healer refused to commit himself to the patient. It was too risky." He paused to emphasize the seriousness of the situation.

"They all say it is only a matter of time until death comes. These bloody physicians. You should be afraid when you need one of them," Owen said.

"No one has offered help; no one has offered the skill or expressed the desire to heal the future king of England. It is pathetic. Most of the physicians know the law," James added. The orphan wanted to know more.

Red Herring explained, "If the patient dies, there will be a trial for the physician to determine whether the healer did everything he could. Did he do everything that was necessary? Why didn't he do this or that?

"No one wants to pay the price for a dead royal body, and the chance of success is slim. Most have said the patient will die regardless of the treatment given. No one will risk his own reputation for a poisoned person, even a royal one." Red Herring grunted with disgust.

"So, now we ride to Jerusalem, the center of the world, to find a real healer," Owen said.

It was going to be a hell of a trip. This path would lead

them into the sultan's territory, which was controlled by Mamluk forces.

Edward's fellowship rode into hostile territory dressed as pilgrims and priests being escorted by a few mercenaries. Their armor, weapons, and gear were in one of the wooden carts they drove. Over these belongings were several corpses—bodies they had fetched from the cemetery. The assassin was tied to a second cart.

According to their story, they were transporting dead holy men to be buried in the Christian cemetery of Jerusalem. These were meant to be two famous monks who had recently passed away, someone named Nickolas and the other—Peter had forgotten his name.

The orphan smiled. Who would believe them?

"We look like cats dressed in mice clothing," Owen said.

"A Welsh cat, indeed," James said.

"Ha, but some say many knights and heroes have traveled this path, the path of humbleness and pilgrimage," the Welshman said. He smiled at the orphan. "You are still alive, eh? Do I look like a humble priest?" He released his viper laugh.

The inexorable heat drained the water from their bodies, causing them to ride mostly in silence. The five soldiers Peter didn't know were dressed as hired blades—mercenaries—the kind that were routinely paid to protect people on journeys to the Holy City. They were dressed in leather armor vests and carried flat-topped kite shields, spears and swords, and kettle helmets. They bore no banners or standards. Mercenaries provided services to the pilgrims who couldn't afford to hire Templars or Hospitallers.

The roles were divided. James, Owen, Peter, and the pale Frank played friars; the others were dressed as their bodyguards.

Hamo Le Strange, the arrogant knight, played a wealthy lord from the Welsh Marches, the lands on the border between England and Wales, which he actually was. But now, he acted as the leader of the mercenaries, and Sergeant David played his steward.

The theatrics were for the Mamluk's scout patrols, who watched every caravan, as well as the pilgrims on foot trying to reach absolution.

"This is ridiculous." James still didn't approve of the idea. For Owen, this was amusing.

Peter understood that Red Herring had protested the plan proposed by Otto and the rogue from the beginning. James couldn't believe that the Welshman had succeeded in convincing Otto and Hamo to do this. The Scottish knight was irritated, but, after a short argument, he had agreed, Owen's smile told Peter all he had missed.

No one could overcome Otto.

Red Herring grunted; he didn't look comfortable in the monk's robe. Even though he had leather armor on under the dress.

"I hate this stinky robe. I would rather be in my full battle gear if an enemy attack us," the Scottish knight was muttering incoherently to himself.

Peter and the rest laughed.

"We are in a hurry," he declared to the orphan. "We need also to catch up to an Italian merchant caravan a few hours ahead. We want to use them as a cover."

"Italians?"

"They arrived yesterday with a paper from the Pope and were planning to go straight to the Church of the Holy Sepulchre. They've already managed to fetch letters of protection from King Hugh, the sultan, and even the Tartars," Owen said.

"I don't know how they obtained such papers, but I bloody want to catch them up and bloody travel under their flag." James was serious.

"We also need to obtain their favor," Owen added.

"And how do we do that?" Peter asked.

They nervously observed the horizon and the nearby hills for enemies. The assassin in the second cart listened in silence.

"This corpse story stinks," Red Herring murmured.

"How will we win their trust and favor?" Peter asked again.

"We will have to think of something," Hamo said and

smiled.

"According to the tavern's rumors, they were travelers guarded by a group of Genoese crossbowmen. Or were they Venetians? We will find out soon," James added.

"Why the hell are there so many mercenaries for some stupid travelers? Perhaps the new Pope needed some fresh holy wine to be delivered?" Owen scratched his curly hair.

"Hey, don't forget that the Pope is a close friend to our Edward," James said.

"Venetian merchants with Genoese soldiers? I thought they didn't like each other," the orphan asked.

"Since the War of St. Sabas, Venetians are richer; they sometimes hire Genoese crossbowmen. It is simple," Red Herring answered.

"We will catch up to them soon, I suppose," Peter said to no one in particular. He hoped they would be safe under the Italians' protection.

David, the short sergeant, didn't say much. The older men questioned Peter about what had happened at the monastery with Julian. The orphan retold his last adventure. He had become a target, for some reason.

The orphan looked at Edward the Saracen. The dark mercenaries had been waiting for him, and now they were after Peter. Why?

The orphan moved his attention to the unnamed last companion, some pale Frank in a torn, dirty robe with a colorless hood. Peter couldn't determine his age, as the man constantly turned his face to observe the landscape. He was the only one who dared to drive the cart of corpses. The stranger hadn't said a word all night.

"Who is he?" Peter asked.

"We captured him a few days ago," Owen said.

"Captured? And now he is on our side?" The orphan was astonished. These days everything was upside down. Red Herring said nothing.

"He is dangerous. We must keep an eye on him," the Welshman said, adding with spirit, "So, we are in the wilderness with an assassin in our cart, a strange man attacked by his own, and an orphan with no war experience—a chased man." Owen nodded to Peter. "We come out for a walk with a couple of corpses. We are riding into hostile territory under the Sun which makes us want to die, leagues away from our home and good ale. It's beautiful, isn't it?"

"Yes, this is what I signed into this Crusade for. Not for riches, glory, and easy women. No, no, we are here by God's will, remember," Hamo said with irony.

"You bastard, you will kill me with your thoughts quicker than the enemy." James finally laughed. Edward the Saracen looked at the orphan.

"How is your head?" the assassin asked.

"How is yours?" Peter smiled.

"Do you know it's not a polite to answer a question with a question?"

"I had no father to teach me," the orphan replied.

"What about the old monk who looked after you?" the assassin asked.

Peter's mood became gloomier.

"He's dead."

Astonished by the answer, Edward the Saracen raised his eyebrows as he said no more but waited for the orphan to explain.

"The men who were waiting for you killed him. Now they're after me."

"He was an old Hospitaller, but a wise one," he said. "I liked him. He was very knowledgeable about herbs and potions. It's sad when such a wise and educated man is lost to the world."

Peter's mouth dropped open. He hadn't known his mentor was a Hospitaller but the infidel had known. The orphan rode beside the wooden cart with the assassin. Peter and Edward the Saracen were watching each other.

"How did you persuade Sir Otto to spare your life and to take you on this mission?" Peter asked.

"I didn't do anything. Lady Eleanor did it all herself."

Peter smiled. "I am one of her guards since yesterday. I saved her husband but have never spoken to her." The orphan paused and said, dreamily, "Now I know what I have to do if I want an audience with Lady Eleanor. I have to try to kill her husband, but not to save him."

All the men laughed—even the assassin—except the stranger.

"What is wrong with him?" Peter asked, pointing at the hooded man.

"He lost his family four days ago," Red Herring said.

"Look over there," one of the men pointed to the shadow on the hill on their left. Peter turned his head and saw horsemen who were watching them. They were about a mile away. Red Herring froze for a moment, then held up his hands and started to pray. The Welshman noticed this and did the same, trying to hide his smile.

"Are you pretending to be a stupid praying monk, sir?" Owen said.

Peter didn't understand at first. The assassin explained to him while observing the horsemen on the ridge.

"This isn't an ordinary patrol. There are too many riders, so they do not look like a scout patrol."

"Yes, and if they want to catch us, nothing can stop us, right?" Owen murmured.

They continued along the road.

Peter turned to Owen.

"Can you teach me to read?"

"Eh, but first I must teach myself." He grinned, as usual. "You don't learn to survive in the wildland like this from books, Peter."

The orphan was disappointed. He had his precious letter and book in his leather bag. He was ashamed to ask Sir James to teach him. He did not want the Scottish knight to understand that he stole a book. He borrowed it, and he intended to return it.

As they rode, it seemed as if they were all familiar with the route, except Peter.

"We are being followed from the moment we crossed the plains of Acre," James said. And now they had seen the Mamluks.

"We need to catch up to the Italians quickly," Hamo said. His voice was bold. He was riding a fine, black destrier and James observed the expensive animal.

"Great warhorse," Red Herring said. Peter noticed James' face showing admiration without a hint of envy. As did Peter; the black stallion was one of the finest chargers the orphan had ever seen. A horse which had been bred and trained for war was one of the most precious possessions a knight could bring into battle. This black stallion had a short back, a well-muscled loin, strong bones, and a well-arched neck. It was a splendid charger.

James had mentioned that he had an honorable stud back home. Everyone knew he had a passion for horses.

"What was the name of the horse master who sold it to you?"

"Simon," Hamo replied and petted the horse. "It is an excellent animal, indeed."

Peter listened to the two knights as they talked. The orphan had heard the story of a recently-failed night raid against the Saracen border patrol involving Hamo. It had turned into a rescue mission of a caravan. Hamo had been hurt, but his fine destrier, which had survived the journey across the sea with its owner, had been pierced by Saracen arrows. An iron arrowhead had cut the steed's main artery; the animal collapsed in agony. Hamo had done what he had to do. It was a great loss to him. He had fallen behind his fellow knights. That night, Hamo had lost his horse and Red Herring had saved his ass. Now, the arrogant knight had a new destrier.

"I hope I will have the chance to restore my honor," Hamo Le Strange said in a low voice intended only for Sir James' ears, and the young knight rode ahead. But Peter had heard.

"Ah, every young knight is a fool. The world won't end from one failure." Red Herring smiled and turned his attention to the ridge.

A dust cloud betrayed the position of the Mamluks.

Pressed by both the time and their enemy, the party ceased its conversation. Their wagon wasn't fast enough, but the task required it to be. Owen and Hamo wanted to speed up, but

James interrupted them.

"If we are pretending to be pilgrims, we shouldn't let some scout patrols scare us. Besides, the path to the Nazareth isn't a war zone, according to the peace treaty."

"Why not? We are stupid and terrified monks, and when we see the fierce Mamluks we fill our pants with shit, don't we?" Owen said. The other Crusaders laughed at this, but not James.

Peter observed Hamo, who proudly rode his new horse. He was clean-shaven, his hair fell freely on his shoulders, and he never lost the smile on his face. He wasn't familiar to Peter from the training zone or barracks, or the streets. But the orphan used to see him mostly in the taverns, and every time he was there, he was surrounded by pretty ladies. He was of an average height but his long, dark gold hair combined with his black eyes made him popular with women.

The orphan understood why these men had been chosen for this mission, but he wondered about the role of the pale Frank.

Red Herring rose from his saddle and observed the area.

"Hamo, please stop dancing around like a stupid, headless lord from the Welsh Marches. Be a real guard leader, as you're supposed to be," the Scot shouted.

"But, I am," the golden-haired rider of the black destrier grinned. He was bold and handsome. He didn't look like a man who obeyed other men but he did it.

"I've never seen him listen to orders from anyone else but Sir James. He thinks he knows better than everyone," Owen said. "He had great respect for Sir James of Durham."

"Why?" Peter asked.

"In the Battle of Evesham, the Scot saved his arse."

Peter looked at the nearly thirty-year-old knight Hamo Le Strange. After a few hours, Peter could notice this. The Scot was the only person who could make Hamo behave properly.

The whole adventure promised a little chance of success. Would they find the physician? Would Edward endure until they return? What time did they have? Peter couldn't answer these questions. But he noticed that they didn't show any sign of despair. Peter also noticed that the men spoke with pride that they were part of the prince's retinue, serving under his flag. And now James' men were fighting for Edward's life; his people loved him.

He was new to this environment, inexperienced, but he could understand that. He also understood from David, that these men hadn't received their wages for almost a year, but they still were holding together, as friends, as real brothers at war on a distant land, full of violence and death.

Peter hoped to be accepted as a real member of the household one day, but he knew these hardened men wouldn't let an outsider into their ranks so easily.

He looked at the Sun and smiled to him. The desert wind brushed his face.

Peter was anxious to see a real Mamluk scout party. His childish curiosity was stronger than his fear. He had never left the city before. He had survived on the street all his life. But this adventure was something different; now, he knew there was a whole other world outside the city walls. Unimaginable land, which waited to be discovered.

"We are going south," Owen declared, "along the sea. The Romans once called this road the Via Maris." He guessed the lad's question.

"You are unbelievably clever, Sir Owen, as well as pretty." Red Herring joked. Everyone knew Owen was an ordinary man, but one of the best archers in the lady's service.

Hamo led the group. His fine armor, gray surcoat, and the black horse he rode distinguished him from the others. He had no helmet and his hair danced in the wind. But his determined and focused face showed more than knightly arrogance and confidence.

"We crossed the border, we are now in Mamluk territory," James said.

The Sun was devastating, making Peter sweat in the intense heat. The events of the past twenty-four hours had left him unclean. At first, he didn't notice a chafing on his inner thigh. This was a mistake. His sweat toughened his dirty underclothes like hardened leather. With every movement, he felt his pants abrading his thighs.

The sweat stung him like thousands of fleas biting at once, without mercy. He felt a constant itching, an uncomfortable desire to scratch his thighs but it was inappropriate in front of other people to behave like a mangy dog. He longed to wash up but, of course, this was impossible. He supposed it would turn into a wound, which he would have to treat. Peter felt shy but he knew he must ask the experienced soldiers how to treat such wounds, even if it was bound to provoke some teasing.

They continued their quest through this sandy land. For now, only the Sun followed them.

After a while, they reached a yellow, rocky ridge and came across a rivulet. Here, they stopped to water the horses and rest. Peter ran quickly from the eyesight of his companions to check the state of his thighs. Most of them sought the shade of a tree; some replenished the water flasks they carried. Peter quickly found some privacy behind a thick bush.

He removed his robe and pulled his pants down, inspecting his skin.

"It doesn't look good" A serious voice from nearby startled him. Owen's face didn't show any sign of his usual, merry mood.

The orphan was surprised; he expected jokes. The Welshman came near and looked at the abrasion on Peter's thighs. The skin was red and raw.

The archer said something in his native language, and the orphan did not understand a single word.

"One of the first mistakes of inexperienced soldiers is to forget their hygiene." Owen said, scratched his neck, and continued: "Sweat and dirt stick on their trousers, then sweat dries on the clothes, thick and hard. Before they know it, they have skin abrasions. In such dry, sandy place, this could become deadly painful."

Owen looked the orphan in the eyes and, with some sympathy, added, "You need to clean it and wash it well, then dry it. Wash your pants, too, with fresh water and let them dry. Put some clean, dry, cloth on your skin. You will need medicine soon or it will turn nasty."

Peter was thankful for the advice, though a little ashamed,

with his pants around his knees; he hoped no one had observed them.

He did exactly as the Welshman said. He hadn't any clean, soft cloth. But he still had bandages on his head, which he removed, washed, and wrung dry. He lay them and his washed pants under the Sun's smile and waited. He wasn't disappointed; before long, the clean bandages and pants were dry. He smiled to the Sun for its help. He tied the bandages around his thighs. The pain was terrible, but he was optimistic after the advice he had received.

Why had this happened to him? Especially now, when he was on an important mission. He was like a new-born baby dressed in old and rough clothes.

He needed not to think about it. But how? Every single step made him feel the pain in his flesh. He closed his eyes and tried to pretend he wasn't in the sandy wastelands, but instead in some safe place. His mind lacked images of good places. He couldn't remember even one.

He finished dressing and joined the others. Peter hoped this was another step to the manhood—a quick step.

***

When Hamo came back from scouting ahead, he said that he had seen a caravan from the ridge.

"Come and see, sir," he said to Red Herring and spurred his stallion to the frontier of the cliff.

"Look on your left." Hamo nodded, patting his animal. Sir James stared at the dusty cloud beneath them and calculated their options.

They saw a Templar party which was attacking a caravan. This, in itself, was not unusual. But the victims of the attack were another matter entirely. The marks of the travelers revealed them as royalty; they flew the banners of Ibelin.

Almost twenty Templars—ten knights dressed in white tunics with red crosses on their chests over their chainmail armors and as many black-dressed men-at-arms with kettle helmets—surrounded their victims. There were already a dozen dead guards around the royal carriage, which was on its side with a door opened toward the sky. On the left of the wooden cart, there was a helmeted man in Hospitaller's clothes, the only guard standing between the knights and the royal servants who surrounded their lady.

James saw troubles. A lot of them.

"We need to interfere," Hamo said.

"No, our mission lies elsewhere. We need to avoid complications."

"No, we need to help the defenseless. Isn't that right?" His eyes looked like the devil's and his tiny smile was provoking.

James knew he was right. But he also knew he couldn't easily control this lord from the Welsh Marches. Red Herring asked himself why he had wanted to involve Hamo in this mission. He was hard to control, he never listened to orders, and he was reckless and arrogant. But he was a real knight—brave, smart, and capable. He never left a man behind. Some day he would govern his own lordship, Red Herring thought. But first, they needed to survive this.

"They need help, yes."

They interrupted the calm that their own men were enjoying by the rivulet.

"Men, there is a battle before us and we will have to come to the aid of a royal person," James said to his followers and they went there.

The monk party turned in haste to the cloud of dust and troubles.

The lady stood, looking fragile, her face hidden by a hood. She bore the marks of the lords of the Kingdom of Jerusalem. She was a royal lady and they rode to help her.

The Hospitaller Knight, dressed in a black tunic with an eight-pointed white cross on his chest over his chainmail, did not surrender. He was surprised. This was a rare situation. The Templars and Ibelin were not enemies.

And Hamo rode forward to meet the Templar's leader.

Red Herring smelled trouble; he looked at his fellow false priests and signaled to them to be ready to draw their weapons.

"Who are you?" the lord of the Welsh Marches asked as he

stood a few paces away from their leader.

"Halt." An ugly face met them. He looked from his saddle toward the monks with demand and arrogance and then to Hamo. "Roger of Sicily. And this is not your business. What is your name?" the leader of Templars said.

Hamo didn't reply, but he stared at the Templars' captain.

The warring action seemed almost over. The royal guards were dead and Hospitaller Knights' bodies lay on the ground, as well. Just one still stood and held the assailants from their obvious target. The carriage and the cliff blocked the knights from two directions. The bodyguard stood between these obstacles with just enough space to face at least two attackers at once with his shield and sword.

The rest of the Templars had surrounded the servants and half of them now turned their attention to the newcomers.

James and his men were two hundred paces behind Hamo arriving from the western part of the road. The Templars and the Ibelin caravan were at least five hundred paces from him.

"Prepare the shields, men," he said. And he turned his gaze to the lady. "Hurry up!"

Two of the Templars approached the last standing Hospitaller at once. One of them made an approach with his shield. The defender stepped to meet him. He realized it too late that was a feint. The other Templar kicked him from behind. The Hospitaller snorted out. He tried to step back and turn toward the second attacker but he lost balance and fell on his bottom.

"Get up!" the taller of the Templars shouted. The knight with the black tunic and white cross over his chest turned toward them. He stuck his sword in the ground, looked at the attackers, and stood again.

"Did you miss me?" The second knight smiled. He kicked dirt at the Hospitaller, who charged. He tried to push the first Templar but the taller knight was solid as a rock and didn't move. The Hospitaller looked surprised. The second knight struck the member of the Order of the Hospital of St. John with his shield with a terrible sound. The defender collapsed.

"Finish him!" Roger of Sicily cried from his horse.

"No!" Hamo shouted.

Hamo's horse reared onto its hind legs and charged. The lord from the Welsh Marches spurred his horse toward the Templar's captain. There was a ferocity at his eyes. He closed on him quickly and pushed his horse to the Knight Templar's, which was pushed to one side and lost balance. The captain was taken by surprise and he fell.

The Italian screamed; his animal had fallen onto his leg. Roger wailed in pain, trapped under his horse. Suddenly, the party of mail raiders in white tunics with red crosses on the chest moved. After them, the black-dressed sergeants with distinguished kettle helmets followed.

Two knights remained near the fallen Hospitaller.

James had his sword in hand, his red hair freed from its hood. He jumped from his horse, following the younger knight. The pale Frank stood shoulder-to-shoulder with Red Herring.

"Stay together with your men and keep your Marcher Lord at bay. Stay behind the carts, use them to block the path of the horses," the Wolf said calmly.

Red Herring understood but was shocked at the way he had received this order. It wasn't a command, nor was it a request. He was angry that someone else had told him what to do. He knew his trade; he was aware of what would happen next.

The sound of the pack of animals' breathing was in his ears.

He turned to shout an order to the others; almost all the false monks had grabbed their weapons and shields and prepared themselves to meet the enemy. Like a pack of wolves, the Templars galloped to their prey.

There was a fire in Hamo's eyes. He turned his charger, seeing the raid closing fast upon him. He galloped to his friends, trying to get back to Red Herring to form their shield wall and meet the charging Templars together. James had seen them before; he knew they were professional killers in the name of God.

But the Templars were also mercenaries, working for whomever paid best.

James felt anger and when Hamo passed near him, he saw

something extraordinary. The strange Frank was holding a green apple with his left hand, looking at the approaching knights.

The nameless Frank was holding an apple but no weapon. He stared for a moment to the fruit and turned all his attention to the charging Templars.

Sir James organized his men, ordering them to stand behind the wooden carts, far away from the reach of the raiders. Owen and Peter had turned around the other cart near the first one to protect their right side. They moved quickly, surprising the attacking knights.

As far as the Templars knew, they were only stupid monks with some inexperienced guards. But below their ragged robes, they were dressed in leather armor. In their hearts, they were some of the best and most trusted warriors of Lord Edward and England.

Unfortunately for the red-crossed attackers, they didn't have this information. Yet. Most of the Templars rode past the man dressed like a wretched monk with an apple in his hands, walking toward the fallen Hospitaller. They were focused on reaching Hamo and the intruders.

***

Peter forgot his pain. The blood in his veins was hot, his eyes were wide open, and the events around him seemed to slow down.

The sword singing began.

The riders hit them hard, trying to break the defenses of the Englishmen.

A baby cried.

The cry cut off the sound of swordplay in the valley like a knife through fresh ham. Most of the men pricked up their ears. Something was in the air, something apart from the crying baby. Even the attackers turned and slowed a bit.

In this moment, the pale Frank removed his hood and, with no hurry, he walked to the Templar Knights who had surrounded the wounded Hospitaller. He left James and his men fighting with the charging attackers behind him.

Peter tried to see through the shields and swinging swords over his head. He wanted to see the stranger. Red Herring and the rest formed a tight wall with their shields, wooden carts, and horses.

The orphan observed the attackers' faces. The religious bastards looked arrogant and confident, battling two-to-one against five guards and some ragged monks who were shaking from fear and wielding tattered shields and swords, bearing no armor. If Peter was in their shoes, he would think that the Templars would win, this was obvious. They weren't in a hurry; they wanted to play with their prey, having been interrupted by these ragged newcomers from their hunt. They looked angry would have wanted revenge because somebody resisted them.

"No prisoners!" Roger shouted from his position, as one of the black-dressed sergeants helped him to rise.

But the charging Templars faced organized monks. They tried to maneuver them from the rear, but Peter and Owen had placed the two carts in their way. Red Herring was shouting insults toward the attackers as Owen, dressed like a ragged friar shooting at them with his bow.

"What a blasphemy! Shooting bastards," the Templar captain cried.

Red Herring's men had wedged themselves into a narrow place in the valley, with their backs against the solid yellow rocks. This little advantage saved them, for now.

Peter was curious, watching the holy knights near their defensive line and the stranger, who had almost reached the rest of the Templars near the fallen carriage and the last guard of the royal person. Maybe she was a princess? A beautiful one, he hoped. Or did she look like an old rag? Peter saw a threat flying to his head and he instinctively raised his shield. He heard something that struck the metal part of the shield and deflected to the ground. He felt the power of the blow, as his left hand ached. Peter glimpsed at the spear which stuck on the ground, an inch from his left feet. Focus, man, he said to himself as he looked forward.

The Frank was behind the two Templars facing the final

Hospitaller. He threw the green apple to the servant next to the woman who held a baby, over the attacker's heads. He nodded to the boy and the servant gave it to the baby to play with.

The cry of the infant stopped.

The Hospitaller Knight was almost on his knees, bleeding, tired, and wounded. One of his assailants succeeded in hitting him from his right and made him lose balance. The other met him with his shield and pushed him hard to fall on the ground.

Peter was behind his shield. The Templars were regrouping and preparing for another charge. But the orphan looked forward. He wanted to see the stranger.

The pale Frank looked focused. His hair was ragged, his eyes looked cold, his gait was that of a predator, anticipating his target's move.

The orphan hadn't seen such movement before. He felt some bad feeling in his stomach, like never before.

With a swift move, the stranger reached the first Templar from behind, grabbed his mantle with his left hand, forcefully pulling him back. He hit him on the neck, below his helmet, like a tavern brawler, with ferocity and brute strength. The stricken man fell, dropping his sword.

The Frank caught it in the air and faced the second man, attacking him and deflecting his swing with skill. With ease—as if he were playing with his dogs—he kicked dust into the Templar's eyes, gaining a moment in which to twist his blade deep into the man's throat. Then he turned and stabbed the first man, still trying to rise from his back. The point of the sword showed through his neck.

The Frank wiped the fresh Templar blood from his face while the second body convulsed near him. It all seemed to happen in a heartbeat before the orphan could blink.

The Frank left the sword in the second corpse, rose, and said something to the nearby servants and the lady. Then he turned and knelt beside the first body. He searched it for a moment and, apparently, found what he was looking for: a short blade and a one-handed Danish axe—a single piece of wood with a crescent-shaped blade on one end. The axe was as long as a one-handed sword.

Peter had seen knights use axes—the soldiers called them horseman axes, or hafted axes—but never in combat. He always connected chivalry, knighthood, and soldiering with the sword. The sword seemed inexorably connected to a man's honor and pride.

The men-at-arms had used to wear an additional weapon for clearing wooden obstacles or smashing enemies' shields during battle. While the orphan was observing the other end of the valley, he received a blow on the shield he held. He supposed his shoulder would hurt him for a few days. He swung his sword, but he cut only the air. Peter observed that the assailant turned his horse aside and kicked orphan's shield. The Templar raised his sword again and Owen put an arrow in his armpit. The rider cried, spurred his horse and ran away.

The adrenaline from his first open-field battle filled Peter with life. He almost forgot the sadness of his mentor's death and the pain from his head wounds and his legs. He was focused on what was happening around him and on the stranger's actions.

"Duck!" He received an order and instinctively obeyed, evading a strike to his helmet. He was already used to the good judgment of Red Herring.

Peter saw a sword swinging through the air above his head, and a sweat drop fell from James' brow as he heard his own heartbeat. Everything was moving slowly around Peter. He had observed this delusion before but had had not discussed it with anyone. He was amazed by his discovery: time slowed when he entered into danger. Was it the same for everybody or just him? He was smiling. Why was he smiling? Was it normal to be like that during a fight?

He looked around at the men with him, James, David, Owen. They were the closest companions he had today, even if he had only met them two days before. He noticed their grim smiles and determined eyes. No one showed any signs of fear or lack of courage.

The fierce and brave Sir James, whose face became reddish in battle and justified his nickname, Red Herring—he was an unforgettable character. His knightly presence on the field was essential and influenced the others. This was the way he thought a real knight and leader must behave in the face of danger and in front of his men to give an example to others, to give them courage, to organize them and to calm them, to be the spearhead of their formation, and to motivate them. To make them be like a family, to defend together as a unit and to want to die for each other. This was a real leader.

Because they were brothers of war, sword brothers, Crusaders for life. No one could take this away from them.

The ragged band of monks became a rogue host of experienced warriors led by a reddish-faced man who looked like an angry bear.

But the Templars were experienced soldiers, doing what must be done in the name of God, or so they said. Shouts and the clash of weapons met each other. Owen was shooting with ferocity on his face. He released arrow after arrow. In the narrow valley, it wasn't hard to deliver. Horses and flesh, mail and battle sounds echoed at once.

But then there was another sound, a new song.

The baby didn't cry anymore but laughed.

Even James and Peter took a moment to look away from the battle and observe what was going on. The baby played with the green apple and was laughing.

The stranger—the "Franj," as the Mamluk called their kind—the pale man was dressed in a tattered shirt and pants but was armed with a short blade and an axe. Two bodies lay near him, the Templar's sergeants who had been left to finish the last guard of the royalty. The sword of one of them stuck up from his body, symbolically. The Frank knelt down, looked over the wounded Hospitaller, and helped him rise. He moved like a dust shadow, like a predator of sands, and his almost white hair was streaked with blood.

The servants stood behind the lady and stared at the stranger. The pale man turned his back on them and looked at the fast-approaching, white-mantled knights. The Templars were split, half surrounding Red Herring in some fierce push to penetrate false monks' wooden obstacle defense, and another five galloping to the Frank, wanting to avenge their fallen brethren.

Edward the Saracen was behind Peter and his eyes and mouth were wide open.

"*Diyaab al-Sahra*, The … Desert … Wolf." His throat was full of sand, but his eyes weren't calm anymore "The Frankish Wolf …."

Peter looked at the assassin, then back to the pale stranger.

"Desert what?" The orphan asked.

David was behind the Saracen; he constantly looked after him. From Sir James' shadow, he had become the assassin's one.

"Shields up!" Red Herring shouted and all of them prepared to meet another charge. This time, the enemy footmen's soldiers were on the move. They were trying to open the route for the horse raiders. But Peter was very curious and he risked exposing himself to danger to see the Wolf.

And what splendid entertainment he received for taking such a risk.

The Desert Wolf had no armor but his cold-blooded face made the orphan's skin prickle. In his left hand, he held a blade and in his right, a one-handed axe. The first rider who reached him was about to swing his sword. Without waiting, the Wolf lunged his knee straight forward to the horse's left flank, unbalanced the animal, and used its speed and acceleration to take it to the ground. The horseman was surprised and shouted as he fell under the stallion.

The second rider was a few heartbeats behind, and his face was distorted by surprise from what he saw that had caused his forerunner to collapse. Suddenly, a shadow, fast and dirty, used the sound of the crack of bones and cries to jump to the right and used his axe to cut the throat of the Templar. Blood and the terrifying sound of bones crashing were flying through the air with the sand. The other Templars passed their two fallen comrades and their horses and tried to turn around. The sergeants ran to help them.

Roger of Sicily was observing from a new horse delivered

by his sergeant and was shouting fast orders. But the Desert Wolf was like a plague, fast and deadly. He grabbed the third rider and pulled him off the saddle. He threw him to the ground and stabbed him.

He never tried to parry the approaching weapon of the enemy but evaded it and, with the speed of a hungry predator, he kissed them with his deadly teeth. After another heartbeat, two of the riders were dead. The first attacker, who was trying to stand on his feet and to meet him, was still alive. But after the fall, the soldier looked dizzy. The stranger approached him with haste and with a swift move of his hand he delivered a fierce, fatal blow, piercing his head directly through the eyes and breaking victim's skull. He left the short blade inside.

"There is no mercy in his soul," Edward the Saracen said. He had witnessed the bloodthirsty Wolf as the rest of them had.

The orphan was silent. The course of the battle had changed. Half of the Templars had been cut down without mercy by this pale, ragged man without armor.

The baby laughed again while holding the green apple with his tender, little hands.

The remaining half of the Templars gathered around their bruised captain and regrouped for another charge, this time taking care not to underestimate the opposition.

Near Red Herring and his men, there were some wounded horses and few knights who couldn't retreat to their companions. Owen took care of the horses. Hamo stepped out from their shield wall and kicked the first standing knight. Cursing, he used his shield to knock down the whimpering soldier.

"Hamo, get your arse back here." Red Herring's voice cut the horizon.

The Templars split again. Five men galloped toward the pale Frank, while the rest charged at Hamo, who was still outside the improvised defense. James rushed from his place and ran to the lord from the Welsh Marches.

"Get back in line, right away," he shouted to the young knight. James felt the danger to which Hamo had exposed his men. The lord from the Welsh Marches turned back to his old position and started running, not even taking the time to look at the pursuers. James was a few steps in front of the first rank and was ready with his shield. He made a place for Hamo to enter behind him, then stepped back, closing the gap to the raiders just in time to meet a devastating blow with his shield. James managed not to lose either his balance or his ground.

But the Templars had lost their chance to penetrate the defenders' line. They rode around the English like hungry predators, unable to reach their prey. They cursed their luck.

All attention was diverted from the pale, dirty defender of the royal lady. At the moment, Peter was free to watch what was happening at the opposite end of the valley. The five men had been reduced to only two on horses, two dead and another twisting from pain on the ground, as a fountain of blood gushed from where he had a hand. The severed limb was on the dusty ground still holding the sword.

The other two riders turned their destriers and were calculating their chances. Meanwhile, the Wolf stood by the wounded knight and, with a single blow of the axe, he blew away the man's skull, creating an unforgettable sound of breaking bones. The blood flew and pieces of the man's brain scattered on the dirt. Some parts were on the Wolf's ragged boots. He had killed the man easily, without seeming to make any effort.

This was like an invitation to the other Templars. Peter's eyes were wide and his jaw dropped a bit, as the Desert Wolf killed them, one by one. The Wolf left no one alive around him, like a butcher preparing meat for supper.

The rest of the Templars slowed down and hesitated, unsure of what to do. They had lost half of their brothers to a single man with a blade and bloody axe. He had no shield and no armor, but he looked like a warrior demon covered with enemy's blood.

The Wolf had given them no chance, not even to surrender.

That wasn't chivalrous. Nor was war.

James must have read Peter's mind.

"There are only two rules in war, lad: To win and to

survive. Remember that."

Peter was frozen to death by fear as he held tight his shield and spear.

"On my signal, ready to advance," Red Herring shouted.

A knight of Roger's men dared to attack the pale frank again.

The Desert Wolf had taken a sword from the last dead body as his right was still holding the axe, from which blood drops were coloring the ground. He was waiting and looking his approaching opponent in the eyes.

The rider galloped toward him with a sword raised, ready to cut him down. The Sun shone on the assailant's armor. Peter thought that the horseman looked like a warring angel, come down from heaven to deliver justice. The mounted, divine messenger looked large and fearsome and was trotting with his horse. His big sword was in his hand, and his head with a helmet was slightly leaning forward. He looked like the last thing a man saw in this forsaken world.

In a few heartbeats, the horse and his rider would be on him—one, two, and the Wolf made a move.

With focus and determination, he ran forward. The rider held his weapon with his right hand, but the running footman suddenly had changed the position and moved on the left side of the horseman, surprising him.

The move was so quickly executed that Peter blinked and missed it. When he opened his eyes, the sword of the Wolf was already between the head of the horse and the raider's belly.

Peter heard the roar of the horseman mixed with the sound of the iron that kissed his chain-mail armor. The song of steel echoed. The Frank was so strong that he didn't lose his balance and the rider was cast from his saddle. Peter heard the dull sound of the body hitting the ground. Blood was wasted as if it were as useless as dirt. The Wolf stepped to the fallen warrior of God and put his blade between his eyes, crushing his skull as if it were but an apple split with a fruit knife.

"Charge!" James ordered and his small band of monks ran toward the remaining Templars.

Roger fled with the rest of his men and the battle was over.

CHAPTER NINE

Via Maris, Holy Land, Sunday, 19th of June, in the year 1272 of the incarnation of Christ

Blood dripped down Peter's face. He ignored it and stared at the Desert Wolf. The adrenaline in his veins overcame his rational thought.

Owen was grinning, as always. "I took down four men," he said.

Hamo looked at him. "So what?"

"Why did the Templars attack us, too?" the Welshman asked. "Yes, Hamo provoked them, but so what? We're on the same side, aren't we?"

A man lying nearby was convulsing. He tried to speak, but his throat had been pierced by a bodkin arrowhead. The sound of bubbling blood and labored breathing was unbearable. The pale Frank approached him and dispatched him from his pain.

Peter was looking at the battlefield. It had been his first open fight and it hadn't lasted longer than a song at the harbor's tavern.

"Is that it?"

"Yes, it's over, for now," Owen said.

"We must hurry; they could be back," Red Herring said.

"Mamluks are watching us," the pale Frank said to James and nodded to the north.

Red Herring stared for a moment and then spat on the ground.

"Damn it. Our priest-cover is over. Come on, lads, get the

valuables," James said.

The orphan noticed Red Herring's men's deftness when they searched the dead bodies. They systematically detached any precious or useful items from their corpses—not only coins but gear, as well. Owen gathered his arrows back. Hamo approached, carrying a Hospitaller's surcoat.

"The royal lady will need bodyguards," he suggested, holding the sleeveless garment up to his body.

Peter was observing the bodies. His heartbeat wasn't decreasing as drops of sweat ran down his forehead. Owen and David had brought the wooden cart as all the plunder was placed near James. Some of the Hamo's men unloaded the false dead saints from the cart to make room for the stolen goods.

"All of you, equip and arm yourselves, quickly," James said.

One of Hamo's men had assembled the free horses and tied them behind the carriage, which was ready for travel.

"False monks!" A young voice said. It was the lady. She approached the men, who were changing their robes without shame. The last standing Hospitaller followed her.

"Who are you?" she asked

"Why did they attack you, milady?" Hamo's voice was gentle.

"Do you know it isn't polite to answer a question with another?"

Peter saw a tiny smile on Hamo's face.

"The first thing to do when you are saved is to say thank you. And then it is customary to introduce yourself."

The lady removed her hood.

She was the most beautiful lady Peter had ever seen, with extraordinary blue eyes, small lips, and a thin nose. She seemed to be his age, or younger. Her long, dark-red hair was tied at the back of her neck. Peter had trouble looking away from her face.

"So, who are you, my lady?" Even Hamo stuttered a bit when speaking to her, but then regained his composure again.

"I am Isabella of Ibelin, Lady of Beirut. I was traveling to Jerusalem when Roger of Sicily ambushed us."

"You know him?" Red Herring asked.

"Of course, I know him. He was once in my service. But the Templars paid more," she added.

"Why did he attack you?" Hamo asked.

"I would like to know that, too," she said, then smiled.

"I think you do, but you keep it for yourself," Hamo said.

"The troubles of royalty don't concern us," Owen said.

"Why, then, did you interfere? And why are you dressed like holy men? You clearly are not."

"We are all holy men in this land, aren't we?" Hamo said.

She looked at Hamo with an innocently questioning look.

Sir James shook his head, cleared his throat and introduced himself.

"We are from the English Corps of Lord Edward," he said.

Peter wondered whether news of the assassination attempt had spread enough for this lady to have heard about it.

"Crusaders?"

"The Crusade is over, due to the peace treaty. We decided to make a pilgrimage to Jerusalem before we set sail to our homeland," James said.

"Dressed like monks?" There was sarcasm in her remark.

"A precaution. We are intruders; beyond Acre and Nazareth, there is a war zone."

She looked at them skeptically.

"And you, milady, traveling with a baby, almost kidnapped? You aren't traveling with many valuables besides yourself, are you?" Hamo asked.

"It is not your business," Isabella said.

With Isabella and her knight were traveling three servants: a middle-aged woman holding a baby, the same who had the apple, a lady-in-waiting, and a lad, younger than Peter, who was Isabella's valet.

"The baby is the reason for our journey to the holy city," Isabella said. "We travel to seek a healer for the child; less than a year old, he suffered from an illness."

"Whose baby is it?" Owen asked.

"It's not your business too," Isabella said.

"It appears it is now," Hamo said gently. The subject was

set aside.

Peter followed his gaze to a dust cloud over the ridge where the Mamluk scout party was watching them.

"We lost our cover; you lost your guards. Perhaps we could help each other," Hamo said.

Isabella thought for a moment, nodded, and turned her back on him, conferring with the wounded Hospitaller. They exchanged some words and then she turned back to Hamo.

"We have an agreement. We will continue as you propose. Let's go." She ordered and returned to her carriage.

The last standing Knight from the Hospital of St. John approached the Wolf and removed the great helmet which those of the order wore in battle.

It was a woman. Her blond hair was cut short and she had sunspots on her face. Peter hadn't seen a female knight before, nor heard of one.

She looked at the Wolf's eyes and, with coldness, said, "Thank you, Ulf Magnusson. Again." She turned her back on him to enter the carriage of her lady.

Most of the men were astonished for the second time. They had never met a woman in knight's gear wearing the eight-pointed white cross of the hospital. And she was a pretty one, though older than her mistress.

She knew the Desert Wolf by name.

"What the hell?" Peter thought. Templars fighting Hospitallers, Mamluks, assassins, a mysterious warrior, a secret mission, a female knight, and a rescued princess. What was the world coming to, and how had he gotten involved in all this?

The orphan patted his new beard, which itched.

This was just the beginning. The orphan wondered what lay ahead.

"We need to find a place for the night," James said. "We are too exposed in the valley."

They traveled as fast as they could; all of them were now equipped with horses and the only thing that dictated their speed was the royal carriage. Edward the Saracen was on a horse next to David. Red Herring and Hamo led the travelers, and Peter and Owen rode close behind them. Along with the warhorses, there were some palfreys, lighter-weight horses, suitable for riding over long distances and to pull the carriage and carry their belongings.

They found high ground overlooking the road. After they made an improvised shelter for the night, David and one other man were on the first watch.

This was Peter's first night out of the city and the events of the day only enriched his excitement. Peter helped Owen make a campfire, fetching dry wood from bushes and fallen old tree.

"This will keep the predators and cold at bay," the Welshman said. "And, of course, it is useful to cook food. But sometimes, we do not light the fire when we don't want to show our position. Then we sing the song of the frozen dreams."

Peter's curiosity was piqued. "Frozen what?"

The rogue-looking Welshman started to tic-tacking with his teeth in some fearsome rhythm, like a song.

"This is the song of the frozen dreams, when you are alone in the dark, without fire, without warmth, and without hope." He paused, and when he was satisfied with how wide the orphan's eyes were, he laughed.

After that, all around them laughed, too. It wasn't the first time the Welshman had told this story to some inexperienced soldier. Everyone enjoyed his humor.

They were all around the fire, except the sentry. Most of the soldiers carried with them some bread, Arab biscuits, and salted meat. Owen had lost two arrows, but there would be a hare for dinner.

They enjoyed the smell from the fire. There was some talking, too.

"We rode all day along the Via Maris," James said. "This ancient, Roman road, whose name meant "the way of the sea," had been used for centuries, even since the time of the legendary Saladin."

"The story of the war between him and Richard the Lionheart was almost 100 years old but was still remembered by the people, the legend having passed from generation to generation, as all legends were. Richard had defeated the great

Saladin near the fortress of Arsuf and Jaffa." Isabella said.

"Do you know that Lord Edward is Richard's grandnephew. He took the Crusader's vow, just as his great uncle had. Just as Saladin, the famous sultan, had opposed Richard, and now Sultan Baibars stood against Edward." James said.

Peter and the rest were tired. They sat around the fire and talked about the failed Crusade of the French king, Louis, two years before. After his first failure, twenty years previously, on his second attempt, he had been more determined to succeed. He had managed to build a large network to organize logistics. There had been a rumor that he had had the Spear of Destiny but had died before using it. It was a pity if it was true.

"He should have bought himself a future, not the Roman spear that pierced God's son," Owen said.

Romans had built roads and whole cities conquered the world, even killed God's son. Peter thought they must have been a fearsome people but, eventually, even the best die. Something had crashed their empire and he was eager to learn it. The Roman Empire—that mysterious, ancient people whose heir was the Byzantium Empire—fired curiosity in the orphan's heart.

The fire cracked; its pleasant heat warmed the front of his body but his back was exposed to the cold night.

Peter turned his back to the others and took the precious book from his leather bag. He looked at the cover page; it was marvelously painted with beautiful drawings of knights and villains, horses, and some creatures he was seeing for the first time. The light which came from the fire was dim but was enough to satisfy his curiosity. There were some letters on the front. He regretted that he hadn't listened to his mentor to learn how to read. The memory of John the monk saddened him. His eyes filled with tears, but he managed not to let a sound out.

"Hello. Is this a book…?" A young, trepidation voice came from his left side. It was the valet, a wiry boy of about fifteen years. Peter gave the boy a predator's look. The boys' brown eyes were a mixture of curiosity and youth. His curly, dark brown hair was cut short. Maybe he was Italian, or a mongrel bred from a Christian and a Saracen, but Peter didn't care.

He decided to be kind after all. "What is your name?"

"Nickolas." His voice trembled. He must have still been in shock after what had happened during the day. "What are you reading?"

Peter was tempted to lie, ashamed that he couldn't answer because he didn't know.

"Eh, ... I wish I knew, but I have to admit that I can't read. I never wanted to learn and never listened to my teacher when he tried to teach me," Peter said. He was older than Nickolas but now felt vulnerable as a man without wit or skills. He realized that a man without knowledge is poor; anyone could steal an object, but no one could take away knowledge.

"I can teach you," the valet said. The orphan saw the reflection of the nearby fire in Nickolas' eyes.

Peter focused his eyes on this scared, little fellow. This was the first time that someone had offered to teach him, other than his mentor.

"What would you want in return?"

Nickolas seemed a little surprised by the harsh reply but appeared to be used to such reactions.

"Tell me your story. I want to be a writer, a chronicler of the past deeds; I want to leave something for the future generations."

Peter felt the ambition and the passion of this boy, like his own. He knew that to become a better soldier and, someday— a knight—he had to learn to read and write. He was ready to learn. He wanted to be a better warrior like the Desert Wolf and he was sure that this book would help him to achieve that. He wanted more than what he had.

He gave the book to the valet.

"My stories for your lessons," Peter agreed.

Nickolas examined it. "A fine book you have."

Peter didn't say a thing. He hoped he had made the right choice.

The two young men sat by the campfire with their dreams: the future warrior and the future chronicler. The world needed them both, the orphan thought.

Owen approached them. "How are your legs?"

"I am not sure. Every move I make feels like someone cut off some of my flesh." Peter said.

"Here, take this." The Welshman gave him a package of bandages.

"Where did you get this?" Peter said, examining them. They were of a fine quality. He didn't remember them from when they had assembled their supplies in Acre.

"Let's just say he didn't need them anymore." Owen gave a rogue smile to the valet.

"Are all of you knights?" Nickolas asked timidly.

The Welshman grinned, then said, "Myself, a knight? Eh. No boy, I am a common archer in the service of Lady Eleanor." Owen looked as proud as if he were guarding the Tree of Life. "A knight must behave in a certain way, but not me."

He nodded to Peter and continued, "Look at him. He is not, either, but with the speed of his deeds and heroics, he will be knighted before the next full Moon." He paused to emphasize what he said next. "If we survive ...." And he laughed, hard. The Welshman sat beside them and nodded toward the Wolf.

"There is a legend of the Desert Wolf and how he had helped the sultan deal with assassins who had tried to assassinate Baibars," Owen chewed the feather of one of his arrows. "The Wolf had managed to get inside one of their main castles. Alone."

"Alone?"

"And unarmed." The Welshman leaned on the wooden wheel of the wagon. "While climbing the main road, he took an arrow in the shoulder but survived." He grinned. "If I was the shooter..." he winked at Peter.

"What happened next?" Peter's shoulders lifted in a shrug.

"He reached the castle, somehow managing to sneak inside during the night. The next morning, the large, wooden door of the main gate opened for the sultan's soldiers. The Desert Wolf met them, covered in blood, sitting and eating a green apple. All the inhabitants of the assassins' castle were dead."

"Is this really happened?" Nickolas asked.

"You can ask him if you like," Owen said.

Red Herring and Hamo came from questioning Isabella and Githa. James told them that the Master of the order of the Hospitallers had assigned Githa to Lady Isabella.

"And how did a fine, pretty lady like her become a religious knight?" Owen asked. Peter was amazed, too. James told her tale, which he had succeeded in acquiring from the knight.

"She and her husband journeyed from the distant North on a pilgrimage to the Holy Land to pray for a child. Soon they received the gift they desired most: a baby. They bought a vineyard and they paid the Templars for protection." Red Herring drank some wine and continued, "But fate is cruel. In a midnight attack, their manor was sacked by the Saracens as revenge for an earlier raid by the Templars. Only she survived—wounded, raped, and thrown away like a rag doll. She saw her husband and child burned alive for the amusement of the Saracens. She remembered the coat of arms of the assailants, never forgetting it. The Templars wanted her land; without a husband and her harvest burned, soon she would be in debt. She had lost everything: her husband, her child, her land, and her future.

"Instead of signing the land over to them, she gave it to the Hospitallers, who leased it back to work so she and her servants could try to rebuild her life. The Templars were left red-faced and they personally led a raid against her. They killed everyone, even the animals. They raped her, beat her, and left her to die."

Peter listened with some disbelief.

"Yet, she survived, and now, look at her: a real captain of the knights. She swore to hunt Saracens and Templars for sport. When you hear the name of Githa of the Hospital, beware if you work for the Templars!" James finished his tale dramatically.

Nickolas was rapt, writing the story down on parchment.

"Isabella of Ibelin. I have heard this name before," Owen said to himself.

"It's one of the great lordships in the Holy Land," Nickolas said. "Lady Isabella was the king's bride but he died."

"I heard this story," James said. "There was a scandal, too."

"Yes, there was a rumor about an affair with a knight named Julian of Sidon," Hamo remembered.

"Julian, again. Small world," Red Herring said.

Edward the Saracen sat near them, listening. Red Herring turned his gaze to him and asked, "Is it true the assassins don't attack Templars or Hospitallers or other religious knights?"

The members of his party around the campfire were silent in anticipation of the answer.

"The assassins' leader demands a ransom for every important life. Princes, lords, wealthy knights, even western kings—if you pay, there will be no attempt to take your soul," Edward the Saracen said.

Red Herring wrinkled his face.

"So, you threaten the lives of the rich for money? An interesting business you have."

"Something like that," the assassin nodded.

"But you did not answer my question."

"There is no point attacking religious orders. They are fanatics; there is no point in killing the Grand Master or some important officer because another fanatic will just rise in his place. It's not worth the effort."

"I heard that, when Lord Edward arrived, his advisers took care of this matter. A ransom was delivered through the Templars to eliminate this risk," Sir James said. This was news to Peter, but, judging from the expressions around the campfire, not to anyone else.

"I never heard such thing," the assassin said confidently. "Although I know there is more than one faction of assassins. A few years ago, there was a plot against the sultan with the support of another faction, so there are at least two factions I know of, but there may be more."

He paused, signaling with tied hands that he wanted some water. Owen complied.

"The sultan survived the plot and made his own regiment—the Qussad, as you know it—only loyal to him. One of his most trusted men organized it and commanded it. All members of the secret intelligence Qussad had left their families to be guarded and cared for by the sultan's personal legion." He drank some water. "If someone dies on a mission, the sultan takes care of his family. But if someone disobeys or defects, ..." Edward the Saracen closed his eyes.

"Sultan Baibars?" James said.

"Yes, Sultan Baibars have a fearsome reputation. After all, he is the Sultan of Egypt and Syria, from Cairo to Damascus. He had repelled the fearsome hordes of the Tartars, he had defeated opposing amirs who didn't share his visions, and he had built an empire. He had also established trade and diplomatic relations with the Byzantium Empire, the Kingdom of Sicily, and many others. He continued to crush your Christian kingdom, piece by piece, castle by castle," Edward the Saracen said.

"We have not surrendered yet," James said.

"There was no sign of anyone brave enough to match him, except Lord Edward," the Saracen said.

"And now the prince would pay with his life, as had Phillip of Montfort," James said. Edward the Saracen raised his eyebrows and looked at Red Herring.

"Do you know that he used to work for the sultan?" The assassin nodded to the Wolf.

Peter looked at James. The Scottish knight didn't look surprised.

"And to punish the plotters, he sent the Desert Wolf to take care of them." The assassin looked with fear at the Frank, who was sitting opposite him. "When you need to terminate a lord, a prince, or even a king, you arrange it with the assassins. But when you need to give a lesson to some disobedient faction of assassins, you send him." His eyes were on the stranger.

Peter's eyes were, too.

CHAPTER TEN

Via Maris, Holy Land, Monday, 20th of June, in the year 1272 of the incarnation of Christ; Near the Qaqun fortress

Peter didn't sleep much that night.

It was his first night in the wilderness. There were unknown sounds—night songs of different insects. He even heard an unknown animal cry near to their camp. He barely closed his eyes.

He had lay down late after working with Nickolas. The young valet was like Peter, a novice in Lady Isabella's service. The young men's ambitions drove them to work even in the dark, even as most of their companions slept.

The book the orphan had stolen wasn't an ordinary one. "De Re Militari," Nickolas read on the cover. It had been written long before by some man called Vegetius—a Roman— and it was an instruction for warfare with colorful drawings. It had been translated from Latin especially for Edward.

"To my beloved one, my Edward, my better half. So that you may become a great general, and an even a greater king. With love, Eleanor." Nickolas read the inscription written inside the book.

Peter took a deep breath. He had stolen a present from the future King of England. This was bad. He felt weak.

"Where did you say that you got this book?" Nickolas asked.

Peter felt miserable and said nothing.

For theft, he could lose his hand. But for stealing from a

prince, he could lose much more. If Peter's party was successful in finding the special physician to heal Edward. If the prince survived.

Yet, Peter felt his curiosity was stronger than his guilt. He was eager to learn. He had in his hands a Roman book on warfare. He wanted to know more.

"Step by step," Nickolas had said. But Peter didn't get much sleep, thinking about his new desire.

In the early morning, before the Sun rose, the party looked at the plunder they had taken. All of the yesterday's monks geared up with the dead warriors' belongings. Peter found a padded leather jacket close to his size and a mail coif, a shaped hood of mail to protect his head, neck, and throat. As he attached a one-handed sword to his new leather belt, he felt almost like a knight. Almost. He understood that he wasn't a proper soldier or a knight just because he had a sword. He needed to learn. He lacked experience and of course, he had to earn his spurs.

Wearing the Hospitallers' surcoats, they were now, officially, the Lady of Beirut's new guards until they reached Jerusalem. Their new cover had advantages but they must also accept the disadvantages: Roger of Sicily would be after them. They had taken on the enemy of the lady's former guards.

To the amusement of the all-seeing Sun, they were led by women. The Lady of Beirut, Lady Isabella, and her knight, Githa. It would look more realistic for Githa to lead them if another scout patrol met them, Isabella insisted. James agreed.

"What luck," Owen murmured all morning.

They were on the road and Peter rode a gray warhorse whose master had been slain. The animal was nervous, like his new rider. The orphan didn't understand too much of horses. He was riding this week for the first time and it was a real challenge to keep on the back of the animal.

"Githa ... What is this name, German?" Hamo seemed unbalanced by the fact that a woman would lead their vanguard.

Red Herring, on the other hand, was enjoying the situation and the murmuring of his younger friends. For him, this was a fun adventure. Red Herring smiled. Peter knew he preferred to be dressed for battle rather than in a monk's robe. He had been warring all his life: in his homeland, in France, and now, here in the Holy Land.

They had set off early, with Owen and David scouting ahead. Everyone rode in pairs, Hamo and Githa rode in the front, James and David were the last and the carts were between them. Nickolas was in the wooden cart behind the main carriage, with the supplies and loot. Peter rode close to him and they continued his instruction, working on his letters. The orphan was determined to learn quickly. He tried to memorize all the important things the young valet said to him.

"Reading and writing are invaluable skills," Nickolas said. "They can change your life. The written word has elevated mankind."

"How?"

"It allows you to move knowledge across the ages, to preserve it for later generations," the young valet said.

Peter was amazed by his words and said so.

"These are not my words, but what my teacher told me." Nickolas blushed.

The orphan would remember them.

"Your teacher is a clever man," Peter said. He continued all morning to study. After a while, he looked at the assassin, examining his expressionless face. It was hard to imagine that Edward the Saracen would escape this journey with his life. The assassin was a wanted man—by his master for his failure and by Julian. Sooner or later, they would know he wasn't in Edward's dungeon anymore. His only chance was to stick with the plan and to hope their mission succeeded. Even then, Lord Edward's reputation made Peter doubt that he would let the assassin live.

The prince had a reputation for a violent temper. He was a loyal friend but anyone who betrayed him was doomed. But Peter understood that the assassin had Lady Eleanor's word. This might be enough to save the man. Regardless, there seemed no advantage for the assassin to try to escape.

The Sun smiled on him again with its full warmth.

Peter guided his horse next to the assassin and looked at the Desert Wolf.

The stranger was riding side-by-side with Edward the Saracen. He was dressed in his usual hood, now was equipped and with a sleeveless, leather vest. The orphan lined his horse up next to the Wolf's.

"Teach me to how to fight," Peter dared to say, his voice trembling a bit.

The Desert Wolf said nothing.

He gazed at the horizon. The orphan stared at his cold eyes, they were like endless pits. Peter wondered what had turned this man into such a skillful and merciless killer.

He looked in the middle of his thirties. His face showed nothing, and he looked like a man who had nothing, had lost everything, and was tired of life itself.

After a few minutes watching him, the young man wasn't sure of anything about him, except that he was a hell of a warrior. Peter was determined to do anything to learn from him.

"Teach me to how to fight, please." This time his voice was steady.

Again, there was no response. They rode side-by-side, following the caravan.

Peter learned that a caravan was a group of travelers or merchants and their goods and conveyances; it could be either on land, with animals, or on the sea, with ships. He was learning so much these days and that made him feel alive. There was so much to learn and to discover in this world. As the circle of his knowledge enlarged, he discovered how many things lay outside of it. It was a strange, new feeling, but Peter liked it.

The local priest in Acre had preached that everyone should work and be humble and fear the unknown. But why? When unknown was uncovered, there was no fear anymore. Why did his religion want to spread fear?

"If you want to live longer, Peter, stay away from him." Edward the Saracen said.

Peter understood but he wasn't on this quest to stay under

an umbrella, watching the storm from a safe distance. He wanted to participate equally with all the others.

He had also realized the main reason he had been invited on this mission.

He was the bait.

Lady Eleanor had gathered all the lambs into one place to seduce the wolves.

Yes, he was one of the lambs ready for the supper, along with the assassin and the Wolf. Except the assassin had proper skills to survive—the Desert Wolf had, too. Red Herring and his fighters—everyone but the orphan. What little experience he had, fighting with thieves and bandits had been on the losing side for the most part. He felt exposed. He needed to train to survive this.

He asked again.

"I have been in the castle's service for two days. I barely know how to hold a sword or a shield. Is that what you want standing by you in a fight?" He was bold to say this and he knew it. He hoped that by pointing out his liability, he would persuade the Wolf to help him.

"On the battlefield, there are two types of soldiers: those who fight and those who die. There will always be a need for both species." His cold statement almost froze Peter's desire. Almost.

"I want to be on the surviving side," Peter insisted.

No reaction again.

"I want to defend myself," the orphan said.

The Desert Wolf said nothing again. Peter looked away as he wilted in the saddle and paid languid attention to the landscape.

After a few hours of riding, they had almost reached the district of Qaqun Fortress.

Red Herring pointed at the rocky tower that showed above the trees on a hill up ahead.

"We tried to capture that fortress a year ago," he told the orphan.

"What happened?"

"Well." James looked as if he were searching the parchment

of his memory. Owen also stared upwards at the fortress that stood on the horizon.

"We had underestimated the situation and the opponent. Edward had war experience, but Templars and the other religious orders—" James spat on the dusty ground. "They didn't follow orders. They smiled and said we were on the same side, but all they were doing was looking for plunder; they didn't want to change the status quo. In the end, it was just us against the fortress."

He looked at the sky.

"There was some resistance, of course. We had an open skirmish with a Saracen regiment. We surprised them, scattering their forces, and won the field that day." James stopped for a moment, sighing. "Owen was fantastic that day; his fingers were bruised from the ferocity and speed of his arrows." He nodded to the Welshman and continued, "But disagreements between the Templars and Hospitallers for our next action in the siege slowed us down. Lord Edward's plan was to organize two wings to launch an attack: one from the north, with the help of Tartar alliance, and our main forces on the south, attacking the Qaqun fortress which controlled the road to Jerusalem. The Tartars failed." There was anger in his voice.

"A sandstorm appeared from nowhere and scattered us like pieces of straw," Owen recalled.

"But this place wasn't an ordinary fortress on a rocky hill. It protected the newly-established market, the center of trade for the whole sultanate. The fortress had been repaired and heavily fortified. We didn't expect it," Red Herring said.

Owen smiled and added, "Sir James was like a real lion that day. He beat the Saracen forces with his small company. Not one of his men was hurt. With a cunning maneuver and great speed, we took them by surprise in the morning and blew them away like a storm from the north."

Red Herring's face showed some regret.

Edward the Saracen broke in. "Lord Edward attacked exactly where the sultan wanted. It was a well-placed trap and he fell right into it. He jumped like a fish into a hot pan."

James stared at the assassin, his brow furrowed.

"What are you saying? It was a full-scale operation that we prepared for months."

"Are you sure about that?" the assassin asked.

Peter's curiosity was piqued.

"It was a full-scale operation, to be sure, but it was prepared by the Qussad and the sultan's spies." Edward the Saracen spoke with confidence.

"How?" Red Herring and most of the men were eager to hear more.

"We had agents and spies everywhere. I assume you did as well," the assassin said. Peter looked at him. He was a persona non-grata, after all; he was the man who had tried to kill their master.

"My primary task was to gather information on your plans and to synchronize our actions against your prince. It was not easy, but I organized things so that his plan would fail. The Tartar forces and your own never managed to unite and achieve their goal. I was able to divide them and to force your prince to attack this fortress. I planted misinformation, manipulating him into believing that the fortress was ill-defended and under repair. I offered him a hook and he bit it." He looked into Red Herring's eyes.

"Our sultan used a principal of your ancient Romans: Divide et impera—divide and rule." Edward the Saracen smiled.

Divide and rule. The phrase was familiar to Peter. He had heard it just the night before from the book. The Romans were dead, but their legacy had lived on in the many nations they had conquered.

"If Edward had succeeded in uniting his army with the Tartars, our advantage would have disappeared. Imagine the heavily-armed Crusaders united with the eastern horde and their mounted archers. This would have devastated us. Baibars was fully aware of this scenario. When Edward sent an embassy to the Tartar horde, the sultan set our goal to mislead him and to prevent the union. Our first and major goal wasn't to assassinate Edward because we weren't sure he could unite the Crusader lords and the pathetic King of Cyprus. It is always a risk to eliminate an enemy's ruler. You never know what will follow."

"But the sultan changed his mind," Red Herring said.

"Yes, your lord wasn't a headless chicken like the rest. He proved to be a prudent and brave leader; he managed to win his father's kingdom back in the battle of Evesham. We learned his record and his reputation." Edward the Saracen stopped.

"He became the main threat to the sultan and his goal to overthrow the Latin kingdom. After he dealt with the Tartars," James concluded.

Peter's ears perked up again. Evesham—he had heard of this battle before.

"Lord Edward made his choice and he lost." The Saracen's eyes looked vivid and he continued. "After the peace treaty, my job was done and I was eager to abandon the city of Acre and return to my family. The order for his assassination was a shock even for me."

"But fate is cruel, isn't it?" James looked at the orphan's face and said, "An orphan foiled your plan."

"What doesn't kill you makes you stronger," Peter said. "The old monk used to say that to me."

The orphan closed his eyes in an attempt to visualize his mentor's face but the image refused to come. Barely a few days after John's death, he was starting to forget his image. Maybe this was human nature. But he couldn't forget his mentor's wisdom and lessons, his kindness, or the way he had looked after Peter.

They stopped for some rest and water.

"John, the old Hospitaller with cooking skills?" the Wolf asked. "The one who lived in the old monastery near the harbor and knew all about herbs and wounds?"

Peter nodded.

Githa, too, had a few good words to say about the old monk.

The orphan was surprised that his mentor was so well-known. Even Edward the Saracen talked about him with respect. Peter hoped that one day, all his friends would respect him in the same way these people respected his mentor.

He heard a whistling sound and saw an arrow hit the ground as kicked up some dust near them.

"It is a warning shot," James said. "Mamluks!"

"They are too many. We can't fight them," Hamo said.

"Stay calm. They will not attack Lady Isabella of Beirut," The Desert Wolf lowered his head and checked his weapons— the one-handed axe attached at the back of his waist to his belt and the short knife on his left side.

"A hundred," Hamo guessed, trying to count the enemy riding toward them through the cloud of dust and sand.

"Two hundred, at least." James was more serious. Owen approached and observed the enemy.

"Why not just let the Frank kill them all while we cook something for lunch, eh?"

No one laughed this time.

"Don't call me Frank." The Desert Wolf's comment made the men shut their mouths.

"If we survive, then it would be a great pleasure for us to introduce ourselves properly and share some beer." Owen smiled.

It was a Saracen cavalry, wild with war cries. It advanced from all directions and filled the road. The ground wasn't visible under their horses' hooves.

"Gentlemen, behave yourselves." Red Herring was serious.

Peter and the rest of the Christians were quiet in the searing Sun. They were surrounded. Some of the Saracens wore chainmail armor; others had leather, lamellar armor. Most held short bows and arrows in their hands, ready to shoot. Those with mail had spears and round shields, and curved sabers at the waist. Most of them wore spangled helms and aventail, a mail which covered their necks. Many of the spears bore short flags of different colors and signs.

They were many and they looked terrifying, like an experienced band of warriors. Sweat had glued the dirt to their faces.

The Saracen captain was a tall horseman. His legs looked

crooked. He was clean-shaven and his brown hair was all but hidden below his white turban. His blue eyes made him stand out from the rest of the Mamluks.

"Lady Isabella!" he shouted.

He waited, a few steps ahead of his men.

"Lady Isabella of Ibelin!" the captain shouted again.

She opened the wooden door of the carriage and stepped out. She was accompanied by Githa.

"We invite you to our camp near the fortress for the night," said the captain. "Our amir is eager to meet you." His tone was peaceful but cold. It didn't sound like an invitation, but more like a command.

Peter turned and saw the same expression in the Wolf's eyes as had been there when he killed the Templars.

The Wolf dropped like a snake from his horse and jumped over a rock on the ground, kneeling behind it. For a moment, Peter didn't understand what he planned to do, but suddenly his vision cleared. The Desert Wolf was trying to blend in with the yellow, dusty background of the rocky desert.

Peter didn't think but followed the Wolf's example; he dropped from one side of his horse and hoped the Saracen cavalry didn't spot him. The orphan hit the ground hard, feeling pain in his bottom and his legs. He rolled over the sandy land and his back hit a rock almost half the height of a man. His eyes started to fill with tears from the impact but he tried not to lose sight of the Desert Wolf.

Some would call this blind bravery, others would call it foolishness. His old mentor used to say, "Peter, do not behave like a frog, which looks at the warhorse and raises her leg, wanting a new horseshoe, too." The orphan smiled at the last thought as he felt like a frog.

It was a long time until the Sun would go to bed and the heat was devastating. He wished he had taken some water. Next time he would know better—if there was a next time.

The sound of the trotting horses and men's voices were around him. Dust danced from so many riders. The desert wind also kicked up the dust and he was hidden by it, or at least he believed so.

Peter hadn't taken anything from the horse. Now, he had to wait for the Mamluks to leave. While he was hiding, Peter heard a man's voice near him.

He didn't understand a word, as the Mamluks spoke in a language that resembles Arabic. He held his breath and hoped to stay unseen. He felt like he was waiting for hours. Sweat drops began to appear on his forehead. His black hair was wet and full of sand and dirt. Like the landscape, or at least he hoped so. Footsteps were closing in and Peter's heart beat fast. He tried to calm down and decide what to do.

Another sound turned the attention of the Saracen in another direction and he walked away. Peter let out a breath of relief. His fingers had become stiff and he moved them a little. At last, he dared to raise his head and look where he had last seen the enemy. But he saw nobody.

The Saracen cavalry, Lady Isabella, and his friends were all gone. Peter saw a big sand cloud moving east and after a while, he lost them from his sight. The Mamluks had taken his friends. But where?

Peter had risen and started to beat the dust and sand out of his clothes when two raiders appeared around a nearby turn.

The horsemen had been sent left to investigate and clear the area, the orphan guessed. They had been waiting for their prey to reveal themselves and Peter, in his foolishness, was visible again. He should have known someone would return to check the area to be sure.

He was like a fish on the hook, weaponless, horseless, and waterless in the middle of the barren desert. Alone, he watched the two professional soldiers ride toward him with their sabers ready to unleash death.

Diyaab al-Sahra, the Desert Wolf, sprang forth and threw his short blade into the first rider's neck while he surprised the second one with his axe. The body of the dead Mamluk fell on the ground, as the Wolf approached Peter, cleaning his weapons off.

"Because of your stupidity, now we have horses," the Wolf said. His voice was like a blade, cutting the air. The sentiment behind his words was clear; the orphan was now part of his wolf pack.

There were Arab biscuits and water in the riders' saddlebags. Peter watched the Wolf as he took what he needed from the fallen Mamluks. He kept his expensive, leather vest armor beneath the mail shirt and put a peaked helmet on his head, leaving his hood lying on his shoulders, ready for use. He took the red scarf from one of the dead men and tied it around his waist, above his leather belt.

He caught the orphan's look and said, "Mamluk officers are distinguished by such red scarves. If someone speaks to us, let me do the talking. Now take his gear." He pointed to the other corpse.

Peter was sure the Desert Wolf had a plan; he would ask about it later. He needed a few moments for his heartbeat to reach a normal rate. In a few minutes, the two had turned themselves into slave soldiers of the sultan.

When they had taken what they could from the fallen Saracens, they rode after the rest.

***

The Night wrapped his arms around the land.

"What is our plan?" Peter asked, but received no answer.

The stars in the sky looked like distant, static fireflies. There was a strange calmness in the darkness.

Peter and the Desert Wolf had approached the camp of the Mamluks before sunset and waited for the nightfall. The orphan looked at the Wolf. He wasn't from this land, but from a distant one beyond the sea. He had to be from the North, Peter assumed. The young lad had seen such men arriving in the Crusader port of the kingdom. They arrived in search of salvation or else were looking for a new life, new future, new start—new something. For most of the Europeans, this land was an opportunity. The poorest fisherman in Normandy could become a lord in the Outremer, the land overseas; a thief could become a royal adviser or a rich merchant. The kingdoms of Europe were full of dogmas and class systems, where everyone knew his place and there was no hope of advancement. One couldn't change, earn a promotion, build on what one had—or even think innovatively. There was only one way, the church said: their way. This was something the newcomers said often when they arrived—and that the dream of a new world had driven them forward to the unknown future. The taverns and ports were full of such stories. Some arrived from England, many from France; there were many Germans and Italians, and some from the North.

The Desert Wolf, with his eyes and hair—he looked like those foreigners, although his skin was different; it was obvious that he had lived on this shore of the sea, as his face had some sun marks.

But he did not belong to this place. How had he gotten here? Nickolas would be intrigued. If Peter could survive this quest, this would become a great story. If he could survive.

"What is your name?"

"Ulf."

"Just Ulf?"

"Ulf."

"I am Peter, son of ...." he paused; he wasn't used to his father's name, Longsword, yet. "...Peter of Acre. What is our plan?"

"I had one before you decided to follow me. Tell me what to do with a bag of bones after me?"

A bag of bones? Peter pressed his tongue against his teeth to keep from responding to this insult.

"Well, what is your plan with a bag of bones at your side?" The orphan spoke with a little irony this time, but the Wolf didn't react.

"Maybe I should tie you to a tree, just in case; I don't want to lose you." Ulf's tone revealed no emotion.

As promised, Peter was left to wait alone with the horses, while Ulf went into the darkness to scout the camp. Dressed like a Mamluk, with his red scarf on his belt, he walked straight forward to the camp, his head covered by his hood. He had a blade on his left thigh, and a short bow attached on his back with a shaft with arrows. Anyone could mistake him for a Saracen.

"It isn't hard to replenish your arrows. Just give an ugly smile to a Mamluk battalion and run like the devil with a shield on your neck. If you are lucky, you will collect more than you need. But be careful; you have only one arse. You do not want to turn it into a pincushion, do you?" Welshman had said the night before at the campfire and laughed.

Peter remembered it and smiled.

Now, he missed Owen and his humor. He could see Ulf recede further and further into the dark, his axe glittering in the moonlight, on his back. Peter noticed he had put short blades into his leather boots. He had never seen such boots before, fine masterpieces of thick, dark-brown leather with a metal lamellar, attached on his shin guard and covered by leather strips to tie up them almost to his knees. It occurred to the orphan that he hadn't noticed them before because Ulf had been wearing a long and dirty old monk's robe.

He wasn't used to being alone in the dark, in the wilderness. There had always been some light from the torches of the towers and castle walls or the harbor in Acre at night.

But here, it was different. He didn't want to be left alone to sit and wait for Ulf to do all the work.

Peter thought about the Wolf's plan to enter the camp and release the Crusaders and Lady Isabella. He suddenly wondered why Ulf would risk his life for theirs. Yes, there were legends about the Desert Wolf and his unnatural killing skills, but what was his motivation to help them now that he was free? Peter remembered the story about how the Desert Wolf lost his family.

"Oh, hell, that bloody bastard." Peter slapped his temple. Ulf's motivation to be with them on this quest was revenge. He wanted to catch the Mamluks who were responsible for the attack on his manor, nothing more. He wasn't one of Edward's men. He had taken no vow to the English prince. Now he had the chance to sneak into the enemy's camp in the night. He had no reason to help them, didn't even pretend to care about them. That's why he had left Peter to wait.

"This is not good," the orphan murmured.

Not only did Ulf have no attention of helping his new

friends; he had used them as bait, as Otto had used Edward the Saracen.

"Damn it," he cursed. "Think Peter, think." He started to move quickly in the same direction he had seen Ulf set out.

He hoped not to lose in the dark.

**

"Marco Polo," the lad said. He looked young.

James estimated he was no more than eighteen years of age. He was tall and skinny. In a few years, he would be handsome. He had to earn some experience and to develop his smile.

"My name is Marco Polo," he repeated with more confidence.

"So, Mr. Polo." Hamo was more well-mannered. "What are you doing in this camp? You are Italian, aren't you?"

"A Venetian," he confirmed.

"And with whom are you traveling, sir?" Githa asked.

"With my father and my uncle, milady." He gave a little pause, probably unsure as to how to properly address to the female knight. She had encountered this reaction too many times to count. "And Captain Andrea Pelu, who led us."

"Led you where?" Red Herring asked the inevitable question.

"Jerusalem." Marco's lips pinched.

"So, you are a Venetian but escorted by a Genoese captain and you were captured in the middle of the road by Mamluks." The Welshman scratched his forehead.

"How do you know that?" The lad was confused.

James' eyebrows heads moved down as his jaw tensed to biting posture, pushing lower lip forward and making his mouth curved. They were captured. They were in the enemy camp, waiting for some amir to arrive and to interrogate them. They had been separated from Lady Isabella and the young Polo's family. Their chances of success were evaporating. As the Welsh archer had said earlier, they still managed to find the Italians.

James noticed the absence of two of his companions, Peter

and the Desert Wolf. The Scottish knight hoped they were fine and would be able to help. But what they could do against a whole camp of Mamluks?

"Hamo, what do you think of our chances now?" James asked.

The lord from the Welsh Marches grinned, then turned his head to the left.

"Soon there will be a storm," he said. "The wind is cold and soon will become stronger."

They were tied in pairs to a beam near where the horses were kept, under a tent-like shelter. The smell of horse droppings was in the air, but the smell of an upcoming storm was stronger.

"So, we pray, and maybe our Lord will provide a savior to hit them with lightning," the archer said and laughed. James smiled too. What else could he do?

CHAPTER ELEVEN

*Holy Land, Monday, 20th of June, in the year 1272 of the
incarnation of Christ; Mamluk's Night Camp, Near the Qaqun fortress*

The orphan looked at the dark sky. The storm would arrive soon.

Peter had seen Ulf approach the sentries, saluting them while straightening his pants, as if he were returning from relieving himself. The Wolf had said something to them; he staggered like a drunk, he stopped and scratched his ass. The soldiers had let him in and he disappeared into the darkness of the camp.

The orphan decided to try the same. He waited a few moments, untied his belt, and started to walk to the sentries, his gaze pointed at his pants and belt. He was clumsy trying to tie his belt but it wasn't acting. Peter's hands were sweating with nerves; it was hard to hold his short haubergeon, a mail coat, smaller than a hauberk, above his pants while trying to fasten them. He dropped his belt, his pants wrapped around his legs, and he stumbled. After a moment, he was on the ground with a silly expression on his face.

The guards looked at him, laughing, and said something among themselves before ignoring him. Peter stood, lifted his pants, and tied his belt. He looked for a moment toward the camp and the rows of tents. The Moon was hidden behind some dark, gray clouds. He suddenly realized that his nervousness had disappeared. He adjusted the Saracen helmet on his head.

He half-turned toward the sentries—four big men—and he nodded to them. They nodded back and left him alone. He was in.

Now what? To storm the camp, neutralize the enemy soldiers, drink some wine, and free his friends. Simple. The orphan grinned. It was a nice little dream, but he had to be serious. He needed to find his friends.

He walked in. Torches and campfires gave the site a little light. The smell of vegetable soup made his stomach howl like a hungry wolf. He had not eaten anything since morning; his belly felt stuck to his back. He walked around, unsure of what he was looking for.

Peter saw a big pavilion. There were no sentries outside. He instinctively turned in its direction. Something wasn't right. It looked like a captain's pavilion, bigger than the other tents. There were spears stuck in the ground near the entrance with flags hanging from the top. The orphan approached it and listened. He heard something familiar and he entered.

The slaughter was over before Peter arrived. The Wolf stood, bleeding, above his prey. The young man looked at Ulf's eyes, but they didn't show any sign of satisfaction. Something was missing.

"He is not here," Ulf said.

"Who?"

"The amir."

The orphan looked around. He saw a dozen bodies, all with red scarfs around their belts, showing their Mamluk officer status. It appeared that Ulf had interrupted an important meeting. All of the Saracen officers had died with a terrifying grimace on their faces. Their throats were cut; some had severed limbs. Everything was covered with blood.

The captain who had captured their companions wasn't among the dead. This massacre could not be hidden. Soon, it would be discovered and then they would be out of time.

Peter cast an accusatory look at the Wolf.

He had blown their cover and hadn't even attempted to save Peter's friends. Ulf turned his eyes to the orphan; they were savage and empty. He took a few steps toward Peter.

"That way, second row, three tents to the north is where your friends are and another party is to the opposite side of the plateau near the horses. Hurry, I will hold them up," the Desert Wolf said and nodded to indicate where Peter should go.

"What about you?"

"Go, I will catch up." Ulf's confident voice was cold, as everything around him. He was a strange soldier, a strange supplier of death for some, but for others, like Peter and the rest of their party, he offered hope. The orphan ducked out of the pavilion and started to run in the dark, following the direction Ulf had shown him.

He held his helmet with his left hand and his sword with his right, to limit the sound of rattling and not attract attention. He soon reached the long tent.

Four guards stood against him. They looked at him, confused.

Peter acted like a mad messenger, raising his hand and pointing toward the pavilion where the dead officers were. He opened his mouth but stopped. He didn't know their language and to speak in his own tongue would be to betray himself. Instinctively, Peter said the last thing he had learned.

"*Diyaab al-Sahra*," the Desert Wolf. He shouted the foreign name and pointed in the direction of the big tent. He shouted again. He never thought these words could provoke such chaos in men's hearts. All four guards ran in the direction he pointed.

The gusting wind was picking up as the nearby tent flapped wildly.

Peter had grit in his mouth. He spat and entered the tent the guards had stood before with hope in his heart. It took a moment for his eyes to adjust to the light inside.

"Sir James?" His heart was wrapped in hope, but no cheers from his friends arrived.

"Who are you?" said a voice from the back end of the tent. Peter froze.

"Peter ... of Acre." He saw at least two dozen Italian soldiers tied to a long, wooden beam in the middle of the tent.

The orphan remembered the Italian merchants whom they had sought to catch up to on the road.

He jumped over the beam and reached the bearer of the voice, drew his knife and started to cut the thick rope ties. Peter talked fast while freeing them.

"Who are you?" the orphan asked.

"Captain Andrea Pelu," the same voice said. "We traveled to Jerusalem when the Mamluks caught us."

"Do you know where is Sir James and his men?"

"Who?"

"My friends," Peter's voice was trembling. His heart beat fast, and he felt a slight dizziness. "A storm is coming. We need to get out of the camp quickly, but before that, I have to find Sir James and the rest." The orphan didn't have any spare time to explain himself; once he had freed three of the men, he handed them his knife and told them which direction they should go to escape from the camp.

Peter ran back outside. Where were his friends? Where the hell was the other end of the plateau? Peter looked around frantically. The wind lashed his face.

In the darkness, a song of chaos, wind, and thunder rang out. The wind whistled in his ears. He bent to avoid a dead bush flying by.

Peter looked at the horizon: darkness and gray clouds. A sandstorm was approaching; he hadn't much time.

He heard the horses. He guessed he was near. Peter had forgotten to count the tents while walking, but he sensed the horses. The smell of horse shit wasn't something you could miss, or forget.

A man with a blazing torch in his right hand stopped him. He looked at Peter's eyes and asked him something in his language. The orphan wondered for a moment how to react, but saw in the Mamluk's eye that the guard recognized Peter wasn't one of his comrades.

Now what?

Peter instinctively pulled out his knife with his right hand, used his left to grab the guard's sword hand and stabbed the soldier in the neck from below.

If the guard had had any doubt about him, it was justified—but it was too late for the poor guard.

Peter's soul didn't belong to himself anymore. He had killed a man. He wasn't the innocent orphan who had started this journey.

He was in shock.

"Peter!" The voice was familiar; it was Red Herring.

"Over here!" Owen shouted.

Everything around him slowed and blurred, like a slow song. Only his thoughts and reactions seemed to happen at a normal speed. Another guard appeared from the dark in search of his companion. Peter was caught in the middle of his deed. He had to act first, and he knew it. The young man lunged forward to overtake the running soldier drawing his sword. Peter surprised him with this jump and hit him in the throat with his left arm. The guard choked and tried to push him away and cry out. But Peter swung his right hand and pierced the guard under his jaw with the bloody blade. Warm, sticky blood ran down his arm.

The orphan looked the Mamluk in his eyes; it seemed to be the right thing to do, to look his enemy in the eyes at his end. Peter pulled out the knife, and the guard fell to the ground, dying in convulsions.

Like a young predator, he felt the euphoria of his first bloodshed.

"Peter, over here!" Shouts from his left made him turn quickly, ready for the next danger.

It was Sir James and the others. They were sitting in the dust behind a fence and were tied in pairs to a plank. But Lady Isabella was missing.

He felt a strange heaviness in his chest. Peter knew that now wasn't the time or place to think about that. He had to save his companions.

He jumped over the fence and used his blade to cut the ropes from Herring's arms, who was paired with Owen. Hamo was with David, and Githa was tied to some unknown lad. The rest were next to them.

Peter gave the Welshman his knife to continue to release

the others and then fell on his knees.

He threw up some water; it was everything he had in his stomach. In a moment, he forgot where he was; the face of his last victim hung before him.

He closed his eyes but could not escape the image of the Saracen. Peter took a deep breath and looked at his palms. Despite the torches, it was hard to see the sticky liquid on his hands. But he knew it was there; he felt the dark blood that marked his deed. He had seen blood before, but this time it was different. He didn't know what to think. The last Saracen was like him—an ordinary, young man near his twenties. Had he had a family? Peter knew not everyone was without parents. But he had heard from Sir James about the origins of the Mamluk. The word meant "slave," and was used to describe a slave raised and trained to be a soldier. They were homeless orphans, like him. They only had their regiment, their war brothers, their faith, and their lineage lord. It was a fierce force, a professional army of trained soldiers committed and loyal to their master, with nothing to lose except their honor and reputation.

Peter felt a strong hand on his shoulder, turned, and saw a familiar face. The face said something to him, but the orphan didn't hear a thing. He looked through him, and he blinked.

The wind lashed Peter's face and returned him into the middle of the arriving sandstorm.

"Peter! You must breathe. Look at me." Red Herring said to him.

Slap! He hit Peter so hard with the back of his hand that his head went back. It was harsh but it did the trick. The orphan shook his head, cleared his vision, and rose from the ground with Herring's help.

Lightning pierced the sky.

Peter blinked and opened his eyes again. He turned his head around and, realizing where he was, focused on the man near him.

"I killed him ...."

"You had to. Now we must go"

"But ... he was like me ...."

"Come on lad, you did what you were supposed to do. We will talk later." He signaled to his men to gather around him. "Everyone, find your gear, get on a horse, and let's get out of here."

Hamo and the others acted quickly. They collected their equipment near the tent close to their improvised prison and geared up. Peter told them where the meeting point was.

"What about the Wolf?" Red Herring asked.

The orphan's heart was divided. He wasn't sure whether Ulf had planned this massacre as a distraction to help the others, or if Peter had simply discovered him after he had abandoned their cause.

"He will be late," Peter said, nodding to the east of the camp, where a sound of a clash of swords echoed through the wind.

"We need to find Lady Isabella," Githa said. Hamo nodded.

"And my father, too," a trembling voice from behind them broke through the sound of the wind.

Githa took the Italian's hand and introduced them quickly. "Marco Polo."

The orphan paid no attention to the young man. Peter's breathing was rapid; he knew that they had to act quickly to succeed. He told the others of the other location Ulf had told him about. James voted against going there; their mission wasn't the lady's safety. But Hamo refused to obey. He wanted to find the princess.

"We must run fast, they will search for us. And the storm will hit us any moment; we need to find shelter," Red Herring said, but everyone knew the temper of this lord from the Welsh Marches. "You and Githa have a few moments before the storm. We will distract the enemy if need be. Now go."

"I am coming with you," Peter volunteered. "I know where they might be. Follow me."

He drew his sword, then turned to Red Herring and said, "Release the horses; they are scared to death of storms."

He led Githa and Hamo back to the center of the camp again.

Why was he doing this? It wasn't because he had a good

soul. He wanted to see the lady once more. What about Hamo? He, too, was obsessed with her. If this was a competition for the princess, what chances did a street rat from Acre have against a lord from beyond the sea? Still, something in his heart drove him forward, hoping to earn a smile from Isabella. Perhaps even something more.

He led them through the camp, his tunic soaked in sweat. They reached a large tent with two guards near the entrance.

Everywhere was turmoil—screams and shouts combined with the wind, sand, and lightning announcing the oncoming storm. Confused soldiers were trying to hold their tents and their supplies to keep them from blowing away. Yet, here, the guards stood strong at their post, regardless of the weather.

Hamo reached the two sentries first. He threw his scabbard at the right guard's face and swung his sword toward the left one. The Mamluk raised his arm to shout a warning but he quickly changed his tactics. The guard pointed his spear toward Hamo, but the Crusader pushed it aside with his shield and his blade landed on the Mamluk's face. Peter kicked the second Saracen's leg; he lost his balance and Githa stabbed him between the ribs from behind. The orphan and Hamo lunged into the tent without caution; something like an unspoken rivalry had arisen between them in their competition to reach the lady first.

They saw Lady Isabella lying on the ground, her dress had been ripped and torn down the front, revealing her pale skin. The brown-haired captain who had taken her here was bending down, grabbing her arm and was with his back to Hamo and Peter. The princess tried to push him away, but he was stronger.

Peter felt a heat in his stomach; disgust and rage boiled within him. He approached quickly and pulled the captain away from the lady. The Mamluk tried to stand and to reach for a weapon but the lord from Welsh Marches used the pommel of his sword to hit his shoulder. The captain roared in pain but the knight hit him again and he stumbled and fell. Hamo kicked the Mamluk in the ribs as Peter helped the lady to get up and gave her a cloak he found on the ground to hide her nakedness. The lord from the Welsh Marches was about to deliver the final blow when he was interrupted.

"Look out!" Githa shouted.

Four Mamluks with angry faces stormed the tent with naked swords in hand. The attackers saw their captain on the ground and charged the Crusaders. The first one, a cross-eyed Mamluk swung his weapon toward Peter's neck, but the orphan was faster. He raised his hand and grabbed the Mamluk's wrist that held the blade and twisted it, butting him in the face with his forehead. There was a sound of breaking and the man screamed in pain. The soldier looked surprised, his nose streaming blood. Peter instinctively stuck the sword above his armor, under his chin. He stepped back and with ease, he pulled his bloody sword out from the dead Mamluk and blocked the second soldier's attack.

Peter heard another Mamluk's scream and glanced over from his fighting to see the man's look for surprise and bleeding face as Hamo hammered his weapon over the soldier's neck. The orphan stood between the lady and the tall soldier he faced while Githa crossed swords with the fourth Mamluk. Peter bent to avoid a sword flying to his head, knelt and stabbed the Mamluk in the thigh. He felt the sticky blood run over his hand. He retrieved his sword and kicked the wounded man's other leg. The soldier's face showed a grimace of pain and he fell on his back.

"Finish him," Hamo shouted, while he pushed the dead soldier back with his shield.

Peter hesitated for a moment. He knew he had to, but when he looked at the enemy's eyes, he saw fear. He raised his blade and froze for a moment. But Hamo jumped over the fallen man and finished him with his bloody sword. He snarled toward Peter, wiping the blood from his face.

Githa pulled her sword from the chest of the last guard. As she rose, another four Mamluks charged the big tent. Hamo, Peter, and Githa lined toward them with bloody swords, as Lady Isabella cowered against the back of the tent.

Peter heard the whistle of crossbow arrows flying past his head coming from behind him. Flying death, the orphan called this sound. He went wide-eyed, ducking behind the dead tall Mamluk, as crying out:

"Watch out!"

He glanced and saw the Italians at the entrance of the tent, reloading their crossbows. Their arrows pierced all the Mamluks with one volley. Only one of them was still moving on the ground, producing pre-death sounds, but Githa silenced him with her sword.

The Genovese captain approached with his men.

"Peter," Andrea Pelu nodded to the orphan.

"Thank you for your help, Mr. Pelu."

"We have to find our paymaster, the head of the Polo family," the Genoese captain said. The storm was provoking a real terror in the camp, but the westerners looked uninterested.

Peter introduced the Genoese to Hamo.

"I want to interrogate this one," Pelu said and pointed the wounded Mamluk captain.

Hamo knelt down, wiped the blood from his sword on the cloak of one of the dead bodies, then got up and crossed his arms.

"Do it quickly. We have to get out of here."

"Where are the others?" The Genoese asked the Mamluk captain. "Where is Mr. Polo?" Pelu asked again as Isabella was acting as an interpreter.

The Mamluk captain said nothing, but Hamo wasn't as polite as the Italian. He approached him swiftly and hit the Saracen with the pommel of his sword on the shoulder. Peter heard the crack of a bone and the Mamluk dropped on the ground like a broken man. Hamo's handsome face looked now fierce. The Saracen emitted a scream and pain was painted on his face. After a few moments, he started to talk.

Isabella interpreted his words. "He says they are waiting for the amir to arrive to question the travelers," the lady said in a calm tone. She had regained her composure. "The Polo family are outside this tent on the west side. The Mamluk had ordered his men to tie them outside so that he could be alone with me."

Pelu went to check.

"Why does the amir want to interrogate Lady Isabella and the Italians?" Hamo asked.

The question was translated. The captain convulsed from the pain in his shoulder. The orphan guessed that there must be something broken.

"It was the sultan's order to check every passing caravan and convoy, even the birds."

"Why?" The Mamluk hesitated and Hamo urged him to continue by pressing his finger into his wound. "What was he looking for?"

"A traitor and an assassin." The pain made it hard for him to speak, but the interpreter understood what he said. "He is searching for a traitor and the sultan is looking to uncover a plot against him. He thinks the Crusaders are involved, too."

"What a discovery; Crusaders to want to kill the sultan," Hamo said with irony.

"Sultan Baibars also thinks the assassination of Edward was an inside job."

The Italian returned from outside and said, "We are ready to go, we found Mr. Polo."

"That's all the information we're going to get out of this man. Let's go," Hamo said. But something was bothering Peter. Why would someone make so much effort to block the valley and question everyone who passed?

"*Diyaab al-Sahra?*" he shouted. The captain's face turned to purple, his eyes opened wide, and he became quiet.

"*Diyaab al-Sahra?*" Peter repeated the question and the Mamluk responded.

"*Diyaab al-Sahra* was close to the Sultan, once. But someone attacked his family by mistake. He doesn't know more," Isabella finished her translation and added, "I think he lied just now."

Peter knelt down to him, looked the Saracen in the eyes, and said, "He is here, in the camp."

The orphan left Isabella to translate his words. He saw the Mamluk's face turn white. Sweat was dropping from the wounded man's temple.

"So, tell me something I don't know, or I will leave you tied up here without a weapon."

Peter was surprised by the coldness of his own voice. "What happened to you, Peter?" he asked himself.

"They were close, the sultan and the Desert Wolf. He was the tool of the sultan's vengeance, years ago, when certain amirs and a faction of the assassins revolted against Baibars. The sultan sent the Wolf ... and the rebellion was no more. Two years ago, *Diyaab al-Sahra* met a woman and he wanted to retire. The sultan agreed, on the condition that the Wolf complete his last assignment. It was nearly impossible—almost a suicide mission—but he succeeded and Baibars kept his word. But now the Sultan feared him: the Wolf was to live in peace; nobody was to touch him and he was not to interfere in the ruler's affairs."

He stopped and glanced to Hamo who stood with his sword pointed to his throat.

"But?" Peter asked.

"But someone dared to attack him. They killed his loved one but failed to kill him."

"Who?"

"I wish I knew." The Mamluk coughed with some pain. "And now the Wolf is unleashed, and he never fails. The sultan knew this; it is because of *Diyaab al-Sahra* that the sultan sits on his throne." The Mamluk captain coughed blood onto his tunic, then continued.

"He isn't from this world. People say he was delivered by sea waves. The Wolf doesn't know what fear or pain is. He excels at two things: survival and killing. He strikes with dedication, determination, and skill."

He paused, coughed more blood, and said, "He is surrounded by death, and now we are going to die."

Lady Isabella stopped translating and made the sign of the cross.

"Is there a connection between the two events? The attack on Edward and that over the Wolf's manor," Peter asked.

The Mamluk's eyes became wide and rounded and stared at the young man as his head jerked back. But the Saracen said no more as he fainted and they left him on the ground.

"We are running out of time and we have to go," Hamo said. They stole between the tents to their escape, using the night as cover.

Peter turned his head back toward the center of the camp, where he heard the sound of fire, swords, and screams. He felt the thirst that made him want to know what was going on with Ulf. Something was stuck in his throat.

They said that curiosity killed the bird.

"I am not a bird," he told himself.

"You are not. But the little creature can fly, what about you?" he answered himself.

"I can hold a sword," he thought and grinned.

Lighting hit the sky again; thunder echoed in their ears.

Golden flashes came from the north. Peter and the rest had almost reached the horses. But he felt he needed to turn back. After all, the Wolf was part of their fellowship.

"I will stay to find Ulf," Peter declared. He slowed his pace and turned his gaze to the dark. "You go. If I don't show up soon, don't wait for me."

"Good luck, Peter." Githa waved and they left him in the dark.

The night was gloomy and yellow. Wind and sand added to the confusion, blurring everything in sight. Peter ran toward the battle sounds. He had lost his helmet and his black hair was visible. But nobody knew his face, nor would anyone be suspicious of another soldier running to the center of the action. He ran, he was oblivious to fatigue and the pain between his legs. As he approached, he looked around the fighting men. He saw a bareheaded man who looked to be their amir and his royal guards dressed in yellow lamellar armors with golden decoration.

Everything was dark, blurred somehow from the wind and the sand, but the figures had their own contours. The outlined shadow of the Wolf was unmistakable.

Peter stopped about fifty paces away from the fighting men. The scene was somehow unrealistic: a fight in the middle of the storm. Why had Ulf embarked on this? To kill a few Mamluks? Peter would ask him if they managed to escape but he wondered if that was what Ulf wanted.

The Desert Wolf stood in the dark, and his axe and blade looked darkened by the blood. Bodies surrounded him like a heap of stones. He swung his blades, blocking the sword of the last attacker and splitting the Saracen's head with his axe. The dead man fell near the others. Ulf was walking in their camp. His confidence and lack of fear froze his enemies' blood. One by one, he had killed any soldier who dared to confront him. For Peter, it seemed that Ulf was only here to satisfy his hunger for blood and revenge.

Most of the Mamluks were now hesitated to advance against him. They breathed rapidly and tracked him more quickly with their widened eyes. They constantly looked at him and their dead comrades. He was surrounded by the countless bodies of brave soldiers who had dared, tried, and died.

The wind and the flying objects around him increased; the storm was here and everyone had found shelter but these men in the center of the camp.

Two guards on horses in their fine golden armor dared to advance, ordered by the voice of their amir. But the Wolf was faster; he knelt, took a fallen spear from a victim and threw it into the first rider's chest. The spearhead struck between the horse's head and the round shield of the rider; it was enough to unsaddle him, throwing him down in the dark. He fell backward with the spear impaling him, breaking the lamellar structure of his armor. A scream echoed.

The second soldier saw the first rider and his fate and slowed his charge. After a moment, he focused and headed toward the Wolf. Peter saw Ulf grab a shield and lunge toward the approaching animal. He slammed the warhorse's left side using, the attacker's speed to unbalance him.

The horse lurched to one side and fell. The Desert Wolf jumped on his fallen target and, with his axe, promptly smashed his skull. He didn't appear to need help or worry about being caught. Ulf's teeth flashed in the darkness—he was actually smiling.

Did he enjoy killing? The obvious answer set the orphan's teeth on edge.

Peter was glad he had listened to his inner voice and come back.

The wind became stronger and blew away shrubs and small objects from the Saracen's belongings like wooden bowls, cups, and spoons. A small, metal item flashed, hitting Ulf on the temple, near his eye. He lost his balance and fell.

The bareheaded amir on his white destrier noticed this and spurred his charger toward the Wolf. Peter saw a chance the amir to put Ulf's head on his wall. All who were there— soldiers, bodyguards, animals—held their breath in anticipation of what would happen.

Peter looked around. He found a spear in the mess of sandstorm, camp, men, and darkness. His target was in front of him. Everything he saw was blurred and the outlines of the figures were hard to see. No one noticed his arrival and what he intended to do. He took a few steps from his position and threw the weapon with all the strength he had.

The orphan had seen soldiers and Crusaders in the training yard near the monastery throwing spears but he had never held one himself. It was heavier than he expected it to be. He wasn't sure of the proper stance or how to hold or to throw the thing. He did it instinctively.

The spear flew.

A strange sound cut the air while the heavy, wooden rod with the iron blade flew. The spearhead reached its target. It clashed against the amir's shield with a crack. The heavy blow of the weapon hit the rider with such enormous power that he lost his horse beneath his legs and found himself on the ground. Initially, he was shocked, bruised.

Then the pain arrived and he screamed.

Everyone ran toward the amir.

By this point, the intensity of the wind became stronger and lightning danced around. In another time and place, this would have been a marvelous sight.

Peter ran to Ulf, jumping over the fallen bodies. He helped him recover and stand on his feet. The Wolf looked stunned but had managed to observe the rider and his collapse from the orphans' spear.

"A fine throw."

Peter didn't say anything. He realized the two of them were separated from their friends in the enemy camp in the eye of the storm. They had to seek shelter and they had to escape the soldiers, who, once they had aided their amir, would be after them.

"We have to go," Peter said.

The two of them moved through the tents as some were blown away by the wind and wooden carts were turned away, provisions scattered. Soldiers were covering animals' eyes and tying them up to calm them through the storm.

Peter turned left and stopped for a moment behind a fallen tent to think what to do.

"Over there," Ulf managed to say. The orphan turned his gaze and realized their good fortune; there were two horses not far from there. The animals were where his friends had been.

"Herring." Peter was relieved to assume that the Scottish knight had left the horses for them; this old bastard knew his trade. Ulf mounted the saddle of one animal. With fresh eagerness, the orphan jumped on another fine-looking, brown warhorse, and they vanished into the dark.

It was the sandstorm's turn to sing its song.

CHAPTER TWELVE

Holy Land, Tuesday, 21st of June, in the year 1272 of the incarnation of Christ; Near the Qaqun fortress

Barak was sitting on his fine, Arab horse.

It was a special one, indeed; its muscles, its bones, its strength, and the way the Sun reflected on its black coat was magnificent. It was a knight's possession, worthy of an amir. But he wasn't one yet. Not yet, but soon. His gaze was directed to the east and he was near the edge of a small plateau, overlooking a cliff.

Some distant wind kissed his face and tousled his raven-black hair. The Sun was starting to climb the horizon of the blue sky. Earlier, Barak had received news about the events of the previous night. He had hesitated, unsure whether to rejoice or not. He had had some close friends in Berrat's camp and they were all gone now, but he was definitely closer to his goal. It was good news despite the casualties of the sandstorm.

He smiled. Intelligence had arrived about an assassination attempt on Lord Edward. Early reports said that the English prince had slaughtered the failed killer. He had traced the group who had left Acre. And in this party, was his primary target, the Desert Wolf. But there was also another target, an assassin.

But then he received another dispatch from a mysterious ally of his master, Ughan.

The report that the assassin had been killed was deception; he was traveling with the Wolf.

Why was the assassin important? Who was this mysterious ally? He helped them. Why? Now he wanted the favor returned: he wanted the party captured. Barak wanted the Wolf, and Ughan's ally wanted the assassin—alive. So be it.

From the moment the party had left the vicinity of Acre, Barak's men had tracked them, observing the group. Every time they had decided to catch them, however, something had happened. At first, they hadn't been sure about the intelligence. But the identity of the travelers had been confirmed.

Diyaab al-Sahra, the Desert Wolf.

Again, and again, this name appeared. Barak had never met him before but he remembered the expression on the sultan's face two days ago. He had missed his chance to kill the Wolf at his manor. There was something mysterious about this man.

But what was it? He had looked like a ragged rat when Barak had met him nearly a week before. This unknown, Christian dog was important, but to whom? He would like to know. He didn't like this; he was used to the simple life on the northern frontier. He liked it there. He wanted to look directly into the eyes of the enemy and to open his belly with his blade.

Then he could enjoy the nice, pale girl's company and drink some expensive wine. Ughan's winery had one of the finest collections of wine from any part of the world you could imagine.

His master, Ughan, troubled him, too. He had become sleepy, fat, and reckless. He spent too much time with his women and not enough with his duties.

Everywhere, people were talking about the Wolf. Barak couldn't forget Baibars' look when he had received the news about the failed attempt to kill him. That had been curious.

He needed to found out more about this man. He needed to find someone who knew him. He wondered where to start looking for such a person.

Hunger drove men forward, didn't it? He nodded in his thoughts. The eternal hunger. His stomach sang the song of the immortal fight. The desire to satisfy his human nature, to fill his stomach and to wash his dry mouth with fine wine drove him forward. He was hungry, but not for food. He wanted more, much more. He would do whatever he must to satisfy his hunger and even more. He was a determined man.

He looked at the valley. The sandstorm had erased everything. The entire battalion was missing. He remembered the legend of the Persian army blown away by the desert sandstorm more than a thousand years before. He had learned of it at the military school where he was raised and trained to be a Mamluk soldier. There, he and his brothers had learned to obey and serve, to fight and die in the name of the ruling dynasty. They were the "owned soldiers," the slave soldiers, the Mamluks of the sultan.

Yet, times had changed.

Now they were the ruling masters. There were some amirs and factions who didn't like the regime. Nevertheless, they ruled the whole empire. They were forging the "Mamluk Dynasty." He smiled and started to dream.

It was time to step forward and to write his name with gold into the history of this land. He felt he was ready. The events were close and the prophet had foreseen his glory.

A year before, he had met an old man who claimed to see the future. The man told of upcoming events, saying that Barak would play a major role. He had hesitated to believe it back then, but all of the things the prophet had said had come to pass. The traitor in their camp, the flood in the spring, even the poison—the prophet had predicted them all.

It had been Barak's decision to keep this man close, to check his wisdom and words.

There wasn't any chance that someone else would ruin his fate. Certainly, not some ragged Desert Wolf.

This name instilled panic in others.

Barak knew the legends had to be greatly exaggerated. He wanted to meet him again to measure their strengths and swords, face to face. He wasn't afraid of this name. And he would not make the same mistake twice; when he met the Wolf this time, he would squeeze his heart—painfully, and with some pleasure. After all, his trade was war and killing, and he was one of the best around. He had led a fearsome and fearless regiment from the northern frontier of Damascus. He had fought with many enemies: Tartars, Bedouins, renegades, traitors, bandits, western knights, even the fanatic religious warriors of the cross. He had crushed them like flies. He had never failed.

His master, Amir Ughan, was a man who brought fear.

Barak disliked him, but he respected him. He made a deadly enemy—clever, ruthless, and ambitious. Once, he had been an excellent fighter who had held a sword shoulder-to-shoulder with Baibars. But the years had influenced and Ughan became fat.

Yes, he indulged himself and had lost his agility. But he looked more clever and deadlier than ever. Now, most men feared him because no one could guess what was in his mind. And he used this to his advantage, as he had used his blade as younger Mamluk.

Barak and his men were almost 200 strong Mamluk riders equipped with bows and swords. They had observed Berrat's men from a distance over the past few days and had managed to hide in the caves of the mountains before the storm. Why had Berrat not foreseen what would happen? Why had he not retreated to Qaqun before the storm? Now his army was destroyed.

Berrat was weak and this was the moment to finish him.

Most of Barak's men were from the northern border. They hadn't had any trouble seeing their brethren die in the sandstorm. Barak had carefully selected them; they were loyal only to him. He was sure his master had planted a spy among his men, as Barak had among Ughan's men. His master liked the games of spies.

Barak led his soldiers to investigate what had been left by the deadly storm. He remembered the Persian army once more. A thousand years before, the Persian king had made a mistake and the desert had ripped his army into oblivion. Without an army, the king could not stand against his enemies. And now, Sultan Baibars had lost a battalion to the desert storm.

Fate was repeating itself. The day would turn to night, then to a day again. Everything was turning around and his chance would come to him, at last. He took a look at his prophet, who always rode after him. He smiled to him, encouraged him. What difference could a little encouragement of a man's beliefs make?

He would find out soon.

"Come, let's go," he said to his men.

***

"So, someone sent an assassin to kill the English prince, and someone tried to kill you." Red Herring nodded to Ulf. "They both failed. Was it planned or just a coincidence?" James smiled bitterly. "Why would someone want to kill a prince? To take the crown? To prevent his politics or actions? To silence him? To remove him from your path? What else would be a reason? What is so important that it should cost the life of a future king? Perhaps it was revenge. But, again, for what?" Red Herring thought aloud.

They were riding on their path again—the whole fellowship, in addition to a Venetian merchant and his mercenary crossbowmen. The men discussed the events, and Peter sharpened his ears with the thought of hearing everything. They rode in pairs but were close enough to talk and to hear what was said.

"As the Italians say, don't have too many irons in the fire." Ulf was riding alongside Red Herring. Hamo was behind them.

"What it means?" The lord from the Welsh Marches asked.

"You have to ask only the most important questions," Ulf said.

"Who was afraid of the prince? Who was afraid of you?" James said.

"That is easy to answer. The sultan," Hamo said.

"But beneath the obvious, why would he be afraid of an English Crusader without sufficient manpower and resources to fulfill his Crusade? Baibars signed a peace treaty and has started to prepare for the Tartar invasion," James said. "And besides, he doesn't want to provoke a new Crusade in his realm."

"Yet, his reputation shows he is capable of such unchivalric deeds as to send someone home, dead, in a coffin," Hamo said.

"Is Prince Edmund, Edward's brother capable of this?" Ulf asked.

"No. He is too young and lacks experience. Besides, Edward's mother and father are still alive, and it is thanks to Edward that they have their kingdom back from Simon de Montfort," Red Herring said.

"Is there a connection between the two events? The attack on Edward and that over the Wolf's manor?" Hamo asked.

Owen joined the conversation. "To kill an ordinary man is one thing, but to kill a future king?"

"And the assassination looked prepared—organized—but as if, suddenly, someone decided to do it fast and made a mistake. With failure, you expose a whole network of men. Why the hurry?" Hamo asked no one particular.

"Look at him." Red Herring also nodded to the orphan. "What was his part in this? Or was he simply in the wrong place at the wrong time and saw something he wasn't supposed to see?"

"Eh… What irony. Yes, I heard his story so far, an orphan, a street urchin from the poor district, messing up a plan. Like a sandstorm," Hamo said.

"Storm?" Red Herring thought for a moment, then laughed. "A storm undermined our efforts at the Qaqun fortress last time. Now, another one appeared in the same region. The sandstorm residence, this is how I will remember this place. It's like divine intervention; every time we approach this place, a sandstorm rises up against us."

"But this time it helped us, don't you think?" Hamo smiled.

"It depended on your point of view. But yes, this time it was on our side." Red Herring smiled, too.

"So, it was you who was responsible for the failed attack on Baibars' fleet last year?" Ulf asked Red Herring curiously.

Sir James looked at the Desert Wolf but said no more.

Peter was curious. A failed attack? What had happened? He remembered news about a sunken Mamluk fleet near the port of Limassol that year, but what was the connection? Red

Herring? He wanted to know. Peter wished he had listened in detail to the story the sailors in the taverns had told.

They rode and they talked. What else could they do? They discussed the sandstorm, the Mamluk camp, and their new companions. The Genovese crossbowmen and their paymaster, the merchant from Venice, Mr. Niccolò Polo. They had found the Italians with their papers of safe access to Jerusalem. This encouraged them in their mission and lifted their spirits once again.

No one had thought they would be free from the Mamluks so soon and without casualties. Even the middle-aged woman and the baby were fine. Peter was happy to see the Lady of Beirut again. She kissed on his forehead him for gratitude for what he had done the night before.

They had all been saved by a cave they had found during the storm. The cave had been dark and scary, but dry and a safe refuge from the storm. They had lost the cart and Isabella's carriage in the sandstorm. Thanks to their luck, they were unharmed.

According to Edward the Saracen, they were safe because of the Wolf and his knowledge of the landscape as well. At the beginning of the journey, all of the members of the fellowship had looked at the assassin with distrust and eyes filled with vengeance. Only Peter exchanged a word with him.

Before they had slept, Peter and Nickolas had once more used the last light from the fire to teach Peter his letters. Vegetius, the author of the book, had been an extraordinary man. The book was replete with instructions and guidelines to war and training. Had it been written for the Roman emperor or was it a way to preserve information for future soldiers? Reading it, Peter wondered how the world was different now than in the time of the Romans' rule. They had a manual which outlined how to lead an army, how to select men who were suitable for battle, how to prevent and address mutiny, how to organize in battle, and much more. The orphan hadn't imagined it would be so interesting to read. He was amazed at himself, how he wanted to prolong the night so he could have more time to read and to learn. He was astonished how the book contained such valuable knowledge.

This book, containing precious information from the ancient Romans, had been a gift to Lord Edward. Every time Peter remembered this fact, he despised himself. But he wanted to know more. He wanted to learn how to read and write quickly and this desire silenced his inner guilt. In the beginning, it was hard for him, although Nickolas helped him. The young valet guided him with patience and skill. Someday, the two of them joked, Nickolas would be a great teacher and Peter would be a great knight. Only fate would tell.

He had slept after the storm like an oak tree—his left side had tingled when he had risen. But he had awoken with an eagerness for new adventures.

Peter remembered a situation in the morning before they prepared to leave the cave.

Hamo's face was different from the day before; he wasn't smiling, as usual. He looked at the orphan with new eyes. Peter was the man who had guided them to save Lady Isabella. He was the man who had first managed to give her a hand to rise from the dust and to earn a smile from her. The ultimate reward for a knight: a smile and thankful gaze from a princess—indeed, a beautiful one. She had taken his hand and stood on her feet. The view was hypnotizing for all who were there.

Peter had no noble origin, no war experience, no money, and no future. But he had courage, and for that, he had earned Hamo's respect, at least he hoped.

But the war for the lady's heart wasn't over yet.

"Peter, come here." His voice was cold, but the youngest member of the Crusader's fellowship approached like a good dog. They measured each other with a look. Hamo's head was tilted back, looking at his nose, his eyebrows were lower. He crossed his hands in front of his chest and looked at the orphan.

"Thank you for your help last night. But you need a lesson or two on how to hold a sword," Hamo said, sounding cold. He drew his blade and raised it above his head.

Peter wasn't sure how to react. Hamo looked like a man

ready to deliver a fatal blow, but was he? Was this an appropriate place and time for practice? He remembered what Vegetius had written: "The good soldier practices every day."

They began to practice and after a moment they crossed swords, the knight drew his face closer to the orphan.

"Stay away from her," Hamo said quietly, only for Peter's ears. The knight struck him with the pommel of his sword and pushed him hard. Peter lost balance and fell back on his butt. The young man looked at the handsome knight but said nothing. Was Hamo jealous? Peter looked at his eyes again. So, Hamo liked the princess too.

"Get up, you have a long way to go, Peter," Red Herring murmured while watching the two men, who struggled like fighting cocks. He drank some water. "But the lad will learn. That's he wants, right?" James said to the Welshman to his left while they had a quick breakfast.

Now, as they rode he thought about it. Hamo was attracted to Lady Isabella as well as Peter.

The Sun was working hard after the night and they continued their quest.

The Genovese captain was near Red Herring and they talked. Peter couldn't understand a word. The Italian language was close to French but different. They used their hands and Peter recognized words here and there which he had heard in church while the monks were singing.

"Latin," Owen said, answering Peter's question. He came close to the orphan. He was a merry rogue, and an orphan, like Peter. The lad liked his company and his humor and he admired his skills with the bow. He felt Owen determined the mood of the party. His enthusiasm seemed endless.

Peter spat out some sand. He beat the dust and sand from his clothes and hair.

The party talked about the eternal city, Jerusalem.

Jerusalem, the city that attracted people from around the world on pilgrimages to the Holy Land.

Peter had only heard about the city; he had never seen it, nor had the rest of the party. Only Lady Isabella, who lived in the realm and was in a diplomatic relationship with the sultan, had visited it.

As they approached the valley near the Holy City, most of the men became silent. Everyone had his own idea of what to expect of the most sacred place of all Christendom.

Peter had been told once that Jerusalem was the capital of the Latin Kingdom. Once, this mighty city had been protected against enemies by large, stone walls. It was near a mountain, but it was said that it had been built there because of a water spring, which provided travelers with the most precious supply on the road: fresh water. Cold water from the heart of the mountain was enough to build a city far from the trading roads and maritime ports.

Yet, this place had become the most important port for men of different races, faraway lands, and myriad religions. Why was this place so important as to make people travel to an unknown land, braving dangers and losing years of their lives in pilgrimage? The orphan couldn't guess. Maybe when he saw the Holy City he could understand it.

Lady Isabella of Beirut told him that the city had no defensive walls now; it had lost its importance since the Mamluks had become lords of this land. It was more of a city of exile; political and military men who had lost the faith of the sultan ended up here, retired. This had caused the city to grow more and more, to change again, drawing the attention of religious men—the Jews, the Christians, the Muslims—as well as philosophers, physicians, and many more. A new monastery for travelers had risen. New districts and markets had developed around the trade in sacred things and the roads to this once-forgotten place were used again.

Merchants flocked to the area, eager to provide whatever was necessary for living. Politically unwelcomed people of the sultan, rich men from the entire empire living there had the money and the desire to return this magnificent city to its former glory—but not as a strategic, military fortress. The appointment of a new governor had also helped. He was from the city of Damascus, and his mandate was a year and a half. Lady Isabella said that this made the governor avoid entangling with political games.

"Corruption is difficult to develop." Her description of the city held all the men rapt, except one.

"Is that so?" James expressed his doubt. "When the duration of governance is so short, this is a foundation to whole administration to lack of activities and to be rotten and corrupted."

"No, it isn't like that," the Lady countered. "Many interests are represented in this city. They fight each other, and that fight keeps the rotten apples out."

Nablus was far behind them; they rode through Samaria via the road to the heart of long lost Latin Empire.

Peter understood that he had missed the city's first period of glory by a century. But now he expected to explore a reborn city full of merchants, different kinds of people, craftsmen, and healers.

"In the recent past, the city stood aside from the sultan's politics, but it is returning to life under the Mamluk government," Isabella informed them. "It will be important once more."

"So, is this why Jerusalem has excellent physicians?" Hamo asked.

For most of the journey, the assassin listened and said nothing. His head was covered with a white silk hood, but Peter could see his cold face. The closer they came to their goal, the more the Saracen looked troubled, as if he bore a heavy burden on his shoulders. Was he worried for his life?

"Did you come here to see the city and feel your God, or to plunder and war for your own glory?" Edward the Saracen asked. The question was directed at the young lord from the Welsh Marches. Hamo's eyebrows lowed on the eyes and clearly knotted, as his nostrils flared.

Peter observed how he the young knight lost his temper, raised his hand and was about to hit the assassin with his fist.

"Calm down, Le Strange," James said. The lord from the Welsh Marches wasn't a man who liked to be opposed. The fire in his warrior's heart was impulsive and sometimes led to trouble. Although his upbringing had made the young lord fierce and brutal when he had to be and to be gentle when needed, he was young and he had yet to learn to keep his temper under control. But Red Herring, as usual, predicted what was going to happen and interfered confidently.

"We are soldiers who follow our prince. We do not ask where he wants to go and fight; we support him. We gave him our oaths; he is our liege lord," James said.

"It sounds noble and chivalrous, but is it so? I am not a child, Sir James," Isabella said and smiled at Peter, who was near her. "Most of the men who arrive on this shore these days don't just seek salvation, you know."

"Of course, you are not a child. And of course," he said, smiling, "we are not here just for the religion or this damned city or rotten kingdom. We are here to earn fame—not only for the prince but for ourselves, our own households—to gain renown and some wealth, too. Although the wealth is not certain. We are not ordinary soldiers; we have taken care of our enemies at home."

"For now," Owen added and scratched his neck.

"We want a new challenge," Red Herring continued. "And where can a warrior find a challenge these days except in tournaments or some minor, local feuds?"

He spread his hands, showing the land around him.

"The Holy Land is in an unstoppable war of religions, land, power, supplies, interests, and reputation. In these lands, civilizations meet and measure their strengths and honor. We were in need of a challenge. We crossed the sea and now we breathe this sandy air and drink this sandy water, fighting for our own glory and for our lord," Red Herring said with confidence. "We bear a red cross on our chests, but above all, we are sword brothers and we fight together, bleed together, and die together. We don't like anyone who gets in our way." He said all this in one breath. His face reddened and he clutched the hilt of his sword. Most of his men were quiet and they all just nodded in agreement.

The honest answer surprised the lady. She smiled, then turned around and said, "He doesn't look experienced, like the rest of you." Isabella nodded to the orphan.

"Who? The young lad? He has only a few days of service,"

James said, smiling, as well.

"The young man who set us free?" Pelu asked.

"Yes," James grinned.

The conversation turned to the events in Acre. Peter noticed Hamo's face darkened—more discussion of the orphan.

The heat became more annoying. Although Peter was all in sweat, his mouth was dry. He drank some water and petted his horse. He was distracted by the pain of his chafing thighs. It wasn't worse than the day before but was not better, either. Today, before they rode again, Owen had given him some medicine, an oil to apply to his irritated skin.

"What is that?" the orphan had asked.

"A balm from Marigold," he said, nodding toward Githa. "The well-prepared Hospitaller always has medicine for wounds. She was glad to lend some to me." Owen gave a sympathetic smile to Peter, but the orphan saw a devilish glow in his eyes.

"Clean the wound, put this on it, and bandage it again. After a few days, you'll be fine." He observed the face of the lad. "You will thank me later."

The Sun smiled on them.

"Jerusalem! Will we reach it alive?" David asked no one particular.

"We are almost there," the middle-aged lady with the baby said.

Red Herring was deep in thought. Every day since their journey had started, he seemed to become more and more troubled. With every step toward their aim, he became darker and more silent. The orphan observed his transformation. What was caused his unexpected mood?

"Soon we will arrive in the Crusader's Jerusalem or what is left of it," Edward the Saracen said with some regret in his voice.

"Why?" Peter was anxious as ever to know.

"Once," he slowly began, "it was a marvelous city with strong walls. It was the political and religious center of the world. Now, it's different."

"Tell me more," Peter said.

"The city is located between two valleys, the Kidron to the east and the Hinnom to the west, which meet in the south at the site of the city's principal natural water source, the Siloam Spring." The Saracen took a moment to drink some water from his leather bag. "Within this physical frame, the secondary Tyropoeon Valley, running through the city from north to the south, divides it into two hills; Mount Zion to the west and Mount Moriah to the east."

"Moriah?" Peter asked.

"The Temple Mount," the assassin said. But he wasn't sure the orphan understood at all or knew these names. Edward the Saracen continued. "The Siloam Spring is the only natural water source nearby, a factor that would have limited the development of the city, but this was resolved by the construction of aqueducts, open reservoirs, and cisterns. You see, whatever weakness the dwellers had, they turned them into advantages."

Peter looked ahead.

"Soon we will be there, approaching St. Stephan's gate— some call it the Damascus gate—at the north end of the city. The importance of this gate lies in the fact that it leads to the main northern road running to Nablus and from there to Acre or Damascus." Edward the Saracen smiled.

From the hill which sloped down to the city, the orphan saw it and his eyes grew wide.

"Jerusalem!" The assassin presented it to them.

"Yes...." Peter barely closed his mouth. It was an enormous sight; even though the outer stone walls were in ruins and only the foundations of them could be seen, the line of destroyed wall showed a magnificent defensive construction and large barbican, an outer defensive work looked like a gatehouse from the past. The entire city was encircled with thick, stone walls at least four meters wide. But this was a past glory. There were no more fortifications or walls, except the citadel and the nearby tower, which Peter later learned was called the Tower of David. The gates were left strong or had been rebuilt by the Mamluk governor, but this was only to control trading and entering into the city.

The vicinity of Jerusalem was full of plural settlements, farms, some monasteries around the hills, and hundreds of pilgrims. There were some outposts of guards watching the valleys and the people who were coming.

The closer they came, the more people they saw on the road. The lad could see pilgrims, merchants, mercenaries, mason workers, and many more.

There also many refugees—men, women, and children fleeing the violence of the nearby Tartar invasion. Peter saw everything from the poor and sick to the very wealthy. Trade flourished with the movement of people.

Peter was eager to enter the city. His heartbeat accelerated. His anticipation was hard to hide, but the others were feeling the same.

They approached it from the north road, following the natural gorge, to the place where the Christian religion was born.

"What was his name?" Peter couldn't remember all the names of all the places and people he had met or heard about in past few days.

"Jesus Christ," Owen reminded him.

Lady Isabella pointed out some old ruins to their right.

"That is St. Stephen's martyrdom and of the church of St. Stephen, or what is left of it," she explained to the horsemen around her. "It is also known as the Gate of the Pillar, or Bâb al-'Amûd, because of the ancient pillar that stands here."

"Once, before the city fell to Saladin, this gate was used by pilgrims entering Jerusalem," she added.

The orphan spat out some dust again. Sand and more sand, all over this land. It was called the Holy Land, but he would have called it the forsaken land. The sick and suffering arrived from all over the world, hoping to find a cure for their bodies or for their souls. Here, they encountered war, mercenaries, bandits, vultures, heat, sand, and death. Particularly the last one, he thought.

Peter looked at the Italians—Polo's family and their escort of crossbowmen. They were well-equipped for war and highly-paid. The Genoese were one of the main suppliers of slaves from Romania and the northern lands to the sultanate. The most precious stock—the future Mamluk soldiers—were raised from these slaves. Even Peter knew that.

Captain Andrea Pelu, the leader of Polo's group, wasn't worried that his master was Venetian.

Peter was behind him on an old palfrey, as they rode in pairs. After they started to slope down to the city, the road was narrow and he saw many other pilgrims traveling on it.

"Thank you for last night," Pelu said to the orphan. Peter didn't know how to react. He nodded and smiled, but said nothing. Sir James and Owen laughed.

"What's so funny?" The Italian captain was puzzled by their response.

"It's normal these days to thank him," Owen said.

"These days Peter saves princes, assassins, knights—especially Scottish ones—ladies and, by accident, some Italians." The Welshman grinned. Everyone who was nearby and heard the joke did, too. Red Herring's timbre was unmistakable when he laughed.

"He isn't used to it yet." Owen continued, "When he adds a sultan's life to his belt, maybe he will learn how to respond." Even Ulf laughed this time. The Italians, too, although it wasn't clear whether they understood the Welshman's accent.

Peter blushed.

He looked down and tried to concentrate on guiding his horse. He felt proud to receive such an honor. He knew that in this group of hardened men and warriors, wasn't easy to get recognition. Every soldier tried, and everyone was ambitious and would do anything to be the most renowned one—just as, in a wolf pack, there could be only one leading wolf and the rest of the pyramid.

It seemed they were brothers in war—brethren Crusaders—even if Peter didn't understand the meaning of it. They were sword brothers who wanted to prove they were the best. And of course, to be distinguished as such, they needed a worthy opponent. A hero is not remembered if there is no worthy opponent to beat. They had not yet met the elite regiment of the sultan in open battle, the Mamluks. Peter was sure that they would.

They reached Jerusalem. Peter was near enough to see the traces of an ancient moat alongside the ruins of the outer wall, near the gate. It was about fourteen meters in width. It had been left by the previous dwellers and now stood covered by sand and dirt. Also visible were the remains of a barbican. The gate itself was enormous if a bit a dilapidated—built from limestone, the height of at least five men. And this was only the outer gate.

"Look at this," Red Herring said, pointing near the gate. "The wall forms a right angle near the passage leading to the main gate."

The orphan didn't understand.

"An attacker would have to change direction within the gate complex and thus expose the right side of his body, unprotected by his shield, to enemy fire, you see?" James said. "This is clever. Whoever built this knew his craft. Maybe the builder was a soldier, too? Only a man with experience of war, who had previously defended a fortress, could have built this." Herring's eyes were wide and his jaw dropped a bit.

"Edward hired such a builder," Hamo said.

The outer gate was protected by two towers. Once they must have been marvelous, but now they were in ruins.

As the gate's sentries approached them, Lady Isabella and the elder Polo rode ahead to provide their letters of safe conduct to the Saracen officers.

Peter and Owen watched the pair talking to the guards. One of the Mamluks said something to Isabella and the expression of her face became fierce. She was talking fast and looked like she scolded the guard. She turned her horse to the rest of the Crusaders.

"He said we must turn around and enter into the city via the west gate, where the Christians must enter." She said it with such irony, loud enough for all the men to hear her.

"Governor's order," Mr. Polo added.

"But he couldn't make me—me, the Lady of Beirut—walk an hour more just to enter it. Follow me," she said with delicacy, "behave yourselves and keep your weapons in your scabbards. You are allowed to enter only by my insistence. I gave my word that you would stay out of trouble. Am I clear?"

She was young, but knew how to act like royalty; her commanding voice was a little harsh.

"If someone disturbs the order in the city, there are heavy penalties. The Christians are the first to suffer and everyone has a grudge against them. You are warned." She turned her horse toward the gate.

Red Herring gave Hamo a stern look.

"You are warned. Stay out of trouble," James said.

"Why always me?" Hamo gave an innocent smile.

"Because you are handsome," Owen joked.

Peter noticed the guards had balked when they read Polo's documents, but the lady had interfered again and they also were allowed to enter.

The orphan wondered if they would be able to pass through, or if they would be caught by suspicious guards. His heart was working so hard that he thought everyone could hear the beating from inside his chest.

The Saracen officer slowly inspected all their dusty faces. After a moment, he waved them through.

"That was easy," Peter thought.

They passed the gate. Now what?

"Wow," James said.

Stairs descended toward the gate. They had lost the cart and Isabella's carriage in the sandstorm. Most of them were on horses, the others followed the riders on foot. Peter was glad they weren't on a wooden cart, because of the steps.

Red Herring and his men looked at the structure of the gate. They stared with eyes wide open as they passed under it. They looked at the fortification—or what was left of it. Even Peter admired the magnificent stones used to build it.

"The guards let us in easily," Isabella commented. "Sometimes they make me wait or let me out for more than an hour."

"We may be lucky today," Hamo said. As soon as they were through the gate, Isabella ordered them to lodge their horses in a nearby stable.

The Crusaders and Polo's men parted ways, wishing each other luck through the rest of their journeys.

"Be careful, you do not want your trip to last as Odysseus'," James said to the elder Polo. Peter reminded himself to ask Nickolas who this was, later.

Captain Pelu and his men followed the merchants toward the Governor's office and then to where their fate would be leading them.

"Where are they going?" Peter asked.

"They are on a mission to deliver a piece of the Holy Sepulcher to the Tartar king. They had papers from the Pope," Red Herring said, "Niccolò and Maffeo, father and uncle of the young Marco Polo."

Peter liked the lad. He was like him: young and impatient. The orphan envied them; they would see a different world. Peter wished them farewell, too.

Isabella showed them which road to follow, as it wasn't hard to understand where the Church of the Holy Sepulcher was or the Dome of the Rock. Peter thought it would be hard to find what they needed. But not the Polos.

Lady Isabella didn't hurry. She sent her followers—the valet, the lady-in-waiting, and the baby them to arrange for lodging for the night and stayed with Githa to observe the Englishmen's next move.

Nickolas bade Peter farewell and returned his leather bag with his book.

"We will meet again, Peter of Acre. Save one interesting story for me." He smiled at the future knight.

The orphan smiled back.

"To find the best physician, we must begin in the herb market. It is this way, along the southern road." Edward the Saracen said.

They followed him. A week before, he had seemed to be one of them. Instead, he was a spy and a traitor. Now, Peter hoped that he was on their side once more. He hoped the assassin wasn't leading them into a trap. He liked the Saracen. He seemed to like them, an ordinary man with an extraordinary profession—to kill men in the shadows. But a soldier's job was to kill on the battlefield, face-to-face with the enemy. Killing in the shadows was hard for the knights to accept.

The streets in Jerusalem were narrow and crowded, five meters at the widest, and paved. It would have been hard to ride an animal on them; he understood why Lady Isabella had insisted on leaving their horses in the stable.

Red Herring was behind the assassin, David, Hamo, and his men were by him, and Ulf, Owen and Peter were at the rear of their group. They moved like predators, their eyes focused, observing every detail that could save their lives. They were silent and they were determined to find their target. Isabella and Githa followed them.

"The streets are crowded. Damn." Sir James didn't like it. The stream of men flowed in every direction along the narrow streets, made up of all kinds of faces, colors, garments, cultures, and races. Peter had never seen so many different men in one place. How would they find their target among so many other faces?

They followed the assassin silently.

"We are walking toward the Street of David," Edward the Saracen said to them. After a few minutes on the road, they turned left and they were in an Arab market. Peter saw cheese, chickens, eggs, and birds placed for sale.

"Syrian exchange," the Saracen said and approached a small, two-story building with open, wooden windows on the first story.

A man with a turban and a chubby face was trying to sell his birds. Surrounding his business were other wooden and silk pavilions full of buyers and sellers. They talked loudly, arguing, smiling, and shaking hands. Peter felt a sharp smell of fish down the street. The trade flourished.

The assassin talked to the fat seller briefly and continued south.

"The man we are looking for is called Ibn al-Nafis. This merchant said he saw him in the Street of Herbs an hour ago."

"Where?" James asked.

"We need to go past the place that was once the Hospitaller

Quarters, along the main street. The Street of Herbs is the only venue in the city where herbs, fruits, and spices are sold, according to this merchant," Edward the Saracen said.

"We are close," Red Herring said. "Be careful," he warned his men.

"Careful?" Peter's mood was ironic; Owen had influenced him already.

"Leave the thinking and acting to the real men and knights." Hamo grinned at the orphan.

Lady Isabella watched and said nothing.

"Hey, don't waste your energy and strength in a boy's quarrel," Sir James said.

They continued. Peter noticed that almost all the streets were paved with great stones. The buildings had many stone vaults, pierced with many windows to allow the natural light through. His mind was absorbed in the city. He was in a dream, walking through the most famous place in the world.

They walked in silence and, after a few crossroads, they entered a little square with dozens of pavilions full of herbs, fruits, spices, and smells. Bearded men dressed in white robes were talking and arguing animatedly.

James and his men approached and Edward the Saracen once again asked questions about the mysterious physician, Ibn al-Nafis.

One of the merchants nodded and stood straighter, showing he recognized the name. The Saracen exchanged some words with him; the westerners didn't understand a single one because they talked fast. Ulf acted as their ears.

Peter wasn't sure what would follow. He thought they needed a backup plan, an escape plan or some strategy if everything went wrong. Peter noticed Hamo's cocky wink at him and his confident smile.

"Why are you so calm?" The orphan asked.

"Relax Peter, think, we are men looking for a physician, the best one. It's a normal endeavor," Hamo said.

But something bothered the orphan. He remembered Lady Isabela's comment when they entered. Yes, the way they had passed through the sentries outside the gate had been very easy. He had a strange feeling in his belly.

Peter looked around and listened to his surroundings. He could hear the sound of the street, people talking, some animals. He saw the pavilions and their merchants and goods. It was a well-stocked herb market, similar to those in Acre, although the prices were different. The men's faces around it were, too—less Mediterranean than in Acre, near the sea. But there were faces with unfamiliar features, who had gathered here from across the Holy Land, Egypt, Syria, and the Tartar kingdom. Bedouins, Arabs, Nubians, and many more whose names Peter didn't know. He looked at their faces. He saw many similarities, but many differences, too.

Suddenly, he noticed one familiar face.

He looked at the man to confirm it, and the man looked back. Rather than the relief he normally felt at seeing something familiar—particularly in a new place—he felt nervousness.

It was the merchant from Acre. The same one who was the assassin's contact. It was in this man's house that he had met Julian for the second time, with Red Herring and David.

It seemed that the merchant had been waiting for them. The thought scared him. It meant he knew they would be coming.

"It's a trap!" Peter shouted.

But it was too late. He heard the sound of breaking ceramic jugs. The whole square exploded. A cloud of smoke surrounded everyone and everything. Peter felt the sharp sweet taste in his mouth, turned his head in the blinding fog and something hit him hard. His body collapsed like a rag doll on the perfectly-paved Herb Street.

CHAPTER THIRTEEN

Holy Land, Tuesday, 21st June, in the year 1272 of the incarnation of Christ; Jerusalem

"Lad?"

He was in brutal pain. His head was going to explode. What had happened?

Peter wanted to sleep but the pain did not allow him. He wasn't supposed to be here. But where was he?

A girl passed him.

He turned his head, but she was gone. He was slow. Where was she? He saw something red, perhaps a scarf. He wasn't sure. It was dark and he mistrusted his vision. Was she real? Had it even been a girl? He wasn't sure. He didn't know where he was. His memories and thoughts were blurred.

He was sure about one thing. She smelled good.

He tried to clear his eyes but realized his hands were tied behind his back. He tried to clear the dust from his eyes using his left shoulder. He was sweaty and shirtless.

It smelled too good to be a prison. It was some soft, sweet smell, like a woman's perfume. Like Isabella's. Unless the Jerusalem's prisons smelled like that.

"Peter?"

Red Herring was near. His voice was a small relief to the orphan.

"How is your head?" he asked.

Peter shook his hair. He felt a little stunned and the attempt to move his neck and head brought him some pain;

nevertheless, he felt there wasn't any other wound or damage. Whatever had happened, he had missed the fun.

"Like an oak tree," he said.

"That's what you said the first time I met you," Red Herring said. The two of them smiled.

"I think I saw a girl when I woke up." The orphan's curiosity was stronger than his pain.

"She was checking your bandage. I wish she had checked mine," James said.

"Are you injured?" Peter asked.

"Not this time, but she makes me think about it." The orphan liked his Scottish humor.

"I thought I was dreaming. Where are we? What happened on the street?"

"I would guess that we are in the main tower of the citadel," James said.

The orphan tried to remember something—anything. They were in a small room with no beds or table. A small window gave them a view of the dancing night and stars. The Moon was bright as ever in the hot night.

They were on the floor, against the stone wall, with their hands tied up behind them. A many-colored carpet was on the floor, as well as several small pillows. There was a bottle with two ceramic cups in the middle of the room on a silver tray. The room was fairly narrow. The door was old and wooden but the orphan hadn't heard a squeaking sound when the girl had left the room.

"What is this place? Strange and cold," Peter said. "How did we get here?"

"What do you remember from the herb market?"

Peter told him that he had seen the merchant's face, the smoke, and darkness. Something hard had met his head.

"It was a trap, yes," Red Herring admitted. "A well-placed one. We should have predicted it, but we were naïve." He stopped for a moment. "They stormed at us, blinded us with ceramic smoke bombs that I just heard they exist and took us by surprise. There were flying knives, smoke, masked men in white robes, daggers—it was terrible. We had no chance to defend or to strike back." James shook his head. His wildly orange hair was matted, it looked darker from the sweat and was sticking to his skull. "I failed to foresee the ambush or to prevent it."

"Don't blame yourself," Peter said. "Who attacked us?"

"I guess we will find out soon," Red Herring said.

"They were waiting for us?"

"We were completely unprepared and overconfident. I did not expect this." The Scottish knight looked tired and helpless.

"Why did they attack us?" Peter looked at him.

James shrugged. "Damn them, we were in the center of a city, how dare they?"

"Where are the others?" Peter's voice was dry.

"In the smoke cloud, I saw nothing. Someone tried to stab me, but I was lucky. His blade slid on my mail shirt. But next, I received a blow that knocked me down. I could see Hamo lying unconscious next to me and you, too." James nodded toward the wall. "And I thought I heard the voices of Owen and David in the next room. But two of my men were killed, I think. O, Lord, accept their souls," Sir James said and stared at the Moon through the window."

"Lady Isabella? Ulf?"

"I lost them from my sight, but didn't hear a woman's scream, that's for sure." He said this slowly. Like Peter, he was only in pants. "Let's hope they are alive," James said. "I heard the attackers were vividly arguing about something. They mentioned 'Acre' and 'Crusaders' several times as they dragged me up the stairs. They didn't seem satisfied. I'm guessing someone escaped from their trap, but this may be wishful thinking. We can only wait now and see what happens."

"Look," Peter said as his eyes fixed the tray with a jug of water in the room.

"But we are still alive, aren't we?" James tried to lighten the mood. If their captors had wanted them dead, they wouldn't be here, Peter thought.

There were two oil lamps in the room, their lights dancing around in the faintly-blowing breeze.

"There is water in front of us, but we can't drink. Maybe it's a new form of torture," Peter said. James smiled then, though only a little.

"If it were Durham ale, I would find a way to drink it, ha," Red Herring said.

Peter grinned.

He was glad Red Herring was with him. He didn't think he could manage to be calm if he were alone.

"Why did they capture us?"

"This is a good question," Red Herring said.

Sooner or later, the truth always came to the surface. His mentor had always said this to teach him not to lie as a child. He had always been right.

The wooden door opened and a short guard entered, followed by a girl and two servants clad in white. The pleasant smell arrived again, stronger than ever. Who was she? Peter asked himself. He grew scared, but his curiosity also rose again like a storm, as he wanted to know who the man was and what he intended to do to them.

***

A man with a fierce face stared into the dark.

Two hundred steps from the citadel, he stood on the terrace of a two-story building, wrapped in a gray cloak. His face was hardened and his battle dress was dusty. He had recently arrived from the desert. He was dressed in expensive gear which only a few men in this realm could afford to possess.

He took a few steps to the parapet and focused his eyesight toward the main tower of the citadel. His right leg ached from time to time. He had fallen from his horse a few years before and broken it. Yet, he never showed any appearance of discomfort. His status didn't allow him to show any sign of weakness.

His right hand was on the hilt of his sword and his eyes stared into the dark streets. The Moon provided a ray of light. The night was in its prime. His cloak reached the ground—it was intended to conceal his garment.

The daily clamor of people buzzing was finished for the day and the sound of the night permeated the city. But he was expecting some activity that night.

The man's thoughts turned to the faded Crusade which had created waves of refugees. This wasn't a bad thing; with the right system of politics, this influx of people could be integrated and used as new labor. After the past years of war and devastation, the land was facing a serious manpower shortage. The refugees were an ideal replacement for the dead. The man smiled. Yes, the policy had to be correct, the law had to comply with the migration or the existing order would collapse.

Some moments later, a group of men approached the gate. These faces he knew well, and they made no attempt to hide them. They were well-known men, Mamluks dressed in lamellar armor and mantles. They greeted the guards and entered the citadel.

After a few heartbeats, he saw Christian knights walking to the main gate of the tower. They were using dark mantles to hide their battledress. But their gait and confidence couldn't be mistaken. Five of them were led by a man with blond hair, who seemed proud and didn't put his hood up to hide it.

"Interesting. What brings them to the citadel?" he thought.

Earlier, the observer had heard that there had been a massive turmoil in the herb market's square. Assassins had attacked some newcomers, left a few dead bodies, kidnapped the rest, and disappeared.

What was this about? Following the wave of his thought, he was surprised to understand from his spy that the assassins had withdrawn to the citadel. The citadel had become the residence of the assassins. It was curious. Most interesting was that the newcomers to Jerusalem were Christians and were looking for the personal physician of the sultan, Ibn al-Nafis.

He was also curious in recent days, after the news he received about the attempted assassination on Edward. He had decided to wait and see what happened. There was a game in the shadows these days and he was interested in revealing it. He scratched his chin while trying to remember where he knew this blond man from.

Yet, he wasn't pleased with what he saw. Westerners, assassins, and Mamluks, all in the citadel of Jerusalem. It wasn't news that would make the ruler happy.

And the last spice to the dish: another party appeared—a Tartar prince and four of his officers. Siraghan al-Tatari, who was the commander of Mongol horsemen, on service of the sultan. There had been a massive Mongol incursion twelve years before, and some of the horsemen had decided to stay on these lands with their families. The sultan spared them and allowed them to settle in return for their service.

How had he let it happen? Assassins, Mamluks, Christian knights, and now Mongols—the same who were allowed to live in these lands—were about to enter.

Well, this was news. He was eager to find out the subject of the meeting of the groups who entered the citadel. He doubted they were gathering to exchange some spices.

Twenty paces from the place he was watching, his gaze was attracted by another shadow.

The man saw him. The Wolf was alive.

Since this man was here, watching, just like himself, it wasn't good. Wherever this man went, death followed. This would jeopardize his agent inside the citadel.

"*Diyaab al-Sahra*," he said to himself.

He watched the lonely man, with anticipation in his eyes. The Desert Wolf was dressed in a ragged robe and dark hood, but his walk and presence couldn't be mistaken. He hadn't changed at all since their last meeting. Ulf walked with calmness toward the gate and after twenty paces he faced the guards.

It seemed as if he hadn't been invited to the party.

No one expected a single man to meddle into the assassin's business and to threaten their residence. The left guard raised his hand and tried to say something. Ulf grabbed his arm, pulled him close, and hit him with his forehead, pulling out a dagger with his right hand and flinging it into the neck of the right guard. He looked at the scared face of the first guard and slit his throat with his own knife. Everything happened so fast that the guards did not have a chance to call for reinforcement.

Ulf knelt down and searched the bodies, then raised from the fallen soldiers, throwing away his robe. He was dressed in leather vest armor, and his almost-white hair reached to his shoulders. The Wolf stopped for a moment and closed his eyes. It was like time was stopped—for him, for everyone. A moment later, he opened the door and entered.

The observer needed answers.

From his watching place, the cloaked man removed his hood and raised his hand, and the streets beneath him suddenly sprang to life.

***

Peter received a blow on his right cheek and fell to the ground.

It was the short man standing next to him who had struck him. Peter tried to think of something pleasant to forget the pain and the desperate situation they were in. He tried to remember Isabella's face. She was so beautiful.

The morning after Peter had rescued her in the Mamluk's camp in the middle of the sandstorm, she had kissed him on his forehead to thank him. It had been a kiss of gratitude, but he wanted more. Her image made his soul fly away from this dark place. Isabella made him want to live another day, to earn another kiss, or something more precious. His body was tired; he felt no desire to continue, but Isabella ... she could light a man's blood on fire.

The short man who was clad in white wanted them alive, but he wasn't sure anymore.

They were in a bigger room, now, probably the main hall of the building. The short man had had them taken here by guardsmen. He, James and the girl were here, as well as Hamo, Owen, and Edward the Saracen. Githa and Isabella were missing, as well as David and the other men.

The Christians were stripped of their possessions and tied, but Edward the assassin stood straight and his hands were free. On a high platform sat a man on what appeared to be a wooden throne. His face was dry and ugly. His white eyes showed nothing except emptiness. He was near his fifties, strong and tall, gray-bearded, and was dressed in rich garments. His right hand was bandaged. On either side of the wooden throne were chairs. Apparently, the host was waiting for more guests.

The hall was spacious. There were two doors, one from which Peter and Red Herring had been dragged through, and one on the opposite side. Sentries were stationed in all four corners, dressed in white robes, their faces covered with masks. They held long blades in scabbards and in the other hand, each man was holding a spear. The two doors each were guarded by four men dressed in the same fashion. The stone walls were lit by blazing torches and oil lamps, yet the light wasn't enough to look better at the host. In the middle of the room, the prisoners were gathered close to each other, on their knees.

"You are just in time," the host said and nodded toward Peter. "Is this the lad responsible for your failure?"

"Yes," the failed assassin said.

"What was written in the orders? To kill the English prince, and not to hesitate. But you hesitated." The man nodded to a guard standing behind Edward, who hit him with a wooden club on the backs of his legs and made him fall on the ground.

"Who are you?" Edward the Saracen asked, trying not to show his pain.

"Who am I? If you're working for Qussad you should know," the man on the throne said. "You are a disgrace just like your father, al-Rida. He was as weak and unreliable as his son is now. His seed was spoiled." He smiled. "Don't you recognize me? I am Shams al-Din, the son of the Najm al-Din, the Nonagenarian. Your father tried to steal my heritage, my lands, and my castles. You should know me well, al-Rida."

Peter tried not to miss a word from the conservation. The old man called Edward the Saracen with another name, al-Rida.

"Maybe you are wondering why you are here. Well, I have prepared a little surprise for you all." A small smirk crossed his face.

This wasn't going to be good.

A servant entered the room and whispered something in Shams al-Din's ear.

"It's about time," the host said.

***

Ulf knelt down and examined the bodies of the two sentries, quickly and methodically. He had seen their clothing before. He found a small tattoo on the left shoulder of each man. A mark, drawn in black ink, which indicated that they were owned by Shams al-Din. They belonged to a faction of assassins, one of the last to survive. Why had their members attacked Red Herring's men in the market? Who had hired them?

He didn't care.

He wasn't curious, like James or Peter. He now lived only to deliver his revenge. For him, it was crystal clear: someone had sent Mamluks to kill him. Someone had sent an assassin to kill a Christian prince. Someone had attacked them in the center of Jerusalem. Only one man had such power and could organize this: Sultan Baibars.

Sultan or not, all who were involved would die. His beloved one—the only light in his life—was dead. Someone would pay.

He had made a deal with the sultan; no one was to bother him, his family, or his manor. The Mamluks had broken this promise. So be it.

Earlier, in the market, he had spotted the trap, but he could tell that the ambush's purpose wasn't to kill them. His trained eye recognized the hidden assassins. He was a little surprised that Peter had also managed somehow to discover the trap. He was amazed by the young man, who reminded him of himself as a youth. He was very much like him—eager, determined, brave, as well as stupid and naïve, just like Ulf had been when he was younger. He shook his head. The memories from his past made him sad.

Now he must be focused. He had a job to do—a bloody one.

Earlier in the day, he had managed to escape the herb

market attack. No one had noticed him as he jumped aside and climbed through the turmoil to the nearby roof while hiding his face and eyes, protecting them from the smoke. He used the ragged robe to protect his breath. He traced the assassins to their lair and waited for the arrival of the night. He had followed them to this place. It was the citadel, with its towers and strong walls. The rest of the fellowship was held there.

The Tower of David stood proud. It was ancient and in need of some reconstruction and repair, but still, it was massive and stood solid and impregnable, like a single stone from the base up. He understood that within it were five iron gates, 200 steps leading to the summit, and a good supply of water. It was difficult to take, and once it had formed the main defense of the city. Even now, it was carefully guarded, and no one was allowed to enter except under supervision.

The Tower of David also encompassed the royal lodgings, the state prison, and the record office, among other functions. The offices within oversaw the entrance of merchants into Jerusalem and collected dues levied on the entry of goods into the city.

He estimated that a garrison of 15 to 20 men was sufficient to guard it but he expected more since so many interesting visiting figures had arrived that night.

A job without sweat, his old mentor would say. Ulf smiled at this thought. The old warrior, whose task had been to train him, had had a strange sense of humor. Red Herring reminded him of it.

Many guards awaited him; they would be prepared when he announced his presence. He wasn't there to save his companions, but to kill everyone else. He didn't care about Red Herring and his men; he had sworn an oath to the lady from Castile, nothing more. He could find the physician alone and bring him to the city of Acre, although he doubted Lord Edward would still be alive. He doubted also that the failed assassin had told James who the physician was: Ibn al-Nafis, the personal doctor of Sultan Baibars. If this fact had been mentioned earlier, they would not be in this situation. Still, he understood the assassin's motives; he wanted a way out and only the belief that the future king of England had a chance to survive could save him. Lady Eleanor was a woman who loved her other half.

As Ulf had loved his. He respected that. She had managed to secure his own oath from him and bound him to her for this very reason.

He shouldn't spare a thought for Peter, but he felt some regret about the orphan. The lad had saved his life in the desert storm, and he didn't like to be obliged to anyone. And Githa, she was a fighter but the assassins had captured her, too. She had been kind to him. She was a proper widow who had chosen the path of the order of the Hospital. He was touched by her fate and couldn't let her be drawn into the mess the Crusaders had put them into.

The Crusaders. Why were they always involved? Most of them lacked knowledge about the situation in these lands. After a year or two in the Holy Land, they were able to learn, but most of them died or left for home before then. Brave and naïve to stupidity.

Fools.

Ulf didn't care for them and he wasn't the man to teach them or to enlighten them. He saw the world in a different way. A wise man, Avicenna, had once said that the world was divided into men who had wit but no religion, and men who had religion but no wit. Baibars had told him this on a hunting mission, not for hinds, but for assassins. And this man was so right.

He also knew that he must not depend too much on anyone in this world; even your own shadow left you when you were in darkness. He tried to smile. He had suffered from this. For this reason, he had used to live alone, to survive and fight alone.

Now, he would seek answers the way he knew, the way he was trained to. He was even more determined to finish it, now. The killing was easy; accepting the answers was hard.

The day before, Peter had asked him why he liked to use this type of weapon.

"Why the axe? Because of the fear?" Peter had asked.

"You're starting to learn, lad," Ulf said. "The weapon itself doesn't matter. This piece of iron and wood is just a tool in a man's hands. The real weapon, lad, is the man. He is the one who swings the sword or axe or lance, with the single thought of delivering death. But the axe delivers death in a terrifying way. Fear is a strong assistant."

He gave the orphan some time to think. After a moment, Peter nodded to thank him for the answer. The lad told him that only a few men in his life had spared the time to answer his questions; most men had beaten him or given him orders.

Ulf looked at the black-haired young man as they rode toward Jerusalem and talked about fear.

"How I can be like you? To fight better and not be afraid of the enemy?" Peter asked.

"Fear."

"Fear?" The orphan's eyes opened wide.

"Fear drives us forward," Ulf said. "The fear of death makes you want to survive, the fear of embarrassment makes you perform better, the fear of losing something—it doesn't matter what—makes you defend it. It makes you stronger. It makes time move slowly, so you can react faster and win." He noticed that Peter was starting to understand.

"To win the fight," he continued, "fear is a natural motivator. It can make you fearless, but first, you need to accept it. Fear makes you battle in new ways. Sometimes it is an assistant; sometimes it is the strongest motivator. But beware; you need to understand that it is a short-term motivator."

"Short-term?" Peter asked.

"After you survive your first fight, you are experienced. The fear is no longer the same."

The Desert Wolf looked harshly at the lad.

"It's like riding. The first time is hard; it's strange and you felt uncomfortable. Now, on the back of your horse, you are trying hard not to fall. But after a week, the feeling isn't the same. I guarantee you that."

"You want to bet?" Peter grinned.

They placed a bet. Red Herring witnessed it and a green

apple was the prize.

"And how does one accept fear?" Peter asked.

"Tomorrow, lad. You can't learn all at once."

The orphan distracted him from thoughts of his dead wife. Now, he would go to the tower to find him. After all, Peter had saved his life during the storm.

He closed his eyes for a moment.

Every time he did this, he saw her image, the smile she had brought to him, and the meaning of life. She smiled at him and whispered in his mind a song:

Here again, you are on the road again
Here you go … you must start over again
Here you go … draw your sword again
Here you go …

Ulf opened his eyes. His eyes were full of tears. He was ready. He looked at the Moon, smiled at her, then pushed the dead bodies of the sentries aside. Now was the time to pay them a visit. He had never visited this tower before.

Ulf smiled. The surprise was on his side. His thirst for blood needed to be satisfied, and he was ready. He gripped the handle of the axe till his knuckles turned white and entered through the wooden door. It was a time for work.

***

A man, followed by four guards, entered the room, and the host saluted the Mamluks. The orphan raised his head.

He knew this face. It was the same man at whom Peter had thrown a spear at the Mamluk's camp.

Edward the Saracen or al-Rida, as the host called him froze looking at the newly arrived amir, as did the rest of the fellowship, or what was left of it. Peter had forgotten his pain.

The golden amir exchanged some words with their host. Then he turned his face to the captives in the center of the room.

The orphan could hear his own heart beating.

The bareheaded Mamluk looked at the prisoners' eyes, one by one, turning to Peter last. The tall amir was in no hurry as he examined the lad's face. Did he recognize Peter? The thought made him prickle with fear. He had almost killed this man, denying him the Wolf's head on a platter, and now Peter faced the Mamluk.

But it had been night, hadn't it? The orphan calmed himself down. He hoped the darkness and the yellowish sandstorm had prevented the amir from seeing his attacker's face.

Yet the eyes of the Mamluk were like fiery arrows fired in the night. There was a prolonged silence in the room. The amir was tall and skinny; his battle dress looked expensive, yet Peter could see where his blow had done a little damage and managed to scratch the lamellar armor with golden decoration. The orphan's eyes widened at the sight of this, and the Mamluk caught his gaze at the same moment.

Finally, the amir turned his gaze away.

"What was so important that you had to go out in this storm, Berrat, my son?" the host asked. But the confident Mamluk didn't say a thing, only grinned in response and sat on one of the wooden chairs. The four bodyguards stood behind Berrat. A servant placed a little table near him and another brought him something to drink and a bowl of fruit, placing them on the table.

"How many assassins do you have in the citadel with you?" Berrat asked.

"Enough," Shams al-Din said. "Why?"

"Sultan Baibars will soon arrive at the outskirts of the city with his royal guards."

Shams al-Din narrowed his eyebrows and touched his beard.

"Don't worry my son," the host said.

Peter reassured his breath, though he was still nervous.

They were caught again. It seemed that Shams al-Din and Berrat worked together. But where was Isabella? Was she alive? His mind and heart were battling each other. This feeling was new for him, and he was eager to drink from this cup. He wanted to taste everything that life offered to him—no less, no more. But he needed to be stronger; the game wasn't over yet. And even the pain and the hopeless situation mustn't be given a chance to crush his desire to live. Peter heard that the door opened with a squeak.

Julian walked into the room.

The young man stared at the floor. His head was pulsating, but not from pain. His heart rate was high. He thought the sound of his breathing was filling the room and would betray his emotions. He wanted to hide, but there wasn't any place for that. He felt exposed, unprotected. He hoped, childishly, that his antagonist would miss him in the crowd.

The blond, western mercenary walked to the host and exchanged greetings. What was he doing here?

Shams al-Din raised his hand and pointed to the hostages, explaining something to the dark knight. Julian's eyes met Peter's. Neither one retreated from the battle of gazes.

Julian left the throne platform and walked toward Peter.

When the knight was just a step away from him, he ducked a little and smiled at the lad. His breath was rotten and his teeth were yellowish. The smile wasn't pleasant; it was the smile of a hunter who had caught his prey—triumphant.

Roger of Sicily was behind him, and some sergeants whose faces were hard to see from his vantage in the dim light.

"We meet again, street dog," Julian said. "And now, there is no place to run." He raised his hand and tapped Peter's cheek a few times, like a lord. "You are mine."

One of the sergeants behind Julian was familiar to the lad.

"Traitor!" Sir James' face was furious.

David. No!

"Traitor," the Scot shouted again, "I will rip your heart out." Red Herring forced himself to rise and lunged toward the short sergeant.

"Scum!" The Scottish knight's mouth was full of rage. His face was reddish and he seemed determined to reach David. James was a strong man and he reached the traitor and headbutted him in the face. The guards in the room reacted with lightning speed. They managed to hold Red Herring and drag him down. Four men were needed to tame him. Screams, shouts, and insults were flying.

"Your time is up, old man," David said and spat some blood from the blow.

David's blade gleamed in the air as he prepared to strike his former master, mentor, and guardian.

Peter observed all this with surprise. He squatted and jumped, aiming his head and shoulder straight forward to the group of fighting men. He surprised David and the guards from behind and managed to divert the blow of the traitor.

But not enough. As he fell, he saw the blade reach the Scot, making a cut on his chest.

Blood splattered. Peter's face was covered in blood. Someone kicked him from behind, another hit him on the head. He instinctively tried to protect his head and eyes with his hands, but it wasn't possible because of the ropes. He tried to look at James.

"Behave yourself, gentlemen," the host said.

The guards separated the men.

The blow that James had received from David didn't look bad, but it would be fatal if the wound were not treated. The Scot didn't show any signs of pain; he was focused on the traitor. James couldn't accept that the dog that he had fed had bitten his hand.

Red Herring was held by six guards now, and his anger slowly evaporated. He had enormous strength, but the odds weren't on his side. Peter felt sorry for him.

"I am Shams al-Din, and I do not allow such behavior in my presence." The host's dark voice was harsh. As he spoke, every muscle on his face vibrated; he seemed to be trying hard to restrain his emotions.

Edward the Saracen's eyes were fixed on the host. Peter was sure now that the spy recognized the man. But from where? He hoped to discover it; he didn't want to miss such a story. Nickolas would have appreciated it, Peter thought, trying to smile. His old mentor had said that every smile was the enemy of the fear. But the pain inflicted on his body was hard to smile through.

Another party had arrived.

The cracking sound of the door pulled Peter from his thoughts. He shook his head and tried to focus again. The pain made him wrinkle his face, but he wanted to view the newcomers, who added to the tension in the room.

He had never seen these men before. They all had tiny thin eyes, round faces with red blushed cheeks and small chins. Their eyes were dark brown, but their skin was like the rest.

Tartars. But they looked more like Mamluks wearing the same outfit. The man who was leading them saluted Shams al-Din and nodded to the rest of the guests. The orphan became more curious despite the fear thriving inside his heart.

"Amir Siraghan al-Tatari, you are welcome," Berrat said.

Assassins, a Mamluk lord, a Templar Knight and a Tartar lord gathered in one place. Why? And their prey was on the table.

"We are dinner for these vultures," decided Peter. They looked like they worked together, or had conspired together.

This did not look good.

A few guards pushed him to sit next to James. He observed the pain and the anger in his friend's eyes. No one was helping him. Red Herring was in trouble, as was the rest of the fellowship.

Peter realized that they were doomed. And he just had started a new chapter of his life. The story of himself as Peter Longsword. Untold, but true.

"Don't worry, lad. Everything will be all right. I want to erase this traitor's expression from his face," James said, nodding toward David. "I know that God will give me a chance. Life always gives you a second chance, sooner or later."

James smiled. It was a bloody smile, and painful, but honest. The guests were talking about something, arguing, but Peter and the Scottish knight weren't listening to them.

"Lad," he coughed, "back in my homeland, there is a place ...." He closed his eyes as if trying to visualize his memories. "There is a castle, the Castle of Durham. It has never been conquered. It's massive, old Norman stones stand today on the peninsula of Durham, on the river bank."

Sir James opened his eyes. "I wish to see it again."

Peter thought for a moment. He felt pity for him. Home, sweet home. At least the Scot had a home to remember and longed to see again. The young man envied him for that.

"I want," Red Herring continued, "to show you this castle." He spoke slowly. "To show you the green pastures, the river, the hills, and the eagles."

Peter's heartbeat was accelerating again.

"My land ... you would love it," the knight said.

"Don't talk …."

"I am sure of it." James stopped.

The two of them somehow managed to be on these far away green pastures back in Herring's home. They weren't in the hands of the assassins, in their base of the citadel. They were free for a moment.

But something brought Peter back to the present.

Silence.

The orphan looked around. There was something strange. Everyone was staring at him. Apparently, he was the problem of them all. He started slowly to realize.

Such men in one place could only be united by a fearful enemy. Who was so violent, who could unite these men and to force them to act together? Who was so powerful as to make them bind their strengths and to use all their imagination to organize a vengeful plot?

Lord Edward was a pawn in this game, Peter thought. The English prince was in the right place at the right time for the plotters. They didn't give a coin about him. Not the Tartars, not the Mamluks, not the assassins—what they would care about a Christian prince stirring up trouble on their playground? What about the Templars?

Peter's mind woke up and began to run at full speed. "So, who was these men's target?"

He could only think of one man who was powerful enough to unite these different groups of people against himself.

Baibars, the Sultan of Egypt and Syria. The Lion of Egypt, some called him. And so he was. What a rise in power this man had experienced—once a slave from the distant land of

Kipchaq, now the most powerful man in these lands. Some called him a Scourge for the Crusaders, others called him Tartar Destroyer and Sultan Slayer.

He was the enemy. These men had chosen their target well. The real man is shown by his enemies, his old mentor used to say.

Peter smiled. From the beginning of this adventure, he had thought there was some strange plot to kill Edward, the Crown Prince of England. But this raised more questions than answers.

Who would want to kill a departing Crusader? His prudence and wisdom in war affairs and his bravery had earned him a reputation. Yet, why would anyone breach a recently-signed peace agreement? Baibars would not risk a new open war. The sultan himself had agreed to this peace between Crusaders and Mamluks. Sultan Baibars wanted to secure his rear after he was about to face a new threat to his realm.

A new Tartar invasion. They had tried twelve years ago. Peter was a child, but he had heard of it and how the Mamluks had won the decisive battle. They arrived last year with an insufficient army but soon withdrew. There was a rumor that they would try again to conquer this realm.

"But ...." he continued to unleash his thoughts. Edward was a bonus, an instrument to lure the real target out. But how? The men in this room all had something in common. They had the same enemy, the same man. Who was the real threat? There was only one man who could unite this party.

Sultan Baibars.

Now, after observing the men invited to this tower, his mind rejected all irrelevant questions and answers.

They feared Baibars. They were threatened by him because he had crushed them, one by one. Eventually, he would drive them out from his dominion. Piece by piece.

Baibars was a determined man, one of a kind. His reputation stretched beyond his own realm.

Peter couldn't believe such a man existed. Listening to stories about him, he felt the sultan was unreal. To force all kinds of men to join forces against him—Christians, Muslims, pagans, even assassins—he must be a real danger.

So, Baibars was their plan. He was the reason they were here right now.

But what was the plotters' plan to lure Baibars alone?

Sweat beaded on the orphan's face. No one would want eyewitnesses who could reveal a plot against the sultan and the English prince.

What about the attack on Ulf's manor? They had intended to remove the one threat to their plan, the only one in these lands who wasn't involved in politics or ambitious but was able to destroy them all: the Desert Wolf.

The Templars and the assassins had taken care of the leader of the Crusaders, the only one who could unite the Latin lords and manage a combined attack on the sultanate. They delivered the assassination order and tried to compromise the intelligence service created by Baibars, using Edward the Saracen. By assassinating Edward, the Templars would ignite the Holy war again and show their loyalty to the plotters. Yet, they would accuse the sultan and his network of spies. Brilliant.

The Mamluks from the north had had to kill the Wolf. A fast strike to weaken Baibars' position. An interesting coincidence was the presence of James that night. But who had made sure the Scottish knight would be there?

The Tartars' role wasn't hard to accept. They were the main threat and they would organize incursion, he thought. They had tried last year and failed.

So, now all they were renegades. And now was the time to strike again. The Tartars would be the main striking force, the orphan guessed.

His mood rapidly changed. Sometimes it wasn't fun to have an illumination. They would all be killed, that much was sure. Enemies' eyes were on him. Could they guess what his thoughts were? Peter cursed and closed his eyes.

***

"You there," Shams al-Din said, looking at Peter. "You were not supposed to be there that night. You ruined our plan." He walked closer to the orphan. "We were preparing this plan for over a year."

He approached the prisoners. "You should have stayed on the street with the other homeless dogs, where you belonged. Mongrel!" Shams al-Din said, stooping down to see the orphan's eyes.

"Mongrel, indeed," Julian smiled and said. "Your father, Longsword, was from a bastard line; your mother was a whore. And you? A mongrel, a street urchin from Acre. Peter Longsword—once a great name, now a label for a dirty cur."

Shams al-Din rose and turned his back on Peter.

"It was a brilliant plan, to assassinate this irritating Englishman—Longshanks, as you call him." He smiled. "Then, our friends, the Templars, would help the assassin to leave the city. No trace, no eyewitnesses, a simple and brave deed."

"Is that your plan? To threaten the recently signed peace?" James asked.

"With the help of our friends, the Templars, who would attack a few villages looking for revenge, we would manage to force the sultan to come to our trap."

"Traitorous bastards," James said toward Julian. "Why?"

"Imagine what this would cause in our Christian world, a future king losing his life. A new wave of future pilgrims, Crusaders and donations to our order and cause," Julian said.

"Yes," Shams al-Din said, turning theatrically to James, "everyone would suspect only one agent for such a mission." Shams al-Din's eyes were filled with passion. "Piece by piece, we tried to overtake the sultan's Qussad network." He turned his face to a man in a corner of the room. "Thanks to him," he said, nodding to the familiar face. It was the merchant from Acre.

"He managed somehow to discover one of the sultan's spies," Shams al-Din said and pointed to the failed assassin. "He was perfect for the job, an heir of a once-great assassin leader, now seeking redemption for his father's sins by working for the sultan's spy network. What more could I want than to ruin the reputation of the family responsible for the death of my father? Fate smiled on us."

"Who, the merchant of Acre?" James asked. Edward the Saracen's face became darker.

"Yes, our spy, the merchant from Acre, contacted Julian," Shams al-Din said. "The world is a strange place, you know. Once Sir Julian was the target of our spy; now we all play in the same team."

The host laughed.

Suddenly, his mood changed, like a hurricane. He turned and struck Peter's cheek with such ferocity that the lad's head was tossed aside.

"You ruined all of that!"

He turned to Edward the Saracen, or, as he called him, al-Rida.

"You are a disgrace to your kin and now you are a true failure." Shams al-Din looked in the eyes of the failed assassin and smiled. "And that's even better. Now you know why this is happening to you and you will die screaming, knowing your entire life has been ruined and that you will leave no legacy, no trace of your existence."

A tense atmosphere was in the room, carefully managed by the host.

"And you ...." He turned his attention to James. "I want to know how you got there—the Wolf's manor. Who told you about it?"

Now, Shams al-Din was furious. He kicked the wounded knight in the chest and his boot became bloodstained. James writhed in pain, as he tried to stand but the guards grabbed him and pushed him to the floor.

"Why you wanted to kill the Wolf?" James asked.

"He is the only man who would be a threat to us and our plan—" He turned to the Mamluk lord. "Your job was to eliminate him, Berrat."

"The Scottish knight surprised the men I sent."

"Yes, but how did the Crusaders learn of the plan?" Julian asked.

"This we must find out," Berrat said.

"Is it important now?" Shams al-Din calmed a little. "Even in these circumstances, events turned in our favor."

"How is that?" Julian asked.

"Don't you see?" Shams al-Din smiled.

"Are you thinking what I'm thinking?" The bareheaded Mamluk looked to the host of the party.

"Exactly; we have them now." Shams al-Din pointed to the prisoners. "Prince Edward's best men." He started to walk around and a big smile spread across his face.

"Their prince is dying. James's men will unleash their anger and with vengeful minds, they will kill in a search for revenge. They will ride to unleash terror, chasing refugees, killing common men ... These dirty barbarians from the west." Shams al-Din said.

"We will dispatch the news to the sultan. We have to be nearby to come to his aid and deliver justice." Berrat added.

Shams al-Din face twitched with pleasure. "Justice for all."

He looked at the other conspirators. "We will welcome Baibars, the Lion of Egypt and we will ambush him. Here is your part, Sir Julian, Amir Siraghan al-Tatari," he said, "You and your horsemen must be hidden. When he falls into our trap, you have to cut off Baibars' escape route."

"Now we need to find a suitable place for an ambush," Berrat said.

"So, your miserable lives will last a little longer than we expected," Shams al-Din said, laughing while he watched the prisoners. Then turned his attention to the person he hated so passionately: Edward the Saracen. "But you, what do you have to lose? Yes, I think that when the sultan finds that you sided with the Christians, your fall will be complete." He ducked to look into al-Rida's eyes. "You are mine now, and your life's song is over."

He rose again, sat on his wooden throne, and ordered for someone to fetch him something to drink.

The Mamluk leader said, "We must act fast, but where?"

"What is the meaning of life if we are always in a hurry?" He twisted his head to the other conspirators. "Bring the women."

"What about the man called the Desert Wolf?" Siraghan al-Tatari asked, speaking for the first time since his arrival.

"Don't worry about him. He wouldn't risk anything to save these men. He is somewhere in Jerusalem and soon my agents will find him," Berrat answered.

"How can you be so sure?"

"No, but I know him; I fought side-by-side with him. Leave him to me. He is my responsibility."

"You failed to kill the Wolf, Berrat, my son," Shams al-Din said. Then he pointed a finger at Peter and Edward the Saracen. "Sir Julian, you failed too. Both of you failed me."

Julian tried to say something, but the host waved his hand to quiet him.

"Please do not compare me with the Templar Knight," Berrat said.

"We will see. Do you know where the Wolf is?"

"He will show himself soon."

"Are you sure?" Shams al-Din smiled at that. "Is he so stupid as to attack us here? There are many guards here, in the heart of Jerusalem,"

"I underestimated him once. Do not make the same mistake." Berrat said. "He is very determined, like an unleashed hound from hell. Next time, we must be prepared."

"I like your comparison," Shams al-Din said with mockery. "Who is he?"

"He was the man who helped us when we took your father's castle."

A strange silence filled the room for a moment.

"Why you didn't tell me that before?" The mood of the host changed again.

"I didn't want your emotions to interfere with our plan." Berrat smiled. "After all, you will get your revenge soon enough."

"Let's hope so," the host looked at the Mamluk

"Springs of Goliath," Berrat said.

"What?" Shams al-Din said.

"The place is perfect for an ambush," the Mamluk said, smiling. "Baibars knows it and he will not suspect anything."

"Let's hope you are right. We will wait for the sultan's arrival and we will be ready." The assassin leader smiled.

"Sir Julian will arrive with his Templars, as well as the Tartars. And the trap is set, but we must hurry." Berrat said.

"We have the whole evening before us. Now let's drink for our future," Shams al-Din said.

***

The conspirators started to discuss some matters but Peter hardly heard their words; they talked silently. The second door opened.

A scantily-dressed slave girl arrived with drinks and fruit for the guests. The fresh air from the windows made her shiver.

Lady Isabella and Githa were delivered by a handful of guards who followed them.

Peter's heart sank. He had hoped the women had managed to escape in the turmoil at the herb market. But no, fate was cruel.

The situation looked bad. Peter swore silently.

The young man felt extraordinarily tired. His shoulders shivered. His eyes couldn't stay focused while he laid on the floor. Now everything was hurting him; he felt the pain from the hits he received in Acre and the scar on his face. His heart cried for his mentor. Although his body was tired, however, his soul was not. Peter was positive that somehow, they would manage to survive this. Yet, he felt almost ready to surrender, not to his enemies, but to the fatigue.

Peter was near Red Herring. He looked at his friend's eyes and smelled the blood.

Suddenly, he heard something.

Shouts.

What was happening?

There were shouts again.

Everyone was alert: the guests, the guards, and even the prisoners.

Something was happening downstairs.

A man entered and he interrupted the host and his guests as they drank. He shouted something. Peter didn't hear most of the part. Shams al-Din and his guests talked quickly and angrily. More and more guards arrived from the door through which Peter and James had entered. They were dispatched to investigate what was going on.

They seemed to be under attack. Peter wondered who would want to attack this strongly-fortified citadel. Perhaps the sultan, but this was his own property. It didn't make sense. No.

Diyaab al-Sahra. The Desert Wolf.

Why the hell he would risk his own safety to help them?

Peter looked around, realizing that he hadn't come for them. He grinned at his naivety. What on earth would bring the Wolf here? His humanity or altruism? The young man's heart smiled.

The prey. Wolf and his prey. Peter observed the faces in the room. It was full of traitors, conspirators, murderers, and evil whisperers whom he suspected had a hand in killing Ulf's beloved one. He hadn't come for Peter and the rest, but for his revenge.

The orphan was sure this man had some humanity left in his heart. He had noticed earlier how he had looked at the baby. There had to be something left in his heart.

Or not.

He acknowledged the fact that, to do what must be done, a man must be brutal and heartless.

"We must run!" Berrat shouted.

"Why? Are you insane? Why should I run from the citadel? Even if the sultan were coming, I would not."

"But you should be running." Berrat grinned.

"Explain my ignorance," Shams al-Din demanded.

"*Diyaab al-Sahra* is downstairs; soon he will be here. When he decides to appear, he is prepared. In a narrow place with tunnels, staircases, and rooms, no one can beat him. The numbers didn't matter. If he has decided to come here to salute you, believe me: no one can stop him."

"How we will stop him?" The eyes of the Shams al-Din were dancing around and panic showed on his face.

"We must retreat now! The only way to beat this beast is on open ground. Then the numbers will be our advantage," Berrat said.

Screams echoed from below—a clash of blades, a scraping on the walls, and cries arose before dying. The terrifying thing was that no one could see what was happening downstairs, but they could imagine by the sounds they heard.

Peter smiled; he saw some hope in the night.

"Sir Julian, please send my regards to your master and tell him about the new plan. Now go, but use the other exit," Shams al-Din said.

The orphan's ears were alert. There was another exit. And what was the new plan?

"What about these rats?" The blond knight's gaze was pointed to the captives.

"We will take care of them, now go." Shams al-Din turned to the Mamluk amir. "You should, too."

"What about you?"

"I'm right after you," There was a little hesitation in Shams al-Din's face.

Terror and darkness were singing from below. Peter heard some screams. Everyone's ears were on alert. Something bad was happening. Someone was dying painfully. And someone was coming.

Only one man could bring so much terror and fear in the conspirators' eyes. He was climbing the stairs of the tower.

The new screams made the host turn around. His eyes looked scared.

"We will meet as we planned." The Mamluk looked at the Tartar leader and nodded to him, saying, "Follow me."

The guests snuck away like a morning mist. The host shouted orders in his language. More soldiers arrived and they obeyed, heading toward the violence downstairs.

Shams al-Din turned his attention to the tied men in the center of the room.

The screams and the darkness were increasing. The orphan could hear men's flesh and armor being pierced, bones breaking, and souls departing their bodies. The sound of killing was nearing the room.

"Our plan will succeed. Even without you." Shams al-Din grinned, gave a signal, and four men surrounded Edward the

Saracen, put a bag over his head, and dragged him toward the exit. He tried to free himself from their grip but failed.

"Take the ladies and kill the rest!" the host commanded and left the room.

The orphan knew he must find what was left of his strength if he wanted to survive. Although he was tired, he knew he had to try harder.

He closed his eyes for a moment and took a deep breath. After a moment, Peter's eyes were focused on his target. He managed to look at Hamo and hoped the knight had the same idea as him. He blinked and held his breath. Everything in his body gave him pain. But the determination in his heart and soul gave him hope.

In that moment, he turned from captive to predator.

Just then, Peter heard two massive blows from an axe on the door, and then the room exploded.

The wooden door was in pieces. A few guards were thrown backward as Peter saw the flying darts from the corridor pierced them. A smoke appeared as the Desert Wolf arrived. He was covered in blood from head to toe.

He looked calm as he stepped over a dead body and entered the room. The smoke ceramic bomb he had used caused havoc, clouds of smoke and red mist, and everyone in the room froze, providing a distraction for Peter, who lunged forward and hammered his fists at the nearest guard, who was dragging Edward the Saracen. He surprised the soldier, as most of the people in the room were staring at the door. The orphan managed to put his target down, using his head and shoulder. Edward the Saracen lost his balance, too, and hit his head on the floor.

The remaining guards near the entrance attacked the Wolf. Yet, his reputation brought fear into their hearts, as Peter could see on their faces and the way they stepped slowly. The short man dressed in white who had previously struck Peter and his four followers who were standing around Shams al-Din didn't move. The host pointed to the prisoners and his personal guards naked their swords and walked toward Peter.

Hamo, Owen, and the rest tried to push the two guards

who were near them, too, while Shams al-Din's personal guards advanced toward the orphan and Edward the Saracen.

Peter tried to stand on his feet. His hands were still tied behind him; he had no armor or weapons, except his heart and mind. Yet, he remembered Wolf's words about the weapons, that the real weapon wasn't the iron or the wooden piece in a man's hand, but the man himself. This was the real danger; the man was the real tool of delivering death. He smiled, realizing what the Wolf's words meant, and his smile was caught by the approaching enemy. The guards stopped for a second. They were confused by the strange joy in the face of this unknown man from Acre. This little moment gave him hope. He noticed a metal jug near him and kicked it hard toward the attackers.

The object hit the forehead of the short man clad in white. His neck tilted backward, and he fell like a tree cut down with an axe.

The rest of his men stopped for a moment, looked at the motionless body of their officer and then to the orphan who guarded their target, the assassin.

The orphan wasn't looking at them but was trying to release his hands. To his surprise, the rope was cut from behind. He smelled the perfume. He turned his face and saw the girl.

She gave him a fruit knife.

Time slowed around Peter again, as he turned to the next enemy who advanced toward him. He ducked a stroke meant to hack his neck and stepped to the left, while he stabbed the man in his armpit with his right hand. The fruit knife was a little, one-edged blade designed for kitchen work, but a deadly tool in the young man's hand. The Saracen cried out, Peter stepped close, grabbed the attacker's sword palm, and stuck the knife in his neck. The blood from the dying man made a reddish fountain and almost blinded the orphan.

He pushed the dead man toward the second attacker who tried to avoid it but stumbled and fell on Peter's feet. The black-haired young man kicked the fallen guard's head and faced the other attackers. The other two men stopped again, they were confused, and their target was armed. Regardless of the smoke, most of the candles gave the fighting men enough light to see each other.

Peter stepped closer to Isabella and pushed her behind him, too. Githa took a sword from a dead guard and stood beside Peter. He was covered with blood and sweat but he was ready for battle, as he took the sword from the fallen guard. He acted as a shield between Isabella and the attackers. His heart was full of determination and vengeful fire.

The girl had freed Hamo and he had knocked out one of the guards. Owen was already armed with a spear from a dead sentry and he thrust it into another guard. Sir James kicked one Saracen, despite his wound. There was a real battlefield in the room; everyone was fighting with someone.

He saw that the Wolf had killed the guards near the entrance and was walking toward the Peter's attackers. Ulf didn't take prisoners. He stabbed one from the back and hammered the face of the other with his axe. Peter heard a death scream and a dull sound of a body which fell on the ground.

Silence. The fight was over.

Red Herring sat down, and Peter knelt near him.

"They will pay, the traitor will pay." James's voice was weak.

Shams al-Din had escaped with the rest of his supporters and blocked the exit door from the outside.

There were dead bodies everywhere.

But it wasn't over yet.

Another sound of alarm rose in their ears.

CHAPTER FOURTEEN

Holy Land, Wednesday, 22nd June in the year 1272 of the incarnation of Christ; Somewhere in the Golden Mamluk Camp

Peter sat quietly, head bowed, shoulders stooped.

He wasn't in Jerusalem anymore.

He remembered the golden officer and his soldiers who had stormed the hall. They had tied Peter and his friends again, dragged them out from the tower and loaded them into wooden carts like cattle.

When he awoke, they were in a tent. It was a hot day and he did not know where he was. He lay in the tent, thinking about the tower. He was haunted by the thought that they had failed in their mission to fetch a healer for the English crown prince. They had lost a few of Hamo's men.

And what they had achieved so far?

"Nothing!" rang in his head. But he knew that he couldn't afford such thoughts.

"Pull yourself together, Peter," he said to himself.

It was hard. His mind was still back in the Tower of David in Jerusalem, poring over images of horror and dead bodies. He had seen the Desert Wolf in action before, but it hadn't prepared him for this. On his way out of the tower, throughout the stairwell was a road of a bloody violence, death, and pain. Peter had witnessed some terrible things; some limbs were cut off, some heads were released from their responsibilities, too. Some necks were slanted in an unnatural position, and some broken bones were visible. There was much bloodshed

227

All these images of death made Peter want to vomit. The last steps toward the outer door were a real test for his stomach. He had leaned against the wall to take a breath and an inscription on the wall had stolen his attention.

"LEGXF," it read.

It reminded him of something, but he couldn't remember what.

Ulf had delivered a ferocious and merciless death to all the soldiers and guards he had met. Peter could see terrifying grimaces of pain and helplessness on the victims' faces.

His fierce determination to dispatch his vengeance seem to fuel his desire to kill them all and at times, Peter could see a little joy in his eyes.

Was it a battle joy?

He had heard tell of men who entered in a state of wild fury during the battle, their battle joy bringing their battle skills to a different level. Some imbibed drinks and potions to accelerate the process, to suppress their conscience, or to forget their fear. Peter had heard that one could buy such a potion in the herb market to prepare oneself before the fight. But he had not seen Ulf take such a potion on the evening of the fight. He had looked calm, and in the next moment he drew his blade and displayed his killing skills. It was terrifying.

His reputation was crucial. Stories about the Wolf seemed like legends, but when the lad witnessed his work, he could say they all were true.

This sight of dead men in the Tower of David was burned into his memory, and he couldn't wash it away. It was like his body was marked forever from inside and he couldn't remove it.

Peter put his hands over his eyes. He had thought that knighthood and soldiering were to protect the weak and the sick and to serve the law or some noble cause. But now he seemed only to witness death—meaningless death and injustice.

Was this the way of chivalry? Was this the path of the defender of the weak, the defender of the law?

If there was any law, it was that the stronger man always

won; the rest obeyed or died. His mind was shaken, as was his heart. He had even become a murderer in this quest. True, his intention had been to free his friends, but this didn't change the fact he had killed men.

"Is this the life you want, Peter?" he asked himself.

Sin after sin, he climbed this doomed road. He was afraid for his soul and his heart. Nevertheless, he only wanted to survive.

Or did he want more?

The glory was ringing in his mind. He was a miserable soul who had lived in the dark, and now he wanted everything from life. He wanted to see the world, he wanted to win every battle he faced, he wanted to taste everything life had to offer. He also wanted to avenge his mentor.

Peter needed some water. He needed to clear his heart and mind of hate and sadness. The young man opened his eyes again and tried to take a breath. He wanted to scratch the wound on his thighs but he had been warned not to do that. He had used the medicine Owen had given him. The desire to scratch was more demanding than ever. Peter tried not to think about it, but it wasn't an easy task.

He tried to focus, but it was hard. His throat was dry and his lips were cracked.

"Water?" No one moved. He looked around. There was salt in his mouth. Peter turned his gaze and noticed he was in a soldier's tent and Hamo was lying next to him. There was a little round table with a jug of water.

Water. His mood began to resurrect.

The cold liquid kissed his lips, blissfully. The only thing a man could want in the desert under the Sun was water. There were two ceramic cups, but the orphan drank directly from the big jug. He decided not to overdo it, having read of the risk to the stomach of drinking too much water in the book with Nickolas. He had drunk enough for now.

He rose and tried to move his limbs, one by one—his shoulders, his arms, and his neck. He felt a little stiff. How long had he slept? A few moments, a few hours, or an entire day? They were short of time for their mission. Peter wondered where Red Herring was.

A short man entered the tent. Some shadows outside hinted that there were guards near the entrance.

"I need to know your names," the man said. Hamo was awake too, and with some effort, he rose from his corner.

The orphan examined the face of this chubby, little man.

"Why? Who gives you the right to ask about our names?" Hamo was in a mood.

"My name is Ibn Abd al-Zahir," he introduced himself, "and I am the personal clerk of the sultan—"

"The sultan, you say," the knight said. "And what does the sultan want from us?"

Al-Zahir looked directly into Hamo's eyes.

"Sultan Baibars wants to question you about your business in his land. But first, he wants to know who stands before him. My job is to gather the information and to deliver it to him along with you." He said it quickly and cleanly. Peter and Hamo didn't expect to receive such a direct answer. They looked at each other.

They gave their names. The chubby man smiled while listening to Hamo as if he already knew him. But about Peter's name and origin, he was curious.

"Peter of Acre, that is a nice ring you have. Please accept my sincere condolences for the loss of your guardian," the clerk said.

The young man was shocked. Hamo was, too.

"Where is our wounded friend, Sir James?" The orphan realized this man couldn't know the name of his comrade and added, "The big one ...."

"Red Herring, as you call him." The clerk paused to observe their reaction to his knowledge. "You could ask the sultan about him." Ibn Abd al-Zahir showed them the exit of the tent.

"So, to the sultan." Hamo grinned.

They followed the short man.

Outside, there were a dozen Mamluks, apparently waiting for them. The faces of the guards who escorted them couldn't be seen through their masked helmets. They escorted them to a large tent with a side entrance. Peter guessed it was used as a field hospital and, indeed, there was a physician inside, examining patients. A line of soldiers stood waiting and they found Owen with them.

A man with an aquiline nose looked at Peter and Hamo. Apparently, he was the one who would examine their health. The orphan hoped this was a sign that the sultan would not execute them, even though the ruler was known for his unpredictable manner and fierce temper.

The physician looked over the orphan's body—the wounds on his legs as well as his head. He received a cup with some bitter liquid, which he guessed was for his health. He drank it at once.

He would live, the old physician told him in a deep voice. The sultan's clerk stood with them, looking at them and asking questions about their journey. There was another clerk behind him who wrote down whatever they said.

Hamo, Owen, and Peter were given clean bills of health. Red Herring wasn't there and they were anxious to know more about him. After a while, they were cleaned and ready to pay him a visit.

"Peter?" a familiar voice from behind arrived.

Isabella of Ibelin was smiling at them. Beside her was the middle-aged woman who accompanied her with the baby in her hands; Githa was behind them.

Hamo spoke first: "I see you are fine, my lady."

"What are you doing here in the camp?" Peter asked.

The beautiful lady smiled at him and looked at the child. "The same as you, searching for a physician."

"But …?"

"We will talk later. I am glad you are alive and safe." She turned and walked away, followed by her small retinue.

"So, we are together again," Owen grinned, tapping Hamo on his right shoulder. "You will have another chance, sir." He stressed the last word, but he knew that, even with the difference in their origins, his friend would never be angry with him.

"A lovely camp we have here," the Welshman added, "but

where we are?"

"Al-Bahr al-Mayyit," the clerk said. "It means the Salt Sea. The Christians call it the Dead Sea, for the sea is so salty that nothing lives in it—no fish, nothing."

"Why we are here?" Hamo asked.

"You can ask the sultan himself," the clerk replied.

After a few moments, they were taken to the ruler's tent. The old physician with the aquiline nose followed them too. It was more like a pavilion, the biggest one in the camp, pitched on high ground with a view to the whole Salt Sea. There were two guards near the entrance, holding spears with the Sultan's flags. A black lion on a yellow background. The Lion of Egypt, Peter thought.

When they entered the tent, darkness surrounded them. Outside it was midday, Peter assumed. He needed a few blinks to adjust his vision to the dim, inside light.

To his surprise, Red Herring was already there, sitting on a little log.

"Sir James!" Peter's mood was better. Hamo and Owen also were pleased to see that their friend still lived.

The guards pushed them to their fellow in the center of the tent, slowly.

"Peter, Hamo, and the ugly-faced Welshman," Red Herring said, looking at them and smiling. It seemed he never lost his humor. "I am pleased to see you are well."

"What about you?"

"I am not an easy target. It was just a scratch; I will survive." He turned his head to the man who followed his friends. "I think we found our man," he said, and all of the Crusaders froze. "Ibn al-Nafis," he said, nodding to the man who had examined Peter and whose nose looked like the beak of an eagle.

"Our man?" Owen gave an ironic smile.

"Yes, the physician. Thanks to him, I will live."

"In the middle of the desert? In the middle of the sultan's camp?"

"He is the sultan's personal physician. Where else would he be? In Damietta, fishing?" James grinned.

Peter didn't say a thing, but he stared at his friend. His heart was pulsating fast, his face smiling—it was excellent news.

"Well, well ...." A husky voice arrived from Peter's left. They all turned their eyes, but the Sun behind the speaker made him look like a dark shadow. He slowly approached the center, where a few lamps were dancing and the light gave the voice a face.

The sultan stood in front of them.

There were some silence and moments of staring at each other.

"You?" James' eyes opened wide.

Peter froze in anticipation. Hamo's face was also surprised, but Owen looked like a duck before supper. The orphan managed to observe all his friends' expressions before he realized what was happening, and he was more curious than ever.

Baibars grinned at James but Peter had trouble identifying whether it was a friendly smile or not.

There was a pronounced silence.

"But ... how ...?" Red Herring tried to say.

The first time he had seen the English prince, he had felt a similar excitement. At last, they were meeting the most famous man in this realm, face to face.

The man had a broad chest, a large skull, broad shoulders, and slim legs. His complexion was reddish-brown, his hair thick, and his eyes were vivid. He looked like a man who hated rest and loved movement. The determination in his blue eyes was like a rock, and the white spot on his one eye made him look fierce.

He was clearly battle-hardened. He looked like a man who wasn't afraid of anything. His reputation made him look even more ruthless. It was hard for Peter to determine his age; he guessed that the sultan was nearly fifty but he looked more vigorous than the younger men before him. He was dressed in a fine, white tunic embroidered in gold and he was barefoot as if he were coming from a bath.

On a wooden stand behind him was his battle dress. His polished armor looked excellent enough to make every knight in the kingdom jealous. The chainmail looked expensive, with fine golden decoration on the borders. Fine equipment, suitable for a true lord.

The orphan had never seen such excellent gear before.

"The Crusaders," the sultan said, then nodded toward James, "and a Scot—a real one—in my lodging."

"My lord …," Sir James managed to say as he was trying to stand proudly, despite his wound.

"A week ago, dressed as a dirty agent, I took you to Ulf's manor. You were thinking that I was a traitor, weren't you?"

"But …."

"Now I am standing in front of you as a sultan. What would you say? Not bad for an old dotard like me." The sultan was known to use interpreters whenever he talked and negotiated with Westerners, but now he spoke directly in their language, amused by their expressions of surprise.

James swallowed with difficulty.

"It is funny," the sultan stood a few paces before Red Herring. "Do you know what the French King Louis said about the Scots to his son?"

Red Herring didn't move.

"He said, 'I would rather have a Scot come from Scotland to govern the people of this kingdom well and justly than that you should govern them ill in the sight of all the world.'" The sultan seemed to amuse himself with his knowledge. "I am curious what a real Scot would say. And now, before me stands a real Scot, and what do you say? Could you properly govern the kingdom of France?"

"Well, …." James still didn't move. "He is right, as usual, my lord, King Louis of France."

"Yes, but he is dead now, isn't he?" Baibars turned the tone of the conversation. "What do you think the new French king would do? Listen to his father or hire a Scot to do the job?"

"I will leave this matter to him, my lord," Red Herring answered without thinking.

Baibars laughed and took a step forward. He walked with a nearly imperceptible limp, but Peter saw it. He had often helped Brother Alexander and he understood this pain.

"It's interesting to think how history will remember King Louis. Will he be known as the Crusader King, the Wise King, the Holy One, or Saint Louis? Or just a failure, an ill-prepared Crusader and indecisive general? Or a king who didn't know how to act as one? Was he a proper king, according to his people?"

The sultan focused his eyes on James, waiting for his opinion. When he didn't receive one, he continued.

"After all, he failed twice in the most important ventures of his life. Perhaps it was because he was stubborn or he was foolish. Or was he just subject to blind faith and couldn't see reality?" Baibars said. "I will never forget how he managed to lose from a winning position in the Battle of Al-Mansoura, but this was the spark that reignited my career." He smiled at James and asked, "What do you say?"

"I will leave this matter to history," Red Herring said. "After all, I have my own puzzle to solve, my lord."

"Yes, the puzzle," the sultan echoed the last word and his eyes were focused entirely on the Scottish knight. He nodded to his servants and food and water were delivered. "We all have our own puzzles to solve."

James nodded.

"Please," Baibars said and invited them all to eat and drink.

Peter knew that the sultan had once been a slave and had risen from the ranks of the Mamluks to become a sultan, worthy to be mentioned in history.

"Owen?" Peter whispered. "He was the man who led you into the Desert Wolf's manor?"

"Yes," the Welshman said, "a few days before the assassination attempt."

This was astonishing news to Peter. Why? His mind was confused. In the last few days, he tried to figure out what was happening. Why had all this happened and what moved these events forward?

"Alone?" the young man asked as he watched the servant deliver more food and drink.

"All alone, and he was dressed like a poor and unscrupulous spy. But this bastard was the sultan. He's got balls. I'll say that for him."

Now it was more complicated than ever.

Sultan Baibars drank some water.

Peter wondered where Ulf and Edward the Saracen were. After the tower, some of his memories had faded.

"So, as I watched the citadel in the dark and how the Wolf came in, please tell me, why I found you in the assassins' nest in Jerusalem?" Baibars asked. "And please, leave the nonsense aside that you were the Lady of Beirut's escort."

"It's funny, but it's true, in some part, my lord …. Yes, we escorted her," James said.

"What I can expect from a Scottish knight, nicknamed the Red Herring—an honest conversation or a hard one?"

"Well." This time it was James' turn to smile despite the pain. "I am so grateful that you allowed your physician to take care of me. And that's true."

"Of course, it's true," the sultan said. "Who wouldn't be grateful?"

"And, to be honest, we came here for him." Red Herring nodded to Ibn al-Nafis, who was standing next to Baibars.

"For him?"

"Yes, my lord."

"And how do you intended to obtain his service?"

"Hiring him or kidnaping him," James said.

"Ibn al-Nafis, did you hear that? They've come for you." Baibars showed some joy in the conversation. The physician didn't say a thing. He seemed uninterested in the course of the talk.

"Do you know why we are here today, near to the Salt Sea? Because of him. A few years ago, I broke my leg and it has never let me forget it. The mud baths in the sea relieve my pain. It was my friend, Ibn al-Nafis, who advised that I come here."

"He is a valuable one, indeed," Red Herring said and told the sultan about the assassination attempt and about their mission.

"Ibn al-Nafis is not only my physician, but he is my adviser and a friend," Baibars said with pride. "A real king can be determined by his friends and, of course, by his enemies."

"That's true, my lord," James agreed.

The sultan sat on a wooden chair placed for him on a small platform to be higher than the rest.

"How do you treat your friends, Sir James?" he asked.

"A true friend is hard to find, but after that is easy; we fight together, we live together, and we share the difficulties and the fruits of life. And we would die for each other." It was an honest reply.

"A fine answer, but do you think I will allow you to take my friend to Acre? What guarantees will you give me for his life? And, more importantly, why I should allow it?"

"Because of the peace, my lord."

"The peace, yes." Baibars smiled.

"And because of your reputation, my lord. I think Your Highness would like to distance yourself from the assassination attempt." James seemed very sure of what he had to say. Peter admired him for that.

"The assassination attempt, yes." Baibars thought for a moment and said, "We will get to this. Now bring the others," he said, nodding to the officer of his guards and observing the rest of the Christians.

"Well, these two, I know from Ulf's manor," he said, gesturing to Hamo and Owen. He then turned his focus to Peter. "But you ... I don't know you, and yet, your face is somehow familiar to me. Who are you?" Baibars asked.

"He is Lady Eleanor's new valet," James said.

"Aren't you too old to be a valet?"

"A new recruit, my lord."

"What is your name, young man?"

"Peter from Acre," the orphan managed to say, trying to bow and to look the question-giver in the eyes at the same time.

"Interesting ring you have, Peter ..." The face of the sultan suddenly changed. "It's as familiar to me as your face."

The small, middle-aged man who had interrogated them earlier stepped forward.

"He is the presumed bastard son of William Longsword,"

said the short clerk, who was near his master, adding, "from Battle of Al-Mansoura, my lord."

"Longsword ...." Baibars was shocked. "You look more like a mongrel than the son of your father."

"You knew my father?"

The sultan stood from his chair and approached Peter to examine his face. "I am wrong; you look the same as him." Baibars could not conceal the astonishment on his face.

The rest in the tent were surprised, too.

"So, an heir of the line of the Lionheart lies wounded and poisoned in Acre. But another heir to his half-brother is standing now, in front of me. The lost son of Longsword." He smiled at this discovery.

Red Herring, Hamo, and Owen also were astonished by that fact. Peter hadn't told anyone what Brother Alexander had said to him about his origins.

"He is the man who saved Edward's life," the clerk added.

"He is the man who saved mine, too," James added, "and Lady Isabella, also."

"And in the tower, he saved al-Rida's son, as well," a woman's voice said from the shadow on the other half of the tent.

Peter turned his head toward the sound but failed to see the face clearly, yet he smelled the perfume. The girl from the tower was here.

Baibars raised his hand and all became silent.

"As far as I have heard, you saved Ulf's life on the night of the sandstorm." The sultan seemed to know everything and was enjoying the situation.

Peter blushed. His eyes pointed to the ground.

"He is one week into his service," Owen said. "Beginner's luck, my lord."

"Beginner's luck, you say ...." Baibars scratched his chin. "I am intrigued by your story, Peter."

A newly-entered guard interrupted them, and two men were dragged in.

"So, Sir James, we have a puzzle to solve, and here are the pieces, one by one."

***

Peter looked at the sultan.

Was Baibars behind it all from the start? Why?

Peter had heard of Sultan Baibars' reputation. He was a capable man who took care of his own business. He was feared, brutal, and determined. His reputation had spread throughout the realm like a song that was sung in every tavern. There was a rumor that he had managed to enter Acre and other cities, dressed like a messenger or a merchant, to observe their fortifications and defenses and to personally collect information on the situation inside before he besieged them. It seemed now that he was capable of such deeds, indeed. He was a bold and brave man and for that reason, he was the sultan. And now there was a plot—against whom? For what? What were his intentions? Peter was confused, but he was determined to see things clearly. His goal was clear but how he could obtain it, for now, was unclear to him.

He looked at the newly-arrived men. There were a full dozen golden Mamluks with gritted swords and spears pointed at one of the two men.

It was the Desert Wolf.

The other was Edward the Saracen. He was only accompanied by one soldier.

"So, the puzzle—or, as I prefer to think about it, just another plot against me, …." the sultan said.

Red Herring looked confused, "Against you, lord?"

"Is it not obvious, Christian?"

"Well…" The Scot scratched his chin.

The only man who had something to lose … is me, not your miserable prince; his life is only a tool."

"But—" Red Herring tried to say something but decided not to interrupt the sultan.

"Why I would risk breaking my freshly-signed peace treaty? Why risk inviting a new wave of Crusaders? Did you know there was a massive threat to this world coming from the east? The Mongols—you call them Tartars. You are history and we will be, too, soon. But we will fight." He paused to take a breath.

James was silent.

"Did you know that the profit from controlling the trade in this region is five times bigger than that of your whole island? England, yes, I have heard of it. Did you know that when your precious Lord Edward arrived and realized there would be no hope, he tried to change the status quo in the overseas lands and lordships? Did you know he tried to change the direction of money, and the pocket where the gold sleep?"

Red Herring said nothing.

"Yes, my honest Scottish knight, and do you know who would make more profit from a prolonged war?" The sultan received no reply and continued. "Templars, Hospitallers, and the other military fanatic orders!" Baibars looked his guests in the eyes. "The Templars and Hospitallers are said to deliberately prolong the war between Christians and Muslims in order to collect more money from the pilgrims." Baibars drank some water. "After the assassination, Edward would become a martyr for these people, a sign that would attract more and more followers and pilgrims from your backward and barbaric world." He blinked for a moment. "And who will benefit from the movement of people and goods? The soulless Italians, the traders, the men who control the sea-roads. The future of the world is to conquer the seas."

"A martyr?"

"The old man from the mountains, Shams al-Din's father, and his assassins worked with the Templars. When the assassins couldn't break the holy knights, they allied with them," Baibars said. Peter had heard this rumor.

"But the old man from the mountains faded in one of my prisons and now his son is trying to restore what is left of his possessions and power. The only ones that could help him are the military orders because these structures only profit from fear, war, and death."

He turned his eyes to Edward the Saracen, who was bandaged on his head and his ribs and, Peter thought, looked like a street dog after a brawl.

"You … what should I do with you?" Baibars asked.

Al-Rida's son said nothing.

"I gave you a chance to restore your father's name …."

"I did what I was ordered to do—"

"Now you are sided with the infidels? Traitor. You are like a snake that will do whatever is necessary to survive." Baibars' face looked furious.

Peter observed the failed assassin. Edward the Saracen tried to look proud, but his reputation was tainted. He looked at the orphan; they were here because of him.

"You will be hanged tomorrow, assassin," Baibars said.

Peter was shocked at the ease with which the sultan delivered the death sentence.

Baibars turned his gaze to him as the guards took the assassin away.

"You prevented one of my best spies to do what he received in a written order, and for some reason, this is some lucky mischief."

The sultan turned to the other corner of the tent. It was a large tent, as Peter had observed earlier, and from the inside, it looked even bigger.

"*Diyaab al-Sahra* …," the sultan said.

The Desert Wolf said nothing.

His face was like a rock and gave away nothing. Nevertheless, he turned his sight slowly to the host. All people in the tent were left breathless. The guards and the golden Mamluks around him were nervous and tight.

"I am pleased you are alive," Baibars said.

"But your daughter is dead!" Ulf said. "Killed by your dogs!"

The sultan blinked for a moment and took a few steps toward the Wolf.

"I know," he said and dropped his eyes for a moment, followed by his head. He murmured something to himself and focused on Ulf again. Peter was deeply struck by this moment. The sultan didn't show any sign of sorrow or emotion from the news of his daughter's death. His presence was absolutely controlled.

"A daughter?" Peter and James looked at each other at the same time.

"Your hounds came to my manor in peace," Ulf said, "and killed her—killed everything—without hesitation. I thought we had an agreement!" The last was said with such vengeful passion. "Why?"

Everyone froze.

"Why?" This time Ulf's tone was harsher.

The orphan and his friends had all washed and been given clean tunics, but not the Wolf. He was covered from head to feet in dust, dried blood, and dark spots on his garments. Even his arms, from the end of his armor to his red leather vambraces, were tarnished by the blood of the previous night's killing.

He wasn't able or hadn't wanted to clean himself, Peter thought. His look was dark and scary, yet Baibars didn't show any sign of being affected by it.

"Why? Why send your hounds to attack us?"

"I didn't give such an order!" Baibars shouted.

"He was the man who sent us to your manor!" Red Herring said quickly. "But we were too late."

Ulf was puzzled and looked at the Scottish knight.

"He was the spy who delivered the location to Otto and guided us to your place. I saw his face."

So, the role of the sultan was deeper than he had thought. Peter's mind was racing again. Ulf turned again to Baibars. "So, you knew that this would happen and did not do anything?"

"I suspected, yes…" the sultan said.

"But she was your daughter, your own blood …." They started to scream at each other, the Desert Wolf and the father of his dead wife.

"Yes, and I tried to fetch help, sending information to the infidels, because they were at least involved in the running plot … and you—you were responsible for my daughter's life, her health, her happiness …. This was the most important mission of your life, and you failed." Now it was the sultan's to unleash his anger toward Ulf.

"You and your conspiracy games, you and your royal ideas

for power and control ....” Ulf's fists became white. “You ....
I gave you everything you wanted from me. We had a deal.”

Peter observed the sultan. He was a real force in ruling his
own empire, he thought. But now his daughter was dead. He
had nerves of steel, still; he didn't show anything, he didn't
reveal any weakness or emotion.

Yet, he had known about the plot and had done nothing.

Peter suspected that the sultan was so eager to know who
the plotters and traitors were, one and all that he failed to
interfere in the attack on the manor in time. Peter thought he,
himself, would want the same. Sultan Baibars had taken a risk
and had failed. And one of his daughters was dead.

For a moment, there was a dangerous silence in the tent.

***

Baibars was focused on Ulf.

“I loved to see a smile on her face,” the sultan said, “and
because of my daughter, I lost your service. You were my ally
and your sword served me well.”

“And now she is dead,” Ulf said.

Baibars shook his head and rose like a phoenix. His eyes
were empty of love and life—instead, they were full of sorrow
and determination. The same determination as the Wolf's: to
punish the men who were responsible. Baibars knew this
gaze—the expression which showed he would never stop
hunting his prey.

Baibars tried not to show his emotions to others.

The lonely Wolf without a cause was the fading shadow of
a past myth. But he was a fierce beast, ready to deliver
vengeance with another song. The sultan knew he needed that
song, which could bring fear into the hearts of his enemies
once more, and it was about time release it.

He looked at the warrior's eyes. He, the sultan, had never
been frightened by anything in his life except for Ulf's eyes.
Every time he looked into his eyes he saw the stone-cold soul
of the Wolf. Whether others and his enemies saw the same?

Baibars shivered.

He, the sultan of these lands, was one of the best soldiers and generals. Although his strength was fading with the passing of years, he had experience winning battles, leading men and battalions, fighting wars, sacking fortresses and towns. He had won in all these endeavors, all his battles.

But whenever he saw Ulf displaying his skills, it was like observing a fallen shadow from the sky, doing God's work.

Now, he thought, he needed to guide this weapon in the right direction once more.

Baibars spoke easily. "In the beginning, it was a lust for power. I had desired the highest position in the kingdom so much. Then I realized everything had a price." As he spoke, he moved closer and closer to Ulf. "The crown was heavy. The power went hand in hand with responsibility for the people," the sultan continued, "Ordinary men and women needed order and safety. The world was in chaos. Someone needed to bring justice and order …."

"And you sacrificed your own daughter for that?"

Baibars ignored Ulf and—as if he were speaking before a jury—he continued, "I needed to be a lion for my people. I needed to be that beast to bring stability for the sake of the realm. And if preventing a treacherous plot meant that someone would be exposed to danger, then I would take that risk again!"

"She was my beloved one and she was your daughter. She loved you!" Ulf nearly shouted this last in fury.

"Where were you? You were responsible for my daughter's life, and you failed!"

Ulf froze.

"*Diyaab al-Sahra* …," the sultan said. "You … what are you? A lonely wolf without a cause. You are a man who needs a cause."

"A cause?" Ulf's face was furious. He leaped at the sultan, managed to wrest a sword from one of the guards, stabbed another in front of him, and faced Baibars. He did it so quickly that no one moved. By the time the guards had reached him, blood had been shed, a golden Mamluk lay dead, and Baibars' life was at stake.

"I have a cause." Ulf grabbed Baibars by the throat.

But the sultan looked calm. Baibars raised his hand toward his golden guards, signaling them not to move.

"Anyone responsible for her death will pay. That is my cause," Ulf said.

Baibars looked at his fierce eyes, responding with the same. The moment was heavy with tension.

"If you think this will bring back your beloved one and my daughter, do not hesitate, do it ... do it!" Baibars shouted.

The naked sword didn't move.

"If you think this would bring order and stability to this land, do it, now." Baibars chose his words with care and spoke them as he would twist a sword into a man's wound.

The blade pointed to the sultan's chest, almost pierced it; the two men locked eyes and would not look away. Ulf's eyes were focused like a predator's on its prey.

The whole tent became darker. What on earth could prevent the vengeful Wolf, grieving for his lost family, from ripping apart the heart of an aged lion?

Silence.

Baibars' heart was starting to beat fast and sweat appeared on his temple.

"Daddy?" A child's voice cut the darkness.

Ulf turned his gaze to the source of the disruption, as did Baibars and the rest of the witnesses.

"Uncle Ulf?" the little girl said.

"Anna?" Baibars managed to say.

The Wolf froze.

***

Peter's eyes were dry. He rubbed them a little with his forearm and blinked a few times. The scene he had witnessed in the sultan's tent made them hold their breath.

They had been interrupted by a little girl, whom Peter supposed to be another of the sultan's daughters. The Desert Wolf had looked at her eyes, raising himself, and Peter saw a tear glide down his cheek.

He stopped his hand from taking the sultan's life. He watched her for a moment and stormed out from the tent, vanishing.

Baibars said nothing, simply stood firm and hugged the little girl. She was beautiful and innocent, close to her sixth year. Her long, golden hair and blue eyes distinguished herself from the rest; her face was vivid and happy. Even when she saw Ulf, she showed an eagerness to hug him, too.

The sultan watched the Wolf disappear.

"Leave him alone," he said to the guards and all were dismissed from the tent.

"Children …." Owen said outside. "It's a bloody family affair, eh?"

"Shut up, Welshman," Hamo said.

"Why? Some day you may have children too, handsome, then we will speak again!"

Red Herring was silent.

The golden soldiers escorted them to their tent. Peter managed to exchange a look with Edward the Saracen who was taken away.

An old Mamluk bearing a white beard asked them in the Christians' language to behave if they wanted to be allowed to move freely around the camp. He asked for James' word, and when he received it, he turned his back on them and began to walk away.

Peter stopped him, asking, "Who was the girl in the tent?"

"It's not your business." The man was harsh.

"Not the little one, the other one?"

The old officer ignored the question, but before he walked away, he nodded to Ibn Abd al-Zahir, the sultan's clerk who was constantly around.

"Who was she?" Peter persisted to know. "The girl behind the sultan. I want to thank her."

"Why?"

"She was in the tower," Peter said.

"Are you sure?" the clerk said.

"She was there; it's the same perfume. She took care of my wound and cut the rope from my hands. She helped me … and

I want to thank her."

Sir James, Hamo, and Owen had surrounded the short man and he appeared to be uncomfortable, surrounded by the Crusaders, who were all a head taller than him.

"She was there," Hamo said. "I saw her, too."

The clerk smiled, then said something to a nearby guard, and the two laughed.

"If she wants to speak to you, she will. If she doesn't, no one can make her."

"Why? Who is she?"

"One of the sultan's daughters, the wildest one," the clerk said and observed their open mouths with a smile. "You had better stay away from her. Take that as friendly advice, free of charge."

"How many daughters does he have?" Hamo was curious.

"Seven," the short man said, then stopped. "Six, now …."

There was an uneasy silence.

They talked a little more, sat near their tent and enjoyed the view of the Salt Sea. The orphan found some water and while they rested, they were questioned by the clerk. He and one of his servants wrote down all they said: their names, their ranks, even their questions to the sultan. They recorded the men's intentions, what they knew about the assassination, what they knew about the Wolf and anything that could be helpful to uncover the plot.

"Why ask all these questions?" James asked. "I doubt the sultan reads it all."

"Our lord likes to be informed. As you know, he created a new information system, a new way of delivering news."

"What is he preparing for?" Hamo asked.

"The Tartars?" Red Herring suggested.

"You know Mongols—you call them Tartars—and their customs?" the clerk asked.

"Only rumors," Hamo said.

"Twelve years ago, the Great Hilegu Khan—the Mongol ruler—tried to conquer these lands. He sent a letter with envoys to Qutuz—the Sultan before Baibars—calling on him to submit to his rule. This letter, although coached in Islamic terms and even containing verses from the Qur'an, expressed the traditional Mongol world view."

"Mongol world view?" Owen lifted an eyebrow.

"The Mongols believe they have a heaven-given right to rule the world," the clerk explained. "All those who resist are rebels who must be destroyed. There is no possibility of escaping, so Qutuz was counseled to submit at once. The letter also referred to the sultan Qutuz and disparaged his Mamluk origins, saying, 'He is of the race of Mamluks who fled before our sword into this country, who enjoyed its comforts and then killed its rulers,'" the clerk quoted.

"Sultan Qutuz killed their envoys," Ibn Abd al-Zahir said. "Did you know that the Mongols never again negotiated or sent envoys to the people who had killed their messengers? Not until they conquered and killed them all as punishment."

"Really?" Peter was amazed.

"As a matter of fact, Baibars was the man who suggested the beheading of the impudent envoys. Shortly after that, the Mongols unleashed their hordes. Baibars urged the sultan to meet them in open war and to teach them a lesson, saying that the Mamluk warriors weren't scared and that they would gladly kill their enemies."

"What happened?" Peter was like a child near the fireplace, waiting to hear the full story.

"The Mongols crossed the river Jordan, and there was a great battle near the Spring of Goliath. The Battle of Ayn Jalut."

"I have heard of this in the taverns," Hamo said.

"Qutuz even received permission from the Kingdom of Jerusalem to pass through safely and to supply his army on the eve of this great danger."

"The overseas barons helped him?" Hamo asked.

"They hadn't much of a choice, had they? Internal conflicts and the ongoing war for power between the Italian traders and the military orders had sapped their man power and resources."

"What happened?" Owen's attention also was stolen by the storyteller.

"On the battlefield that day, our brave Captain Baibars and his loyal Mamluks fought bravely and fiercely against their hordes and squadrons. You must know that the Tartars, at this point, didn't know what a major defeat was. We beat them, annihilating their forces."

"So, Baibars had balls, eh?" Hamo said.

The clerk continued, "Baibars believes that they will return and try a new invasion. The Mongols will never forget that the Mamluks served them their first defeat. Even after the death of their Khan, his son has continued his politics against our realm."

"And we, the Christians, are in the middle of this war between Mamluks and Mongols," Sir James concluded.

"Exactly. And you should know, too, that Baibars lost his home and family, far away in his homeland, because of them."

"The words from the Tartar's letter— 'He is of the race of Mamluks who fled before our sword into this country, who enjoyed its comforts and then killed its rulers'—this referred to Baibars, too?" Peter asked.

"Yes."

After a while, the Sun went down and Hamo, Owen, and James went to sleep.

But there was something that bothered Peter. He followed the clerk and persistently asked him questions about his father and the sultan.

"You are an annoying mongrel, like a fly—a horsefly."

"I want to know," Peter said.

"Why? These are things from the past."

"I didn't know my father," the young man said with some sadness in his eyes. "I was raised by old monk, without a family, without knowing my origins and without a future. Until last week, I had not heard the name Longsword."

"I have heard of Brother Alexander and Brother John, who raised you."

"You have?"

"Peter of Acre, are you sure you want to know about your father?"

"Yes!"

"So, listen, I will tell you what I know, but it isn't a pleasant story." The short clerk took a breath and continued. "The father of your father was the illegitimate son of King Henry of England. He was a half-brother of Richard the Lionheart. You have the same blood as Edward has. You are from the same bloodline of warrior kings. They are constantly looking for someone to fight, something to conquer and win. Your father had the same madness inside him." Ibn Abd al-Zahir, the sultan's clerk, paused while they walked through the camp.

The stars and the Moon began their night concert and before them was revealed a magnificent view of the sea. Its waters reflected the heaven's lights.

"Look at nature, Peter; it knows its business, and we men are like ants walking on this land." He smiled, looking the stars. "There is always someone bigger and stronger who can crush us."

"My father?" Peter prompted.

"William Longsword led his men without fear into battle. At Mansoura, he followed the Count of Artois, the brother of the French King. I heard they didn't like each other. Longsword was accused of cowardice in the face of battle by the Count. Templars were blamed for the same. The reckless Crusader, the Count of Artois, was to wait for the whole army to cross the branch of the river Nile. But, instead, he was greedy for glory and for booty. He charged the streets of Mansoura and doomed all his followers. For he had made a fatal mistake. The narrow streets weren't suited for horsemen. Baibars, who had organized the defense, was a great soldier and took the advantage."

"And?"

"The pride, lad, the pride of your father cost him his life. You are not a knight or a man with status, so you don't know what that means. Maybe you should ask Brother Alexander."

"Why Alexander?"

"Because of his knight's pride, he can't go home," Ibn Abd al-Zahir said.

"Tell me more about my father."

"Your father, Peter, bore the sign of an heir of the great

warlord king. He did not want to be accused of cowardice in the face of the enemy, leaving the battlefield and his brethren. He had come to the realm of war to earn honors for himself." He looked at Peter's eyes and they stopped near a camp fire.

"He would have rather died than lay down his sword. He paid dearly for his pride. The French count fled and drowned while trying to cross the river. But Longsword stood and fought to the death. I could never forget his black hair and his determined eyes. You are like two water drops. He swung his longsword, his great destrier biting and fighting, and fought like a demon that day. Our captain knew that if he wanted to crush the attack he must take the fight on his own.

"Baibars stood against your father and with two more officers, he fought him. They begged him to put down his weapons and surrender, but he refused. So, it became a fight to the end."

Peter's eyes were dry. He didn't know the man the clerk was talking about, even if William Longsword had been his father. He felt nothing but the anger of a missed childhood and regret that he hadn't had a proper father or mother's care. Why had he wanted to know more? He couldn't explain the desire inside of him but he was glad he had asked.

"So, Baibars killed him?" the orphan asked.

"He wasn't a sultan back then, only a loyal officer who defended his brothers, his soldiers, and did what the warrior's fate commanded: to stand and fight the enemy and to win."

There was silence while the two men watched the night and enjoyed its music and the reflection on the water's surface below them. It was clear their conversation was over and Peter suddenly felt tired and wanting to hug the bed.

"Thank you for the story," the young man said. The orphan wished the clerk good night and went to his tent. So, Baibars had killed Peter's father.

A shadow waved its hand toward him, gesturing that he should follow. Peter didn't think, just obeyed. After a few moments of walking under the Moon, a hand grabbed his arm and dragged him into the nearest tent.

"Peter Longsword, an illegitimate branch from the

bloodline of the Lionheart, the bastard line. How you ended up in this mess?"

A dim light came from a candle she held. The orphan looked at her. She was nearly Peter's age but younger. Still, he had so much to learn in his life. She was at another level, that was for sure. Isabella, the Lady of Beirut … was not she a danger to their mission? Dangerous to all men?

"I never managed to thank you properly, Peter," Isabella said.

"For what?"

"For saving my life, twice." Isabella smiled gently at him. "At the Mamluk camp and again in the tower."

She went to a wooden chest and placed the candle she held on top of it. She turned toward him, her head was tilted forward and slowly, step by step, she approached him, barefoot, looking at his eyes.

Peter managed to look around the tent. There was some light and they were alone.

She dropped her dark robe and stood before him in a light nightdress. The orphan had never seen such a sight. Despite the dim light, he could see, through her dress, the form of her body and her pale skin.

"Wake up, Peter. She is a princess; she has no business with you," he thought. Nevertheless, his heart was flying with lust and desire.

"Peter of Acre … or do you prefer Longsword?" She talked slowly. "You are my savior, my bravest knight …."

"I am not a knight …" the orphan faltered.

"You are the knight of my heart."

"I am not a knight at all."

"But soon you will be …." Her chest was almost touching his. Her whispering voice was upon him now. The orphan could smell her perfume.

"Now, I need my hero … to hold me tight."

Peter lost his breath. He was bewitched by her charm and her beauty. She smiled seductively. Yes, he wanted her, too; she was the one thing that filled his life with purpose: to fight for her, to love her, to die for her. The princess and her beauty.

She kissed him.

Emotion and passion erupted within him.

The orphan from Acre and the princess stood, close together, in the dark. His heart was working fast now. He was conquered; his mind tried to resist, but he didn't listen. He had the greatest urge to satisfy this hunger, this passion, this desire to hold her, to touch her. He knew this could never last, a lady with an orphan from the streets. This was a doomed union; still, he enjoyed the perfect moment with her. He knew it wouldn't last long, he hoped he knew the consequences, but still, his heart was conquered.

Was he in love? He hadn't used this word before; what was it?

"Enjoy it, Peter," his inner voice commanded. He couldn't see any reason not to. He had nothing to lose … except his soul, his heart, and his mind. For this one-of-a-kind woman, he would gladly present his heart. The orphan and the princess—he smiled at his thoughts.

The Moon was the only eyewitness of what lay ahead.

He returned the kiss.

***

Peter walked as if in a dream, smiling, back to his tent. The Moon was vibrant and the stars were dancing on the skyline.

"Hi."

He was surprised by a vivid voice accompanied by a familiar perfume.

Peter turned his head toward the voice.

"So, you are the lucky bastard, Peter." He lost his speech in the dark, but not his smile.

"Hi?" she repeated.

"Hi …." the orphan said.

"How are your wounds?"

"I will survive." He looked at her eyes. It was the girl from the tower. "Why did you help me in Jerusalem?"

"You looked like a man who needed to be saved." Her lips were small but were in an easy smile.

"Why you were there?" Peter asked.

"You need to ask my father these questions, but you must know, he has only one weakness …."

"His daughters?" the orphan asked.

She smiled at him.

"But …." The young man tried to observe her face, and their eyes met under the Moon. Her brown eyes were big and deep, and she stared at him. She didn't look like a younger girl—not at all. The girl who stood before Peter was a real woman; she looked the same age as him. Her long, black hair was curly but well-maintained. Her cheeks made a little dimple when she smiled. She was shorter than Peter, thin and fragile-looking. Nevertheless, Peter knew she wasn't defenseless.

"What were you doing in the Tower of David?" he repeated the question.

"Where is the best place to hide a weakness?"

"Weakness?"

She smiled and watched him.

"You are the weakness of your father. But of course, you are."

She enjoyed his reaction.

"You are so clever, Peter of Acre."

"Are you mocking me?"

"Nope, just a fan of you and your way of thinking." She was laughing.

Peter was smiling, too.

"But how …?"

"It wasn't hard to find a job as a nurse with my skills," she said.

"You have skills?"

"Yes, Peter, I can wield a fruit knife when necessary." The two smiled and laughed again.

Her eyes were always warm. She never removed her smile or the curiosity from her face. Yet, she didn't say much. She seemed pretty and mysterious.

"What was that between the sultan and Ulf? Family affairs?" Peter didn't want this night or this conversation to end. She looked into the orphan's eyes.

"My father said that sometimes, bravery is mistaken for stupidity, and vice-versa. He says that most men are neither brave nor naïve. Sometimes even the stupidest man can be the bravest one. But it's rare to see a clever man do a brave deed, to have the courage for it. Prudent men calculate the risk, always.

"*Diyaab al-Sahra* is the cleverest and the best killer I've seen. Believe me, I've seen enough. He also is not bound to anyone, you know. Even to my father."

"But he worked for him."

"My father, the sultan, saved his life."

"His life?"

"After a fierce storm, years ago, near the sand beaches of Arsuf, there was a shipwreck and the Wolf's body was delivered ashore by the sea waves. The newly-crowned sultan was hunting and he was near the coastal line."

Peter listened carefully.

"He saved the life of a man that day. His body was all in scars from battles and torture. On his entire body. Baibars saved his life. He thought of it as a sign of his rule. After a time, he left him to live nearby. Yet, this man from the distant land called Norway returned the favor, saving the sultan's life from mercenary killers who ambushed him in the woods."

"All alone?"

"Yes, alone; this is how my father understood about his abilities. And Ulf only wanted a bucket of apples for his help."

"Green ones?"

"Yes, how did you know?"

"I guessed," Peter lied.

"After that, the sultan hired him; he asked him to perform certain tasks for him. He saw in Ulf's skills and thirst for blood an ultimate weapon to use against his enemies—the ones who were difficult to bring onto an open battlefield.

"I saw what he left behind in the tower," he said.

"As you already know, he is unstoppable in close fights. He is an outlander, yet no one has seen such rage and coldness as are in his eyes. He is a master in delivering death to his opponents. The sultan's opponents. Baibars managed to use him well; he sent him to the most dangerous places, after the fiercest enemies you could imagine. Ulf always went silently, disappearing into the desert and then returning with the next trophy under his belt. The other Mamluks started to call him the Desert Wolf, *Diyaab al-Sahra*. There were no impossible targets for him. He saved the sultan from several plots, as well."

She paused, watching the stars, and continued. "One day, Ulf faced the lord of the realm and said that he wanted to retire from this kind of life because of my sister."

"Just like that?"

"Yes, just like that."

"Was she pretty?"

"My older sister was more than that, much more; she somehow managed to calm his thirst for blood." She closed her eyes while talking. The orphan guessed that she was trying to imagine her sister's face again. "She turned him into a calm farmer running an ordinary manor."

"A man like him, a farmer?"

"He was more like an engineer, weapons and war adviser for my father, but he ran his estate well."

"I can't imagine it."

"Baibars was on the brink of losing his best weapon. Yet, the smile on the face of his daughter persuaded him. Still, the Lion of Egypt asked for proof of the warrior's love for my sister. He wanted something in return for her hand."

"And what is that?" Peter asked.

"The last fortress of the assassins. The ones who didn't recognize my father's rule and didn't show any kind of respect. They were difficult to control; their promises could be swapped for gold. My father gave the Desert Wolf the deadliest mission: to crush them all."

"What happened?"

"What do you think?" She released a smile. "Ulf killed all who he found in the fortress."

"But someone survived?"

"As you saw in the tower, a few had fled before his arrival and hidden, such as the son of the old man from the mountains. Al-Rida's clan were foes of Shams al-Din. The gray-bearded host with the dry and ugly face you met in the citadel in Jerusalem. Baibars used this rivalry for his own ambitions and forced the assassins' clans to kill each other before the arrival of the Wolf. He almost succeeded. In the end, with the help of *Diyaab al-Sahra* he took their last fortress and he had scattered them like a herd of sheep."

"It seems that the son of al-Din has returned," Peter said.

"Yes, Shams al-Din, the Son of Nonagenarian. There is another plot to kill my father. The players include greedy Templars and their Italian partners, and some renegade Tartars, the ones my father allowed to settle on his land. But the worst is that one of the elite Mamluk regiments have betrayed my father, too.

Peter's eyes were curious.

"My father gathered intelligence on this group. He learned of a plan to attack Ulf's manor."

"Why he didn't send his own battalions to save her?"

"His most trusted Mamluks were far away. Do you know there was always a struggle between the amirs and their own ambitions? Who can Baibars trust when an amir plans to send a battalion from the northern frontier to sack sultan's own backyard?"

"So, he didn't trust much to his own, did he?"

"What king does?" She looked at the Moon. "Now the sultan needed the mice to come out from their hole."

"How he could make them do that?" Peter asked.

"How do you think? It's like hunting, you need a bait."

"Yes, and they revealed themselves to us in the tower. Now they needed bait, too."

"Ironically, yes, the two sides used the same tactics." She looked at him. "This is like a game of chess, eh?"

"I can't play chess," he said.

"There is a Scottish proverb that your friend told me earlier, 'Forgive your enemy but remember the bastard's name'," she said. "My father used to say that, when you are at war, there are no rules except to win." She spoke confidently. "And during the middle of a battle, you can earn revenge. You have to remember who your real enemy is and challenge him on the battlefield. As you know, a war is upon us. It is only a matter of time. To survive, we will need the best warriors, knights, killers, and commanders."

"We?" Peter was confused.

"As you see, Peter of Acre, you are involved, too. You were hunted, almost killed. You are an obstacle to the new power which is about to rise."

"But ...?"

She dragged him near a campfire, knelt down, took out her knife, and began to draw in the sand.

"Look, here is Acre—your dying prince is there. Here is Jerusalem." She pointed with her finger. "Now, we are here, east. We are surrounded by renegades, who also blocked the path to your home."

Peter looked at the improvised sand map and said nothing. She pointed again with her finger at the sand, north of Jerusalem.

"Ughan's men and his allies are moving," she said.

"What we are going to do now?" Peter looked at the stars then back to her.

"My father always has a plan. We will see." Her eyes were beautiful.

Darkness was all around. Some clouds wrapped the Moon and most of the stars; the song of the night became soundless.

Peter looked around. He saw some tents and some tired sentries.

A shadow moved.

The orphan's eye caught it and it was gone in the blink of an eye.

He looked at the girl and the two ran, following it.

He jumped over a campfire, flying like a hawk after prey. He heard her steps and breath behind him.

After a few heartbeats, he was near to the rear of Sultan Baibars' tent, and something wasn't right.

"Where are the guards?" she asked.

A noise from inside the tent made him turn.

Peter had no time to say anything. Everything around him

was moving slowly, and he felt he was on a wave again. The wave of destiny.

The wind blew at him like during the sandstorm. But this was different. It was like a blurred song surrounding his face. His hair was dancing and his eyes were drying. The wind was playing with his face. The wind was everywhere: around his neck, in his ears and his eyes, between his shoulders and on his back. It was a whispering song for a dance, a slow one. Still, he was determined to follow his instincts and to find out what was bothering him.

Peter rushed into the ruler's tent. He lunged toward the enemy. This time, it was Baibars' life which was threatened.

An assassin dressed in dark clothes held a bloody dagger in his hands, aimed at the chest of his target. The sultan had fallen on his back, and the body of a dead assassin lay near him. The old lion had put up a fight. Still, he had almost lost his life. Almost.

Peter introduced himself like a hurricane and hammered the assailant's back, using his speed and shoulder to hit him hard. As a guest in Baibars' camp, he was unarmed. Still, he remembered what Ulf had taught him. The man himself was his most dangerous weapon, not the iron in his hand.

Baibars eyes were wide open from the surprise of seeing Peter. After a moment, his daughter arrived. She was quick and stabbed the intruder in his neck as he struggled to stand again.

"No ...," the sultan shouted, "I wanted to question him." But it was too late. She pulled the knife from the attacker, who fell dead near her.

There was a third man, watching from the dark. He had naked his sword and was ready to attack Baibars as Peter and the girl entered. She started to shout orders. A noise coming from soldiers and cries cut the silence of the night. Sultan Baibars was in danger.

The third man tried to approach the ruler but hesitated. His indecisive step exposed him from the darkness. Peter caught this move in the corner of his eye. He rose from the ground and started to run toward him.

The hunt began. Peter focused only on the man in front of

him, who ran fast but turned to see who his pursuer was. The orphan didn't think but instinctively tried to catch him. The two men left the camp behind in the darkness. Peter saw a slope ahead of them and curves formed by rocks. Though tired, he didn't give up. He knew the assassins were part of the problem, and as soon they eliminated them, they would be free to continue their mission. He followed the man down the slope in the night, barely able see where he was running.

Peter lost his footing, falling into a small, underground cave near the rocks around the Salt Sea.

He opened his eyes as he stood up and felt a pain in his back and his right shoulder. The young man looked around. It looked more like a tomb, and he stumbled over skeleton bones.

"Damn it." He cursed his luck. How would he get out?

He could hardly see in the dark as the only light came from the Moon through the opening above his head. Peter searched the cave with his hands. He found something wrapped in an old piece of leather. It was too dark to see what it was but he felt the coldness of an iron, which was as long as his elbow. He leaned against the wall.

The cave could be his resting place, as it was for the poor fellows whose remains he had found here.

He evaluated his situation. Peter stood again and tried to climb, but his attempt was unsuccessful. He couldn't find a hand- or foothold. The underground cave was small; judging by his fall, he assumed the height to be about three meters and the width seemed about four. The orphan could see the Moon through the place where he had fallen in. He cursed again.

"Peter, how did you get down here?" he asked himself, then sat down. Finally, the night and his weariness drew him to sleep.

He awoke when he heard his name spoken. He looked up at the cave entrance. He saw a silhouette of a daughter and a father, surrounded by a dozen golden helms lit by the smiling Moon.

A rope was dropped. Peter climbed, escaping the darkness. The assailant was long gone.

The assassination attempt had failed. The assassins must have been truly desperate to attempt such a dangerous task.

Peter and the rest walked in silence to the camp.

"In debt to an orphan from Acre!" Baibars said at last. "Such irony! You have certainly earned some fame in a short time."

Peter just stared at the lights of the camp. He had just saved the life of his father's killer.

"You, Longsword, you have saved many important lives in just a week: Edward, Ulf, James, Isabella of Ibelin, even the life of the Genovese captain is under your belt. You saved my life too. And now all of us owe our next breath to you."

The sultan laughed. The world was falling apart, and what was he doing? Laughing.

Fate was merciful, wasn't it?

He looked at Peter.

"With this deed, you have signed the death sentence of your kingdom."

The orphan was puzzled. He had expected some gratitude, but not this response.

"The Christian kingdom—or, as you call it, the Kingdom of Jerusalem—is doomed. You know why? Because I am determined to conquer it. It is on the land I have claimed."

"But you had no rights over this land!" Peter dared to speak.

"But you did? No, nobody had rights over this land. This is a realm of God and we are just creatures passing through."

The orphan wasn't sure he understood this.

"The right is on the winner's side, Longsword. And who is the winner? The strongest? No. The cleverest? No. The most prudent? No."

He left Peter to think about his last words for a few moments.

"The winner must be all these things, but most of all he must have a cause. The winner trains hard; he prepares himself. He invests his life to be ready when the right time comes. But what links all champions? Devotion to a cause. My cause is to unite Egypt and Damascus, to unite the Muslim world and to fight back the hordes from the east. The Mongols," Baibars said. He smiled at Peter and continued. "So, remember, my dear savior, the devoted player with a cause always wins. Your kingdom, unfortunately, is not ready and never will be. Even if new Crusaders arrive, they will not save your kingdom from its fate."

"But ...."

"Nobody will," Baibars said. "Either I or the Tartars will overrun you soon. Your leaders are too greedy and think only for themselves. Your world needs an overall change—a new structure and new laws, even a new way of thinking. But you are far behind us." The sultan took a breath. "The threat from the east must be repelled by a united force. Your kingdom lacks this. Who do you think has the better odds?"

"Odds of what?" Peter asked.

"To destroy your kingdom first? The Mamluk empire or the Tartars?"

Peter was astonished by the savage look on Sultan Baibars' face. This man was different from the others he knew. The orphan was speechless. Was there irony in his voice?

"Saving my life has earned you my favor, but you have doomed your kingdom. What irony. Be sure that the Mamluk empire will finish your coastal dominion. There will be no words for rights or demands. I will win. There is no question about that."

"It's not over yet," Peter said quietly.

"But you must remember this day. The day you saved my life. You will be rewarded. I expect such duty to protect their master from my soldiers. But from you, I didn't expect it, and I am thankful," Baibars said.

A three Mamluk officers interrupted their conversation with news It was in a language Peter could not understand. As the sultan listened to them, his face twisted with rage.

Even with the pain in his leg, the most powerful man in the realm ran toward the other side of the camp with a determined stride. His retinue—including Peter—followed him through the darkness with flaming torches. Suddenly, all was alive in the camp and there was chaos around it.

"There had been a second attack," sultan's daughter explained to Peter what the soldier had said.

While all the guards in the Mamluks' camp were running to their master after the assassination attempt, a second wave of assassins had stormed in from the opposite side and managed to infiltrate the sentries and to kidnap Isabella and the youngest daughter of Baibars, Anna.

They had vanished into the night, leaving a written message for Baibars.

Peter learned later that the conspirators had demanded that Baibars meet them in a specific place if he wanted to see his daughter again. After two days, on Midsummer, Baibars had to march to the meeting point: Ayn Jalut, the Springs of Goliath. The sultan had to come for his daughter at midday.

Peter understood that Sultan Baibars hadn't time to gather an army; he had only his most trusted battalion at the ready. He also knew that the assassins would lay a trap. What was Baibars to do?

The sultan had to use all the force he had: his intelligence network, the Desert Wolf, and the Crusaders guests.

The little princess was missing, along with Isabella and Edward the Saracen. Githa had been wounded but not the sultan.

The enemy had their bait. But they had made a mistake—a bad one.

***

The Sun was almost on his trail.

Peter, James, Hamo, and Owen sat in front of the tent in the camp and waited to find out what the Sultan's next move would be. The orphan looked at his find from the cave—an ancient Roman iron vambrace with an inscription on one side. There was some rust on the iron armguard but it was remarkably well-preserved. It was a small piece of armor, not heavy, and covered his arm from the wrist to the elbow. It was a perfect fit for Peter's left forearm.

James took the item and looked at the inscription:

"LONGINOS," it read, and below this, "LEG X FRE."

Peter remembered, from the Vegetius book, that Roman soldiers had inscribed symbols of their names and legions on their armor. Who was the man to whom this piece of armor had belonged? He had seen such letters in the Tower of David.

"Maybe it belonged to a Roman soldier?" Peter asked.

"In France, a monk told us a legend about Longinos. During the crucifixion of Christ, a man who was a blind Roman soldier thrust his spear into Jesus's body," James drank some water and returned the iron vambrace to Peter. "Some of Christ's blood fell over the soldier's eyes and people said Longinos was healed."

"Healed? Are you serious?" Peter grinned.

"Hey, these are not my words, but the story which the French monk told us," James touched the bandage over his wound. "I wish I can heal so fast."

"You're saying this vambrace is from the time of Jesus?"

"Maybe it is, maybe it is not. It is curious," Red Herring smiled at him. "The ancient Romans called it a 'manica' or something like that and it was a part of their segmental armor. Every legionary soldier owned it."

"How do you know so much of the Romans?" Peter asked.

"In Durham, my family has a full set of armor in our armory. The Romans lived on our lands, far in the north of England."

Upon reflection, he decided not to reveal it to others except his friends. He feared that the church might want to claim his discovery. Red Herring approved of his decision.

"It's a lucky charm and it's only for you, lad. But if you want to sell it, call me first."

Ibn Abd al-Zahir, the sultan's clerk arrived with puffy eyes.

"Follow me!" he ordered and guided them to the sultan. Peter hoped they would learn their destiny.

Rather than lead them to the sultan's tent, the clerk turned toward the slope. Soon they reached the shore of the Dead Sea.

Baibars was dressed in a tunic and was in the water up to his naked knees. He saw their arrival and walked toward them.

The golden Mamluk soldiers surrounded him at every step. Nevertheless, the sultan looked calm. He raised his hand to the orphan, beckoning him closer.

"Walk with me, Peter Longsword."

The others stared but said nothing.

They walked side by side for a few steps. Baibars looked toward where the Sun would soon be rising. When they were far enough that no one could hear them, he smiled at the lad.

"I wish to walk with you and to know the man to whom I owe my life."

Peter didn't know what to say.

"First, again, thank you for your deed, as it wasn't your duty," the old man said, looking the younger man in the eyes. "Second, I would like to know what were you doing so late with my daughter in the night."

Peter was shocked by the request.

"We ... talked," he managed to say.

"Just talk?"

"I wanted to thank her for saving my life in the tower," Peter said.

"Fate is unpredictable," Baibars said, smiling. "One saved life leads to another; she saved you, and then you saved me. Such irony. What you think?"

"I am glad she saved me," Peter said.

"I am glad she saved you, too."

Baibars changed the subject.

"This man, Ulf, is unbeatable, one-on-one. Even if there are ten soldiers against him, he will win again. But do you know what would make him a better warrior?"

"What?"

"A cause, as I said before. The cause makes you a better man, makes you value life and the precious little things in life ...."

The sultan raised his left hand toward the landscape.

"...the Sun, the warmth, a smile, love, a child's laugh, the satisfaction when you build something in your life more than a straw hut," Baibars said.

"... a smile?"

"Someday you will understand that you can't buy a smile—a simple child's smile." He stared at the lad. "Take this knowledge in advance, but you must accept and understand it first before you can benefit from it." The older man smiled. "All these things form your own cause, something more to fight for than survival. To fight for the things and people you love—that, my friend, gives you a cause"

"A cause."

"Yes, and it makes you a better man, hence a better warrior. A warrior fighting for his own cause can match ten men who don't have one. No one can change that, and guess who will win?"

"Ulf."

"You've seen what he can do, imagine what he is capable when he has a cause."

Peter said nothing, swimming in his own thoughts.

"I've witnessed him when he had a cause," Baibars said, "I'd never seen such determination and such devotion before. I almost felt sorry for the forsaken souls whom he stood against."

"At the last fortress mission?"

"Are you intending to follow his path?" Baibars asked.

Peter wondered for a moment what to say.

"I wish I could fight like him, to take my revenge on the man who killed the closest thing I had to family."

"An honest answer, but you should beware of the path of the vengeful warrior." He looked the orphan at the eyes and said, "It will drain your soul."

A rider arrived and interrupted them.

It was the woman from the tower. They returned to the others, and Peter felt the curious looks of the others upon him. Everybody wanted to know why Baibars had taken him for a private chat.

The daughter of the sultan brought something wrapped in a piece of linen cloth. She dismounted and gave it to her father. The short clerk, the physician, and a dozen golden guards stood around him. Red Herring, Hamo, and Owen were ten steps away from the shelter and there were another dozen

Mamluks in the area.

Ulf dragged himself from nowhere and stood behind the girl, showing no aggression.

"Last night, this man saved my life," Baibars said and gestured toward the orphan.

All eyes were on Peter.

"Not again," Owen said with an ironic smile.

"This gift is to remember your courage and your name."

The sultan unfolded what his daughter had brought. It was a sword, a real Crusader's blade.

It was a magnificent masterwork, a little longer than the more common 'hand-and-a-half'. The blade seemed expensive; it was four-sided—like a flat diamond—and had a reinforced triangular midrib. The sword possessed a stiff cross-section and reinforced tip, and the round pommel had a cross on it.

Peter's jaw dropped a bit as he remained silent. This gift definitely surprised him. He felt like a child receiving a long-anticipated gift from his father. The weapon seemed versatile, a custom-made masterpiece. Now he felt like a child, his eyes full of joy.

"Peter," Baibars said. "With my grateful joy, I present to you this gift and I am indebted to you. Peter Longsword—" The sultan offered his hand. "—to whom I will be obliged forever. You are my blood-brother, now, and I am yours."

One servant had appeared and brought an old scabbard to dress the blade and the sultan gave it to the orphan.

"This was the sword of your father, William Longsword, which I have possessed since the victory at Al-Mansurah. Now, I return it to you, its rightful owner."

Peter noticed all eyes were on him waiting for his reaction.

"Blood-brother?" Owen smiled. Red Herring slapped him on his neck to silence him.

"You may also name your prize, whatever you want from me," Baibars added.

All this shocked Peter. The sword of his father was presented to him from the sultan. The man who slew him. The father whom he never knew. His image was somehow strange and distant for him. He wanted to learn more about his father.

And Peter had saved his father's killer who made him his blood-brother.

Such irony and Fate loves it.

***

Ten years before, Baibars had met a Templar Knight named Matthew Sauvage. The knight had been a prisoner, but a great man, nonetheless. Baibars had made him his blood-brother. This decision gave him benefits. Since then he had used their personal friendship to negotiate agreements and truces with the Christians. Now again, he trusted his instincts and made the son of Longsword his blood-brother. He just knew he had to do the same way with Peter as he already owed his life to him.

Sultan Baibars looked at Peter's innocent face.

When he was in prison in Karak thirty-two years before with his then master he met a prophet. This old and crippled man had said to him back there that: Three great warriors would define Baibars' fate, a prophecy had decreed: one to threaten his life, one to fight on his side, and the last to be the first two combined.

"Is he the one?" Ibn Abd al-Zahir asked.

The Lion of Egypt didn't answer. He was back in his memories.

He had been young and ambitious, but he hadn't lacked bravery. He thought of himself as anything but a coward. He had survived many things since he had met the old, dying prophet.

It rang in his head as if it had happened just the day before.

"One to threaten your life, one to fight on your side, and the last to be the first two combined, but more dangerous than others." The old man's words echoed in his mind.

One he had met at Mansura. William Longsword.

He was the only one who had almost killed Baibars. The sultan hadn't seen such zeal, devotion, and bravery before. This knight, a dark-haired Christian demon, had almost succeeded in killing him. Baibars managed to escape death by virtue of luck and the help of one of his friends.

One had saved him. The Desert Wolf. Ulf was the one who had fought on Baibars' side. He had been delivered from the waves; there had been a shipwreck and the Wolf was the sole survivor. Had it been luck again? Baibars had almost given an order to kill him. But his heart had decided against his mind's decision. This man had turned the odds in his favor. He was the man and the sultan he was today because of Ulf.

Since then, Baibars had asked himself when the third one would appear—the third great warrior from the prophecy. He had encountered many brave soldiers, but none could compare to the other two.

And now he thought he had met him, at last: the third one. Peter Longsword, the orphan from Acre. The man who had saved his life. The son of William Longsword, in whose veins ran the blood of the Lionheart, walking on the steps of the Desert Wolf.

Baibars was amazed by this.

Fate had a strange sense of humor.

CHAPTER FIFTEEN

Holy Land, Thursday, 23rd June in the year 1272 of the incarnation of Christ; Somewhere north of Jerusalem; St John's Eve

"You are insane!" Sir James scolded him. "Why not simply let the bugger hang? Why?"

"It is not right that the man dies like this. It doesn't seem right." Peter had difficulty explaining.

They discussed the favor which Peter had asked of Sultan Baibars: to spare Edward the Saracen's life. The orphan had pity for this man. He couldn't explain it, but he felt it wasn't right for him to be hanged like a helpless rat. After all, Peter owed him for sparing his life in Acre.

"He is a treacherous bastard. Remember that. He switched sides. No man who does that can be trusted," James said.

Peter looked at the Scottish knight. James had never been a fan of Edward the Saracen.

The enemy had struck fast the night before. In the tower of the citadel, they had been exposed and had managed to escape by an inch. The conspirators had sacrificed many lives to slow down the Wolf.

Today, the enemy had the upper hand. Today, they had the one thing that could break a man's will and desire to fight: Sultan Baibars' most beloved child, Anna.

But Baibars wasn't an ordinary man. Neither was Anna's Uncle Ulf.

The Desert Wolf had rejoined their group just before Peter received the sultan's gift. Fast as the wind, another spy had arrived with news of a force gathering between them and the city of Acre. Ughan's northern battalions marched south, alongside the river Jordan. A renegade Tartar army led by Siraghan al-Tatari had already reached the Iron Hills northeast of the fortress of Qaqun to join forces with Berrat and Ughan's soldiers. Soon they will all come together and wait for the Sultan to arrive.

The enemy had but one crucial blow to deliver and the path to the throne of the Muslim world would be free.

"Call your battalions?" Ibn Abd al-Zahir suggested.

"My most trusted one was annihilated in the desert storm, led by Berrat." Baibars looked accusingly at Ulf and the orphan.

"The traitor," Ulf said.

"The betrayal of the closest people hurts most," al-Zahir said.

"Is there a betrayal that does not hurt?" Baibars looked stone-faced toward the clerk.

Another rider delivered more news. A small raiding party, probably from the night assault, was heading north toward the northern battalions. The sultan's network was working; even far from civilization, he received news.

"So, Anna and Lady Isabella were taken north." James nodded.

"Why do you bother? You can make another daughter," Ibn al-Nafis said.

Baibars looked at his friend's face. "I am the most powerful man in this realm. I cannot allow the renegades to determine my decisions. Yes, I can make as many daughters as I want. But I cannot leave any of my children at the mercy of my enemy." Sultan's tone was stone-cold.

The answer shocked the orphan. So, it is not for his daughter's sake, but for the sultan's pride. Peter bowed his head and looked at the dusty ground. He preferred to think that it was all about Anna. Baibars turned to him and said, "'If you want to go fast, go alone,' a wise man once said. 'If you want to go far, go together.'"

Ulf wanted to go alone. But Baibars insisted that they

should be as many as the souls who had been kidnapped: Anna, Isabella, and al-Rida's son. Peter and Hamo volunteered at once.

He remembered his night with her and his protective instinct kicked into high gear. He wanted to see her again, her smile and her face. Her angel's face was so innocent, like Anna's. Ivar the ostringer, the personal guard and falconer of the young lady, volunteered too.

They would ride as if there was no tomorrow, and if they failed...

The rest would stay behind to gather as many trusted soldiers as possible in a day and then marched to the meeting point. On St John's Feast day, Baibars was to come for his daughter at midday at Ayn Jalut, the Springs of Goliath.

The meeting would be bloody. Peter didn't think for a moment that the sultan would leave everything to diplomacy. Not this time. He had lost one daughter. One more had been kidnapped.

"Five to go." Dark humor rose in Peter's mind. But this act of the enemy had crossed a line—the bloody line of pride. There would be no peace for anyone.

Peter grinned. The end of their quest was near, like a song. It promised to be deadly and momentous. The song would be sung for a child's rescue, a princess, and a kingdom. There would be sword brothers, bravery, knighthood, and revenge. The song would be marvelous.

Yes, revenge. Everyone had his path to follow.

Peter noticed that Baibars looked calm. He remembered the expression he had worn while they walked and talked on the shore of the salt sea.

"The enemies have their bait."

"Anna," Peter said.

"But now the Wolf has his cause once more. Anna is a little copy of his beloved one, my eldest daughter." The sultan looked like a heartless bastard; he spoke of the situation as if it were another ordinary opportunity to battle. He looked back at the conversation he had with the other daughter. If they were the sultan's weakness, why would he bring them with him to the desert? Why would he hide her in his enemy's lair?

Because he didn't trust anybody.

Still, he showed nerves of steel. No emotion, no panic, no rushed decisions, no bad temper toward the circumstances, although he was known for it.

"They made the mistake I was waiting for," Baibars said to him. "Like in a game of chess. The son of Nonagenarian, Shams al-Din. He tried to play the game of the kings. Some succeed at this, others do not. Will he succeed? I doubt it."

"A mistake?"

"Anna!"

"You hoped they would kidnap her?" Peter asked.

"Don't be silly. I am a father. Do you really think I hoped for that? But, yes, they made a rare mistake. They have tried to eliminate *Diyaab al-Sahra*. Why? Because they fear him. And they should. Now, his vision is clear; he knows who the real enemy is."

Baibars looked at the sky.

"They captured the wrong person. They kidnapped the wrong target," the Sultan said. "And who do you think will bring her back?"

"Ulf?"

"Berrat and Ughan, the men you saw in the citadel in Jerusalem, must pay for their actions. And not only them but their families and all who were involved. This time, Wolf has not only to kill but also to save the life of a child." And to make the world a better place, Peter thought. For that intention, the world needs its beasts—the most bloodthirsty predators—on his side.

"Even you have a motivation and a cause: your Lady of Beirut," Baibars said.

He was right, Peter thought.

"In your eyes, I see the hate you bear toward me. I understand that. But now the spy games are over. The masks have fallen away. It is time for our turn," Baibars had said earlier to Ulf.

Sir James was invited to stay behind to join the sultan's war council. Owen stayed to watch after him. He wasn't sure if they were sultan's guests or hostages.

The demands of the renegades were that the sultan should be in a specific place on Midsummer to exchange the old man of the mountains, Shams al-Din's father, for Anna.

There was one problem, Peter understood: the old man was dead. There could be no exchange.

"What, then?"

"The plotters will reap what they sow," Baibars said, his face twisting. "War is coming. And we must face it."

"Lads, I wish I could ride with you." Red Herring's face sank; he was a man of action, and staying in the camp was difficult for him.

"You should fully recover first, Sir James, but we will meet again," Hamo said.

"Watch out lads, do not do anything stupid," Red Herring shouted at their backs.

They left the camp: the Desert Wolf, Peter, Hamo, and Ivar the ostringer. They rode like demons—fast as if a whole army of angels pursued them. This was a race for lives and salvation—for Anna, Isabella, and the two Edwards. But they were also after death; they were on a hunt.

Sweat covered Peter's neck. He was dressed in a white robe with a hood over his head. The heat was harsh though the Sun wasn't up yet.

"Here we go again," he thought, "riding toward the unknown." The whole story was happening so fast.

Peter looked in front of him, where Ulf was riding. Hamo rode behind Peter and Ivar was last. Ulf knew him from before. The young man examined Anna's bodyguard. His nose looked like the beak of an eagle; it was fitting that he was an ostringer, a falconer. Peter had asked Ivar about his bird—a golden eagle he kept with him—and had learned its name was Igor. It was a marvelous creature. Peter knew it was expensive to possess one; it was a hobby for royals. Not simply nobility; only royalty. They took pride in competing with each other, hunting with birds of prey. The golden eagle was one of the best hunters.

"Igor can catch even a wolf," Ivar had said.

Anna had a hobby; she loved eagles. Especially golden ones. For that reason, her father had presented her with this man as her personal bodyguard, one of the best falconers in the world. Ivar was like a nursemaid to Lady Anna. Nursemaid, guard, and falconer—Peter was jealous. Where was his father, to give him such presents?

Ivar was tall and stocky; he had a big brow and blue eyes. His light brown long hair was usually tied at the back of his neck. He seemed to be in his late thirties but he possessed fearsome agility. He spoke rarely; he didn't ask questions and didn't say much.

They were riding at full speed toward their target, never mind the heat. It was a wild chase against time. They were running against the odds.

And they rode, four men toward countless enemies coming from the north. Peter didn't count himself a proper soldier yet, somehow. He had been bound to this story from the beginning, but he didn't feel ready to put himself side-by-side with the men who were riding with him.

Peter felt somehow rejuvenated. The end of the game was near. In the past week, he had seen a whole new world. He felt drunk as if he were drinking deep from the cup of life.

He wanted more. He was ready to unleash his vengeful thoughts soon.

The Sun had awakened long ago.

They were dressed like locals, not only because of the heat. Hamo's destrier had been brought to him from Jerusalem and now he was happy again. The others rode some of the sultan's best horses. They didn't give rest to the animals, nor themselves. The River Jordan was on their right; they followed its bed, climbing cliffs, descending slopes. Ulf spurred them hard.

The kidnappers had almost four hours of advantage. Still, they were dragging a child, a woman, and a wounded and tied assassin; they must be slowed down. Or so Peter hoped.

"Look, down to our right!" Hamo shouted.

There was a dust cloud a few hours ahead of them.

"Our target?" the orphan asked hopefully.

Ulf said nothing. They traveled fast and light, with no additional bags—just the clothes on their backs, some light leather armor, their weapons, plus some water and Arab biscuits in the bags around their necks—nothing more. A wise man would say they were mad to go through the desert and the wilderness like that, but Peter trusted the judgment of the Desert Wolf.

"Rainstorm is coming," Ulf said.

Peter looked at the sky, but there was nothing except the smile of their unstoppable follower, the Sun.

"What rainstorm? It's almost Midsummer in the desert." Hamo also examined the horizon.

"The last few years, there were storms, rains, and floods during this time of the year," Ivar said.

"We survived a sandstorm a few days ago, too," the orphan added to no one in particular.

"The land and the weather are changing," Ulf said.

"God is punishing us," Hamo said.

"Any weather—good or bad—affects everyone and everything. Even the wildest creatures," Peter said.

"They are near," Ulf said.

"What we will do when we catch them?"

Hamo and Ulf said nothing. The orphan wasn't sure he was ready to face the obvious answer.

As sunset approached, they were close to their prey. They reached the end of the cliffs and observed the river bank and what lay ahead.

Peter surveyed the landscape. There was a place to cross the river—a natural slope down to a gulf, where the riverbed branched like narrow sleeves which were crossable during the summer—a natural path created by almighty God.

There were ruins on the left bank of the river from a fortress which had once guarded the passage. The stone wall—or what was left of it—was about six meters high. There were also the remains of an old bridge; pieces of destroyed rocks, rotten trees, and planks were visible. Someone was rebuilding the fortification, Peter could see. Carts, stone, and wooden parts had been delivered and were stored on the right side of the river. The entire place was full of workers and soldiers who protected the raw materials and oversaw the builders.

"Someone must be in a hurry to complete the work during the summer," Hamo said.

Most of the reconstruction was finished. The fortress was square-shaped, with a four-sided wall and a tower on the eastern end. It was an old-fashioned design. They were building over the ruins, without clearing the ground, and they were in a hurry.

"In France, I discovered that builders of fortification and castles now prefer round towers, as they resist catapult and trebuchet fire better. The round tower will not crumble so easily," Hamo said.

"But this was built long ago," Ulf said.

"And now someone is rebuilding it," Ivar observed.

"Mamluks from the north?" Peter asked.

"Perhaps," Ulf said.

The Saracens were working on it fast, and it wasn't cheap to bring so many resources and workers to one place these days.

"In the time of Saladin, this border castle was erected by the King of Jerusalem against the agreement they had with the sultan back there," Ulf said. "The Knights Templar, in their greed, insisted on imposing taxes on the passage. It was almost done when the Sultan's force overran the fortress. According to the story, there were no survivors; it was a bloody slaughter. The Christian king arrived too late and when he saw the smoke from the fire, he turned back his horse. Saladin razed it to the ground. Still, he left some stones to remind the Crusaders what would happen to them if they broke their word."

"When was that?" Peter asked.

"Long ago ... even before Richard the Lionheart's arrival, before Saladin broke the Kingdom of Jerusalem. It was when the kingdom of the Christians was strong and great," Ulf said.

They saw that their prey was taking cover for the night inside of the fortress.

It would be an interesting night.

"Now what?" the orphan asked.

The Sun was almost down behind the hill.

"No campfire," Ulf said. "Now we'll wait."

Peter felt like a child before a game. Darkness hugged the passage when two battalions arrived at the fortress from the north. Peter's group observed them as the soldiers crossed the river. He estimated at least 200 Mamluks and more than 200 Bedouins. The Mamluks looked different than the golden soldiers of the sultan, as if from another realm. They were disheveled and dusty as if they had marched all day long.

They dismounted and started to make a night camp around the fortress. Some of the Mamluks entered, but the Bedouins were all left outside the walls.

"Sir James told me that most of the Bedouins obey the old man of the mountains, the same man who led the assassins, the father of Shams al-Din," Hamo said.

"The Bedouins believe that no man can die, except on the day fate decide for him. For this reason, they don't wear armor," Ivar added. He held a small knife in his right hand and was making a whistle from a piece of wood. "They also believe that, when a man dies for his lord, or for any good purpose, his body passes on to a better life, happier than before."

"No armor?" Peter wasn't sure he heard right.

"In battle, they carry nothing but sword and spear. Nearly all of them are clad in furs," Ivar said. "They lived in the realm of Egypt, in the realm of Jerusalem, and in all other countries that belong to the Saracens and infidels, to whom they pay heavy tributes every year. They are the real desert masters. They can smell when there will be a battle and booty." Ivar looked at the whistle in his hand and tried it. Nothing occurred and he continued to use his knife to shape it.

"Look," Ulf said, pointing below. "The Mamluks are wearing the colors of Ughan."

"It looks like the Bedouins are in alliance with the Mamluks of the north, then," observed Ivar. "Ughan's battalion. Still, they cannot be trusted. They have always been on the side of the old man of the mountains. And Shams al-Din is his direct heir."

"They are gathering their forces," Peter said.

"And rebuilding the fortress to control the passage of the

River Jordan," Hamo said.

"We will wait until the Moon gets tired. Then we will enter." Ulf said.

"Four versus 400? That's without counting the guards and the workers."

"Are you scared, young lord?" Ivar challenged him.

"I am all things, but not scared."

"But you should be."

Clouds hid the horizon.

Peter pulled an apple from the bag.

"You were right about riding and that the feeling isn't the same after a week," he said and gave the fruit to Ulf. "Why green apples?" The young man sat down beside him and bit one fruit too.

"I like them." Ulf stared at Peter. "When I was a child, every time I was sad, my mother gave me a green apple."

"Your mother?"

"Yes, a green one. Now every time I look at this fruit I see my mother's face in my memories."

"Where is she now?"

He did not say more, but instead, he looked up at the sky and his face became bleak. Peter didn't ask again.

After some time, he observed that four riders arrived and entered the fortress. They were dressed in dark clothes, unlike the rest.

Mercenary knights? Could it be Julian?

"Look!" Peter pointed at the newcomers.

"We must hurry," Hamo said. "They may have come to take them away."

"Why? They won't go into the desert at night. If they're here to take the prisoners, they will rest and leave in the morning," Ulf said.

They waited in the dark.

For a moment, Peter thought about Isabella. He couldn't remove this woman from his head—her smile, her eyes, her soft hair, her pale face. He had seen the way Hamo and other men looked at her. It was like magic when she entered the stage; all eyes were pinned on her. She was a beauty, and she was charming. Above all, she had been clever enough to survive all these years in this forsaken land. This was a rare combination: beauty, and cleverness.

On the other hand, he thought of the sultan's daughter, the one who had been in the tower. She was more like him—not necessarily noble in her behavior, but wild; the fire of youth was in her face and heart. She was adventurous like the orphan; she possessed more than prettiness and a smile.

Peter smiled. He had forgotten to ask for her name. He asked Ulf, who only grunted and responded that this was a question for her.

The young man urged himself to focus; now wasn't the time to think about women, even if he was on course to save one.

"Where did you learn to fight like that?" Peter asked Ulf.

"I had a teacher," the experienced warrior looked at the sky then turned his eyes to Peter. Ulf told him that his master had taught him, as a boy, how to use both his hands. He had beaten Ulf—hard—when he favored one hand.

"My teacher was constantly telling me that if I wanted to live and to deliver my message or revenge, I needed to be more, much more than the other soldiers. To be that man, you must be completely dedicated and train hard. It is a continuous process."

"Training is continuous?" Peter asked.

"Yes, I trained all my life to be such a warrior, to survive and to win. And then I met her ...." Ulf paused. "But now she is gone."

Peter observed the Wolf's face. He looked lost in his dark world.

His face was empty, his emotions lost long ago.

"Only one thing can ease the pain," Ulf said.

"What?"

"Release the anger."

"Does it help you?" Peter asked.

"No," the warrior said and looked at the sky. "But I know only this way, to kill them all."

The conversation was over for now. The orphan sat down

and fell asleep. He was so tired that even the light drizzle which had begun to fall lulled him.

Ulf woke him up. Peter rubbed his eyes and stood. He noticed the rain had put out all the campfires in the fortress. It looked like the drizzle was going to rain all night.

"Where have you been?"

"Scouting." He tossed four Bedouin outfits, marked with blood, at their feet.

Peter stood and wiped out the water from his forehead. It had even gotten in his ears. There were a few hours before sunrise.

They folded their weapons in their clothes and tied them up on their backs. They left behind all their mail armor and anything else that could reflect the moonlight. Ulf ordered them to leave the shields, too; he didn't want to risk someone slipping and alarming the guards. They put the new garments on over their leather armor. The rain didn't stop but only grew thicker. No stars could be seen in the sky and the Moon was missing, too.

This would be a night of knives—silent and deadly—Ulf warned them.

"Do not hesitate! If you do, you are dead. Worse, your friends will be dead, your mission ruined, and your princess lost." The harsh Northman emphasized again, "Do not hesitate! Just do whatever you must. When the enemy starts to wake up, you have to thrust, stab, kill, and silence him." These words were still in the orphan's head.

At the tower in Jerusalem, Peter hadn't had enough time to think; he had been tired and vengeful. He had killed a guard without hesitation. The situation had been one-on-one, eyes open, face-to-face. He had delivered justice for James. But now … in the dark, while the opponents were sleeping, he felt strange. He tried to imagine what would be in guards' place. To sleep and someone to enter in the night to cut your throat. But it was like the Desert Wolf was reading his mind,

"It is their responsibility to protect and not let us inside. If you leave the door open, wolves will attack your herd."

But first, they had to find the ladies.

They crept through the night, as the sound of the unstoppable rain covered their steps. They approached a part of the wall on which there was a wooden scaffolding. The darkness was their hideout.

Two sentries were hiding from the rain under a tent, leaving one part of the stone wall unguarded. The newly-erected pieces of stone were attached with mortar, which was wet and muddy. Ulf showed them how to put their short blades between the stones and climb up, step by step, in the darkness. Soon, they had all jumped over the wall, and they were on the third story of the fortress, a hundred paces from the tower.

Peter saw a light at the top of the tower. There must have been a guard on the top, hidden from their sight and under some shelter to protect the torch from the rain.

Ulf nodded toward the light and gave them a signal to wait in the shadow of the tower. While the orphan and the rest were waiting, Ivar climbed and, after a few moments, the light was shaken and a tiny sound announced that no guards would see them from the top.

"Maybe they aren't here and this is a trap," Peter suggested.

"Trap? For whom? For you? For me? Or for him?" Hamo said with irony.

"Quiet! Look to your left, second story—the wooden garret windows with the tiny light from the inside," Ulf said.

They froze and looked where he was pointing. They would have to walk along the parapet on the wall, the length of the fortress. The courtyard was full of tents and sleeping men; a few campfires were still dancing, but the sentries were hiding from the rain.

"A lot of soldiers," Peter noted.

"War is coming, and for that you need soldiers. The renegades who want to overhaul the sultan and his authorities will need a lot more than these men," Ivar said.

"Why?"

"Baibars is a dangerous man. He is a soldier, a captain, and leader of men. Beware of an old man in a profession where men usually die young," Ivar said.

Ulf signaled to them to shut up. Then he pointed through

the yard and observed a stone arc. Stone pieces of the structure, left from the Crusaders' builders, still hung over the two walls, connecting them. The entrance under the arc would lead them to the inner yard of the fortress. But they had to go over it.

Ulf began to climb over the arc, step by step, and then he slid on the slope to the opposite side. Peter and Hamo followed his example. For a moment, the orphan thought he would fall. He looked down and observed some improvised shelters, constructed in a hurry to protect the sleeping men from the torrent. His heartbeat accelerated and he sweated.

A hand grabbed him and steadied him.

"Look at me, Peter!" Hamo's voice was quiet, focused on the young man. Darkness was around them, but the orphan could see the fire from the camp reflected in Hamo's eyes.

"I am fine," Peter faltered.

He dragged himself to the other side and took a deep breath. They climbed over the roof. It was tiled and slippery from the rain. Ulf transferred himself close to the window and hung down on its left. It seemed so easy when Ulf did it. He peered inside and raised his right hand, showing two fingers.

The orphan heart was pulsating hard; he was afraid the enemy would hear it.

So, in the room, there were at least two guards. But what about the rest? Peter looked at the opposite building, the place they thought the enemy held the captives. They must cross the inner yard to enter it. Under other circumstances, it would be easy. But now they were in the middle of an enemy camp full of soldiers.

The Desert Wolf caught a part of the wooden beam and hung, relaxed his body, and released himself. Peter heard the dull sound when Ulf landed, and turned around like a cat and moved against the wall in a heartbeat.

Peter did the same; he was used to running among the ruins of the Genoese quarters in Acre after the Saint Sabas war, and he was nimble. For Hamo, it was much harder to land lightly and leap quickly against the wall. But he managed it, somehow.

Standing, Peter observed that they were in the inner yard; it was smaller, with a stone well in the middle. There weren't any sentries here, only the rain dancing on the tile and the mud.

The stable was in the courtyard, but Peter could hear a little noise from it. The horses weren't calm. The drizzle would turn into a storm, the orphan predicted.

They were soaked as if they had been swimming in their clothes, and their faces were hard to recognize. Their four shadows approached the first door.

Ulf was near the wooden door, which stood ajar. Light from inside was dancing and making shadows on the wall. At least two men's voices could be heard inside.

When the Desert Wolf had explained to them what the plan was, it had seemed easy: To wait until the dying parts of the night, to enter under the cover of the night, to find Anna, Isabella, and Edward the Saracen, and to retreat. Easy, like a walk in a garden. The orphan hadn't imagined this journey would be soaked with water, darkness, and patience. Not to mention the danger.

They heard voices clearly speaking their language.

"Christians?" Hamo's face was in wonder.

"The four riders," Peter assumed.

To succeed in this endeavor would be equal to a miracle. Still, he knew the kidnapped souls wouldn't have a chance without them. One chance was all they needed now. And some luck.

Distant thunder cut the sky and echoed for a few heartbeats. This was a sign; soon there would be more lightning in the sky.

Peter closed his eyes for a moment and tried to focus.

What was inside the door?

The rain was singing, *tap, tap*. It seemed as though it would never stop.

***

Dark riders were all over the place.

"Kill them all," Julian shouted, joy in his voice.

Ughan said nothing. He had agreed with the Templar's

proposition. He turned his gaze to survey the whole valley. The city of Nablus was sacked with ruthless speed.

"Uncontrollable refugees are a threat to society," Ughan said. "Isn't that right Berrat?"

He nodded toward the man on his right. The bareheaded Mamluk was watching. It was dark; soldiers were puttering around with torches. The screams and cries had almost died out.

The united forces of Ughan's personal battalions, Julian's Templars, and Berrat's men had surprised the inhabitants. They let the old, the women, the children, and the sick leave through the desert and executed the rest.

"Uncontrollable refugees are a threat to society," Berrat repeated to himself. He had learned it from his friend, Baibars—now the sultan, but not for long.

They created a mass of refugees. From his experience, he knew the sight of these helpless, crying people inspired hatred of the government because it showed that the ruler had failed to protect his own people and taxpayers. It also brought fear to the mind of the opponent. And now Sultan Baibars was their opponent. Whether this strategy would work the time would show.

They were prepared. They had been planning this. It wasn't an ordinary attack to satisfy the hunger for plunder; it was with purpose. They used these tactics against the sultan.

Baibars was the ultimate enemy. He wasn't a pale commander with yellow spots around his mouth; he was an old man in a profession in which men usually died young. And Berrat knew his friend well.

Were they still friends?

They had shared everything, up until Baibars had become a sultan. After that, the danger was for Berrat, but not the spoils of victory. This had tainted their friendship. Berrat wanted more. He knew he must wait for the perfect moment. He had waited so long, it was painful. He had established control over the sultan's network and used it well for his personal benefit.

He managed to unite Ughan and Sir Thomas Bérard, the leader of the Templars under one cause. Siraghan al-Tatari, the

Tartar lord had not been easy to persuade; he still remembered the kindness Baibars had shown to him and his men.

Berrat had needed to provide a letter from his faraway lineage lord to persuade him. It had cost him a hefty sum to bribe the convoy, and a year to get it. But the effort had paid off.

The assassins, on the other hand, had not been hard to convince. All one needed were a bunch of promises, a bag of gold, and to push the finger into the wound. Shams al-Din was blinded by his desire for revenge of his father's fate. The assassins' leader was easy to manipulate.

Berrat smiled. His plan was almost complete.

Barak had failed. The orders had been clear: kill *Diyaab al-Sahra*, take his wife—the sultan's daughter—and start the second stage of the plan, assassinating this impudent English prince. This would bring the peace accord to an abrupt end, make the military orders look for payback, and draw Baibars onto the open battlefield.

His daughter would be bait. Baibars had a weakness, as any father would. When they met, they would capture him.

The plan had been simple, clear, and clever. Yet, this dog, Barak, hadn't managed to finish his task. He was astonished how Red Herring had managed to interfere with the attack on Wolf's manor.

He had underestimated Otto; he suspected this knight was different from the others, but still, he couldn't determine how they had obtained the information. He would be seeking answers later, discovering who had sold this news.

The assassination had failed, as well. But a new opportunity had arrived. The Crusaders had acted stupid and helped him. It didn't matter now. They, the renegades, were close to their goal. The end was near, as was the victory. Berrat had waited a lifetime for such opportunity. Now, everything was set and he was ready.

Berrat and his brother in the conspiracy were so close to achieving their plan.

A Wolf and an orphan had stood in their path.

He had almost caught the Wolf on the night of the

sandstorm. But then the orphan had appeared from nowhere and saved him—for now. No one could avoid the inevitable.

Yet, the Wolf had almost ruined their plan when he had appeared in the tower of the citadel. They had managed to recover; now they had Anna. But the sultan already knew of Berrat's betrayal.

Now, he must face his old friend on the battlefield—this wouldn't be settled otherwise. The battalions were mustering: Templars, assassins, Tartar cavalry, his loyal Mamluks, and some from the north, Ughan's own. He still was anticipating an answer from the Hospitallers; they wouldn't want to be left without a share of the plunder and fame, and they would want to avenge their assassinated prince.

It was a dangerous plan, plotting with everybody, using their own weaknesses and greed against them. But Berrat had been playing this game a long time.

Now, they delivered terror to the inhabitants of a village after village, as they approached the meeting place.

"Sir Julian," Berrat grinned. "Why do you want so much this woman, this Lady of Beirut?"

"It's not your damn business," The Templar Knight grunted from his horse.

"I saw her in Jerusalem. I can understand your desire. Maybe I'll take her for me?" Berrat said.

Julian clinched his jaw after the Mamluk's comment.

"We'll see which one of us she will choose," Berrat winked at him.

"Isabella is mine." Julian's eyes flashed.

The bareheaded Mamluk laughed in the dark then he noticed a wounded man, a shepherd who was trying to drag himself out of sight of these bloodthirsty assailants. The bareheaded officer stepped over his back and stabbed him with his sword.

One more village to sack. He looked at the Moon. He had done his part—he hoped his agent would manage, too. The trap was set up. A Lion was anticipated.

***

"We will enter like we are returning from a night watch," Ulf said. "We are soaked and wet, dressed like the rest. Who would suspect us?"

"At least the bath is free," Hamo said, adding, "as the Welshman would say."

They laughed, their laughter lost in the harsh song of the rain. Peter missed the archer's humor.

The Desert Wolf looked at them with amusement. Hamo and Peter nodded; they understood his plan, for it was simple enough. They would enter, kill the guards, and save the ladies. Who needed a better plan? Peter had sarcasm in his thoughts. He couldn't figure out how Ulf was always a few steps ahead—always prepared, intelligent, and insightful. The orphan was eager to learn from him and quickly obtain these skills, but even when he witnessed events, he was blind to what was really important.

"You can't learn everything in a night. You need to fail—this is the best experience," James and Githa had said to him. But there was one catch: in battle, you could only fail once.

Their fourth companion was silent. Ivar had an additional task.

The Desert Wolf nodded to the window of the second story. The rain continued to fall.

He said something to him, but Peter didn't hear it clearly. The man with the aquiline nose started to climb the scaffolding toward the second story. Slowly, he tried not to slip on the wet surface. He would be their insurance, their hidden backup if needed. He would be their eyes and ears for what was happening outside. He would be their eagle guarding them.

Ulf looked at the two men behind him.

"Ready?"

They nodded.

Their leader opened the door, the rain drowning out the sound.

The dim light inside the room shuddered as the fresh air entered with them. It was quiet and for a moment Peter thought it became darker. Fate looked dark, and a moment later they were in.

Peter and the rest had drawn their hidden weapons and were ready to use them. The young man looked around. They entered a spacious room, common to the second floor. From the left and right there were closed doors. At the far end, there was an internal wooden staircase leading to the next floor. There, Peter saw two doors on the left and two on the right, with a wooden railing in front of them.

An oil lamp was dying slowly near him.

They took a few steps forward, their backs to the stone wall. Peter's eyes were trying to adjust to the light inside.

It was quiet.

"Well, well. I knew you would come," Edward the Saracen's voice arrived from above. Peter raised his head. The assassin stood on the second floor to the left of the orphan, placed his hands on the wooden parapet and was surrounded by three more assassins with naked swords.

The left door on the first floor opened and four men clad in white appeared, pointing their spears toward Peter's party's bellies. The young man heard the wooden door opened from the right and he turned his head to see what was coming. Through the door on the first floor, four dark knights arrived with swords in hands. Their faces were unfamiliar to him. On the second floor above the knights, another four assassins with white tunics stood.

"It's a bloody trap," Hamo said.

It was the moment of truth; all masks had been removed. Edward the Saracen—al-Rida—had managed to lay a trap without anyone suspecting him. He had been a rat from the beginning.

"You were supposed to be dead," al-Rida shouted at Ulf.

The orphan managed to catch Edward the Saracen's eye. Peter couldn't believe that he had advocated for him before the sultan. His eyes had looked so innocent.

"You killed everyone I loved," al-Rida screamed at Ulf. "You killed my father, my brother—every single male in my family. Now you must pay. Did you watch your wife die?"

The orphan tried to find some hope. He looked at his

companions. Not one of them looked prepared to surrender.

"When I saw you, Wolf, as we left Acre, I thought our plan was doomed. But I suddenly realized that this mission was due to my failure. Barak hadn't fulfilled his task to kill you. But seeing you agonize over the guilt of your beloved one's death ... It was worth it. Your pain was a bonus to me. Sometimes it is better not to kill your enemy but to make him suffer." The assassin smiled. "You lost, Desert Wolf."

Ulf didn't move or say anything.

"It was a simple plan: kill the Wolf, assassinate the crusading prince, and force the Christians to seek revenge. This would coax the sultan from his hole to address this outrage. And then, the Lion would be in our trap. Simple, eh?"

Peter narrowed his eyes toward al-Rida. Simple, eh?

"When we left Acre, I thought that the mission hung in the balance, but fate has a strange sense of humor, don't you think?" the assassin asked.

Hamo raised his eyes. "What do you mean by that?"

"Didn't you see how the things turned? Now you are in my trap surrounded by my men," al-Rida said.

"Did you know that David was a traitor?" Hamo asked.

"I suspected, yes. The Templars have always had at least one traitor nearby ...."

"This little rat, he will pay ...." Peter now understood that when one betrayed a sword brother, there was no forgiveness. Could there be any forgiveness for treason?

"Peter of Acre, my little orphan, you played your part beautifully—you were so predictable. Thank you for your help, my friend," al-Rida laughed. It was the sick laugh of a sick mind.

"I thought you were on our side," Peter said.

"I have never been on your side, Christian."

The young man gritted his teeth and tried to stay calm as he focused on the assassin's face. He was right, the orphan acted predictably.

Al-Rida turned his gaze toward Ulf.

"When I saw your face, Wolf, as little Anna entered the tent, I realized what my next move would be. She stopped you just as you were about to do what I desired most: kill Sultan Baibars. I had planned it for so long. When Barak failed to deliver your head, you became a deadly blade in my hands, pointed at all Mamluks, including the sultan. But the little girl changed everything, didn't she?" Al-Rida spoke from above as he crossed his hands in front of his chest. He smiled, but it was a new one, which no one had seen before. It displayed a long-hidden hatred. He looked like a man who had just caught a fish in the river with his bare hands.

"Wolf, now you will kneel in front of me and ask for mercy for the life of the little princess as my family begged you before you killed them!"

Peter observed the nervousness of the men in front of them with weapons pointed toward him, Hamo and Ulf. He knew his friends saw it too. It was a bloody trap. This rogue had played his part perfectly. No one of them had suspected anything. Still, al-Rida and his men all waited for their response.

Ulf's eyes were cold. He didn't say anything just listened to the assassin.

"Kneel, dog," al-Rida shouted, "Or you will die and the little lady will watch it!"

A scream from the upper story cut the air. Was it Anna? It was hard to identify; the rain outside sang through the open windows: Tip, tap, and again, tip, tap….

"Kill them all," Ulf said. With the same music, Peter and his fellows charged. They thrust, cut, and swung their weapons.

Ulf grabbed the spear of the nearest assassin and dragged him toward him. He stabbed him in the chest with his sword and used his body for protection from the flying darts from above. Most of the flying daggers were directed toward the Wolf. He was fast like a cat and managed to use the dead man as a shield. In a flash, Peter instinctively raised his left hand as a dart hit him. He heard a metal kiss as the dart struck his Roman arm vambrace. He had forgotten all about it but was happy about his luck.

Christians, traitors, mercenaries, assassins, Mamluks—it seemed all kinds of soldiers were trying to kill them. But it wasn't so easy. The Wolf turned around and used the spear of the dead man to pierce the next assassin just below his chin. The orphan lunged forward with his long blade and surprised the third enemy. Peter impaled with his weapon the man in front of him and he felt the warm blood on his hands. He pushed the man back as he pulled the sword out from his belly. More blood mixed with entrails spilled on the floor as he saw the body fell. Peter swung his long blade to the right and hammered the head of the fourth assassin and his face covered in blood from the stroke. Hamo used his sword to deflect the spears toward him and stabbed one of the dark knights with his knife in the left eye.

Darts from above had stopped. Peter and his friends had mixed with the fighting men and there was a risk for the assassins to hit one of their own. Four of the assassins from the second floor stormed toward the stairs but Ulf was already there. The young man managed to see him using his axe and sword to meet the attackers as the orphan crossed swords with one of the knights. He saw the knight's eyes flickered. The situation wasn't anymore in the control of al-Rida. It seemed that the newcomers would win. Peter heard the sound from Wolf's axe delivering death followed by a scream as he tried to push aside the tall knight in front of him.

Edward the Saracen shouted.

A man appeared beside him holding Anna—her mouth was bound, as were her hands.

All the fighting men froze.

"Stop it! Look upstairs, you desert piece of shit," al-Rida said. Yesterday the orphan had thought that Edward the Saracen was on their side. Now he was their enemy again.

Double or triple agent? He was confused for a moment, but suddenly it all was clear to him.

He was an enemy.

"Do you want her pretty face to be spoiled?" Al-Rida touched the face of the little princess.

"Anna?"

"Lay down your weapons, or her beauty will be gone!" Al-Rida said.

"Coward," Hamo said as he retrieved his sword from the chest of last fallen dark knight, pointing the blade down. Peter saw the sticky blood slid down and a few drops spilled on the ground.

"I wanted so much to meet you in a situation like this, Wolf." Al-Rida swallowed, then continued, "You are a dying breed—a warrior with no cause—but living in a world full of enemies. And it's all thanks to you."

They all heard a woman's scream.

Isabella showed herself on the wooden parapet on the left above Peter and his friends.

"Rats!" she shouted.

Isabella kicked a nearby soldier.

A Saracen stood behind her and tried to silence the lady. He grabbed her, raised her over his shoulder and dragged her back where she had come from like a doll. She didn't stop screaming.

"Take her inside," al-Rida said.

The window opened and a figure was delivered through it by the night wind and rain. A pair of daggers flew. The building became a warring chaos again as Ivar knocked over the man holding Anna. The little girl walked around the assassin and stood behind her ostringer who stepped forward and faced another enemy with knives in both hands.

Peter and Hamo intuitively lunged toward the rest of the assailants, pushing aside the spears pointed toward their chests, using the surprise from their companion's arrival to their advantage. Ulf kicked a man in the groin near him, stepped up over his back while he was in convulsive pain, and jumped up to catch the wooden beam of the parapet. In a flash—almost too quick to track with the human eye—Ulf had hoisted himself onto the upper floor and inserted himself between al-Rida and the man who held Isabella.

Peter kicked the enemy who was in front of him between his legs and struck him over his ear with the pommel of his sword. The tall dark knight yelled with pain and fell backward as the young man raised his eyes. He saw that Edward the Saracen realized his own life was at stake; he was panicking.

The vengeful wolf breath was on al-Rida's face, and no man could resist that. The assassin turned his head and saw Ivar who cut his opponent's throat and pushed him aside to fall on the first floor as he stepped toward al-Rida. The Saracen was trapped. And Peter and his friends had managed to overthrow the mercenaries fighting downstairs.

"No!" Edward the Saracen cried. He looked powerless to prevent his plan from being ruined in front of his eyes.

"Die, bastards!" Hamo shouted and hammered an enemy soldier on the first floor with his sword. Blood flew.

Al-Rida stepped back. He tried to say something, but the Wolf swung his blade toward the assassin's neck. The spy stumbled, lost his balance, and rolled, throwing himself through the parapet over the dead soldiers on the first story.

The blade of the Desert Wolf had cut his right ear, but he was falling to freedom. Just before the traitor landed, the assassin flicked his right hand and a dagger flew toward the legendary Desert Wolf. Peter glanced at him to see that he tried to avoid the weapon, but the blade slid over his leather armor to his left side beneath his ribs and hit him. Ulf did not react but stared at the assassin.

Al-Rida fell on the back of one of his men, twisted like a cat, spun on his feet and looked up the stairs. His eyes caught Ulf's for a moment.

"We will see you soon, Wolf," he said and turned, pushing aside one dark knight. He approached Hamo and swung his short blade through his shoulder. The young lord from the Welsh Marches grunted and grabbed his wound.

Al-Rida looked with a vengeful face at Peter, kicked the open door, and vanished in the dark.

The rain sang its melody with rage.

*****

Peter looked through the open door at the night in disguise under the rain.

Ivar and Ulf put to bed all resistance left in the building. Peter looked at the faces of the dead assassins as well as the dead dark knights, but no one was familiar to him.

One was still breathing. It was a member of the dark knights.

"What is your name?" Hamo demanded.

"Antonio of Soana ...." The man had a younger face.

"Who sent you?"

"None of your business ...."

"It seems that soon, it will be not yours, either."

A spasm of pain contorted Antonio's face. He had a nasty wound in his chest.

Hamo pressed his wounded shoulder with his right hand, raised his sword with his left and put the tip of his blade over the right eye of Antonio.

"This conversation can be hard for you, or short."

Antonio stared at the trembling hand of Hamo and watched the dark blood running down his opponent's elbow.

Ulf stood and observed them while holding Anna, hiding her face from this exchange. Ivar brought Isabella from the second floor and went to search the dead bodies.

"Who sent you? I won't ask again," Hamo said.

"It's not your damn business," Antonio said.

"You will die here. I can say a good word for your courage or not. It's up to you. What will you choose?"

There were a few heartbeats, then Hamo released the weight of the sword and it pierced the eye of the doomed man. He screamed and blood stained Hamo's boots.

"The Count of Nola." There was a second scream, and the lord from the Welsh Marches forced his blade down under the weight of his body, silencing the pain of the dying man and splitting his head like a melon.

The sound was unforgettable. Isabella didn't tremble. It looked like she was used to such things.

"Why did you kill him? There are so many questions to ask," Peter said.

"He told us enough," Hamo said.

"Do you know the count?"

Hamo nodded.

"Soon we will have another problem," Peter said, watching

the inner yard. The sleeping men were awakening, raised by the alarm of the running assassin.

Hamo fell to his knees. His face looked pale.

"No …." the Lady of Beirut yelled and ran to him. Isabella sat down beside Hamo and hugged him. She gently touched his face as she raised her head and looked at Peter for a short moment. She had smiled at him, but now she was holding Hamo's face. She was kissing his competitor.

"My love," she said to Hamo as her trembling voice echoed in orphan's head.

"I will be alright, I just…" Hamo grabbed her hand and placed it on his cheek.

She had chosen the knight. Peter felt an indescribable weight in his chest as his heart would burst out of jealousy. Isabella hadn't chosen the orphan. Did they know each other from before? The orphan's mood became darker. He had lost, but he didn't understand why.

He was watching the bleeding Hamo, his sword brother, and the lady Peter desired. Deep inside, he wanted his friend to die.

The moment he had this thought, he felt even more miserable. This feeling tore apart his soul and his mind. Lady Isabella had drawn a line between him and Hamo.

A very deep line.

Over the past few days, the two men had become closer. The knight had taught the orphan some sword techniques and skills but, more importantly, he had let Peter enter their inner circle of sword brothers. He was a good man, regardless of his behavior toward outsiders.

Peter's face twisted in a dark grimace.

A hand patted his shoulder.

He turned with a ferocious expression.

The Desert Wolf, his face stone cold, said, "Peter, keep your eyes on the door."

Ulf pressed his shoulder and nodded toward the task. The young man instinctively obeyed in silence.

"Remove his jacket and bandage his wound. You need to stop the blood," Ulf said.

"You are wounded too!" She said.

"Just a scratch," Ulf said as he smiled to Anna who hugged him.

Ivar returned from upstairs. "It's clear, except this little soul," he said. He was leading a scared, little boy, perhaps the same age as Anna.

"Anna, I need your help. Can you take care of this boy?" Ivar asked his princess.

She nodded.

"You are so brave, little girl," the falconer said.

"I missed you, Uncle Ulf." She had been smiling from the moment she had seen him. She hugged him again, she hugged Ivar, and then she went to the scared boy.

"What's your name?"

Under the sniffles and some tears, the children started their friendship. While they were talking, they went and sat near Isabella.

Ulf nodded at Isabella, who now took care of the children and the wounded knight. Battle was coming and the rest of the party needed to figure out how to escape this mess.

Peter was at the door, watching the rain and how the enemies gathered, preparing to attack the building.

"It's bad," the young man said.

Ulf grinned.

"We can try to sneak out from a window on the eastern side to the river," Ivar said as he turned his gaze toward Hamo and the children.

"But to swim in this rainstorm, in the dark …."

"…it's suicide." Peter finished the sentence.

Ulf turned to the orphan.

"We have to go out. We must surprise them while they are sleepy. Come!"

Regardless of the enemy's numbers, the Wolf always acted as a predator, as a hunter—never a lamb.

"After a few minutes, you have to follow us, we'll attract their attention so you can escape," the Wolf said.

Ivar nodded.

Peter followed him. He looked at his friend in the arms of

the lady and felt a pain inside.

Ulf opened the door and stepped outside, into the rain. Peter Longsword followed him and closed the door behind him. Was he mad?

The young man and Ulf stood, shoulder-to-shoulder, against the inner yard's occupants. Next to him, Peter felt this man had the power of ten men, the courage of twenty soldiers, and the speed of an eagle.

The legendary warrior raised his eyes. His fist became white from holding the pommel of his sword. The blade was hungry, as was his soul. Someone had to pay for his loss and the prize would be a bloody one, Peter thought.

No one could stop Ulf from taking his revenge, he thought. Only death. But no one could evade death. Death was certain, and so was the pain.

Ulf's face was hard as stone, and the determination drawn on it could make even Death avoid him tonight. He was holding his one-handed Danish axe, and his sword was on his left. Peter remembered about their talk for training and Ulf's teacher. The importance to use his two hands, to be more prepared than the other men. Peter glanced at the Wolf, he looked prepared.

Ulf looked forward.

The enemy had nowhere to hide.

The orphan observed the expression and readiness of the experienced killer next to him. Peter's own mood was darker. But he was also scared as he knew how many soldiers were in the fortress. The dark mood of desiring the death of his friend was burning his chest—he never thought such things before. But that thought made his fear disappear. Peter drew his sword—the sultan's gift, the sword of his father, William Longsword—from its scabbard. Somehow, it felt like a natural extension of his hand. But the weapon was useless without its master as Ulf had told him before.

Peter looked forward, too.

"Protect your back, lad, and never hesitate. Remember, do not play with the prey; move fast, aim at their weak points: the neck, the limbs, the armpits. Every single strike must deliver pain, wounds, or kills. The screams of wounded and mutilated men bring fear and terror to the hearts of the others," Ulf said.

The Wolf and his dog stepped forward.

Suddenly, everything turned slow around Peter. He felt as if he could evade the rain drops in the dark. Soldiers were gathering in the yard, organized by the assassin. They were arming themselves in the rain; some were putting on armor, while others did not; they looked like children searching for their toys. It was chaos. They were surprised by the fact that two men approached them.

Peter saw that the Mamluks did not seem concerned. The Wolf and his follower ran toward them, with a purpose to deliver their message.

***

"We must find a way out," Ivar said, looking out through the door.

Hamo's wound was bandaged, but his face was pale. He had lost a lot of blood. Still, his confidence was high around Isabella.

"Let's follow them," Hamo suggested.

"Are you crazy?" Isabella asked. "You are injured and we have two children with us."

"He is right," Ivar said. "We still have the element of surprise. And the rain and darkness will help cover our actions."

"But how …?"

"You heard Ulf, we have to go," Hamo stood and touched her left cheek. She saw the blood on his hand and stared at him silently.

"Aren't we going after Uncle Ulf?" Anna asked. She held the boy's hand, introducing him. "His name is Rave."

"Yes, darling, just a moment," Isabella said.

Hamo retrieved his knife from one of the dead knights and held his sword. "We must force our way out. The faster we move, the better our odds." He bowed his head and kissed her. "I was so scared about you."

"I'm fine," she placed her hands around his neck. "But now I am scared for you."

Hamo stepped aside, took a shield from the dead knight near him and grinned.

"Don't worry, I'll survive."

The sultan's daughter hugged her ostringer and gave him a smile.

"I knew you would follow us, with Uncle Ulf."

"But now we must hurry, my little princess." Ivar's voice was gentle. "We must go through the rainstorm. It is cold and dark. Can you handle it?"

"Of course," she said, smiling at him. It seemed as if captivity hadn't left a mark on her vividness. "But can we take Rave with us?" She looked at the scared boy behind her. Somehow, she had managed to make him trust her.

The severe man with the aquiline nose smiled back.

"Of course, we will take him." Ivar turned and asked the trembling boy, "You are not afraid of the dark, are you?" The boy was dressed in rags, his skin was dirty, and his brown eyes looked scared but curious. The boy nodded and huddled together with his new friend.

Ivar and Hamo looked at each other.

"I'm ready," the lord from the Welsh Marches said.

"So, let's go," Ivar said and pushed the door open wide. "Whatever happens, you stay with me, Anna."

The little girl nodded and took the hand of the man. They went outside and their feet slapped on the wet ground. The rain was singing its song savagely, kissing their faces. The night almost managed to hide what lay on the wet soil; the rain washed the blood away.

Two figures were standing twenty feet ahead, darkened from their deeds, and smiling like a pair of wet cats. Dead bodies were strewn all over the inner yard.

***

Peter and Ulf stood under the stone arch, blocking the entrance to the yard to cover the others while they found a way

300

out. Peter first thought that Hamo, Ivar, and the rest would leave the way they had entered, but then realized that climbing wet stone walls was perhaps beyond the princesses. He smiled at his own naivety. He hoped they would manage to survive.

They had succeeded in killing a dozen soldiers. It had been easy. But that was only the inner yard—there remained the courtyard and the Bedouins outside. They had only three strong men who could fight.

They needed a miracle, and they needed it fast.

Ulf ordered Ivar and Isabella to get up on the stone wall of the fortress with Hamo and the children. "Run between the embrasures and arrow loops. Watch your step. We are coming right after you."

Another group of mail warriors with spears and swords approached from the courtyard. Behind them, another party was awakening. Al-Rida was trying to rouse the sleeping men to attack the entrance that Peter and Ulf guarded.

"Give me that spear, Longsword," Ulf said, wiping the rain from his temple.

Peter passed it to him and watched the man cut some of its length with his axe, effectively turning it into a throwing javelin. The Wolf aimed and threw it. It was a hard shot in the rain but his throw was powered by his desire of killing all who stood against him.

Al-Rida's eyes tracked the incoming threat. It was a hard blow dispatched toward the traitor. The spear point hit him from one side, close to the left shoulder, although the rain had managed to minimize the strength of the throw. The weapon glanced over the mail shirt hidden under his leather vest. Though the spear didn't pierce it, the hit was hard enough to knock him down.

The man who had deceived them all fell in the mud. The Saracen stood; he was shaken but managed to mount a horse and vanish into the darkness.

The Mamluks lined up against the men guarding the inner yard while another group tried to cut off the path of the fugitives on the wall. A tall, middle-aged Mamluk captain with black hair on his helmetless head commanded his men. He led them and approached Ulf. He was only ten steps away.

"Surrender! Put down your weapons!"

Ulf didn't say a thing. His arm moved in a blur and, before Peter could fully register the movement, the Wolf's knife was sticking in the captain's throat. The distance was close enough that the man didn't have a chance to react. He fell on his knees, slowly, his hands trying to hold his throat, but the weapon had broken his trachea and his blood mixed with the rain. His face met the mud and death.

The other Mamluks hesitated. Who was so bold and dared to oppose so many of them and to kill their captain? Another officer stepped from the ranks.

"Who are you?"

Ulf didn't answer him. He turned his back and spoke to the orphan.

"Remember, Peter, anyone who gets past me, kill him. Do not hesitate. This is not a game!"

"Who are you?" the Mamluk asked again. He looked younger than the previous officer.

Ivar led the children and Isabella toward the stone wall on the left and started to climb the wet stairs. Ulf turned to see where they were. "Ivar! Take the children and the woman out of here." It was not a request. The falconer nodded as if he had received an order to buy supper.

"As you command, *Diyaab al-Sahra!*" Ivar said.

"*Diyaab al-Sahra?*" The Mamluk was confused. But not the rest of the squad—they hesitated. There were almost twenty of them, many of them younger soldiers. He was sure the soldiers had heard stories about the Desert Wolf from older soldiers which made them hesitate to engage the famous warrior. A legendary opponent stood before them. Fame was waiting to be won, as well as respect.

Peter felt again how everything turned slow around him. He thought he could see the raindrops falling, one by one. He could see through the moves. It was a strange feeling for him. He held his sword and a round Mamluk shield he had taken from the first wave they had attacked. He wasn't accustomed to using a sword and shield yet. The morning lessons he had taken with Hamo had given him some confidence at the time, but he didn't feel that way now. Still, the shield gave him some protection.

Peter witnessed what a reputation could do. It drove ambitious young soldiers forward, toward risk. It filled them with the desire to win the fight. Twelve Mamluks couldn't resist the temptation and attacked the Wolf, trapped in the rain storm in their yard. They marched, practically ran toward him, trying to catch him off guard. The sound of their feet splashing the mud and the freshly-formed puddles added a strange element to the night of sounds.

Diyaab al-Sahra waited for them as raindrops dripped from his forehead. The orphan's heart was beating in his chest. The Mamluks were approaching him with naked swords and war cries.

Peter saw their eyes were focused at *Diyaab al-Sahra*.

And the first Mamluk, a bulky man, thrust his weapon toward Ulf.

But it was not the sound of the clash of the weapons which echoed; it was the sound of fury and skill. Ulf was so fast. He stood, restless, then—when the enemy was just a few steps away—he suddenly lunged forward. The enemies were running in rows of four, but the first one was a chest ahead. The Wolf pointed toward him. He raised his hands, holding his weapons, and caught him with his axe. The blade met the neck of the first, crushing it with the combination of speed and ferocity. Ulf dragged him and pushed the doomed soul toward the next arrivals. It happened so fast, and the Wolf didn't try to evade enemy's attacks. He moved quickly, knowing exactly where to stand, to stab or to cut.

Like a hot knife through flesh, his blade twisted and splashed. Sounds of broken bones and screams cut the night. Ulf was merciless, delivering pain and wounds with every move. Some of the waves of Mamluks tried to surround him, but he was three steps from the arch which formed a narrow passage. One man almost succeeded in wedging himself next to the Wolf, but he kicked him toward Peter who was behind Ulf, leaving him to the mercy of the young man.

The orphan saw the fear in the Mamluk's eyes. The soldier was young as him. Peter knew what must be done, but he hesitated, thinking.

"Kill him!" The harsh shout erupted from the warrior in front of him. Ulf didn't miss the attackers in front. Peter knew that if he didn't act, they were doomed.

The orphan was a bit clumsy at first, but he put the sword deep into the chest of the Mamluk, looking into the dying man's eyes as he did it. Even the darkness of the night and rain, he saw the fear drawn on his eyes and felt his pain.

The Desert Wolf was unstoppable, nobody got past him, and his weapons delivered death. He used his axe in combination with his sword very skillfully. One man fell with a crushed skull, another attacker hit the mud with a severed limb, a third was pierced directly between his armor and chin. Fountains of blood danced with the rain.

The northern warrior knew his trade. With every step and every move, another soul was released or mutilated. Ulf was darkened from the flying blood. The rain tried to wash his face and attire, but there was always more coming.

Ulf was like an overwhelming plague. If he caught you, you were finished. The hesitation between the Mamluk lines was growing as the lines were coming more slowly. *Diyaab al-Sahra* was doing his work and his follower, the black-haired young man, finished everyone who fell behind him. The fight was surreal, the rainstorm and lightning adding drama to this wet, bloody, dark clash. It looked as if Ulf were enjoying it.

Peter felt exhausted from the killing. The heaviness of his wet clothes and the tiredness of the fighting was drained his strengths. Although Ulf and he fought in the narrow part to the arch that allowed only a few people to face them, still the Mamluks were too many. They regrouped and another line of twenty men advanced.

Hamo came down from the wall, drew his sword, and joined the fight with fresh fury and savagery. He stood on the right side of Ulf as Peter was on his left. The lord from the Welsh Marches struck his shield over the head of a Mamluk who tried to stand from the mud and kicked him in the ribs after he fell.

"Why are you still here?" Ulf shouted.

"We are trapped," Hamo said. Peter glanced up quickly to see Ivar and Isabella were left on the parapet wall with the children. A small group of four soldiers blocked their path and approached them.

But the falconer was a skillful fighter, too. He used a spear to pierce the first attacker, then, without releasing the blade, he pushed the spear and the attacker aside, sending the four men toppling over the side of the stone wall. Another four Mamluks stood before them.

"Damn it!" Peter held his sword tight. Their only option was to fight to the end.

Ulf's cold eyes turned to the next wave of warriors ready to attack. He met the first with a false move to the left and suddenly swung his axe to the right. There was a sound of the skull below the man's eye being crushed and a splashing of blood and brain which hit the next attacker's face. Then Ulf turned, using the back of his axe to hit the second man's shield arm. A scream followed, and another piercing move—this time with his blade to the ribs of the third assailant. Ulf evaded the attacks of the enemies with confidence. He moved like a predator in his prime, using all his abilities to dispatch death and to deliver his message to the opponent.

Lightning lit up the sky; a few moments later the sound hit the ground and the last victim fell under the Northman's axe.

Silence replaced the fight.

Even the dying cries had stopped. Peter caught his breath. There were still many Mamluks in the yard. The enemy was watching them. They were the three men who guarded the entrance to the inner yard—the Wolf, the orphan, and Hamo— sword brothers in the rain, Peter thought and grinned to no one particular. He looked at his companions. Their eyes held nothing but a fighting spirit, which made the Mamluk soldiers stop to regroup again. The rushing attacks hadn't delivered anything significant except death for their fellows.

Peter wiped the water from his forehead. Hamo did the same. Ulf was like a rock; he didn't show any sign of fatigue.

He looked like a man who encouraged the enemy. Evil desire lit his face as if he enjoyed the killing. This scared the orphan. The Desert Wolf was merciless, brutal, fierce, fast—he butchered the enemies like cattle. He turned so fast, swinging his weapons in his hands in the rain, ruthless. The rain mixed with copious amounts of blood. This scared the young man more.

Just then, a Bedouin group arrived in the yard. They were led by an old man, nearly the age of the sultan. But they didn't attack. It seemed that they were looking for something.

"Dad!"

A child's shout rang out from the walls.

A wind arrived and the rain was blown away.

***

City of Acre, Thursday, 23rd June in the year 1272 of the incarnation of Christ; Edward's Chambers

Why was time so limited in this world? Why did it sometimes seem so prolonged?

What defined the difference? Who decided who would live longer—was it God or fate which played with us?

Edward's mind played at these questions. He was observing the departing Templars through the windows of his chambers. His lips pinched on his pale face. The poison in his blood had stopped spreading, but still, he was fading.

There was knocking on heaven's door. No, it was his door, to his chambers. His eyesight was tired, as was his mind. His heart was fighting.

He remembered, from his childhood, the old warrior who had taken care of the youngsters' training, his harsh methods. He had never missed a chance to show his disappointment when the boys didn't try hard enough. He had used to say that it wasn't a bad thing to enjoy what one did for a living but the best joy came with victory.

The young Edward used to hide in the barn, watching this old bugger and how he trained the lads. But one day, he was

caught. Even though he was the son of the King of England—
the crown prince—he was brought to take part in the training.
Young Edward didn't object; he preferred to be treated like the
rest. It was his father who didn't approve of his son being
trained alongside commoners.

Edward's health was poor in his youth. He remembered
when he was seven years old he fell ill that he was unable to be
moved for a couple of weeks. Yet his uncle smiled and allowed
him to train. So, he trained with the others from that day on.
This elated the young prince. Sometimes he thought the old
warrior was especially harsh on him, the future king, but he
didn't know why.

"Winning is everything," the instructor never ceased
murmuring. "Only the victorious are respected." Still, his
frustration when the youngsters didn't try hard enough
brought forth fury and punishment. He wasn't much of a
talkative man, but a man of action. He would slap a boy on the
back of the neck just for sport, to keep him on his toes. He
was like that—always sneaking up on them, always making
them nervous around him, afraid what was going to happen.
Yet, young Edward survived. He grew and matured, all thanks
to the old warrior and his way with them.

And now, he couldn't even remember the man's name.
Edward had been very grateful to his teacher for showing him
how to be a man—a real one. How not to surrender, how to
be prudent and forward-looking. The old man had often
repeated that they should be determined and the boys were,
including Edward. He had been the best of the group.

There was knocking on his door again. A sound of wood, a
scratching on the surface, was followed by a familiar voice.

"My lord?"

Otto and Eleanor entered.

"A letter arrived through a messenger," she said, "for your
eyes only."

"I think it's important to accept him right away, my lord."
Otto's eyes looked alert and focused.

Edward turned his attention to his wife. Her eyebrow heads
rose and came closer together and she had a slight smile drawn

on her face.

"I am eager to find out what news he brings," Eleanor said. Edward stood despite the pain. He nodded and the guards let three newcomers into his chambers.

A man with a nose like the beak of an eagle entered the room. He was introduced as the messenger but he was old for a courier.

All morning, Lady Eleanor and Otto had discussed the events of the past several days. There had been no word from their friends and their mission. The previous day, there had been a bustle on the streets; the Templars had dispatched themselves to an unknown destination with most of their knights, ready for battle.

But not the Knights of the Hospital.

"I had used all my power to discover where the Templars had ridden but… nothing." Otto scratched his nose.

"Sir Thomas Bérard, the Grand Master of the Order of the Temple rode with his men too," Eleanor added.

"It's unusual for their movements to be so well-hidden. Even the Hospitaller Knights, who hadn't gone, were silent on the subject," Otto said.

"I think they knew," Edward said.

"I suspect we will find out soon, my lord."

Edward turned toward the three newcomers into his chambers and examined them.

An old man stood before them as a messenger, accompanied by two younger men for protection, golden-armored guards. Only one man could afford to send such an envoy: the sultan.

"Speak," the prince said.

"I am bringing you a gift, a request, and an opportunity, Lord Edward," the messenger said, then stepped two paces forward and passed to the towering prince two letters bearing the seal of the Sultan of Egypt.

A little cloud of emotion waved through the room. Edward, Otto, and Eleanor stood speechless.

Edward unfolded the first letter, he read it twice and passed it to Otto. While the knight examined what was written, the prince read the second letter, and passed it to his friend, as well.

"He wants what?" Otto looked surprised, almost shocked.

"He asked us gently," Edward said. Eleanor was curious and took the letters from Otto's hands.

"Gentle, indeed," she confirmed. Edward looked at the eyes of the old man and was thinking, but said nothing.

"In a good will, the sultan sent you a symbol of trust," Eleanor added, watching the thoughtful look of Edward and his adviser.

"What's that?" Edward managed to ask.

"Hope, your majesty," the messenger said.

Edward's mind was working fast enough. The time had come. Decisions had to be taken, a fate to be followed.

"My heart is alive again, my lord," Eleanor said, nodding to her husband. She approached Edward as the corners of her mouth curved upward and kissed him gently.

A gift, a request, and an opportunity, what more did a knight need?

CHAPTER SIXTEEN

Holy Land, Friday 24th of June, St John's Feast day, in the year 1272
of the incarnation of Christ; the Second Battle of Ayn Jalut

The Sun was vivid as never before.

What to say about the heat? It was a life-draining torture device; it sucked the life and the water out of you. It made men sweat and thirst; their necks fried under the Sun and their throats burned. Wasn't the Sun supposed to be merciful?

There were some clouds on the skyline and the sunshine pierced through them like a long spear touching the ground. These arrows flew in different directions, dancing around their master, the Sun. You couldn't mistake him, you couldn't miss him—he had been there, every day, since the birth of the Land, and he would be together with her until the end in an enduring, loving relationship. The Sun was the ultimate master of life and death, the warmth-giver, the reason everything grew ... but sometimes, he was so dreadful. There was no other force like him. Now he was in the front row, sitting in anticipation of something. But what? What would follow?

And the birds? Where were they? He missed the sounds of the birds. Baibars waved his hand forward, showing his followers, they were almost there: the Valley of Death.

The sultan rode ahead. He expected an ambush. He knew. Everyone knew. Even the birds knew, but they were missing

It was hot like an oven. The sand was hot. The air was hot. After the rainstorm, now the Sun had decided to dry out every drop of water. The effect of the water evaporating from the surface was devastating. It was like boiling eggs.

He felt like an egg. Trudging forward, feet heavy, as well as eyes.

Although they were late for the meeting, he knew there was no need to hurry; the enemy was already there. The renegades. The traitors. They were there, anticipating him, the sultan.

Baibars looked behind him. He was followed by one of his best regiments, the most loyal to him as well as the best soldiers around. But they weren't enough for what lay ahead.

What were the strengths of the enemies' force? He calculated, and this he did well. All his life, he had trusted his instincts and his judgment. They would be five to one, in favor of Berrat and his allies. Did he have a chance?

He had learned in this life that if the heart beats, there is hope. And his heart was working fast and hard. There would be an encounter; the meeting was near. He knew it was a trap, but he also knew he must enter into it. Why? Because if you wanted to hunt a bear you had to face the beast. If the renegades wanted to hunt a lion, they must face him. The Lion of Egypt, that was what the people called Baibars.

He liked that. He had fought all his life—for a single piece of bread, through his first battle, to his first promotion. Did he have to surrender? Never!

He looked back to his followers and their worn, determined faces. Baibars' force comprised almost 600 strong, mail-clad, mounted Mamluks from his personal royal guards—his most trusted—and a hired battalion of almost 100 Genoese crossbowmen to follow him. He knew his men would follow him to the end.

Why? He might be naïve, but he knew.

The timing was crucial. And thus, he was on his own plan. He knew he had to take a risk once more. But this time, he was risking not only his head on a stake but the life of his little daughter as well. Not to mention the bloody empire. Even without him, there would be this realm; it had survived through the ages—through the Romans, through the Crusaders. Only the future would show what would happen. Now, he only cared about his daughter—his seventh daughter,

Anna. He saw the little princess and the precious smile on her face. This image was fading, but he hoped to prolong its existence in his memory.

After the death of his first one, his legacy didn't matter. His future was tainted. His next day didn't count for apples.

An empire for his beloved daughter? Was it worth it?

How had he let this happen? He would never forgive himself. He had been so confident he could manage it again, like his precious game of cat and mouse with the last conspiracy. But he had failed.

Now, he was determined not to fail again. Because this was a game of death; the losers would be left a head shorter.

He was almost there: Marj Ibn Amer. The valley where he had met the Mongol invasion, long before. He had fought and he had won. The battle of Ayn Jalut. He remembered what his friend, Ibn al-Nafis, had said twelve years before.

"Our country was far from that land which those infidels, the Mongols, conquered, but then it became their neighbor. And our people had to fight the infidels and resist them. To do so, we had to obtain two things: a large army and a brave sultan to lead them. Without these things, it would have been impossible to fight these infidels, the Mongols, with all their conquests over the many lands and their numerous armies."

He remembered it like it was yesterday. It had been a Friday, just like this day. Baibars had convinced the sultan of the time to meet the Mongol invasion and to beat them. They had met them here, at Ayn Jalut, the Goliath's Spring.

The Goliath's Spring was an all-season spring at the foot of the northwest corner of Mount Gilboa, a few leagues west of the village of Baysan.

Baibars knew that Ughan would move south, taking up position near Ayn Jalut, just as the Mongols did, so many years before. There was little doubt that the renegades would be the first to arrive and take up position, just as the enemy had done at the last battle at this site.

It had been twelve years since Baibars, upon reaching a nearby hill, had found the Mongols camped there. He hadn't been a sultan back then—not yet. Some scholars had advised that the Mamluks should arrive at the location first and set up an ambush. But that hadn't happened; instead, they had encountered a prepared enemy who tried to ambush them.

Along the northern foot of the Gilboa ran a river which provided water for the Mongols' horses; the adjacent valley offered both pasturage and good conditions for cavalry warfare. Its other advantages were evident; the Mongols could exploit the proximity of Mount Gilboa to anchor their flank. It also offered an excellent vantage point, as did the nearby Hill of Moreh.

To win, they had needed to fight like demons. And they had won, all thanks to him, his strategy, and his determination to win. Baibars had fought like a lion. He had employed the tactics and the sultan of the time, Qutuz, had taken the fruits of his efforts. But he had paid for them in time.

At that time, they had won a massive victory. They had been the first to defeat the Mongol horde.

Some historians said that, in the battle of Ayn Jalut, which had been fought out between people of the same race, the infidels of yesterday had defeated the hordes of hell to become the Muslims of tomorrow. Baibars disagreed with this verdict. Yet, this victory had defined his destiny. And not only his, but that of the empire, too.

He had fought all his life. He could continue to fight and to be victorious. In his veins ran the blood of a winner. And the winner took all and wrote history as it suited him.

Ughan, Berrat—all his former friends had taken part in this great battle against the Mongols.

Now they would fight him.

This was a logical place for the renegades to await him. But he knew the landscape as well as they. Better; Ughan and Berrat had fought here, but Baibars had planned and executed the attack that had won the previous battle. That was his advantage. Still, his numbers were not as he would have liked. Ughan knew this.

They had wanted to meet the sultan here.

"What are they thinking?" Baibars wondered as he approached the valley. His face was stone cold. He had always known one way and it was straightforward: conspirators and people who wanted to overthrow his reign had to be faced. They all had to be beat. The traitors had no other fate.

Even though he had never failed in battle before, Baibars wasn't calm. He hoped for news from the Desert Wolf. Ulf had failed once—to protect the sultan's first daughter. This was the pain that had haunted the sultan's emotions since then.

He would never forgive either himself for exposing a member of his family to danger or Ulf for not keeping her alive. Still, he hoped the Wolf would manage to bring his youngest daughter back safely. He was the key to this battle now. He was the blade that could cut this knot out of Baibars' neck.

The Desert Wolf, *Diyaab al-Sahra*, and his thirst for blood could be useful again. But could Baibars trust him? He thought he could trust the way Anna looked at Ulf and the way the Wolf had returned that look.

This was funny: an empire, an entire kingdom was hanging by a thread because of a smile. The innocent smile of his youngest daughter.

He closed his eyes. Anna's image warmed his soul. He was ready as never before.

***

The sultan and his host of warriors entered the valley.

The sound of running water whispered its song in James' ears. After the rains, a lake had formed around the spring and at the foot of the mountain. It was not big but was enough to spur them all. Yet the newborn lake surprised them; it was hard to cross with the cavalry. James hoped it would be the same for their opponents.

Sir James of Durham and the Genoese captain, Andrea Pelu, led the Genoese crossbowmen. They had arrived the previous night from Jerusalem. It was a bloody coincidence that they had been there. Baibars had offered Pelu's men a year's pay to fight for him for one day. Pelu had left his previous paymaster after not receiving his promised payment.

He was desperate to earn something for himself and his men on this journey. This was not an unusual business for him; he often traded with the sultan, bringing him slaves or goods from the Black Sea, and sometimes his men fought for gold. Trading in war, it was prestigious to fight for royalty, no matter the side or the religion.

James had a very different motive. He owed his life to the sultan, whose physician had cured the wound he had received at the Tower of David in Jerusalem. The sultan had asked him to return the favor, to fight on Baibars' side and bring his daughter back. In exchange for the use of James' sword for a day, Baibars had offered the cure for his friend, Edward.

It was a dilemma for the Scottish knight. He had come to this land to fight for the Christians against these infidels. What should he do? His heart and mind struggled with the question. In the end, the sultan had convinced him that if they lost this battle, soon there would be no Christian lands over the sea. He chose his friend and his pride.

The arrival of the Genoese had angered James at first—that these money-lovers fought for the enemy, but then his anger cast away. He was glad he had a chance to fight side-by-side with Christians, even mercenaries.

They came from the south and stopped near the foot of the mountain. Their backs were turned to the newly formed lake from the rains and floods that bordered Mount Gilboa. Behind them was a river running east. He looked ahead and saw the enemy and his battalions located northeast at the foot of the Hill of Moreh. The renegades waited until the sultan and his men were in place and emerged from over hills.

This wouldn't be an ordinary battle. The world was changing. A sultan versus his own—Templars, Tartars, and assassins. Not to mention the Italians on Baibars' side. It was madness. There were Italians mercenaries with the Templars, too. But Red Herring knew that the Venetians and the Genoese were foes and always fought for power, for trade routes, for gold, and for prestige. Their desire to once again take on their rivals was evident. James observed the right wing of the enemy. He saw a battalion of Templars led personally by their Master, Thomas Bérard.

"Damn all traitors," James shook his head in disbelief. "If my father was here he would scratch my neck for those words," he said to the Italian next to him.

"You know, Sir James, in war everything is allowed, except losing! So, we must win. Nothing else matters." Pelu smiled at that.

The renegades were so many, he thought. Still, he didn't see any signs of the enemy crossing the river on the newly formed lake, to trap the sultan's forces from behind and prevent his retreat.

Ughan hadn't managed to complete his trap; he hadn't positioned his soldiers on Mount Gilboa so he could attack them from the back.

There was hope.

Or they were very well hidden and he could not see them.

James spat on the ground. It would be a bloody afternoon.

***

In the middle of the valley, the leaders of the two armies met. On one side stood the son of Nonagenarian, Shams al-Din; Berrat; and Ughan, who was followed by Siraghan al-Tatari. They were all on black horses with the exception of Berrat. He was riding an excellent white warhorse.

Berrat observed his followers, Shams al-Din looked tense and was placed his bandaged hand over the saddle. Ughan's eyes were alert as the leader of the Mongols, al-Tatari, was constantly scratching his chin. The bareheaded Mamluk turned his sight to the opposite side, the sultan. Baibars had chosen Ibn Abd al-Zahir to accompany him and the Crusader, Sir James. His old friend's face didn't betray any single emotion, while the clerk seemed nervous as he looked around and drops of sweat ran down his forehead. Berrat looked at the big red-haired Crusader. This was an unexpected move from Baibars to bring him here. Why? He didn't understand. James' head was tilted back looking down the nose, as his eyes were alert and narrowed. The knight didn't hide his disgust toward him.

The air was hot as if the Sun anticipated what would happen next. The men were all on horses and stopped a few paces away from each other. There was a moment of waiting and the tension grew.

"Do you bring my daughter?" Baibars began.

"Do you bring my father?" Shams al-Din countered.

"All this for an old man who didn't recognize or respect my rule?" Baibars' words were sharp.

"He is my father!"

"Not anymore. He passed away," Baibars said.

"How?" Shams al-Din's face lacked the control of emotions the sultan had. He looked like a child about to cry.

"He was old. It was his time," Baibars said.

"Put down your weapons and surrender!" Shams al-Din shouted. "And we will not harm your daughter."

Sultan Baibars said nothing.

"Surrender, my friend," Berrat said, "And you may live long enough to see your precious Anna once more."

"I want to see her now! Show her to me!"

"No," Ughan said.

"Why?" Baibars gave a small, twisted smile. "Isn't she with you?"

"Surrender!" Shams al-Din repeated.

"Shut up, dog!" The sultan's cold voice cut the hot air. "You lack your father's wisdom and manners. He was a prudent man before losing his mind. But you? You will lose your head today!"

Shams al-Din's gapped mouth stared. Ughan and the assassins' leader were astonished by the sudden change in Baibars' voice. They had the upper hand and more soldiers. But Berrat knew his old friend, Baibars, well. Was there any chance that this fight would blow over? No. Now they knew that the afternoon would be hard and bloody. The Lion hadn't come here simply to give up his crown. He had come to make his last stand.

"What you want, Berrat?" the sultan asked.

"I want everything. And I want it now," the bareheaded Mamluk said. "I am tired of being your shadow. I want everything. Your time is up."

"And you think you are ready?"

"More than ever."

"You started a civil war on the eve of a new Mongol invasion. What chance did you think you had to rule? Your actions opened the doors for the horde. Do you think your Tartar allies will be satisfied with this? They are always hungry for more land, plunder, and slaves. They do not build anything; they just destroy, pillage, and conquer. The Romans conquered but they also built. Even we build. Not the Tartars."

Sultan Baibars looked at Berrat's eyes.

"And you, my friend, unleashed them."

"No."

"Berrat, walk away from these renegades and I promise you a quick death, and your family will be unharmed," Baibars said.

"You offer me reconciliation?"

"Traitors do not deserve that."

"After so many years of loyalty, a man deserves only a quick death?"

Baibars face was expressionless.

"I will take my chances today!" Berrat scratched his bare head. "As I see it, our soldiers outnumber yours, five to one. What do you think? What are my chances now, my friend?"

"You just lost your chance for an honorable death, traitor."

"But what are yours? Who are these people standing next to you?" Ughan aimed to break the unresponsive face of the sultan. "Your numbers are insignificant and you are even forced to use infidels to fight for you. What humiliation! Look at who you have brought with you: a wounded Crusader knight and a short clerk."

Shams al-Din and Ughan laughed. Berrat did not.

He looked again at Baibars' two followers. So, he, the sultan, had purposely chosen them to display a lack of respect for his opponents' status. He was determined to show them that they were nothing, only a fading past. That he was the real ruler. Berrat felt that his lips set in a grim line.

Sultan Baibars nodded to the clerk. "He is here to write about my sunny walk in the desert today. The day I met some criminals and killed them while walking with my daughter and enjoying the Sun. Your names will fade into dust and oblivion."

The Lion of the desert would fight to the end. Berrat knew that. He determined that they had one chance to bring him down and they must seize it or they would be annihilated and their families would be pulled violently and painfully from the world of the living.

He knew his old friend well; Sultan Baibars always had a backup plan and was always prepared. He wasn't a man to be underestimated; he was the bravest soldier and leader of men Berrat knew and this scared him to death. He had always wondered how it would feel when they met again after the sultan found out about the plot and his treachery. He always felt some veneration when he stood before him—this time was no exception.

"I spared your life Lord Siraghan al-Tatari and let you live in my realm. Is that the way you repay me?" Baibars' blazing eyes turned to the Mongol. The round-faced horseman bowed his head and said nothing.

The sultan stood up in his saddle and looked around.

"If you can't show me my daughter, there is nothing to talk about. I will give you one last chance. Surrender or die!"

Shams al-Din's jaw sagged. Ughan and Berrat were shocked by the sultan's impudence too.

***

Baibars turned away from them. He rode around them, slowly, and shouted aloud, addressing the renegade battalions standing on the opposite slope.

"You, my friends, are standing on the wrong side of the valley." He said this to one specific Mamluk battalion, which he hoped had still not decided which side to take. He knew he could be wrong, but he had to try. He knew he must earn some time.

Baibars was the master of this realm, his empire. He had developed an efficient network to deliver news around the kingdom. The enemy knew they couldn't afford to waste time. They had to overcome the sultan and to establish a new regime of mercenaries, traders, and military orders to rule.

"Think again!" the sultan said. "You are on the wrong side. I will give you a second chance. I will spare your lives and that of your families. This is my last word."

There was some moaning in the ranks of Berrat's Mamluks. Yet, it was hard to see their faces.

Silence.

"You are too late, my friend." Ughan gave a poisoned smile and laughed.

"You are insane!" Shams al-Din shouted.

"Still, I am the sultan," Baibars gave them a twisted face.

"Not for long!" Ughan said and he gave a signal. A rider delivered a few bags to Ughan, who opened them and threw what was inside onto the ground. Dead carrier pigeons.

"Your cries for help won't reach their recipients," Berrat said.

"If you say so!" Baibars returned to James and Ibn Abd al-Zahir.

There was a moment of a silence. Nobody spoke.

"So be it!" Baibars shouted. "The next time we met face-to-face, it will be in the middle of battle. The steel of my blade will be the last thing you see!" He turned his back on them and rode to his men.

It was time to prepare for a fight.

Baibars positioned himself and his men with their backs to the lake near the northwest end of Mount Gilboa. It was a huge risk. But he had taken big risks all his life and he didn't regret it.

He had received intelligence via his spy network that a fresh northern battalion belonging to Ughan was marching toward the valley. Another battalion of Bedouins had joined the assassins, too. However, he hoped some of his most trusted friends—subjects he had made amirs long before—would answer his call. He must wait and survive while his own Mamluks arrived from the south, too.

But the front line of the enemies was ready to charge his

little force.

***

James looked at their own soldiers and position.

They were near the southern curve of the valley which ran alongside the mountain. Baibars' force was almost 700 men. The sultan had divided his army into three sections: 200 on the left flank, 200 on his right, and 300 in the center. Baibars had ordered almost all of his men to be unsaddled. A group of men had been dispatched to take the horses behind the battle line. The animals were tired from the march through the desert and they needed some water and rest.

It looked as if the sultan's plan was to meet the enemies on foot. Red Herring and the Genoese were in the center, and they formed a defensive line of men nearly 50 meters long. The first two rows of the line were of men with shields and spears and behind them were positioned the archers. The left flank and the right aligned in the same way.

James was not on foot; he was on his fine battle horse and observed the whole line. Red Herring turned his sight toward the enemy. They were positioned on the opposite side of the valley, almost a league away, on the slope of the Hill of Moreh. They formed six battalions. The Templar Knights were placed on the right flank of the enemy. James estimated that they were about 300 strong knights and their sergeants. Behind them, there was a small detachment of the assassin's corps, but he couldn't count them.

In the center of the enemy lines were positioned Berrat's Mamluks and behind him, Ughan's forces: almost 600 strong, heavy horsemen. This was the main force that would be unleashed on them. Red Herring had fought many battles; he knew one day, he would die on such battlefield. He hoped only to die in a great battle that was worth the price.

He turned his face to the right, where the Tartar hordes were positioned on the left flank of the enemy. They were almost 2000 light cavalry archers, divided into two battalions. When their leaders returned to their forces, they slowly started to regroup and to form into squadrons. The squadrons of hell, somebody called them. James would face this kind of soldiers for the first time. He had heard they had been beaten once, by Mamluks led by Baibars almost twelve years before.

He hoped they received the same fate today.

He raised his eyes toward the end of the desert. It was almost midday of Midsummer, the day that St. John the Baptist was born more than 1000 years before. How did people know that? Because of recorded history.

It was always the winners who wrote history and he hoped to write his own history today. The sultan had allowed him to make his own standard: a white background with six red herrings over it—three on the first row, two on the second, and one on the third row—with red crosses between them. He was proud to be fighting under his family colors once more. He hadn't left his homeland unwillingly. Edward hadn't wanted to leave behind the knights who had fought on Simon de Montfort's side. He had offered them letters of protection for their lands and family for four years while they joined him on a Crusade. Sir James's Lord offered someone to take the vow instead of him: Red Herring.

But now, he wondered, where was Peter? Was he alive? And Hamo?

He reckoned the enemy's united forces of assassins, traitor Templars, Mamluks, Tartars, and Bedouins were more than 3000, fully equipped with mail, spears, swords, and bows, strong and made confident by their numbers.

A horn sounded in the valley.

The enemy's left wing was on the move. They would attack in waves. The Tartars' two battalions were divided into five assault squadrons—horse archers. They marched close to the middle, between the two lines, and prepared to unleash their missiles.

They approached and they accelerated their charge.

"Shields up!" Red Herring shouted. The defensive line acted as one and built an iron wall.

"Archers, on my mark," Pelu shouted. Owen was behind him.

The first squadron was almost there, ready to release their missiles at Baibars' right wing. They rode as one unit. Had they practiced that? Red Herring knew how hard it was to be disciplined while charging.

The first unit threw their missiles and turned to their left. Then the next squadron arrived. The five squadrons charged in succession. The Tartars' intentions were to send wave after wave at them. They approached, accelerated their charge, threw their missiles, and turned to their left, again and again. They traded their horses for fresh ones. The enemy tried to overtake them with a rush, hoping that their shield wall would fall apart.

Two arrows stuck in James's shield. He cut them with his sword. He heard the song of the flying arrows and the dull sound when an arrowhead hit its target. He saw a man near him with an arrow pierced his left eye and he fell flat on his back as he tried to scream and died.

"Shields men!" He cried out again under the rain of the Mongols' arrows.

The enemy's right wing, where the Templars were, didn't move. They were waiting for the right moment to charge and to scatter Baibars' thin defensive line.

But the land was soaking wet from the previous night's rainstorm; although the upper soil layer had dried in the Sun, beneath it was mud. The attackers progressed slowly and the horses seemed nervous.

Then the Red Herring heard the sultan.

"Release!"

Sultan's archers shot their arrows and the Genoese were shooting, too. They waited for the enemy to turn and shoot their bolts. The volley's sound was unforgettable. Owen, who stood behind him, was shooting with his longbow.

"Die, bastards." Owen's harsh accent and his dusty face distinguished him from the others. It was a rare view, a Welshman and a Scot fighting alongside Genoese crossbowmen with the elite of the sultan.

Death was flying—sounds of missiles penetrating armor and flesh echoed in the valley, mixed with the cries of men. The Tartars were light-armored; most of their protection was leather, as they wanted to be fast and deadly. But the soil didn't let them. As they turned, they showed their unprotected side. The archers behind James smelled blood. Horses were crying, men were dying, and blood was flowing. One third of a squadron was annihilated from a single volley. The next squadron hesitated at the wounded bodies of their own. James hoped they had enough arrows.

The Mamluks and the Templars seemed to be waiting for something. He saw movement in the ranks of the knights. It was a signal for the Christian knights to prepare for a charge.

Sir James had feared this. He knew what the mailed horsemen of the Crusaders were capable of. They were unstoppable, and they would sweep them like a steel hurricane. The sultan's first line consisted of armored Mamluk, but they didn't possess such large, thick shields as the Crusaders had, nor their long lances. The encounter would be deadly.

On Herring's right, a cloud appeared and the northern Mamluks battalion flourished their standards: Ughan's banners. They were the same as one of the enemy battalions.

"Holy Mother!" James said. They were doomed.

Cheers from the enemies arrived. It looked like their long-awaited reinforcements had arrived. The Templar Knights were on the move.

***

Peter's heart was working fast.

He felt tired but elated too as he knew what he must do. He didn't feel fear, but the opposite—there was joy in what lay ahead. He wanted to fight in the battle, the madness of this coup d'état.

He knew a coup d'état was achieved by force—by killing, by assassination, by attacking the peaceful common folk or by war. All this to fulfill someone's ambition for power.

Ambition—this word was dangerous. When a madman had too much ambition, there would be a bloody coup d'état.

And now it was happening. Everything was set up; every player was ready on the chess board. Peter was eager to join.

He raised his eyes and observed the horde he led. The horse horde. Clouds of dust from their ride masked the lack of soldiers on the backs of the poor animals. Ulf and Ivar had taken the horses from the Mamluks they had overwhelmed in the ruins the night before.

By some stroke of luck, the boy they had found with the princess, Anna, was the son of the Bedouins' leader. The Mamluks had taken the boy hostage to force the Bedouins to fight on their side. Their leader had good relations with the sultan, but he was ready to break them for the safety of his heir. After Peter and his friends released the boy, the Bedouins had turned against the Mamluks and forced them to surrender, all for a child.

Now, they hastened their horse pack toward the battle. They wanted to unleash their charge toward the enemy and instill chaos and fear. Still, they had a task to do, a brave and knightly one. To arrive on time.

Peter and Ulf rode ahead of this horse army without warriors. The real soldiers were the battle trained stallions; their wild run posed the real danger.

Ivar, Hamo, Isabella, and the children followed behind. They were close to the valley. He could see the clouds from the battle and the two opposite forces standing against each other.

"There," Ivar pointed the flags of the sultan.

"Go!" Ulf shouted. The ostringer, Hamo, Isabella, and the children rode away toward the force of the sultan under the cover of the dust the horses made.

Peter looked at the Sun. He was ready. Today was St John's Feast day and he hoped to have a chance to avenge his mentor.

"Charge!" he shouted in his mind and smiled. He hoped the horses would understand it.

He and Ulf led their headless chicken army toward the battlefield, aiming at the Tartar squadrons.

The march of the horse was unleashed.

***

A cloud drifted in from the right. More horses were riding

in from the northeast.

"Ughan's battalions," some of the Mamluks shouted. So, the reinforcements of the renegades had finally arrived—James looked at the banners and his heart sank. The disruption of the horses had bought them just a few moments of time, but that was over. Ughan's forces would turn the tide against the sultan once again.

"Damn these bloody traitors," James said as he observed the newcomers. He wiped out the sweat from his forehead, squinting at the incoming battalions. Something was wrong. The horses were not slowing as they approached the Mongol squadrons. James looked closer. The horses were unmanned, tied together and guided by a few riders. They were not with the enemy. It was Peter on one of the horses.

James watched as a cloud of frenzied horses cut into the Tartar squadrons from the right with demolishing speed.

Disorder, confusion, and panic erupted. Men fell, trampled by their own horses. In the sudden turmoil, the Templars ceased their charging—for now.

"Bloody hell," James' jaw dropped a bit as he observed the horses penetrated the confused rows of the Mongols. He saw dust and shadows as he heard screams of fallen men trampled by hooves of the galloping horses. He saw hope again.

Screams rang out from behind Baibars' line.

A hidden battalion emerged from the mountain to the slope and lunged aimed to hit the defenders of the lake from behind.

"Owen! Pelu!" James cried as he pointed to the enemy in their back. "Turn the archers."

But a new Bedouin battalion arrived from the east following Peter. They were led by an old man, nearly the age of the sultan. They did not attack sultan's forces, instead, they cut off into the hidden enemy battalion which was about to attack Baibars from behind through the mud and the lake. They had been waiting, hidden in the trees and bushes on the high ground and, to strike the sultan's forces at the right moment. The moment the northern battalion arrived seemed to be the time.

For a moment, James was sure their miserable resistance

would end. But as he noticed the two forces of the Bedouins clashed each other he grinned.

"This was the plan, eh?" Red Herring thought. But he knew he had been lucky. He had never anticipated that Ulf would manage to bring Baibars' daughter with bonuses: a battalion of Bedouins on his side and riderless army penetrating the wing of the traitors.

"Father!" Anna smiled at him from the back of the horse she shared with a boy her age. Ivar nodded to the sultan, as did Hamo and Isabella.

Soon Peter arrived, managing to escape from the chaos of wild running horses, followed by the Wolf.

Still, the enemy force was larger and the battle wasn't over yet.

"They still outnumber us, three to one," Owen concluded.

"I can count, you bloody Welshman," Hamo jumped from the horse and even through the pain, he embraced his friend. He saluted the Red Herring too.

"I am glad you are well, Sir James," Hamo said.

"Peter! You are still alive," Baibars' face looked happy. He hugged his daughter while Ivar told him what had happened in the ruins the night before. "I am inviting you to join my little war against these traitors. What do you say?"

The orphan looked at the Sultan then to James, who nodded to him.

"I am where my friends are," Peter said.

"Good, now prepare yourselves, they will come again!"

The battle was temporarily on hold as the Tartars tried to regroup. The horses that were left without riders soon stopped or ran away. The wind cleared the sand cloud over the battlefield.

Another horn sounded through the valley. All men, no matter the religion or side, looked west.

The Crusaders had come.

Edward and his knights were followed by Hospitallers and some Templars who didn't follow their master, Sir Thomas Bérard. The view was magnificent; the Sun reflected off their shining armor and shields. Their banners flew above their helmets. There were almost 200 of them and they were followed by marching 200 men-at-arms and almost the same number of archers.

"Isn't he supposed to be dying?" Owen grinned.

"The sultan promised to send his friend, the physician, to Acre if I fight today and write a letter to Edward," James said. "Hamo, can you recognize the banners?"

"Yes, sir. Robert the Bruce the elder and the younger are there, as well as de Grailly and de Vescy."

"Otto?" Red Herring asked.

"And the fox, too," he confirmed. "I see Lady Eleanor's banner, too!"

In astonishment, all their faces were amazed. She had recovered well from the recent birth of their baby and now she was riding next to her love, Edward, in her small armor suit.

The towering Prince of England rode a white charger and bore his coat of arms: a red background with three golden lions. He was the tallest knight. He was dressed for battle, his fine chainmail with golden strings showed the enemy who was leading these knights. The presence of the prince meant that he was personally interested in the events in the valley.

Edward led his men with confidence. He looked in excellent health as he finally stopped with Ibn al-Nafis and his men near Baibars' forces.

For a moment, James wondered if the prince would take the enemy's side and overthrow the sultan. Yet, he knew the prince was a real knight, a man of honor who—most of all—believed in knighthood and brave deeds. He was like a reborn King Arthur. He would choose his friends' side and deliver his revenge toward the traitors.

The prince approached Baibars.

"I salute you on my battlefield, Lord Edward." The sultan looked at the princess. "Milady, Sir Otto ... I hope you are in good health once more?" He addressed this last Edward.

"I am grateful for your present. Your friend is a master in the art of healing." Edward's harsh accent was vivid again.

Baibars smiled at Ibn al-Nafis and said, "You did a wonderful job, as usual, my friend."

Then returned his gaze to the Crusader.

"You came to my realm as an intruder. Still, we reached peaceful terms not long ago."

Edward said nothing.

"Now, a group of renegades and traitors are mounting a coup d'état. They tried to kill you, provoking war, then they tried to assassinate me, too. They kidnapped my daughter and now, we must face them in the name of peace!"

Edward looked at the enemy line.

"As a wise man once said, 'War must be for the sake of peace,'" the Englishman said. "I am here today as a sign of sincere gratitude. I owe my life to you and your physician. What I hate most is a betrayal. I am here, also, for my friends; I cannot leave them to fight alone, to defend their names and mine alone. I brought them here; I will take them back home."

He looked at James and nodded.

"I want revenge for the treachery. If they could make an alliance to fight you regardless of their religion, we can unite to protect the peace we made and the land."

Peter and James observed the two men: the sultan and the English crown prince. All men on their side of the valley witnessed the Crusaders and Mamluks join forces to fight the traitors.

"So, we have terms. We fight, we win for the peace, then we go home."

"I agree to these terms, Your Highness," Edward confirmed. The two men shook hands in a sign of agreement. The real predators in the desert would fight together, united against the renegades.

***

Edward's knights positioned themselves on the left wing. The center was formed from the men-at-arms and their long, thick shields. Archers rallied behind them with the Genoese crossbowmen. On the right wing, what was left of the sultan's men regrouped. There were many fewer of them since the first attack.

"Because of you, I lost a good and experienced battalion in the sandstorm, but now—again because of you—I have my daughter back," Baibars said to Ulf.

Peter observed them.

"I am in debt to you. But now I must protect her. Once more, I beg you. Fight for me, one last time."

The Desert Wolf looked at the sultan, then at the enemy line.

"They must pay for my loss," he spoke slowly. "This I will do in her name, not yours."

But this was enough for the sultan.

The two opposite sides watched each other. The defenders' line comprising Baibars' regime and Edward's was short and thin. No longer were Muslims fighting Christians; instead, today's lords were up against those who wanted to rule tomorrow—renegades with no scruples, no morals, who were willing to use people's faith to set them against each other.

The Tartar squadrons were preparing to attack again. The renegade Templar Knights also were ready and waited for a good moment to charge Edward's flank.

"They will have only one chance to crush us and leave no witness alive. If they fail, their future hangs in the balance," James stood near Peter. "They had opposed Emperor Fredrick, years before; now, they stand against Edward. Sometimes, they did things only for their prosperity, but this time, the whole order depended on their decision."

"I can't believe they will fight against Edward," Peter said.

The sultan rose from his saddle and said something intended only for Edward, but the orphan was close enough to hear.

"Watch and learn, young prince." Sultan Baibars smiled proudly and turned his fine horse to his troops.

It was not only Mamluks who formed Baibars' line of defense; there were Mamluk foot soldiers, English men-at-arms, loyal Templar Knights, Hospitaller knights, archers, the Scottish regiment of Edward, Genovese crossbowmen, and Githa.

"The battle of the traded souls is about to begin," Baibars

shouted.

The soldiers looked at him in silence.

"Because, they—" He pointed with his sword toward the opposite side of the valley. "They traded their souls for gold and power, regardless of their fate, their oaths, and their comrades. They trade our souls and our lives, too … into oblivion." He paused, and observed the eyes of the men, assuring that he had their attention.

"Who gave them this right? Who are they to think they could guide our path or choose for us? Do they have that right?"

The eyes of the soldiers, Mamluks, Crusaders, mercenaries, and royals were wide open and staring at the sultan. Peter tried not to miss anything from the speech. For him, this was new: a sultan speaking to the common men—his men—in the face of a battle. He felt this would stay with him for life.

"Do they have this right? No!" Baibars shouted. "We forge our destiny by ourselves."

The sultan's face was red now; his passion could be seen in his eyes.

"Together—" He stressed this word and raised his voice again. "Together, we fight as men who stand against the traitors, the same brethren who once were on our side, who once fought shoulder-to-shoulder with us."

He pointed at the enemy again, riding in a circle on his horse, giving enough time to all in the ranks to consider his words. Peter noticed the message being conveyed along the ranks, from one soldier to the next. Baibars stood again in his excellent armor and looked at his soldiers' eyes, even the Christians.

"The enemy wants to steal our legacy, to steal our land, our women, our pride, and finally, our lives and souls." His face became darker. "Does their desire for power and this betrayal give them this right? No! No! We built this realm with our own blood, with the blood of our friends, even with the blood of the Crusaders."

He looked at the westerners. "At this point, we are a sword brothers, united to defend our kingdom, our land, our homes, and the peace, together—Mamluks, Saracens, Crusaders, Englishmen, Scotsmen, Genovese—even our women are here to fight, and for what?"

"Welshman too!" Owen shouted. A ripple of laughter ran near the archer as Peter grinned too.

The sultan let them think a bit, and continued:

"To fight together for our right for our destiny to be chosen by us alone, not by traitors or by the enemy. Twelve years ago, we soaked the land with the blood of the Mongol invaders." He talked slowly. "And now, we have a chance to show the enemy, once more, that they can't take what doesn't belong to them."

Baibars took a breath. "This is our homeland, and we will fight for it."

He looked at the eyes of his men.

"Together." Peter was looking at the sultan's face. He looked determined.

"Do you want our land overtaken by these vultures who have never raised anything? They only steal, kill, enslave, and loot. They call themselves the conquerors of the world. I said to them once and will say to them now, No!" Baibars raised his sword.

"No!" he shouted again.

He shouted, repeating this to the soldiers until they joined in the song and their mood was ready for battle.

"No, no, no," they all chanted as one, slapping their shields.

"We fight, we kill, we kill them all on this field."

Peter had a tear in his eye, watching these men find the courage to fight and to protect what they loved. He felt a little pat on his shoulder. Owen smiled at him.

"What about dying? He forgot to say some would die, you know," he said. "Peter Longsword, do not die today, and you will have a fantastic story to tell."

The battle of traded souls was about to begin—the second battle of Ayn Jalut.

***

332

Edward dismounted and embraced Sir James, then nodded to Peter, Hamo, and Owen.

"I am glad you are alive, my friend!" the prince said.

"I am glad you live, too, my lord," Red Herring said.

"Only thanks to you, men!" He meant not only his Scot friend but all of his fellows.

Lady Eleanor approached and, with a tear in her eye, thanked Red Herring, Hamo, and the rest.

"Longsword," Edward said, facing the orphan, "in our veins flows the same blood that binds our fates. I owe my life to you."

"Sir …." Peter lost his words.

Lady Eleanor looked into the young man's eyes. She smiled at him and kissed him on his temple.

"You are blessed, Peter, to find your destiny and your path." She turned her eyes to Owen, saying, "My beloved Welsh Master archer, I am glad you are here with us today. Thank you for your support."

Owen was at a loss for words. He rarely was. He bowed and kissed the princess' hand. "In your name, milady."

Otto cut off the sentimentalities.

The tactic was clear. Edward suggested and Baibars agreed that they would use the same strategy used by Richard the Lionheart near Jaffa, long before. It entailed a shield wall with crossbowmen and archers behind it and mounted knights on the wings.

"We all have to be disciplined and not to leave the shield wall until Edward says—no attack until the signal. The infantry will meet the enemy's charges with their shields and lances, and the missiles from the archers will do their business as usual," James explained to Peter.

By Edward's order, all defenders had a red scarf tied on their right arm near the shoulder to distinguish the sword brothers in the bloody battle and the killing madness.

The Scottish knight would command the heavy infantry in the center, supported by many good knights on foot. Edward would command the knights on the left wing. Owen and Captain Pelu would lead the shooters. Hamo stood in the shield wall, too, despite his injury. Peter joined the shield wall, shoulder-to-shoulder with Red Herring and Ivar. He looked at the men around him; their shields overlapped and their helmets and weapons gleamed in the Sun. Edward's regiment, which had stayed with him in the Holy Land, was full of his most loyal knights. They were eager to show their warring skills to the enemy.

It was strange how the situation had turned around. A few days before, Edward had almost died. Now he was on his horse once more, commanding his fierce warriors, allying with the man whom he had thought was responsible for the assassination attempt. But even fierce rivals sometimes united their strengths against a common threat: the traitors.

It was a shame, Peter thought.

Everyone despised traitors. And he hoped to face Julian. He had to avenge the death of Brother John, but he wanted to do it for himself, too. Peter wouldn't miss this opportunity for anything; it was so rare in life to have a chance for payback. He fastened his leather belt and checked his sword in the scabbard. With his right hand, he held the spear he had received from one of the soldiers.

The ladies were positioned behind with the baggage wagons with some men-at-arms for protection. Githa had joined the knights from her order.

"Wait for the signal!" Edward shouted. "Do not lose your ammunition, do not miss!"

"Our crossbows are the deadliest range weapons," Andrea Pelu said with confidence.

"You are a dreamer, Messer Pelu, even after a hundred years. If one day, we meet each other on a battlefield, your crossbowmen's arses will belong to our longbows and we will use them like pincushions," Owen laughed. His fellow archers laughed, as well.

So, a little challenge between the bowmen and the crossbowmen had formed. The Genoese and the English archers of the lady, led by a Welshman who was also tasked with protecting her. Peter had heard that Lady Eleanor followed Edward everywhere and everyone in the ranks adored her.

Peter glanced at the English prince who smiled at Eleanor and she returned the smile. Edward was on his stallion and observing his troops. His face was calm but resolute, like a man who knew what he was doing. He had a reputation for a man who had participated in many tournaments. But now the tournaments were in the past. An open field battle lay ahead, where his soldiers' experience and the strength would be pitted against the best in the world: Mongol hordes and the elite Mamluks. Peter wondered if he would endure. Edward had charisma and his people followed him without hesitation. But was that enough to lead his men and to survive this battle?

"Prepare yourselves! They are coming," James shouted.

The enemy unleashed a full-scale attack toward their line.

The horses of the enemy were trying to get across the surface, a strange mix of dry sand and mud. The song of running water near them was drowned out by the galloping horses of the enemy. Ughan's center and their left wing of Mongol squadrons were on the move. Their other wing, where the Templars were stationed, was on hold for now.

When Red Herring saw them coming, he gave an order and the infantry stuck the points of their shields in the sand and pointed the spearheads of their lances toward the advancing enemy.

They stood shoulder-to-shoulder, their shields side-by-side. Peter was impressed by the discipline of the English Crusaders and their Scot regiment. Like one long hand, they arranged themselves to face the enemy and to back their own cavalry. They also stuck their spears into the sand, ready to meet the approaching horsemen.

The Sun took his seat on the first row, ready to enjoy the bloody event.

They would use the same tactics used 80 years before by Richard the Lionheart, the daredevil king, still known in this land for his bravery and deeds. Peter hoped the strategy would work.

The enemy charged against them for glory. The opponents before their eyes had come here to win. They all were traitors, depending on the point of view, even some would say fighters for the new regime. Their shouts and battle cries were full of venom, hunger, and determination, like sea waves crashing on rocks.

"Hold the line!" James shouted.

The shield wall of the defenders was hit hard into the center by the Mamluks. Peter was almost blown away by the fierce strength which the enemy riders forced against them, trying to push them back or to jump over their heads. The horsemen used the animals' force and pointed their speed and blind direction to the shield wall with the single goal of penetrating the iron wall.

But the spears between the Crusaders' shields did their job; screams rang out. Although he was pushed back, Peter was supported by the men on his left and right and the warrior behind him. The young man felt a pain in his left arm from the first struck he had received, and his shield deflected another blow from the top of a mounted Mamluk.

But they didn't break, nor did their spears. The iron-clad infantry line built of shields held. They pushed their spears onward and upward toward their assailants.

The horses' cries—a dying howl—echoed into the valley as blood spurted. The terrifying noise mixed with that of the thousands of hoofs which tried to trample them. Still, they resisted.

Peter would die to prove to his sword brothers he was worthy. "Or foolish," he thought. It was such irony that courage was often confused with stupidity; the foolish and the brave were sometimes one and the same. And Peter laughed, freeing his soul, ready to die for his friends. He smiled and stabbed a rider with his lance, piercing his scaled armor and penetrating the flesh. Peter used more power to pull his weapon from the dead body than he had to deliver it.

He pushed his shield a few inches forward and unbalanced the horse before him to pull his spear out more easily. In this part of the battle, it was unthinkable to be left without a primary weapon on the front line. And he felt that he had chosen the right move. The poor animal tried to escape the death trap formed by the Crusaders. The shield wall did not step back. The enemy cavalry pushed desperately in an attempt to destroy their defensive line, more and more attackers arriving and pushing forward.

It was a fight, thick and face-to-face, but the riders didn't manage to penetrate the shield wall. Now, they were stopped and left to the mercy of the spears and archers. The mud was a death trap for all, especially for the warhorses. The air filled with grunting, shouts, and insults spoken in many languages. Edward's men's fury and unity would make eyewitnesses write songs about this day.

The Battle of the Lake, or the Battle of the Traded Souls.

They were young, they were bold, they were naïve, and they had the guts to stand against multiple enemies and to survive. But at what cost? Peter wondered. He heard a scream from a man near him. He glanced just to see one of their own soldiers' skull was splintered from a blow and his blood mixed with brain flew.

The Mamluk mounted archers' arrows flew toward them. But they used their superior shields and armor to deflect them and to stay protected.

If you want to be king of the hill you must first remove the current one. They were the bait, standing near the lake in the mud. But the Mamluks were deceived because they were standing against fully prepared warriors with not only one leader, but two of the best warlords of the time: Prince Edward and Sultan Baibars.

That day, the Sun became a witness of something rare: two men of wildly different ages, lands, experience, religions, and motives, united to prove, once more, that they deserved their thrones—to fight back and to defend the holy realm from the renegades.

They fought for peace that day.

And for what else? Renown echoed throughout history. Who would be the king of the hill?

This day, the hill was full of kings; all men fought together, as brothers, like real kings. Nobody gave an inch of ground to the enemy, as swords sang, shields were like drums, and the echoed sound made the Sun enjoy the culmination of this story.

Peter pierced another horse in the neck, and blood covered his face and he tasted it. He looked to his left and saw the battle-frenzied look of his closest relative these days, Sir James. His face, his hair, and his reputation had earned his nickname, Red Herring. He fought like a fish on land, tossing, hitting, biting, and hurting all the Mamluks who dared to face him. He raised his long, German blade and slew another rider through his shoulder, even though the enemy had the high ground from his saddle. The orphan helped to unbalance the animal. They formed a deadly duo.

Ivar was like scorpion tail, fierce and unstoppable. He cursed and swore, swinging his one-handed sword. But Red Herring was the main target, distinguished by the Scottish tartan tunic above his waist. He had the reputation for being the toughest fighter amongst the Crusaders on this cursed land. He was the most precious trophy after the sultan and Edward himself. His reddish face, full of rage, was like a flag for the attackers. They pushed toward him, hoping to cut off his curly head.

But it wasn't so easy to obtain. Although his health wasn't fully restored, he didn't give the enemy a chance, as Peter saw from up close. Red Herring swung his magnificent sword, which shone in the Sun and was as red as his master, covered in blood. He used it like a peasant used his shovel and he didn't hesitate to stab forward with it like a spear. He thrust his sword left and right, cutting all attackers who dared to approach him. He was like a windmill, covered in blood and anger—a fierce warrior from northern England. And he didn't miss the chance to curse the enemy.

"Pigs," the Scottish knight shouted.

Red Herring cut off the limb of a rider who dared to swing his curved saber over the head of the orphan. The Scottish knight managed to parry the stroke and to deliver a deadly counter blow over his elbow. The finest German blades cost a fortune but in such moments, one could understand their reputation of fierce durability. Certainly, Peter understood, watching the severed limb and the terror in the eyes of the dying man.

Sir James laughed. His desire to battle drove all around to follow his example. All men he faced and most of the second wave of attackers understood that it would be hard that day. They were forced against wild men from a faraway land, where the coldness made them strong, brutal, and fearless.

But the Sun was heavy and did his work for both sides.

The soldiers of the defenders started to tire from the heaviness of their battle gear and swinging and thrusting their long spears without pause. Every time they showed signs of fatigue, wings of knights approached the enemy riders, ready to advance, in full armor, with their lances. This forced the enemy horsemen to withdraw and regroup.

The renegade Mamluks retreated every time Edward's mounted knights approached from the wing and ordered their mounted archers to fire as many arrows as they could toward the Crusaders. The men on both sides knew that the Cristian knights were capable of a massive charge, as an unleashed force of steel. But Edward did not pursue the enemy and was back in his position with his main force as the renegades rode away to their own line.

"He has learned his lesson," James was staring at the English prince. "He lost one battle because of lack of discipline before."

After they repelled the enemy cavalry and borrowed enough time for the infantry to replace the wounded in the first row with men from the second row, they drank some water.

Peter tried to catch his breath. Hamo who stood next to him grinned with his pale face wiped out the blood from his sword.

"Longsword, you are still alive, eh?"

"He does well thanks to your lessons," James said. "Kill them," he pointed toward the enemy wounded riders who was in front of them and couldn't retreat to their brothers. And they killed them, ruthlessly. Peter stabbed a rider in the back who was lying with a face toward the ground. He didn't like this act but deep in his mind, he knew it was the right thing to do.

He looked at the Sun with a hand close to his forehead. He hoped one day this sin would be redeemed.

It was a strange mix of armies and skills. Every time the renegade generals sent a wave of men toward the united forces of Baibars and Edward, the Genoese crossbowmen and Owen's archers met them with their missiles. The cross bolts were like flying death to the horsemen; their body armor was nothing against the arrowheads. Meanwhile, the Crusader's archers could not be reached by Ughan's horsemen. They were protected by the best-organized and disciplined soldiers—Edward's retinue, which had been hardened by many battles and were wild in their hearts, seeking glory and recognition over the sea.

Every time the opposite wave was repelled, Baibars' Mamluk mounted archers followed them like a plague and delivered them death.

The killing continued all afternoon.

The renegade Mamluks and Mongols tried to push them to the lake. Peter hoped their supplies of arrows wouldn't deplete soon. The combination of longbows and deadly crossbows were a formidable obstacle to the attackers. The arrows and bolts pierced the attackers' armor and their horses with endless volleys, making the landscape an inferno. The soil and mud obstructed the enemy's cavalry and advancing infantry. The sultan's mounted archers did not stay behind.

The men-at-arms on foot and dismounted knights formed a fierce, defensive wall around their own shooters and were determined not to let anyone infiltrate their temporary kingdom near the lake.

The prince ordered his knights to dismount and help the footmen, men-at-arms, sergeants, and Genovese crossbowmen. Their back was to the lake and the enemy was pushing hard to drive them to the water but the infantry held them with the help of the dismounted knights. The English archers were led by the Welshman, and Owen looked very proud of this fact. The personal bodyguards of the sultan also fought on foot.

Peter observed that all of their men fought like cornered, wounded animals. They resisted and showed their teeth. The death they delivered by their missile volleys, combined with the iron wall, was a masterpiece of warfare. It seemed to Peter like something Vegetius would have written down for future generations if he had seen it.

He smiled. They were making history; this was innovative. The separate groups instinctively fought together. Their proud desire to prove themselves better than the Mamluks or the Italians or the knights was unimportant in the grand scheme. What mattered was their discipline and teamwork and their common goal—to win and to survive in the name of peace.

Still, their numbers were decreasing. A man behind the orphan fell with an arrow in the eye. Another screamed near him, cut down by a deadly saber swing. The fight was merciless. Peter could taste it; there was blood and entrails all around them. The battlefield smelled like a bloody bog.

Peter and the Red Herring were shoving back one more attack. One of the assailants stepped up against the young man and swung his spear. James cut the wooden shaft as Peter pierced the rider as he saw his spearhead coming across the enemy's neck. The surviving Mamluks and Mongols after the last attack retreated to regroup once more.

There was a little time for the defenders for water and calculation of the strategy. The opposing leaders sent against them all they had—Tartars, Mamluks, knights—but they only had mounted archers.

"The Master of the Templars, Bérard, didn't believe in the effectiveness of archers on foot," Sultan Baibars said from his stallion watching the enemy line.

"That's true," James confirmed.

"The renegade Tartar lord, Siraghan al-Tatari have the same opinion. He didn't think any force could stand against their enormous and savage horde," Baibars said.

"But they are lightly-armored and our missiles cut them down like an autumn harvest," Owen commented.

With a single volley, they had erased an entire line of riders from this life, sending them to the underworld so fast that the attackers couldn't retrieve their wounded. They were so many that they were forming an obstacle to the following attacks. Peter could see the determined faces of his sword brothers and their unwillingness to surrender to the enemy's endless efforts. They looked ready to fight to the last man standing.

But the enemy weren't toothless and they were numerous. They had knights, Mamluks, and Mongols on their side. They almost succeeded with their plot, the fat Ughan sweating near his comrades in his cruelty, with Berrat on his left and his officer, Barak, on his right.

"Traitorous bastards," Baibars shouted.

If Peter told anyone that he had seen a Christian prince and a Muslim sultan united against mercenaries and traitors, who would believe him? These weren't your ordinary heroes from a tavern story. They were Edward and Baibars, the towering prince who was called the Longshanks and the Fearsome Sultan, the Lion of Egypt, the Slayer of Crusaders. More than twenty years before, Baibars had stopped the Crusade of King Louis IX of France. In the same battle, Peter's father, William Longsword, had been slain by Baibars. Longsword had had the same blood of the Lionheart and the same blood flowed in Peter's veins—a royal bastard's blood.

And in this rare moment, he didn't give a coin. He was on the same battlefield as his friends, Red Herring, Hamo, and Ulf, and with great men like Baibars and Edward. Even Lady Eleanor, dressed in her battle gear, stood next to her beloved, warring husband. She was like a mother eagle who had brought together all of the men from the west. It was especially impressive that she had managed to unite different factions after an assassination attempt against her husband.

Peter felt proud. Yes, he would always be the street urchin raised in the poor district of Acre but he had put this behind him. Now, he fought for his new name. But, most of all, he fought for his own personal revenge, for the old monk, the man who had been like a real father to him. This vendetta made him determined to find Julian in the heat of the battle and to confront him. He knew, deep down, that this moment would arrive; fate always gave you another chance to fulfill your destiny.

Peter looked around. There were a lot of dead men from the both sides. He saw few archers lying with arrows stuck in their chests. There were drawn a grimace of despair on their lifeless faces. The young man wrinkled his face from the smell of blood and entrails scattered on the battlefield as if he were in a butcher shop at the market in Acre.

Despite their courage and termination to fight to the end, he could see some desperation on the defenders' faces. Their shield wall became thin and it looked like the enemy's force wouldn't melt enough under the rain of arrows.

The Sun was watching. The heat was on their temples, and all the men were sweating beneath their armor.

***

The other men called him "seaborn," born from the sea. But he had quickly become the Desert Wolf. His reputation and his Frankish look had earned him his legendary status.

But he was beyond this. He wanted a calm place, far away from trouble and war. Yet, he had found that a man couldn't flee from violence; it was everywhere. The world was surrounded by war and bloodshed. Killing was everywhere. Humans were the only species that killed each other. And for what?

The attacks had stopped for the time being. The enemy was regrouping. The entire battlefield was silent.

Ulf stood behind the shield wall, where the other wounded were dragged out and bandaged the wound on his left side under the ribs. The cut wasn't deep but it had been enough to bleed and make him weak. It was a race against time—the more he bled, the sooner he would leave this world. He looked at the bandage. It was darkened from the blood. The pain was an awakening for him. He remembered his beloved one. She was gone and he missed her. Everything he had loved, once, had gone; maybe his time had arrived, too.

He smiled. Not yet. Not until he had silenced all of his enemies. They were in front of him, ready to advance. He noticed how the Crusaders—what was left of them—formed their shield line, with the archers behind and the cavalry on the two flanks: the Mamluk elite horse archers and the English knights. There would be massive bloodshed today. He didn't want to miss his chance to exact his revenge. It occurred to him that he had trained for this moment all his life, learning how to survive the pain and to fight without retreat and fear. This was his trade.

He looked at the wagons behind the soldiers. One face smiled at him and waved him vigorously with a hand. Anna. He tried to return the smile. She winked at him, and her hair shuddered as her nanny lifted her on her shoulder and headed for the wagon with her. Anna sent him a kiss and laughed.

Lady Eleanor, Lady Isabella and the other daughters of the Sultan were around the wagons with a few maids and some guards. Ulf's gaze caught the eyes of the wife of Edward. The Spanish princess bent her head in gratitude and he nodded.

It was time. He tied the leather straps of his boots below the knees. He put on his tunic and tied his belt around the sleeveless chainmail. His shoulders weren't protected, but he needed the range of motion, to be able to turn, to move, and to evade. He knew all too well that, if he received a stroke, he would be a dead man. Ultimately, all men were mortal. The pain from his wounded left side gave his face a twitch. It was an elixir for his soul. He knew perfectly well that this adrenaline wouldn't last forever.

Ulf stood up, turned to Githa. He stared at her. She did not smile but looked at him sadly. She had already stood in his way twice. Two years ago, he found her half dead in some burning ruins and took her to the hospital. A few days ago, when they met Isabella, it was the second time he saved her. Ulf had noticed that she was somehow accustomed to his company now.

He reached out and took his one-handed axe from her. He attached it to his belt, on his back. He put two daggers into his leather vambraces and attached one short blade to his left boot. The leather of his boots was hardened with small iron pieces, light but effective when used to kick an opponent.

He approached the Hospitaller officer and she offered him a cup.

"From Ibn al-Nafis," she said. "For the wound."

He nodded his thanks and drank it. The bitter taste sent an alarm throughout his body. He was familiar with this elixir; it was for soldiers, to give them strength for one last battle. He hadn't needed it until now. But the wound he had received from al-Rida had made him weak.

He touched her lips.

"Ready?" he asked.

He knew she was looking at the fierce expression of a determined man, that his eyes showed no mercy. He knew she wouldn't try to talk him out of his decision; she knew him better than that. She nodded silently and took a leather bag from the ground and followed him.

The desert wind had arrived. The Desert Wolf also showed himself and his almost-white hair, darkened with blood and sweat.

The enemy watched him. Ulf was tall; his hair and his stance couldn't be mistaken. He jumped over a piece of rock and took a look at the battleground. He was calculating, giving the traitors enough time to know he was coming for them. He remembered a fierce battle from long before and the battalions that had come and broken like sea waves on the rocks.

He smiled; in his hand, he had a green apple—his last. He remembered the face of the little baby when he had played with the apple a few days before. It was a natural joy, true and uncorrupted, not hidden from anyone. His smile was slight as he enjoyed the memory of this little baby. His beloved one had born his child.

Ulf was wounded and bleeding, but he rose. He held his green apple in his left hand and he took a bite of it, enjoying its taste one last time. Then he turned to the opposing army.

He raised his right hand and pointed a finger at the enemy's leaders. Githa stood next to him and gave him the leather bag. He took it and pulled out of the bag the severed head of the Mamluk officer he had killed the night before. He raised it high enough that even the Sun could see it. Githa stabbed six lances into the ground near where he stood, with their spearheads pointed to the sky. He stepped to the first one and put the head of Ughan's officer on it.

The Desert Wolf turned his gaze to the enemy, five empty spearheads standing beside him.

No one dared to move; all men stood, paralyzed as if they had been stung by a poisonous spider. Ulf let his mantle drop to the ground and he put his shield on his back.

He watched the enemy.

There was no going back. Ulf removed his blade from its scabbard and pointed to Berrat. He stood for a moment, closed his eyes, and tried to imagine—for the last time—the face of his beloved woman.

He smiled.

"My darling," the wind whispered to him.

"I will see you soon." He squeezed his eyes shut. "Don't cry for me, my darling, I will be with you soon. Don't cry for me ...."

Ding, dang, ding. The bell of an imaginary temple sounded heavily.

He was, once more, in his favorite garden with his woman, the love of his life, the reason he felt alive. In his head rose the image of his beloved one. She smiled to him and whispered into his ear:

Die my darling, but not today
Raise your sword, my darling, and prepare
Make it sing for me, my darling
Sing, my darling, with your blade
Die, my darling, but not today
Kill, my darling, and kill in my name
Avenge my soul, my darling
Avenge my soul, today…

His heart was bleeding. The only way to silence this song in his mind was to make someone else bleed. It was simple.

His eyes were still closed. It was about time to sing his song, the song of his trade: war. He had forgotten the last time

346

he had heard it.

The music in his ears was the echo of sorrow, of lost battles, of thousands of cries ringing in his mind. He would be dead soon. Time wasn't on his side. It rose like a sea wave in a storm with no fear. There was no past or future, only now.

...Think of me, you're always in the dark
Think of me, you're never in the dark
I am your light, your light, your light
I will never break your heart...

"I will never break your heart," she whispered and kissed his temple. His beloved one disappeared.

His heart was now full of calm and determination to earn retribution. A wise man had once said that war was for the sake of peace. Yes, peace would exist after all men had been dealt the punishment they deserved. But this, now, wasn't for the sake of peace, but for the sake of personal pleasure. Revenge. It was time for payback and nothing could take it away for him, not even the bleeding wound on his body.

Ulf opened his eyes. He looked straight forward, then to the sky.

He was in the desert once more, near the lake. For her, he was readier than ever. He was covered in sweat, bleeding, tired to the bone—but he wasn't through yet; his thirst for blood wasn't satisfied.

Every living creature waited for the Desert Wolf to make his move. He had never disappointed his spectators and he wouldn't disappoint them now, not in the face of the gods and the one who was always above them, the Sun.

He walked straight forward, toward the enemy line. It would be fun. Bloody fun.

***

Peter took a moment to observe him. A week before, Ulf had been a ragged man dressed in a tattered robe. But now, he stood between the two armies like an unleashed demigod

347

warlord, dressed in his red-brown leather armor and boots which had been a gift from the sultan. His beloved Danish axe wasn't something a man's eyes could easily forget. He also had a double-edged steel sword, longer than the average one-handed swords.

The pale god of war stretched his neck and shoulders. What was in his mind?

Peter glanced at the sultan and then to the prince. He saw that Baibars looked at Edward and nodded. It was time to test the odds.

The wind became stronger. It was late afternoon. Ulf was walking slowly, observing the enemy line. After around one hundred and fifty paces he stopped.

"They will just shoot him," Peter said.

"He is beyond the reach of their arrows," Owen said. "A clever bastard."

"What is he doing?" Peter asked.

"We can't hold them much longer," James said.

"So, he intends to kill them all?"

"He will provoke them. And try to kill one of their leaders. It will affect the morale of the enemy and they will have one leader less to follow."

"But they will kill him. It's suicide."

"Probably," James said, "but in the turmoil, we may have a chance."

The defenders of the lake watched, as did the enemy.

Silence.

"Berrat! Show yourself, you coward," Ulf shouted. The bareheaded Mamluk and the former right hand of Baibars couldn't be mistaken. He stepped forward.

"Do you want to surrender, *Diyaab al-Sahra*?"

"I want your head," Ulf said.

"This is not a man-to-man challenge, my friend. First, you must win the battle." He shouted loud enough that every soldier in the valley could hear.

Peter smiled. No one dared to stand against the Desert Wolf but evading the challenge would be a sign of cowardice. Berrat had no good options.

"Or you can only kill children, women, and old men?" Ulf shouted.

"Your wife yelled like a whore!" Barak retorted.

"Wait your turn, dog. Officers are first to die," Ulf said.

Berrat was silent.

"So, are you afraid of me, slave?" Ulf used the Frankish word to insult the tall officer. "The desert storm saved you from me once, but now the sky is clear. Come out and face me."

Peter realized what the Wolf was trying to achieve. If Berrat accepted the challenge, the battle would be delayed. Soon, the night would arrive and they would manage to escape or reinforcement would arrive. If Ulf won, their leaders would be one head less and Wolf's spears in the sand would have one more head of a traitor to show. The Sultan of Egypt had the power to grant them amnesty; Berrat's soldiers would have to choose their side once more. The odds could tip decidedly in the sultan and Edward's favor.

Yes, there was a chance that the Desert Wolf could lose the fight. After all, he was wounded. But this would give the defenders more motivation to fight for their lives. The renegades had no good options.

The orphan was on the front line with Red Herring and they were eager to hear everything. Ulf stood outside the reach of their arrows. The land around him was littered with wounded horses and Mamluks—some dead, others still alive. Screams rose from the dying ones and dark blood mixed with the sand.

A rider, near to the Wolf, was pinned under the body of his dead horse, pierced by three arrows. It looked as if his leg was broken; he couldn't move and his face was grimaced with pain. The Desert Wolf repeated his invitation to Berrat once more, then approached the wounded soldier and hammered his skull with his axe, quickly and ruthlessly. The dull sound of broken bones and spilled blood echoed in the valley.

Ulf's eyes didn't flinch. Watching the enemy line, he shouted, "Berrat, dog … come to me!"

A crow flew above. Ulf noticed the bird on the clear

skyline. The messenger of the gods was here—all eyes were now on this valley and the miserable lake. Peter thought his journey in this forsaken land was about to end. Would he see Acre again? It all depended on Ulf now.

Why were there crows here?

Peter observed the blood on Ulf's axe; the dark liquid was flowing down the blade and a red drop fell on the sand near the warrior's right foot. Blood on the sand. It called to mind an image of blood and snow ... but that was from long before. Now it was sand; the landscape had changed but the circumstances had not. All in all, it was the same: in the battle for power and money, the story never changed—only the kings, the princes, and their opponents. Most of them—the lofty rulers—never fought their own battles; only the poor soldiers, knights, and ordinary peasants died for reasons they could barely understand. The world would never change—only landscapes, clothes, and weapons. That much was undeniable. Even Vegetius wrote it so many years before.

Peter observed the enemy line. Yet, he had seen Ulf kill a wounded and helpless man before and he had learned that the objectives defined the actions. After all, the Desert Wolf wasn't a knight or some chivalrous fool in search of salvation. He was a ruthless and skillful killer who dealt in dispatching souls from this world.

So, the enemy made their move.

Berrat had made the decision instinctively. His pride was hurt; he knew he couldn't match the Wolf one-on-one, so he chose not to risk it but, instead, to advance with his soldiers and to win this battle.

Peter blinked and in the moment after Ulf crushed the skull of the wounded Mamluk, Berrat, Barak, Ughan and the men around them charged toward the Desert Wolf, seeking to conquer the heart of their opponents' resistance. The warrior stood alone on the open ground and horseless. By killing the most renowned warrior on this side of the sea, would increase renegades' chances of success against Edward and his experienced knights and Baibars' royal guards. Peter's jaw dropped.

The renegades broke their lines and, in a wild charge, advanced on the pale warlord, who simply waited for them. Berrat rode his fine Arab horse with such determination that Peter was sure the horse could feel his rage. The bareheaded traitor looked focused on his target. The galloping hooves of the horses around him gave him confidence; he wasn't alone. He turned his face to the left and right—almost a quarter of their army followed him. The Wolf would be a legendary trophy and they wanted his head.

Both sides seemed thunderstruck. Berrat, Ughan, and their Mamluks were in the center; Master Bérard and his loyal Templar Knights were on their right wing, and the Tartar lord was on the left with his scattered horde.

"Now!" Edward shouted. Peter glanced at the English prince who raised his sword. He noticed Sultan Baibars was ready too.

It was time. The young man looked at Red Herring.

"Advance!" Sir James shouted. The whole defensive line started to run as one. They needed to move a hundred paces at once to position their archers within range. It was a magnificent view of discipline and moving armored battalions into formation. Red Herring started a song and the rest of the squad joined him.

Come with me, my brother,
Come to fight at once
Come to me, my brother
Share your bravery with us
Fight like demons and kill them all
Kill, kill, kill ...

The spirit of the infantry was confident and their wild march showed that they knew exactly what to do.

The enemy cavalry was almost upon Ulf, who was farther from Peter and the rest of the defenders. The young man knew they needed to reach him fast and to form another shield wall. He was tired, he was in sweat, but he ran side by side with his sword brothers toward their fate.

351

***

Ulf waited for Berrat and his Mamluks, drawing his sword from its scabbard and letting the leather sheath fall to the ground. He remembered his uncle teaching him how to kill a wild boar when he was a child and he smiled. Killing people was like hunting. Instead of a hunting lance, he held a Crusader blade. He had witnessed how they were used like spears in battle.

He held the sword a few inches behind its crossguard and looked at his target.

Berrat was the man who had given the order to attack his manor and to kill his family, the man who was responsible for the death of his beloved one. He had golden lamellar armor above his mail shirt, but the German blade was the finest sword a man could possess and Ulf had one in his hand. He looked at his enemy. Once, they had been close, shared one fate, fought for one cause. Now, one of them would kill the other.

The Mamluks rode toward him, Berrat leading with Barak near him. They were almost within spear-throwing range. Ulf waited; he wanted to be sure. The Mamluk amir looked amused and raised his right hand with his saber.

The Wolf threw his message, lunging his body forward and twisting his hand as he released the long blade like a javelin. It was a marvelously-balanced weapon; it flew it with a vengeful purpose and fury which no armor could stop.

The missile pierced the charging rider a little below the throat with the sound of crushed bones, flesh, and failed armor. Berrat's body was knocked back onto the ground.

This ignited the battlefield. The leading warhorse, having lost its rider, also lost its motivation to run forward. Ulf, who had drawn his axe with his right hand and held his shield in his left, ran toward Berrat's animal. Using his shield, he struck the horse aside. The blow pushed the warhorse to fall on its right, turning it into to an obstacle for the next horseman.

A rider tried his luck swinging his blade at the Desert Wolf, but Ulf acted in haste, jumping over the fallen horse and leaping off it at the next rider. He swung his axe and smashed the skull of another rider as he pushed the previous one to the ground. It was like a sandstorm of flying blood and screams. The riders tried to surround the footman, but he surprised them with his mobility and speed as he delivered death with just a touch.

One rider pushed him to the ground, but Ulf turned back on his knees like a cat, jumped toward another assailant, caught his shield with his axe, and pulled him down with such ease that the horseman looked like a child. While the man was falling, the Wolf pierced him through the neck with his blade and pulled a sword out from inside his shield. It was a bloody cloud of horses and people, the wounded Wolf biting them all. There was no sign that the riders would prevail. They slowed their speed, turning their horses slowly, trying to surround their target. But he gave them no chance. He jumped, stabbed, and pierced. He swung his axe, slinging his shield onto his back to protect him from behind. Ulf pushed hard against the enemy, delivering chaos, shedding blood, and detaching a number of limbs. He operated like a woodman cut his wood or a singer sang his song.

But the mounted Mamluks were too many. Even leaderless, they were professionals trained for war, not for a ceremonial parade of armor.

They tried to regroup. Most of them were stopped and trying to turn their back toward him and to face the advancing infantry of the Crusaders.

Arrows began to rain down on the Mamluks.

***

The line of defense had moved their position so fast that it surprised the enemy. They were within shooting range again and the unmovable horsemen, blocked by the turmoil around the Desert Wolf, had become target practice. The first volley cut down a whole line of riders.

Ughan and his horsemen tried to charge the left flank of

the Crusaders' shield wall. The penetration failed and he turned around. Missiles flew from both sides. The Genoese reloaded their weapons—they were not quick but their effectiveness was enormous. Owen's archers made up for their lack of speed. They felt comfortable behind the long shields of the men-at-arms and they shot faster than the horse archers of the enemy.

Edward and Baibars were on the wings, holding their positions. If they charged, they would leave their infantry unprotected. They had to await the perfect moment. The English prince had learned his lesson: discipline was the key.

Ughan was forced to stop because of the coming revolved and scared horses lost its masters from Crusaders' arrows. The animals blocked his way as he cried out his orders. The soil was heavy and muddy. Berrat was down. Ughan was caught in a trap between the defenders and his own cavalry. This was their chance.

"Sir James, Now!" Edward shouted and pointed forward.

Red Herring raised his sword and shouted, "Sword squad, at the ready!"

The assault squad was ready. Twelve men—the bravest, wildest, stupidest ones—were ready to leave their mark on history. They raised their shields from the ground. The chosen ones—a dozen from Edward's fierce warriors—had been given the task to penetrate the turmoil of the battle and to seize the enemy's leader, Amir Ughan, and to end the resistance of the renegades. At the battle of Evesham, Edward had used this tactic: an assault party from his best battle-hardened warriors in a spear formation.

"Right, men. It's our turn to steal the glory. You know your job! Go, go, go." James gave a devil's smile to his followers, who had volunteered for this mission. His sword brothers were as ready as ever.

Peter stood on James' right and Ivar next to him; Bruce the Old was on his other side as Hamo too, and Jean de Grailly behind them with his long sword. The young man didn't know the rest, but he trusted them with his life.

They ran, the twelve men, under the whistling sound of the flying arrows, toward their target—the kill that would end the battle.

Peter glanced at where the Templars were watching the course of the fight but they still didn't join. As he ran he thought he saw the blond hair of Julian. There were almost at their target as he heard the battle cry of the renegade Templars and they charged.

Peter and the rest of his companions penetrated the Mamluks around Ughan.

Sir James was like a wild animal; he pierced the line of soldiers around him. Screams and cries echoed through the valley; blood and death spilled. Peter lost his kettle helmet after a stroke he received from a rider but he managed to pierce the soldier down with his spear. Ivar parried another blow aimed at the orphan's head. They were almost at Ughan. His personal guards were charging toward James and his followers. Peter clutched his shield tightly and held his spear pointed at the advancing horses. The cavalry hadn't enough time to quicken their pace and this was fatal. Peter felt that the adrenaline conquered him. He hid behind the shield and met the horseman's strike in front of him. Then he swung his spear and pushed the rider off the horse. With a jump, he approached the fallen man and hammered the shield over the Mamluk's head. The young man turned and a horse pushed him on the ground and he dropped his spear. His heart was beating fast as he kneeled and felt a strong arm around his shoulder which helped him to rise.

"I did not teach you to lie in battle, Longsword," Hamo grinned and used his shield to strike an enemy in front of him. "Come on, there is a plenty of opponents for both of us!" The lord from the Welsh Marches swung his weapon and cut down another Mamluk.

Peter stood and drawn his father's sword from its scabbard and joined Hamo. His left hand was trembling from the blows he faced with the shield, as he thrust his blade forward and met the throat of another rider. Blood was on his sword as he ducked to evade a strike from above and swung his weapon toward the next rider.

The enemy was so many. His eyes met with the Mamluk on

his left. His heart shrunk as he knew he couldn't turn so fast to meet the attack. But an arrow stuck in the rider's chest and he fell from his horse. He took a breath and heard the grunting voice of James around him. Peter turned around and saw his friends who fought fiercely and killed the disorganized bodyguards of Ughan. James cut down fast and ferociously the last man who stood near the enemy leader. Ivar lunged forward and grabbed their amir and unsaddled him from his stallion. Ughan was in their hands as James kicked him like he was a homeless dog.

"We got him!" The Scottish knight shouted. Peter felt some relieve in his chest as he observed that the Mamluks seem to hesitate now.

"Watch out!" Red Herring shouted.

Peter ducked instinctively, turned and observed what was coming. They all froze. The Templars were charging toward them. Peter inhaled sharp breath as his stomach shrank and he cowered behind his kite-shaped shield with a flat top. He wiped out the blood from his face and looked at the galloping enemy. They were in trouble, he thought an instinctively stepped back. He looked around and saw the determined faces of Hamo and James around him. They also prepared to meet the Templars.

"No mercy!" Peter heard Edward's war cry. He glanced at his left and saw the horses and the movement of armor, steel, and men. Their own flanks from mounted knights and Mamluks led by the English prince and the sultan were riding up from either side to protect them as Edward and Baibars would try to hit the enemy like a hammer from two sides.

Now we had to stand, Peter thought, and the knuckles of his fingers whitened by the force he used to hold his sword.

The ground was shaking from the galloping force of the warhorses. He observed the Templar Knights, who were approaching fast. They looked like a wave of steel which would trash them out from the battlefield. He held his breath as he watched the more dangerous threat of what had come before them.

We were doomed.

Peter had almost blinked when his eye caught Julian's blond hair. He had expected this confrontation; their meeting seemed inevitable.

But—just in time—Edward's horsemen arrived.

Riders flew through the air as lances pierced their targets. Horses fell to the ground and blood and dust covered the fighting men. The clash of swords and spears and broken armors and shields echoed in the valley. All men were frenzied into a savage killing. Blood was spilled, swords were broken, shields splintered, souls dispatched. Great was the noise of the battle with the ring of iron and the clash of steel, warrior's battle cries, horse song and flying arrows. Yellow dust and sand were everywhere, preventing Peter from seeing clearly. He caught a glimpse of Edward, towering above them all, was swinging his long weapon.

Peter saw Owen and his archers.

"What are you doing here?"

"I'm out of arrows," the Welshman grinned and joined the melee with a spear followed by Pelu and the Genoese archers. Peter and the rest of the assault squad joined the fight with their last strengths.

The sultan's forces cut into the enemy line, as well. There were no more clear battles or lines. The mix of soldiers under the Sun in the dust was staggering.

Julian passed near Peter. He saw him at the last moment and managed to turn around. The young man pierced the flank of his horse and forced him to fall under the heaviness of the animal.

"Murderer, I am here," Peter shouted.

Julian stood and faced the orphan.

"Dog, we met again."

Peter threw away his shield and held his sword with his two hands.

Julian grunted and launched an attack toward the orphan with his sword pointed at the young man's chest. Peter advanced his left foot to the left of the blond knight, receiving Julian's strike in the middle of his sword. With his right foot, he stepped out of the way to the side and caught attacker's blow at the mid-sword. Allowing his sword to run off toward the ground, he quickly responded with a downward blow toward his opponent's arm. But the blond knight stepped back and evaded the orphan's sword.

They watched each other's eyes, their hatred flowing toward each other. They had fought before but Peter was no longer the orphan he had been a week before. He had witnessed death; he had even delivered death himself. He had matured.

Julian advanced with his left foot and swung his sword from below, aiming at Peter's left arm. The young man stepped back slowly and he heard the knight's blade scratch his Roman vambrace. The Templar smiled, raised his sword over his head, and rushed forward again.

They crossed their swords again and looked each other as Peter felt the rotten smell from Julian's breath.

"Who is going to save you now, mongrel? You will die like the old monk, dog. A street urchin useless dog. Where are your mom and dad?"

Peter's nostrils flared and he gritted his teeth. Julian pushed the young man who stepped back, lost his balance and fell in the dust on his back. The blond knight approached him with his weapon ready to bring death. He raised his right foot and placed it on Peter's chest. The orphan felt the pressure from his attacker's weight as he recognized his boots he saw the first time he met Julian.

"You escaped my sword twice, dog, but now you will die, you and your friends."

Peter's rage wrapped his mind and heart.

"No," the young man shouted, "my name is Longsword. And I will decide my own fate." He kicked Julian's left thigh then he rolled left and jumped on his legs. "Longsword," He shouted again as he lunged forward and faced him again. Peter raised his weapon and crossed it with his opponent's at mid-sword. He immediately advanced and grabbed Julian's blade with his left hand, kicking under the knight's kneecap with his right foot. Julian howled in pain and Peter hammered his sword ferociously over the knight's right arm and he cut off the Templar's wrist.

His enemy screamed and blood flew from his arm.

Peter looked him in the eyes. Julian's eyes burned with hatred as his lips set in a grim line and his mouth nervously contracted. The young man heard the dull sound of his opponent's sword falling on the ground, followed by the Templar's cry. Peter didn't think; he just executed a technique that Hamo had taught him during their practice session one morning on their journey. He backhanded Julian's surprised face with his pommel, and the knight collapsed backward. The young man observed his opponent's severed right hand, still holding the sword.

"Die bastard," Peter shouted.

A rider passed near Peter, and he stepped back, over a dead body, and almost fell on his backside. Sand clouds rose, and he couldn't see a thing around him. He jumped fast, but Julian had disappeared into the fog of the battle.

"Where are you?" the orphan shouted toward the fighting men.

Something hard hit Peter's head and he fell to the ground. The orphan turned and stared at his attacker's face.

David stood over him with a bloody sword and was about to finish him.

"Because of you, our plan was ruined. You must pay," the traitorous sergeant said.

Peter saw David raise his sword above his head.

"Die, mongrel!" the traitor shouted and his face twisted in a terrifying grimace.

"Ungrateful dog." Red Herring appeared from behind the sergeant's back. "Remember this bastard's name: David, a piece of dog shit."

James executed the traitor, piercing the short man's neck with his sword. Retrieving his weapon, he then decapitated his former sergeant and put his head on the spear of his banner.

A horn sounded three times.

Sir James of Durham helped the orphan to stand and, side-by-side, they observed the battlefield. Hamo leaned on his sword and grinned.

"Longsword, you survived after all," he said and together, they observed the formidable battalions of golden Mamluks who emerged from the hill. The sultan's reinforcements finally had arrived. After seeing this, one part of the enemy's soldiers began to surrender and the others started to retreat.

"We've won, lad!"

"The bastard disappeared!"

"Who?"

"Julian."

"But I saw you cut off his hand. He must be lying somewhere on the field."

Peter took a deep breath and wiped the sweat from his forehead. He stared at his trembling hands. His throat was dry as he needed water and rest. They survived and he smiled.

***

"No! We had to win, we had to...," al-Rida stared with cow eyes to the battlefield. He was at a safe distance from the fight.

"Everything is ruined," Sir Thomas Bérard, the Master of the Templars said as he stood near him. "This pompous bastard Edward showed up and we lost."

The assassin sat on his horse and the muscles in his face tightened. No, there has to be another way, he thought.

"It's all your fault. You had to kill him when you had a chance," the thin and bleak master said. "But you failed me."

"Nothing is lost yet," al-Rida thought for a moment. "I can kill him now."

They became silent as they watched the newly arrived battalions of the sultan.

"This dog somehow managed to call for a help," Sir Thomas said with his gapped mouth stared at the horizon.

Al-Rida's eyes were searching the bloody field.

"Here he is," he pointed toward the last moments of the battle. Some Mamluks still tried to resist, others fought in groups to avoid the inevitable. One part of the Mamluks just fled. And he saw him. The towering prince of the Englishmen. The man who turned the course of the battle. He was riding his white war horse, still fighting and giving orders to his men.

A Templar Knight with pale face approached his master.

"We have to leave that field, my lord,"

"Where? We will be hunted," the master said as his eyes rolled skyward. "Where is Julian?"

"He rode to kill Longsword," the pale officer said.

"Longsword?"

"Yes, the bastard son of William Longsword, my lord."

"Peter, the black-haired young man, the orphan from Acre?" Sir Thomas asked.

"Yes, the man I spared his life," al-Rida confirmed.

"He was under our noses during all these years and we were blind to notice him," the master said.

"My lord, we have to go," the Templar officer looked nervous.

"I can kill Edward now, my lord," the assassin said again.

"What will this bring to us? Our plan failed."

"But without the word of Edward no one will believe that you are involved, my lord," al-Rida said. "It will be your word against the word of his men."

Sir Thomas Bérard took a minute to think about it.

"Maybe you are right. Can you do it for me, for the way I saved your life?"

"This is a matter of honor," al-Rida said. "I will do it for myself." The assassin focused on his target. He failed the last time but now it was different. There was no more the surprise effect. He drew his saber and was ready to face his fate once more. He knew that this time he couldn't fail. He had to do it, because of his reputation. A week ago, he hesitated, he liked the prince. But now, observing how he had come and helped the man they wanted to destroy, Baibars, al-Rida wanted him dead.

And he rode to meet Lord Edward one more time.

***

"Look!" James shouted and pointed toward Edward.

Peter turned his gaze left and saw Edward the Saracen

battled his way through the rest of the melee with his horse to the English prince. James, Hamo, and the young man were about fifty paces away from them. They raised their swords and ran toward their prince.

"He is mine!" Edward said and his eyes flashed. All of his knights who were around him stopped. James, Peter, and Hamo approached and stopped as they observed the two Edwards.

Lord Edward rode toward the spy. He used the strength of his warhorse to push the other's animal aside and the Saracen fell from his saddle. The towering prince's face looked focused. He jumped from his stallion and faced, once more, the man who had tried to assassinate him. The same man he had allowed enter his inner circle of friends. The Saracen rose and recovered his saber from the dust.

Edward of England didn't hesitate but lunged forward with his sword aimed at his opponent's neck. The spy stepped aside, evading the blow, and counterattacked, swinging his blade. Despite his height, the prince wasn't clumsy at all. Lord Edward parried the blow and grabbed his opponent's tunic, dragged him close to him, and headbutted him with his helmet. The Saracen cried out and tried to step back, but the prince struck him again. The traitor swayed. On his forehead was a bloody mark left by the prince's helmet. He dropped his saber and looked the Englishman in the eyes. Lord Edward stuck his sword in the ground, took the spy's dagger and thrust it deep into the neck of the traitor.

The Saracen fell on his knees and looked at the letters of the scabbard, covered with blood, in his hands. The failed assassin stared at Edward as he tried to smile and collapsed in the dust.

Peter approached and looked at the man who spared his life a week ago. Now he was lying dead. He knelt down and read the letters on the scabbard. He still had a lot to learn to read, but these letters he already knew.

"Honor bound, Edward of England," it read.

Peter stood and looked at the prince. Lord Edward chopped off the spy's head and put it on a spearhead so that everyone could see it.

"He never forgets treachery, lad," James said, and shouted toward Edward, "It was a good hunt, my lord!"

"Sir James," Edward said, nodding. "Yes indeed." He smiled.

"Some of the Templars fled," James said.

"There is no place to hide," the prince said, petting his warhorse.

Owen and Pelu and the other infantry were in charge of the many captive renegades.

It appeared that Master Bérard had escaped, wounded. He would be hunted down later. Siraghan al-Tatari had managed to escape as well. Half of the men who were on the side of the traitors had died bravely. The other half had fled upon the arrival of Amir Qalawun, the most trusted friend of the sultan since Berrat.

Peter looked at the Sun and smiled. It was a good day, he thought. He had to find something to drink because his throat burned him from inside.

"What are we going to do with the prisoners?" Owen asked. "I say let's kill these traitors."

"No, the prince and the sultan will decide their fate," James said.

Peter heard the sound of women's screams and rose up from his resting place.

Barak managed to bypass the united forces of the defender's line. He attacked the baggage wagons and the women and the children who were positioned between their forces and the lake. Lady Eleanor, Lady Isabela, Anna and the other Baibars' daughters were in danger.

"Run men!" James shouted. But there was no need to order them as Peter, Hamo, and Owen already were running toward the threat.

The young man could see Ughan's officer stormed toward Eleanor with a dozen men who had stayed with him in a desperate attempt to catch her. He clenched his dirty big fists as he approached her and kicked the nearby guard.

Peter glanced at Barak, running toward the ladies and

unsheathed his sword. Lord Edward spurred his horse toward his wife and the rest of his knights followed him. Owen took an arrow from a dead horse and shot one of the riders.

But Ulf was already there, wounded and weaponless. He caught one of the Mamluks and pushed him down from the saddle. Peter foresaw the danger but still was far away. He was using his last strength to run, closing in on the scene—twenty paces away, then ten paces. No, he couldn't reach it in time.

"Sword!" Peter shouted and threw his father's sword toward the Wolf.

The warrior saw it, managed to catch the weapon, and lunged at Barak. The fight was short. The ladies witnessed the justice delivered from up close. The Desert Wolf's commitment to finish his job was brutal; he gutted the man who was responsible for his wife's death like a fish, leaving him no chance. The rest of Barak followers scattered when Edward arrived with his knights.

Peter found his sword later in Barak's chest. The Mamluk's body was cut to pieces by Ulf and his head put on one of the six spearheads. He sat and propped his elbow on his knee. Now he definitely needed something to drink.

Shams al-Din was found alive among the surrendered renegades, tied to four horses, and torn apart. What was left of his body was thrown to the dogs. His head took its place of honor on the next spearhead. Ughan was still alive under the guard of James' men.

The united forces of Baibars and Edward had won. The Battle of the Lake—or, as some described it, the Second Battle of Ayn Jalut—was over. Many brave men had died.

But nothing was over yet. Two men warring for their own beliefs and realms had fought, united, but tomorrow, they would be enemies again.

The war of the religions would continue.

HISTORICAL NOTE

This piece of historical fiction is based on an article I read about a failed assassination during the Ninth Crusade. The target was Edward I, the future king of England. The reason for delaying his departure from the Holy Land after the truce so long is unknown. The birth of Joan of Acre, Edward's eighth child, was one possible reason to stay; Eleanor needed time to recover her strength.

The reason for the delayed assassination attempt also is a mystery. I decided to tell one possible version of the story through Peter—the bastard son of the notorious Crusader, William Longsword—a common man who obtained glory for saving the prince's life.

The Second Battle of Ayn Jalut did not take place. But twelve years earlier, there had been a battle in which the Mamluks had inflicted a heavy blow to the ambitions of the Mongols to conquer these lands. It was there that an officer distinguished himself from the others with his courage and leadership—the future Sultan Baibars.

It was a real challenge to meet the characters of Edward and Baibars with Peter. These men were extraordinary and left impressive marks in history. They divided opinions and they possessed much mental strength and determination. Our orphan will certainly learn from the best.

Peter Longsword will ride again.

ABOUT THE AUTHOR

Dimitar Gyopsaliev was born and raised in Plovdiv and now lives in Sofia with his wife and his two kids. In addition, his family inspired him to write. Dimitar and his son Branimir are very curious and constantly explore any good story. Longsword is such a story.

Made in United States
Troutdale, OR
11/24/2024

25259701R00231